I0671313

Darkness INTO Dawn

Book Two: The Unraveled Trilogy

Theresa Sederholt

Darkness into Dawn
Copyright© 2014 by Theresa Sederholt

All rights reserved. This book or any portion thereof may not be reproduced or used in any manner whatsoever without the express written permission of the publisher except for the use of brief quotations in the book review.

The author acknowledges the copyrighted or trademarked status and trademark owners of the following wordmarks mentions in this work of fiction: Jackson Memorial Hospital. Starbucks. Nutella. Jammie Dodgers. Doctor Who. The Wicked Wit of Winston Churchhill by Enright Dominque. American Express Black Card. The W Hotel. Apple, iPad, iPod. Cardiff Bay. The Doctor Who Experience. Disney World. Rolex. Sing Sing and Attica Prisons. Bon Genie. Savoy of London. Barneys. Raider's Inc. GQ. Prosecco. Cartier. Tiffany. S'Mac. Jewel Cayle. Chae Richardson 'Courage is not living without fear. Courage is being scared to death and doing the right thing any way' quotation. Abracadabra Rose. Bond Cuff links. Friends. Netflix. Scotland Yard. Skype. The Battersea Dog and Cat Home

Music 'One Direction "Half a Heart," 'Ellie Goulding "How Long Will I Love you?," SafetySuit "Never Stop" and "Red Pieces," 'Nickleback "Never Gonna Be Alone," 'The Righteous Brothers' "Unchained Melody." 'David Garrett' "Bring Me Back To Life."

This is a work of fiction. Names, characters, businesses, places, events, and incidents are either the products of the author's imagination or used in a fictitious manner. Any resemblance to actual persons, living or dead, or actual events is purely coincidental.

ISBN: 978-0-9862598-1-4

Publisher: Theresa Sederholt©
Cover designer: Tracy Beavers: TBeavers@roarmarketinggroup.com
Cover designer for paperback: Cover to Cover Design
Editor: Jacquelyn Ayres
Formatter: Champagne Formats

Chapter One

Jaxson

IT'S A COLD WINTER day in New York City, but the sun is shining. I decide to take the ladies out for a bite to eat while I wait to hear from Max. I'm very distracted, and I know it's from the anticipation of his call. I'm not good at waiting, but I have no choice. I push my food around the plate while Raven and Jackie talk about our baby. I want to get married before the baby comes, but I haven't broached that subject yet. Lately, it seems I can't get anything right with Raven. As I look around the restaurant, I realize we must look ridiculous sitting here with six security guards and a dog, but what the fuck do I care? I would have a hundred security guards if it meant our girls were safe. As the waiter comes with the dessert menu, my phone chirps with a text from Tony to call him stat.

"Ladies, I need to make a call. I'll be out front." They are so engrossed in baby stuff, I don't even think they notice, but it's okay. I'm glad to see Raven having some normal girl time. I make my way through the restaurant and out the door.

"Tony, what's the problem?" I ask as soon as he picks up. He starts talking but I can't believe what I'm hearing. I'm in utter shock. Everything he's saying sounds like white noise. "Tony, my jet is in Miami. I need you to charter a private jet for me to leave within the hour—at any cost." Ending the call, I go back inside to collect the ladies and pay the bill.

"Jax, what's wrong?" Raven only has to take one look at me to know when something is terribly wrong. I think she can see the fear I'm feeling on my face.

"We need to leave now."

She brings her hand up to her throat, and her eyes instantly fill with tears. "Jax, you're scaring me. Please, what's wrong?"

Before I can say anything, Jackie turns white and starts shaking. *Fuck!* "Jax, its Maxwell, isn't it? I can feel it." Her tears start falling. I'm trying to hold onto both of them.

"Ladies, I need to leave for the airport—now!"

Raven, puts her hands on her hips as if ready to stand her ground. "We are going with you. No arguments, Jax!"

I want her with me, close to me. I need my lifeline, my beautiful girl. "I'm not going to argue; let's go."

WE RACE TO THE airport where the jet is waiting for us. I get every-one settled in the main cabin before heading to the office area. I need to make some calls. I know I should be strong for Raven and Jackie, comforting them. I can't. Right now, I'm best at setting up top doctors and dealing with the authorities on the ground. All I know is that Max and Vincent were shot, and it's bad. My phone rings, its Bella. I don't want to deal with her right now, but I have no choice. I know she won't let up.

"Bella, I'm really busy at the moment." I try to rush her off the phone.

"Jax, it's all over the news. Where are you?" she cries.

I take a deep breath, trying to steady my nerves. "I'm on my way to Miami with Raven and Jackie."

I hear my mum in the background, trying to say something. "Jax, hold on, Mum wants you." She doesn't even give me a chance to protest.

"Jaxson, you go get him and bring him home. And you tell him he hasn't seen mad!" Her voice cracks and she starts to cry. When my mum cries, it shreds me.

"Okay, Mum, I love you," I whisper. I hang up and sit in my chair with my head in my hands. I don't hear her come in, but I can feel her, my skin tingles whenever she's near. She takes me in her arms and holds me gently. I don't have to say a thing; she knows what I need and she knows that, right now, she is my lifeline. I need to be strong for everyone else, but with her, I can just be.

WE TOUCH DOWN AND there are cars waiting to rush our security team and us to Jackson Memorial Hospital. We head towards the ICU where the nurse informs me that only family members are allowed. I was prepared for this and hand her Max's HIPPA medical release form. We made preparations one night, in a drunken state, hoping they would never be needed.

"Let me go in and assess the situation, then I will be back to let you know what I find out. Please stick with Jackie and your detail," I beg of Raven.

I look over at Jackie and I realize, she's not said a word since we left the restaurant. I hope Raven can help her, because I don't think I can. As I walk into the room, what I see shocks me. It rocks me to my core. My best friend—the man that I consider my brother—looks pale and weak. "Nurse, when will the doctor be here? I want to talk to him now."

"Sir, I just paged Dr. Scott. He is with the other victim now."

I growl, trying to rein in my temper. "Vincent is *here?*" I think I just scared the shit out of the nurse.

"Sir, by law I'm not allowed to discuss other patients."

While I wait for the doctor, I call Tony. "I'm here. Apparently, they have Vincent in the next room. I want extra guards put on his room and around this whole fucking hospital! I want you to find out everything you can about the status of his condition." I inform the nurse that the man in the next room is a murderer, rapist, and kidnapper. She glances at me, but says nothing as she checks Max's vitals. Dr. Scott finally comes in. I get up and shake his hand. "Dr. Scott, I'm Jaxson Phillips, I have Maxwell's medical power of attorney. What's the prognosis?"

He looks over Max's chart. "The next twenty-four hours are critical. As you know, he was shot in the head. I was able to remove the bullet, but his brain is swollen. I had put him into a coma to give his brain a chance to rest. His heart stopped during surgery, but there shouldn't be any affects from that since we were able to restart it rather quickly. My concern, right now, is Mr. Fleming's brain. He was shot with a low-velocity bullet. It entered the left side and stayed there. We were able to surgically remove the bullet, however, there is a lot of swelling. If the swelling goes down, then I'm hopeful Mr. Fleming won't need any additional surgery. That's what these monitors are for, they measure the pressure in the brain,"

I'm not a betting man. I always need to have all the information. I leave nothing to chance. "What are his odds?"

He begins examining Max, checking his reflexes and pupil dilation. "I can't really say until the swelling begins to subside. The fact that he survived so far, tips the scales in his favor. He is in good health, although like I said, the next twenty-four hours are critical."

I growl again. I feel my frustration with this man growing by the second. "What about Vincent? The other man he was brought in with."

He nods, "I'm not at liberty to discuss the status of his condition with you."

I want to rip this guy in half; he is so fucking calm. "You have no idea how sick and twisted that evil man is."

None of this seems to matter to him. "Dr. Scott, I know Vincent was shot, is he going to live?"

"Mr. Phillips, all I can tell you is he has not regained consciousness yet."

I'm not going to get anywhere with this guy. "Okay. First, for security purposes, the two women outside need to be in here. Second, when can I move Max?"

"Sir, do you understand the gravity of this situation?"

Now this guy is really pissing me off. "Dr. Scott, let me explain a few things to you. First, I do understand the *gravity* of the situation. Second, that man in the other room kidnapped one of those women, out in the hall, when she was seven. He killed her father in front of her, raped her mother, and then kidnapped her again just a few months ago. So now I ask you, do you understand the *gravity* of the *fucking situation!*"

"Sir, I understand your frustration, however, I need to consider the well-being of both of my patients." He tries to calm me down but everything he say's only enrages me more.

My patience is at the end of its rope and I'm ready to just punch this fucker. "I think maybe, just maybe, you should be thinking about the welfare of *all* of your patients, since the man in the next room poses a major risk to this hospital. You need to understand that he is a major crime figure with his own army, gunning for him. So how fucking safe is everyone *now?*"

The fucker nods his head, and narrows his eyes, but concedes my point. "Let's see what happens in the next twenty-four hours. The two women can stay in here, but the guards need to remain in the hall. Is that understood?"

I nod. "If that's all you can do then, I guess that will have to do. I have ordered more guards in and around this whole place," I inform before he heads to the door.

"Okay, if you deem that necessary." He sighs then leaves me alone with Max.

"Max, I don't know if you can hear me, but Mum said you're in big trouble, so you better get your arse back to us quickly or she will probably be on the next plane out here. Jackie is here, and I know you probably don't want her to see you like this, but I'm sorry, I had no choice." No movement. Not that I was expecting any. I thought maybe the mum threat might do something though. Fuck. It's killing me to see my best friend lying here so defenseless. I need to be strong for him, no matter what happens. I pop my head out in the hall and wave them in. Jackie still looks deathly pale. Raven is hanging onto her, trying to offer comfort and support. They head over to me.

"Dr. Scott said that they've placed him in an induced coma, hoping to bring down the swelling of his brain. The next twenty-four hours are critical. Come." I put an arm around each of them, and bring them into the room. Bo follows closely behind us. Jackie moves away from me and sits on the bed, stroking his cheek. Raven is shaking and crying. Fuck, I don't know what to do for either of them. Raven pulls herself together, and goes to Jackie's side, offering her silent support.

Now, we wait—something I am never good at.

Chapter Two

ITS BEEN A FULL twenty-four hours and nothing—no movement whatsoever. I have tried to get the girls to eat something, but they won't. "Raven, think about the baby, please eat something." I plead with her.

Suddenly, I hear a commotion outside. I leap up. "Raven, no one leaves this room!" I open the door, and standing there, trying to push her way through six guards, is my mother!

"What the . . . why are you here?"

Oh no. She's giving me that look . . . the same look she gave me when I smashed her new car. This is not a good thing. "Jaxson James, where else would I be? Now please tell these men to let me pass right this minute!"

I don't need to say another word, I nod and they let her in.

"Where is he?"

I put my arm around her for support. "Mum, he's in a coma, the doctor said the first twenty-four hours is crucial but it's past that now."

She pushes past me towards Raven and Jackie. "I have protein smoothies for everyone. Maxwell, I flew all this way; you need to start waking up."

All heads turn towards Max, and I have to laugh; we all expected him to wake up, just out of fear of my mum. "Jaxson, call the doctor in here. I want to talk to him right now. I'd also like a private moment with Jackie, please." Raven, Bo, and I step into the corridor while we wait for the doctor.

Anwan

I WATCH MY SON leave the room, his head down, bearing the anguish for all of us. I fight my urge to unveil so many things he doesn't know. I can't tell him. I made a promise so many years ago—a promise I won't break. All I can do is pray Max fights hard to find his way back to us.

I gently stroke her back, trying to offer her some sort of comfort and support. "Jackie, I know neither one of you are ready to admit this, but I know love when I see it. Don't give up hope; he will come back to us." As I squeeze Jackie's shoulder, I'm reminded of the pain this man has suffered; more than anyone should ever have to endure. I take her hand, "Jackie, you're his lifeline. He just doesn't realize it yet." I sigh at the continued silence. "Jackie, please look at me." She lifts her eyes towards mine. "I've known Maxwell for a long time. He is a fighter— as tough as they come. I can see the love in your heart for him; he's such a good man. He doesn't give his heart away on a whim. Just give him all the love you have; he'll know." I can only hope my words are getting through to her.

Jaxson

"JAX, DID YOU KNOW your mom was coming?"

"No, sweetheart, but I figured she wouldn't stay away. Max is like one of her kids. She is very protective when it comes to all of us."

She stammers, "Is Vincent n-next door?"

My whole body goes tense. "Yes. As soon as Max can be moved, I will be taking him home. Since the hospital is not allowed to give out any information on Vincent's health, I had Tony do some digging. It seems Vincent was shot in the head, however, the doctor couldn't remove the bullet. It is uncertain if he will ever recover. And before you ask, there is not a reason in the world I would agree to let you see him."

"Oh," she whispers.

I'm not giving in on this one, "Yeah, *oh.*"

STEPPING BACK INTO THE room, I see tears streaming down Mum's cheeks. *Fuck.* I can't take this. *Fucking Max.* I swear I'm going to kick his arse. The doctor finally shows up, and I think my mum is about to rip him a new one. "Dr. Scott, I understand, from my son, that you put Maxwell in this coma. I'd like to know when are you taking him out?"

Dr. Scott takes a step back. He seems to be intimated by my mum. She has a way of demanding without demanding. She makes you think it was all your idea. I swear she should be running the government.

"Well, the pressure in his brain has decreased significantly. His vitals have been stable for the last twenty-four hours, so I will start easing him off of the sedation. Then, I'm afraid the rest is up to Mr. Fleming. He is strong and healthy. All the signs are positive that he can come out of this; however, you need to understand nothing is one hundred percent. We won't know if there is any damage or the extent of it until he wakes up."

My mum is stroking Max's arm, never taking her eyes off of him. "Jaxson, I want him moved from here, and brought home so I can look after him myself."

The doctor's eyes grow wide. "Dr. Scott, you heard my mum; when can we move him?"

He takes a deep breath. "Where will you be moving him to?" He raises his voice and takes upon a condescending tone.

The urge to punch this fucker is back again! "I will have him transported by private jet to a facility in Manhattan." *Did he just roll his eyes at me?*

"Lets give it another twelve hours, and then I will recheck him. How much notice do you need to arrange everything?"

I never flaunt who I am or how much money I have, but this is one of those times. "I have a jet on standby. Mount Sinai Hospital has been waiting for Max's arrival—they have been from the minute I received the first phone call. When we land, there will be a helicopter waiting to fly us to their rehabilitation center. Is that sufficient?"

He seems taken aback from all of this information; his eyebrows dart up and the corners of his mouth give a slight frown of contemplation. "Yes. Like I said, I will re-examine him in twelve hours to see what progress he has made." He leaves, and once again I'm left—waiting. *Fuck!*

I have three women who are depending upon me, looking to me for some sort of answers. I have none. My mum, bless her, finally gets Raven and Jackie to, at least, eat protein bars. As I stand in the corner, taking in the room around me, I realize my mum, who is usually my rock—tough as nails and so strong—is scared. I see it on her face; her lips are trembling and she seems to be fighting not to cry. It slays me that there isn't anything I can do. All the money and power in the world means nothing.

TWELVE HOURS PASS, AND the doctor is back again. He announces that the pressure in Max's brain has continued to drop and he can be moved in the morning, and the rest is up to Max. *What the fuck does that mean?* I swear I really want to punch this fucker. Raven must sense my frustration because I feel her take my arm, pulling me towards her.

"Jax, do you have a nurse to travel with us?"

"Yes, she's on the plane already, waiting for us."

Once again, I'm fucking waiting! Raven goes back to Max's bedside to be with Jackie. I decide to head out into the hall and see what is going on with Vincent. I see a flurry of activity, so I decide to pull one of the guards aside to get some answers. He informs me that Vincent is being moved to a federal facility—indefinitely. He will not be able to stand trial for any of the crimes he is accused of until he regains consciousness and is capable of understanding what he is being charged with. So my fucking tax dollars are now paying for him. Only Max can tell me what happened in that room. Why didn't he just kill the bastard?

MORNING COMES, AND I actually get Max and everyone else back to New York City without any drama for a change. While Max is being tended to, I pull Jackie aside to talk.

"I need to know what you need me to do for you."

She looks at me, but it's like she doesn't see me. "Jax, I just want to be with him, to help him."

I hug her. "I understand that, but what about work? Do you want me to handle that for you?"

"I can't think about anything but Max." *Oh fuck.* She's crying again . . .

"Okay, what about your parents? Just tell me what you need handled, I will take care of it all for you." I pull back from our hug.

She starts to shake uncontrollably. "My parents don't know about Max."

I get it. I'm not a moron; she hasn't told her parents about Max because they will probably flip over the age difference. "Okay, I'll take care of everything for you. Look, I had them put a bed in the room for you to rest, but you have to eat, as well. You will be no good to him if you are weak from lack of nourishment."

She shakes her head, "Jax, I can't."

I pull her close. "Here's the problem, when Max wakes up and he sees that you didn't eat, he will kick my arse, so please, eat."

I, at least, get a smile. "Okay."

She heads back into the room to be with Max. I don't know when it happened, but she's in love with him. And I realize I've been so busy with all the drama in my own life, that I didn't even see this happening. What kind of friend does that make me? Why has Max held back on this? Once again, I'm left with more questions than answers!

Chapter Three

Jaxson

I MADE SURE THAT Jackie's work understood what was happening, and they gave her a leave of absence. I paid her rent for a year, so she wouldn't have to be concerned with it. I then had to make the decision to move Max out of the rehabilitation center. I know Max, he would not want to be in there. More importantly, he wouldn't want Jackie there, so I moved him to his place. I put the nurse in the guest room, and I moved Jackie's personal belongings back to Max's penthouse. Now, it's back to a waiting game. My mum and Mrs. Osla come by daily to check on him and to make sure that Jackie is eating. As I head back across the hall to my place, I realize that Raven has a doctor's appointment tomorrow. It's been four weeks since Max was shot. For me, time has stood still. But for our baby, life goes on.

I walk in the door and smell something strange. As I head into the kitchen, I see the most beautiful sight—Raven is attempting to cook me dinner, and I must try *not* to laugh. Just then, she turns around. "Jax, I wanted to try and cook for you, but I'm not having much luck." *She bites her bottom lip; what a beautiful sight.*

She is standing in the kitchen, amongst a mess that I can't believe one person could possibly create. I am overwhelmed with my love for this woman. "Raven, I love you. I love everything about you. I love the fact that you have no clue when it comes to cooking. I love that you want to do this for me. But right now, I need you—*bad.*"

That's all I have to say; she drops everything and takes me in her arms. No words are necessary; she just gets it. She strokes my back, her simple touch offering so much comfort.

"Jax, whatever you need from me, just take it."

When did I become such a lucky bastard? I lift her in my arms and carry her to our bed. I slowly undress her, taking in her beautiful body. I kiss those amazing lips, and then nibble on her ear, slowly working my lips all over her body. Her skin is so soft and silky. I feel the subtle changes to her body as I glide my fingertips up and down her hips, and then reach up, and begin stroking her nipples until they peak for me. I reach up and nibble on *that* ear. *Fuck, I'm so hard.* I look into her beautiful eyes and slowly sink my cock into her warm body while cradling her in my arms.

"Raven, you have unraveled me layer by layer without even trying. I need this—us, in the *happy place—really* slow and gentle."

I move slowly, in and out, and I feel my heart race. I know I can't last much longer. She pulls my face towards hers, resting her forehead on mine. "Fall with me, Jax."

I'm there, the top of the cliff and I'm going to fall. All the tension and pressure I've been dealing with for the last four weeks comes rushing to the surface and I explode with such force, I think I might pass out. We lock eyes, and I know she understands everything I'm dealing with: my need to keep everyone safe, my impatience with Max's recovery, the baby, and all the unknowns. I don't do unknowns. We just lay here, enjoying a temporary moment of solitude together.

"Sweetheart, tomorrow you have a doctor's appointment, it will be four weeks."

"I know, Jax, it's also been four weeks that Max has been unconscious. He will come back when he's ready, not on your timeline but his."

I don't have to explain to her how important Max is in my life, how much I need him around me. She gets it, but more importantly she get's me. I smile thinking of her attempt at cooking. "Did you really try and cook dinner for me?'

She laughs, "Didn't quite turn out the way I planned."

My heart feels like it's going to burst. "Raven, I love you and everything about you . . . that's all."

Jaxson

MORNING COMES AND I'M still buried balls deep. *What a beautiful way to wake up.* As I watch her eyes begin to flutter, my cock jumps to attention. I swear that bastard has a mind of his own. *Calm down, buddy, she needs her rest.*

"Hmm, Jax, who are you talking to?"

Oh shit, did I say that out loud? "Good morning, sweetheart."

"Jax, were you talking to your cock, again?"

Need a change of subject—*quick.* "No, Raven, he was just saying good morning."

I tilt my hips up so he can give her a proper good morning.

"You know, Jax, talking to Mr. Cock will get you sectioned."

I throw my head back in a fit of laughter. "*Mr. Cock?* Is that what you've named him? I think you're the one who might get sectioned, sweetheart."

"Well, he may as well have a name, since you're always talking to him." She reaches up and kisses me with those puffy, soft lips. The taste of her is surreal. "How about if you and Mr. Cock give me a proper wakeup call," she suggests.

I tilt my hips up again, swiveling them around while I hold her firmly pressed against me. "Oh, sweetheart, I love proper morning shags with you."

I stop and watch her with wonder. "Jax, why are you stopping?"

I pull myself into a sitting position and bend my legs more. "I want to sit up and watch you gliding up and down my cock, so I can have this vision etched in my mind for the rest of the day." I tilt my hips up again, as her beautiful hair cascades around her bare breasts. I reach up to stroke her nipples, but she pushes my hands away.

"Just watch, Jax, and enjoy the show."

I'm such a lucky bastard. She's gliding up and down my cock, while she rolls her nipples between her fingers. I reach around and grab onto that fabulous arse, and slam into her. "Raven, I can feel you quivering. Come on, sweetheart, it's beautiful."

As she throws her head back and her lips part, I know neither one of us are going to last much longer. Leaning forward, I take one of those beautifully engorged nipples and drag it between my teeth. She clenches my cock from top to bottom, raking her nails over my nipples. That's it—her nails, dragging across my nipples is what throws me over that cliff. And my sweetheart is right there with me, screaming my name.

She sprawls across my chest as I stroke her back, both of us trying to steady our breath. "Jax, you don't have to come to the doctor with me. It's just a routine check-up."

My arm tightens around her. "Do you really think I wouldn't go with you? Really, Raven, I thought you knew me better."

She leans up and kisses me, "I just want you to know that I understand if you can't."

"Nothing will stop me—ever."

"I love you," she whispers.

I kiss those beautiful soft lips, "More, sweetheart, always more . . ."

Raven

WHEN WE ARE FINALLY ready, Jax and I head out to my doctor's appointment. Manhattan traffic seems to be light for a change. We arrive at the office right on schedule. We checked in, and get settled in the waiting room. I look around the room and take notice of all the women staring at him. I wonder if the feeling like I want to rip their eyes out will ever go away. He is so beautiful that words escape me. The women don't care that he is there with me, they stare at him; he pays them no mind. Just as I feel like I might combust, the nurse calls us back. The visit is as I expected pretty routine, that is, until the doctor informs me that I need to gain some weight. Jax actually asked the doctor for an approved foods list! I swear I want to ring his neck. *Oh whom am I kidding?* I love this neurotic, passionate, intense, over the top man. As we

15

step outside, Jax turns his phone on, and it's going wild. His face lights up with the biggest smile, he doesn't have to say a word, I know—Max is awake.

Jackie

FOUR WEEKS, AND HE hasn't moved! I finally had to call my parents and tell them everything that has been going on. Come to find out, Jax had already spoken to my dad. He assured him I was heavily guarded.

I love Max so much. All I can do is hope that my love is enough to bring him back to me. I sit on the bed and hold his hand; I need the constant touch. "Max, when I was a young girl, my grandmother gave me a crystal pendant. She made me promise to keep it with me always. She said it would protect and heal me. I've worn this pendant everyday. I don't think my grandmother would mind if I gave it to you. I think you need this more than I do." I take it off, place it in his palm, and silently pray. Please, Grandmother, I beg you; bring him back to me. I won't survive without him. This man is beautiful, and I have fallen so deeply in love with him. I don't know when, or how it happened, but I know my life will never be the same again. "Please come back, Max, please." I sit back, getting lost in the sound of his breaths and the different thoughts that parade through my mind. Silence can be so loud at times.

Jax has been here everyday, and I realize that he and Max are a lot closer than I thought. I wonder if Max is aware how many people love and respect him. The nurse flutters around the room doing her work, she keeps humming and I swear I never hated humming until now. The only thing I want to hear is his heavy accent; it's low and as smooth as silky, dark chocolate. I love when he whispers in my ear. I'm so tired, but I will only take naps, just in case he wakes up.

His beard is speckled with grey and so very soft. I've decided to read to Max everyday. I found a book in his office, *The Wicked Wit of Winston Churchill* by Dominique Enright. It figures Max would have something like this; it's just short, funny quotes. As I read to him, I hold his hand. He starts to slowly move his thumb in circles over my hand, and I freeze. I take a deep breath and lean down to take a closer look at his face. His eyes are fluttering, and before I know it, he slowly opens them. I have to force myself to breathe before I pass out! Machines are beeping, and the nurse runs over to us.

"Please, step back while I examine him." She smiles and pats my arm before turning to him. "Welcome back. I'm your nurse, Nicky. Do you know your name?"

"Head hurts," he groans.

"What's your name?"

"Maxwell Fleming . . . head hurts . . . tired." He closes his eyes. I silently beg for him to please stay awake, but he's out again.

Within minutes everything in the room seems to come to life along with Max. After being paged by Nicky, the doctor shows up to examine him. He says it wouldn't be uncommon for Max to be in and out of it for a while.

Jax comes running in. "Jackie, what did he say?"

"Not that much, Jax, just that his head hurts, his name, and that he was tired."

"Jackie, he will come back to us. If he knows what's good for him, he better do it quickly." He tries to tease. "Did you eat at all today?"

"Yes. Your mom was here earlier; she brought sandwiches for everyone."

He takes a deep breath. "Jackie, can you give me a few minutes with him, please?"

"Sure, Jax. I'll go next door and visit with Raven for a bit," I say around a yawn. I hate to admit it, but I'm dog-tired.

Jaxson

SHE LEAVES, AND NOW it's just us. "Okay, Max, if you can hear me, then you better start waking up, 'cause I don't know how much more I can take—and yes, right now, it's all about me. I'm doing your job and mine, plus dealing with Jackie, Raven, Bella, Mrs. Osla, and—*my mother!*"

Nothing. No response, *really, Max?!* "Okay, mate, have it your way, but don't say I didn't warn you." As I turn to leave, I could swear I hear him growl, but when I look back, he isn't moving.

I step out of the room and for the first time, since he was shot, Raven and Jackie are smiling. "Jackie, we are going next door. If he comes around again, please come and get me."

"Of course, Jax. Raven, you look tired; go rest. I promise, if there is any change, I will ring you." She heads back to Max's room as Raven and I go back across the hall. Raven is so tired. I pick her up and carry her to the bedroom.

"Jax, I can walk, you know."

"Sweetheart, humor me please. Have a nap, and if anything changes, I promise to wake you." I watch as she crawls into bed with nothing on but my dress shirt; she's so fucking beautiful. If I were a gentleman, I would buy her beautiful lingerie. But whom am I kidding? When it comes to this woman, I'm far from a gentleman. Seeing her, in my shirt, makes my cock stand at attention. If I don't leave the room now, she won't get her nap. I adjust my raging hard-on, knowing there will plenty of *cock heaven* later.

Maxwell

I HEAR EVERYTHING, YET I still can't bring my mind to the surface. Everything is cloudy; a dense fog. I wish Jackie would stop crying. I hear her sobs, and feel her trembling, but I can't pull myself to the top. Something is in my hand. I squeeze it tightly. My head hurts. I surrender into the abyss.

How much time has passed?

What is that God, awful humming noise?

Jackie is reading my Winston Churchill book. Her voice soothes the pain in my head. There is something in my hand. I vaguely remember Jackie putting it there to help me heal. Mrs. Philips is here, even though she scares me, I find comfort from her—but I would never tell her that. I must be pretty bad off if Mrs. Osla is here, too. "Maxwell . . ." she whispers in my ear.

I need to let Jackie go. She's in pain because of me. When did I let myself fall in love with her? I won't be someone else's burden. Raven will hate me for hurting Jackie, but I can't do this to her. She deserves to be happy, and she deserves to be loved. I'm nothing but a shell of a man.

Oh my head hurts, and the fucking humming has got to *stop!*

Jaxson

I DECIDE IT'S TIME to call in reinforcements, since Max has left me no choice.

"Hey, Mum, what's going on today?"

My mum never beats around the bush, and I don't expect her to start now. "Jaxson, what's the problem?"

She is as reliable as *Big Ben.* "Why do you always think there is a problem when I call you?"

"Jaxson James, I'm your mother, and I know that you don't call me in the middle of the afternoon for a chat. So, again, what's the problem?"

Fuck, middle name and all. "Okay, Mum, Max woke up, but then he closed his eyes again. The doctor said all of this is normal, and we just have to wait it out. I'm trying to deal with work, Jackie, Raven, the baby, and Max. He needs to wake up, Mum."

She laughs, "Don't you mean, *you* need him to wake up?"

"Yeah," I whisper.

She takes a deep breath. "I'm on my way. I'll bring Mrs. Osla again, that should put the fear in him." Before I can say anything else, she hangs up. Now I need to prepare for the floodgates that I just opened.

Jackie

ALL I CAN DO is wait and pray that he will come back to me. There was so much not said between us. *Why did I hold back?* I knew the danger. I should have gone with my heart, not my head. I close my eyes and let the tears fall.

"Max, I need you in my life. I don't know when it happened, but I'm putting it out there now—please come back to me, baby. I need your strong arms around me. I'm not going away, no matter what. Oh, Max, come home to me, baby, any way that you can, please."

Nothing. Not even a flinch. Time seems to crawl by. Nicky, the nurse, checks his vitals every hour, while Jax and Raven come in and out, all day long. Mrs. Phillips comes by once a day with food, usually around noon. Today, she's been here twice and she brought Mrs. Osla again. They are probably here to try and scare Max in to waking up. I look at the two of them and I can't figure out why Max is so afraid of these sweet ladies. Okay—maybe Mrs. Osla—but I don't understand a word she says anyway.

"How's our boy doing today, Jackie?"

I smile. "He woke up for a few minutes, but then he went out again. The doctor said we have to wait, so wait, I will. You're here twice today, Mrs. Phillips, is everything okay?"

She nods, "Yes, dear. Please, call me An. I figured I would come back with Mrs. Osla and check on Maxwell again."

"Would you like me to step out?"

She takes my hand, "No, dear, you can stay. I just need to say something to Maxwell."

She leans down and whispers something in his ear, and then steps back. Then Mrs. Osla, takes his hand and says something, but I'm not sure what. I couldn't hear, and even if I did, Max is the only one who can understand her. They turn to leave and I can see tears in their eyes. "Oh, Max, I hope you realize how many people love you. You might not have any blood relations but you have something so much more, something people search for their whole lives, and it's right in front of you—pure love." I put my head beside his, trying to sleep, but the only thing that comes are more tears.

Raven

I WAKE FROM MY nap, feeling flutters. I realize the baby is moving! I go to look for Jax and see him sitting by the bar, staring out the window with a glass of scotch. He seems lost and so very sad; it breaks my heart to see him like this.

"I know you're there, sweetheart."

Hmm, "I know you do . . . you always do. I have something that might cheer you up a little." I walk up to him, take his hand, and place it on my tummy. His eyes widen as he gazes at my tummy, seemingly fighting to hold back the tears. "That's our baby, Jax."

He pulls me closely, "Sweetheart, it's so amazing that you have protected this little one through so much. I'm in awe of you."

I pull his head up towards mine. I need to see his eyes; they say so much. "Jax, what's got you so sad today? Max is starting to come to. I thought you would be happy."

"You know I'm not good at waiting."

I kiss him softly. "I knew you and Max were close, but I never really knew how close. How did you meet him?"

"I met him at a Pub in London."

"I know that already, but how?"

He takes a deep breath. "I closed a major deal, and I was *out on the piss.*"

"You were *what?*" I can't help my confusion. I have no idea as to what the hell that means.

He laughs. "I forget that you don't know all my slang. Drinking—you know—celebrating. I got into it with a group of people; booze was flowing and it soon became a brawl. Max stepped in to help me, and made sure I didn't get into it with the coppers. I offered him a job, and he joked that I couldn't afford him. He called me 'pretty boy,' dropped me off at my hotel, and told me to go back to the States. The next day, I saw him on the local news while guarding one of the Queen's grandsons. I stayed in London until I was able to find and convince him to work with me—not for me. We became closer than brothers. And honestly, I never thought friends, like Max, even existed. That man would lay down his life for me, and I would do the same for him. I have so few people that I trust; I can't lose him."

I hug him. "He will be okay, Jax. I know it."

"How can you know that?"

"I have faith."

"*Faith?*"

"Yes, Jax, faith. "

"Jax, what else is bothering you? Don't say *nothing* because I can tell; your eyes give it away."

"I'm juggling a lot of balls right now, and I can't afford to have anything slip through the cracks. Lives are at stake. I usually have Max watching my back, but that's not an option right now."

"What do you need me to do for you . . . to lighten the load," I offer.

"Just having you here safe with me helps. God how I love you, Raven." The sincerity in his voice is almost too much for me to handle.

"What did the doctor say today after he examined Max?"

I feel his whole body tense. "Everything is positive."

I glare at him. "Jax, you are the most direct and honest person I have ever met, so what are you not telling me?" I search his eyes, looking for a way in. He leans in and gently kisses my lips, working his way towards my ear. *I can't let him distract me.* "Jax, you can't distract me with your kisses. What aren't you telling me?"

Jaxson

I KNOW I HAVE to let her in; it's just hard for me. I've only shared everything with Max. I swear I'm going to kick his fucking arse! "Nothing, I'm fine." I don't think she believes me, however, the alarm on my phone, indicating it's time for her to eat, has gone off. Perfect distraction. "Oh, time for you to eat, sweetheart."

She freezes. "Wait! First, you try to distract me with a promising visit to the *happy* place. Then, you have an alarm going off on your phone, reminding you to feed me? You're not going to answer my questions, are you?" She watches as I stroke my chin. I decide to distract her further and give her my crooked smile. It always seems to do something for her. This time is no different.

"Sweetheart, are we going to the *happy place?"*

"Not if you don't answer my questions."

I can be such a bastard if I have to be—she has no clue. "That's okay, sweetheart, I can hold out—can you?"

I lean in and nibble her ear, leaving a trail of soft tender kisses down her neck, smirking all the way down! I unbutton her shirt and latch onto one of her nipples, flicking it with my tongue. Slowly I release it and lift her hand towards my mouth and kiss the inside of her wrist—that does it—she leaps up and wraps her legs around my waist. I carry her to the kitchen and place her on the cold counter as I go back to kissing and licking one nipple, and then the other. I know I'm not going to be able to hold back much longer, so I stop.

"Jax, what the fuck? Why are you stopping?"

"First, no blue language; the baby can hear you. Second, I told you I can wait. You need to eat—doctor's orders."

She takes a deep breath, "Okay, so let me get this straight, you can swear up one side and down another but I can't?"

I smirk again, and I swear, I think she wants to pull my hair out. "Sweetheart, I only swear when you're taking me to the *happy place;* that doesn't count."

"Why?"

I need to make her see reason here. "Why, what?"

She huffs like she's getting more frustrated. "Why doesn't it count, Jax?"

"The baby is sleeping then."

Her eyes go as wide as saucers. I can tell she thinks I'm crazy. "Raven, don't look at me like that. I know what you're thinking."

"Oh trust me, Jax, you have no idea what I'm thinking right now."

I bite back a smile. "Let's eat. I have mac and cheese, tomato soup, or peanut butter and jelly. Which would you prefer?"

Raven

I OPEN MY MOUTH to speak, but nothing comes out so I shut it again. He's nuts. "What happens if I swear in my head?"

I watch as he mulls over my question. He cocks his head to the side, and gifts me with such a beautiful smile . . . *Oh fuck, I'm done.* "Raven, I don't want our baby's first word to be *fuck.* I don't think I'm being unreasonable." God bless him; he's serious.

I throw my hands up in the air. "Fine, I'll take the mac and cheese, please."

As he dishes out the dinner I go and curl up by the fireplace. We eat, both of us quietly lost in our own thoughts.

"Jax, since we've been back, our lives have been like a whirlwind. And then, everything with Max . . . we really haven't had any time to talk."

"Where would you like to start?"

I put my food down. "Well, maybe we can start with Erica."

"What about her?"

He's not going to make this easy. "How did you meet her?"

"I met her in a bar. I thought it was random, only to find out much later that she had set the meet up. Did she say anything to you while you were being held captive?"

"Only that she was surprised you would fall for someone like me. She still believed you belonged to her. What exactly did she do to you?

Jaxson

WELL, ASIDE FROM FUCKING with my mind, which she doesn't need to know. "She stole millions of dollars, and put me in a position that could have sent me to prison. It was only with Max's help that we unraveled everything she had done before it couldn't be reversed."

"How did you find out what she was doing?" She pushes her plate away, and I want to argue with her to eat, but I'm not going to push my luck.

I smile, remembering those events. "It was Junior."

Her eyes grow large. "Michael? What did he do?"

I push my plate out of the way, as well. "I went to take a shower, leaving Erica to keep an eye on Junior. She had to make a phone call when I wasn't around. She gave Junior my phone to play with, hoping it would keep him quiet. He didn't realize what he was doing, but he recorded everything. The next day I noticed there was a video on my phone. It was of Erica on her phone, plotting her next move. I gave it to Max and the rest, as they say, is history . . . a history I wish I could erase."

"Why didn't you prosecute her?" I watch her eyes pierce mine as she's trying to understand this cluster fuck of a mess.

"Joseph asked the same thing. With the American justice system and her money, she wouldn't have gotten much jail time—if any. I decided I was going to black ball her from the very thing she loved most—the business world. When her grandfather found out what she had done, he disowned her. She lost everything."

She seems speechless and I'm not sure if she's mad or trying to understand. "So she opted for revenge, and that's why she went after Junior and ultimately . . . me.

"I can't change the past, sweetheart, all I can do is go forward with the knowledge I have, and try to protect everyone as best as I can."

"Now that Vincent is in custody, do you think I can go home?"

Home? Is she out of her *fucking* mind?! Okay, I need to remain calm here. I don't want to freak out and scare her. "No."

"Why not?"

I have to pause, and take a few calming breaths. "Just because Vincent is in custody, it doesn't mean that you'll be safe. He is the head of a major crime family. There are other people out there that might think—to get to him—they should get to you. We don't know who else knows your true identity. We also need to consider your mother's safety and the safety of our baby. Vincent's people went after Jackie just to get to you! Why do you even want to go back to your apartment?" Her eyes burn into me.

"Jax, I would *never* put anyone else in danger. However, I need to get on with my life. I can't and I won't live in fear. You are the one who told me, *if I let fear rule me then fear wins.*"

I get up, "I need to go check on Max." If I don't, I know I will come unhinged.

I NEEDED TO WALK away before I blew a gasket. The last thing I need is for her to pull a *runner.* I need to make her see the light—*my light.* We will be together forever

Arriving over at Max's, I walk into his bedroom to find Jackie, diligent as usual. "Hey, how's he doing?"

She looks so sad. "No change, Jax. Do you want me to give you some private time with him?"

She really is such a sweet girl. "Yes, please. I promise not to be long."

"It's okay, Jax, I'll go next door to see Raven." And with that, she's gone.

I stand here looking at my very broken friend, and I can't help but feel so responsible for all of this. "Max, you fucker, you need to wake up. I can't handle this on my own." I pace with my hands in my hair. Suddenly, I hear him.

"At this rate, you'll pull all your fucking hair out."

I freeze. Is my mind playing tricks on me? I stare at him. His eyes are still closed. "Max?"

He growls, "Who the fuck else were you expecting, mate?" *Only Max would go from unconscious to fucking cheeky in no time flat!*

"How long have you been awake?"

He takes his time answering me. "I came to earlier and then went out again. Calling in your mum and Mrs. Osla? That was low, even for you, you bastard."

I laugh. "I was desperate. Why didn't you say anything to Jackie? She's been here the whole time, crying and praying for you. Who's the *bastard* now?"

He clenches his jaw. "I need you to do me a favor."

I step closer to the bed, "Of course, what do you need?"

He barely opens his eyes, "Help get rid of Jackie."

I'm stunned. Did I hear him right? "Why?"

He's fisting his hands, and I swear he wants to punch me. Which all things considered, it wouldn't be the first time. "Why can't you, for once in your fucking life, do what you're told without questioning it?"

I smile at him, "Because that's not me, and you know it. Now why, damn it?"

His breathing is becoming rapid; this can't be good for him. "She deserves to be happy and safe. I'm in no position to offer her either one of those things. I don't know if I will ever be whole again. I'm better off alone. This is another reason why I don't do relationships."

I'm searching his face for an answer I already know. "You love her, I know you do."

He doesn't say anything for a while. I think he might have fallen out again, but then he opens his eyes. "Just get her to her parent's compound. She will be safe there."

He closes his eyes and lets out a low growl.

Jackie

I WAS GOING NEXT door to visit Raven, but then I remembered I needed my phone for when my parents call. And that's when I heard it. Max was awake and talking to Jax about me. He wants me gone! My heart feels like it's shattering into a million slivers of broken glass. I run next door to Raven's. She takes one look at me, charging through the door and her smile drops.

"Oh my God, Jackie, what happened?"

I can barely get the words out. "I heard Max talking to Jax, but you can't say anything. He wants me gone, Raven." I fall apart in my best friend's arms.

"Jackie, no. What do you mean, he wants you gone?"

"He said he's better off alone, and this is another reason why he doesn't do relationships."

"Maybe that wasn't what he meant. He's probably scared he won't be himself again. I think you need to talk to him." She tries to comfort me.

"No. I will not be humiliated. I don't have to beg someone to love me. I can't believe I gave myself to him, and now he wants nothing to do with me? I thought what we shared was special. How stupid and naive was I?" I sob.

"You are no such thing. Are you sure I can't talk to Jax about this? Maybe I can find out what's really going on," she offers.

"No. I'm going to my parents for a while," I say adamantly.

"I'm here for you, no matter what you need, Jackie. Please don't forget that."

"I know, but right now, I think what I need is time and space. Can you arrange the flight for me?" I ask, wiping my tears away and trying to pull myself together.

"Of course." She hugs me.

Raven

MY HEART BREAKS AS I watch my only friend's life and dreams crumble around her. The worst part is, there isn't anything I can do about it. She heads off to the bathroom to freshen up and collect herself.

Jax comes back, and he looks about as bad as Jackie does. "Jax, I need you to do something for me, and please don't ask questions. Call your pilot and arrange Jackie's flight home."

His eyes shoot up to mine, "She knows?"

I nod, "Yeah, she knows."

"Okay," he whispers. He makes all the arrangements.

JACKIE AND I HEAD out to the airport. She's about to board the plane, when I take her hand and stop her. "Jackie, before you get on that plane, I need to know one thing—do you love him?"

Her eyes fill with tears, "Raven, what do you think? I've only ever given myself to him. I love him with all of my heart and soul. But I won't beg to be loved back; it's his choice." And with that, she is gone.

The ride back to The Tower is a long one. When I finally get there, I head upstairs to find Jax. I see him sitting in the dark, staring out the window. I walk up behind him, putting my arms around him. "Hey, do you want to talk?"

He shakes his head. "No, I just want to hold you in my arms all night long."

"Eventually, we will have to talk about it."

He sighs. "Eventually, doesn't have to be tonight. Tonight, I need to hold you in my arms, and make sweet, passionate love to you." He gets up and lifts me into his arms. He carries me to our bedroom, undressing me as we go. He lays me gently on the bed, cocooning me with his body. He sinks into me so slowly. When he's all the way in, we lock eyes. "Please don't ever leave me. I think I would die." With that, I'm done. I pull him close and let him lose himself, knowing we both need each other.

Jackie

I PUT MY SEATBELT on, and listen to the flight attendant give me instructions about my safety. Can she give me instructions on how to save my broken heart? I watch the lights of New York City fade away into blackness; a blackness that clouds my heart and my soul. How could I have been such a fool? For the first time in my life, I actually wanted to give myself so totally to someone. Yet, he tossed me out like a pair of old shoes. I thought I really knew who he was. I thought he had morals, and valued the gift I gave him. He couldn't even tell me himself, he had Jax do it! I feel like such a fool. All those months, I shared so much of myself with him. All of my hopes and dreams, tossed aside. I've shed so many tears for this man; I don't think I have anything left. I feel so empty inside, like something died. I put my IPod on and hit shuffle. The first song that comes on is "Never be the same" by Red. Oh how true—I never will be. I curl up, close my eyes, and let the darkness take over.

Chapter Four

Raven

MORNING COMES TOO QUICKLY, and Jax is already getting ready for work. I have nowhere to go and no one to go with. My only friend is now thousands of miles away, hurt and shattered. There is nothing I can do about it—or is there? I'm lost in my thoughts when he barrels into the room, startling me.

"What's the matter, Jax?"

He smiles, "Nothing, just making sure you're real after last night."

I laugh, "No worries. I'm very real, and getting larger by the day. I need to go shopping for some clothes and I have other errands to run. I will take my guards and I know to always keep my guard dog, Bo, close, so don't worry, okay? I think I'm going to ask your mom and Bella to meet me for lunch." I'm not going to bring up going home right now; he has too much on his plate.

He smiles, "That's fine, just don't lose your detail. Make sure you have your phone turned on and with you. Your breakfast is ready. I will check in with you later." He leans down and gives me the softest kiss. "Oh, and just to remind you, I'm madly in love with you, that's all."

Just like that, he's gone. I head out to the kitchen and see breakfast is all set up with a single Abracadabra Rose left on my tray. I don't know how he does it but he just renders me speechless, even when he's not in the fucking room. *Oh shit!* I'm not supposed to think swear

31

words.either. I can't believe I just thought that, and I can't help but laugh. Before I leave, I plan on visiting Max; this is not over by a long shot.

I GET READY AND head next door. I need to talk to Max; he can't possibly think that he can just dismiss Jackie like yesterdays news. I run into Max's doctor just as he's getting ready to leave.

"Hello, Dr. Steven, I'm Raven, how is Maxwell today?"

"He is awake and doing better. He starts therapy this afternoon."

Oh, I wonder if he will need any help with it? "What kind of therapy does he need?"

He gives me an impatient huff, "I'm sorry, but I'm not at liberty to discuss the matter with you."

And with that, he's gone. I walk into Max's bedroom and find him sitting in a chair, staring out the window. His back is to me, so I take the time to study this man. He's hurting just as much as Jackie is.

"I know you're there, Raven."

I smile, "How do you know?"

He lifts his hand, "Your reflection in the window. Don't worry; I don't have eyes in back of my head. I take it you're here to get some answers."

I'm not going to make it easy on him. "Actually no, I'm not. I already have all the answers I will need."

He turns and looks at me, his eyes wide. "Really? What might they be?"

I laugh, "You know, sometimes you and Jax can be such cavemen! I know you love her, and I know that you're pushing her away because of that love. You think your life is too dangerous and that she would be better off without you. You don't know if you'll be one-hundred percent again, and it has you scared. So you did what Jax would do, you shut down and block out all the people from your life who love you, the people who give a shit about you. Oh fuck. You see what you did? I'm not supposed to swear, or even think of swear words, and you have me swearing like a fucking sailor!"

His bottom lip is between his teeth, and his eyes look amused. "Well, Max, are you going to answer me? Or are you just going to sit there?" I ask and the amused look changes drastically.

"Raven, first, yes I love her, but look at me. Look at all I have been through. She is so innocent, precious, and pure; then there's me. I'm a broken man, for many reasons, but all the more—broken. Doesn't she deserve the best of the best? I love her enough to give her a chance at that. Secondly, I can't help it that you want to swear at me, and I find it very funny that you go along with the crazy arse fucker."

I know I'm glaring at him, I can't help it—he is so stubborn. "What makes you think you're not the best of the best? We don't get to pick our soul mates; I believe, God, does that. And I know he's crazy, but I love him, so no swearing in front of the baby!"

He seems to be at a loss for words. "I'm going to run errands, do you need me to do anything for you?"

"No, but don't lose your detail. Take Bo and your phone." He orders. I laugh and wave as I'm running out the door.

I HEAD DOWN THE elevator with everyone in tow. It's a beautiful afternoon, so I decide to walk. I call Bella to set up lunch. "Raven, is everything okay?"

I can't help but laugh. She's so much like Jax, it's funny. "Hello to you too, Bella. Yes, everything is fine. I wanted to know if you and your mom could meet me for lunch today? I need help with a project."

She's quiet for a minute, probably not sure how to deal with someone who isn't a bulldozer. "Sure, when and where?"

I give her the details on where and when to meet, and now I'm off to go clothes shopping. I get to Bloomingdales. I stand outside the store and cry. I should be doing this with my best friend, instead, I'm alone. Adding to that, I'm walking around with two guards and a dog! I try to go in, but then I'm reminded about the last time I was here with Marco. How did my life get so fucked up? As I stroll down the street, I find a small maternity boutique and head on in. I pick out some jeans, tops, and running clothes, figuring it's a good base to start with. As I go up to the counter to pay, I discover that one of my guards has already paid for me! "What do you think you're doing?"

He looks down at his feet, seemingly embarrassed by the situation. "Mr. Phillips requested that we get you anything you wanted."

I take my package and leave the store. This is ridiculous. I decide to head to Jax's office and give him a piece of my mind. This man has taken over my entire life. I can't go home. I can't shop without all eyes trained on me. I'm becoming a prisoner with invisible walls. I enter the *Raider*s building and walk up to the security desk. The guard, hands me a badge with my picture already on it. What the fuck is this man up to now! I get into the elevator with Bo and both guards positioning themselves in front of me. As we make frequent stops, people are getting on and off. A group of girls get on, and they are discussing their evening plans. It makes me want to cry. I miss Jackie, and even Marco; he was such a tortured soul. I didn't even realize that he was in love with me. As I watch these girls, I realize beautiful women surround Jax all day long, and soon, I will be a cow. I'm fighting my tears as the doors open and I head out towards Jax's office. Mrs. Osla lets me know he is in, but on the phone. I tell everyone to wait outside the door for me. The guard informs me he has to look inside the room first; this is stupid, but whatever.

As I go inside, I lock the door behind me. He's still on his call and he seems to be getting very pissed off. Oh, I don't want to be the person on the other side of that call. Wow, I don't think I have ever seen Jax this mad. He slams the phone down and opens his arms. I can't help it, I run straight into them. This man makes me crazy mad, and then crazy in love. Will I ever know what normal is?

"Sweetheart, this is a wonderful surprise. There's not something wrong though, is there?"

I'm fighting to hold back my constant tears lately. "Oh, Jax, everything and nothing."

"Okay, are you upset with me?" he asks apprehensively.

"Yes and no."

"How about you tell me what you did today, so far, and then we can take it from there." I can tell he's really trying to be patient with me.

"I had a talk with Max, and he really pissed me off," I say after finally calming down.

"I can understand that, he does it to me all the time. Sweetheart, you can't force him to face his demons, you can only support him."

"I know that, Jax, it's just that they are both hurting, and for what—stupid pride?"

"What else have you done today?" He leans back on his desk.

"I went shopping for clothes. I couldn't bring myself to go into Bloomingdales. The last time I was there was with Marco." A lump forms in my throat.

Jax picks up his phone and hits a button. "One second, sweetheart," he holds up a finger to me, "Mrs. Olsa, please hold my calls and cancel my next meeting. Thanks." He hangs up.

I can't believe he just blocked out that time for me out of nowhere. "Jax, you have to work. I'm a distraction; I'll go."

He pulls me tightly up against his chest, running his fingertips down my cheek. "You'll do no such thing. It shatters me to see you upset." He leans in, lightly brushing his lips over mine. "I'd stop the world for you, Raven."

"Jax, I want to go shopping, pay for my own stuff. Do you know how I felt when the guard paid for all my clothes? I felt cheap, like I'm being kept by someone. Let me tell you, it's not a good feeling." I watch his reaction, but he keeps a stolid expression. "Well, what do you have to say for yourself?"

"Sweetheart, every time I open my mouth, I make you cry, so please excuse me if I'm a little apprehensive here. While we are on full disclosure, I replaced all your credit cards with a Black American Express Card. There is no credit limit. I figured you might want to do some shopping for the baby."

I can't believe what I'm hearing! "So let me get this straight; you went into my purse, took out all of my cards, and then replaced them with one that you think I should have?!" I scream. He is so in the doghouse now. "Why, Jax? Why would you do that? You need to make me understand what the fuck you were thinking!"

He glares at me. "Don't swear, the baby will hear! I remember when we were preparing for Junior, it was very time consuming and expensive. I took care of everything for Bella."

Well that's news. "Why did you do everything for Bella? Why not Michael?"

He kisses my lips softly, and then leans in to nibble on my ear. "It's not my story to tell; it's Bella's."

"I want to see my mother; I think it will be safe. I would also like to check on Jackie. She's my only friend, Jax." I can't be made to feel like a prisoner.

He nods, "Let me run everything by Max first, and then we will figure out the next step, okay?"

"Okay, I have to go. I'm meeting your mom and Bella for lunch and probably some shopping. I'll see you later. I love you." I lean in and kiss him, he holds me so tight.

"Jax, are you okay?"

He smiles, "Yeah, just needed to make sure you're real, sweetheart. I love you more."

I realize that as strong and powerful as he is, underneath, he is still that little boy whose dad walked out on him, and my heart breaks.

Jaxson

I KNOW I'M NOT going to get any work done, so I head over to check on Max. I get to Max's flat. It's very quiet. I watch him sitting in a chair, looking out the window. How did everything get so fucked up for us? "Hey, Max, how are you feeling today?"

"Jax, if you're here to tear me a new arsehole, you're too late. Raven beat you to it."

I laugh, "No I'm not here for that. I'm here so you can tear *me* a new arsehole."

His eyes shoot up to mine, "What the fuck did you do now, mate?"

I have taken up Max's pacing. "That's just it, I don't know what the fuck I did. I don't think I'm unreasonable. I don't understand why she got so mad that I had the guard pay the bill when she went shopping. I then had to confess that I replaced all of her credit cards with the Black AmEx. She really went nuts over that one. I don't want to come across all crazy, but I just want to lock her in the fucking penthouse and throw away the key! Her emotions are all over the place; she cries easily. I feel like I'm walking on eggshells."

"Well, what are you going to do?"

"Fuck if I know what I'm going to do. Max, why else would I be here."

He laughs, "Oh, Jax, it's a good thing I know you so well; a lesser man might be offended by you. Maybe she needs more from you?"

I stop pacing and stare out the window. "Max, I'm not a total moron; I get that. *Fuck.* I've wanted to marry her from the first day I met her, but again, I can't come across out of control and possessive. If I ask her now, she will think I only want to marry her because she is pregnant. If I don't ask her now, she will think I don't want her. I'm so fucked either way. Maybe locking her away isn't such a bad idea." I sigh. " I know you don't want to talk about Jackie, but it's a problem." I wait for a reaction. His jaw gets tight and he closes his eyes, probably trying to gain some control. I can see his pain, both physical and emotional.

"Why is Jackie a problem?" he almost whispers.

Why do I have to spell everything out? "Jackie is Raven's only friend, and right now, she is held up at her parent's compound in Switzerland. Raven needs her friend, and I'm sure, by the look of Jackie when she left here, she is in need of Raven. Plus, Raven wants to see her mum, and I can't say I blame her. If it were my mum, I would be fighting tooth and nail to get to her. I told her I would talk to you and see if it's possible that we make a trip to Switzerland. What's your take on that?"

He takes a deep breath, "Well, I talked to Tony today and he brought me up to speed on everything. Vincent is still being held at a federal hospital. He hasn't regained consciousness, yet. Vincent's lawyer, Mr. Deveno, has been pushing the Feds to have Vincent moved to a private facility. Duke has been brought back to New York. He is being held in solitary at Sing Sing prison, awaiting trial. You know that no one is ever one-hundred percent safe, Jax, that's just life. If you want to get her out of the country for a little bit while she is still in the earlier part of the pregnancy, then I would say go for it. Make sure you have all the necessary security with you, at all times. I can't travel with you, but I will help with all the arrangements if you need me to. I can monitor things from here. As far as Raven is concerned, you love her—that's never been a question. So what are you waiting for? You go after whatever you want and damn anyone to hell if they get in your way . . . so, get the fuck out of your own way, mate."

"This is why you're my best friend." I slap him on the shoulder. I wish I could help him figure things out; I know this is destroying him. But until he let's me in, all I can do is wait. I leave him to his thoughts and head back across the hall to plan my next move.

Raven

I MAKE IT TO the restaurant just as Bella and An pull up. When we're all seated, Bella jumps right in, "So, what did my brother do now?"

I can't help but laugh, "That's not why I asked you both here, but now that we are on that subject, he went into my purse, took all the credit cards out of my wallet, and replaced them with a Black AmEx card!"

Bella is laughing. "Raven, you need to understand that sometimes my brother can be an idiot. I'm sure he has no concept of how a women's purse is very private and personal."

Finally, someone who understands! "Well, I'm glad someone else sees how crazy he can be. He also told me that if I swear, or even think of swear words, the baby can hear it, and he doesn't want the baby's first word to be a swear word!" An is biting her lip, trying not to laugh, but even she seems to see how crazy her son's behavior is.

"Raven, my son can be a little intense."

Bella and I turn toward her and at the same time, we burst out laughing.

"You should have seen him when I was pregnant, you would have thought he was the father. He wouldn't let anyone come within ten feet of me. He wanted medical reports on everyone I came in contact with. I had three cleaning ladies quit because of him!" Bella reports before taking a sip of water. I want to ask her more about her pregnancy—where Michael was—but An is fidgeting and seems very uncomfortable, so I decide to drop it.

"I asked you ladies to lunch today to help me with Max."

"What's wrong with, Maxwell? I spoke to Jax, and he didn't say there was a problem." An's voice cracks and she turns pale.

I don't know how much Jax told her. "He pushed Jackie away. She went to her parents' compound in Switzerland. She is a total wreck; her heart is broken. I went to see Max this morning, and he's so lost. All he would say was that she's better off without him, and he doesn't do relationships. Jax told me to stay out of it, but I can't—they love each other. What has Max so rattled that he would push her away? He couldn't even tell her to her face; he made Jax do it. None of this sounds like Max to me."

An seems very upset, but Bella doesn't seem so rattled. "My brother and Max have been best friends for a very long time. They have relied upon each other for everything. They are closer than brothers; their bond is unbreakable. I'm sure he knows more than we think."

"An, what do you think we should do?"

"Raven, let me think about this for a little bit. You just be a good friend to Jackie. I like her a lot. Her parents raised her very well; they should be proud of her." *She seems really upset.*

I nod, missing my friend even more. "I'm sorry if I upset you, An, I just want to fix this."

She is so much like Jax, trying to be the strong one.

"It's fine, dear, please don't worry. I'm going to leave you here with Bella. Enjoy your lunch, ladies." She gets up and abruptly leaves.

"Bella, did I say something wrong?"

"No, Raven, it's not you. For some unknown reason, when it comes to Max, my mum can be very overprotective." She grabs a roll and butters it. I want to press her for more answers, but I don't have that comfort level with her, yet. God, I miss Jackie so much.

Pretty soon we are lost in all things baby.

WE FINISH LUNCH AND I decide to head back to The Tower to get ready to go for a run. I realize today will be the first time I go for a run with Bo by myself and I'm excited to see what he can do. I finally meet Jax's housekeeper, Sofia. I change so fast, even I can't believe it. I head out the door. I inform my detail of the route I want to take and get approval from them. We enter the park, and after a quick stretch, I take off; it feels wonderful. Running gives me the time to organize my thoughts. Bo seems to love it too.

As I acclimate to the pace I'd like to stay at, I think about Jax's housekeeper. I honestly can't believe this man has a housekeeper that looks like a cross between a Playboy Bunny and a Hooters waitress. No wonder he didn't tell me. He can't be so dense to think that I wouldn't be upset, especially since I'm going to look like a fucking cow soon. I need to figure out what I'm going to do.

I love Jax—heart and soul. I know that he loves me, but now there is a baby involved. I need to have stability, and so does my baby. I need to see my mother. However, I also need to consider her safety. I don't even know if she will know who I am. I could never forget her; her beautiful blonde hair and crystal-blue eyes.

It's amazing when you run through Central Park with two bodyguards and a big dog, no one comes near you. When we get to the end of the run, I head over to the vendor for a warm pretzel and water. I decide to sit on a bench and enjoy the sunshine. One of my fondest memories is of Marco and me, sitting on a park bench and people watching. We would make up stories about some of the people; Marco's were always funny. I still can't believe he is dead, and how little I really knew about him. Before I know it, the tears are flowing. I'm such a jumble of emotions. Bella said it wouldn't get better, so just deal with it and know that for the rest of the pregnancy, I will basically be *bat shit crazy*.

I get up to go across the street, and Bo stops. His hair is on end as he lets out a growl that freezes me to my spot. My guards are around me in an instant. I don't see any threats, only a very beautiful lady with long, black hair and dark glasses. She is watching me and it's making my hair stand on end. She takes a step forward. Bo crouches down, baring all his teeth! My guards lift me up and run me out of the park. Bo is walking backwards and growling, watching her every move.

We run into The Tower, and when I get upstairs, I head right to Max's place. I need to tell him what happened. He gives me his full attention as I relay the story. He gives the guards a quick nodding jerk of his head. They return it with a curt one and head out of the room. My guess is that was some sort of coded way to tell them to dig for answers.

"Raven, are you okay?" He brings his focus back to me.

As I calm my racing heart, I realize no matter how broken he is, we all rely on him so much . . . whom does he get to rely on? "Max, I was just rattled, you know Bo never did anything like that before. Who do you think that was?"

"Well, if I had to guess, I would say she is your father's sister, Annabelle. One of your guards took a picture with his phone and sent it to Tony. Hopefully, he'll have an answer soon. I know you think we are being hard on you with security, but do you see how danger can pop up anywhere?"

"Can this woman be as dangerous as Vincent?"

"Raven, even though women are generally not regarded as dangerous within the structure of a traditional organized crime family, Vincent structures his differently. He's an animal; the lowest of the low."

I walk over to the bar, and grab a bottle of water to help settle my nerves. "Max, what do you know about the structure of Vincent's organization? Does he have a wife or children?"

"Surprisingly, no. He relies heavily on Annabelle and his consigliere, Mr. Deveno."

I take his hand and squeeze it tightly. "Max, I understand about the security, but how am I supposed to live a normal life?"

He grimaces. "How do you think Jax would be able to live if something happened to you and the baby? Take it from me, he wouldn't. It would destroy him."

I'm not sure if he is talking about me anymore. "I get it, Max, and I'm sorry to unload this on you, especially with all the crap you are going through."

I reach in and hug him, I whisper "Thank you." As I leave, I turn and look back at him. He's facing the window, his shoulders slumped. My heart is breaking for this man.

I GO NEXT DOOR and find the place empty. I decide upon a long, hot shower. I set everything up, lighting lots of candles, and I put on Jax's IPod. I really can't imagine life without this shower. I sense him before I see him; I know when he enters the room. My body starts buzzing, and the closer he gets, the louder the ringing in my ears is. I turn around and I'm hit with those beautiful eyes. I pull him close to me, reaching up and running my finger over his soft lips. I need to be in control. He is always so dominate, but he knows when I need to feel in control, and has no problem giving it to me.

"I need you, Jax. I need to wash away the day. I just need you and me."

He leans in, slowly kissing me. "I'm here for you, baby, always." He runs his hands down the back of my thighs and lifts me up. I wrap myself around his rock hard chest. He just holds me so tightly.

"Tonight, baby, I'm your pleasure god, everything I do will be for your pleasure. Do you trust me?"

I don't even have to think twice, "Yes." And with that, he carries me into the shower. He starts massaging my back very slowly, and then, he balances me on one of his knees while he washes my hair. All of the tension I felt before flows out of me.

"I love your hair; it's so silky. When you drape it over my cock it's just—wow!" he breathes. He lets me down gently so we can take turns washing each other.

We get out of the shower; he wraps me in warm towels, and then starts to dry my hair. I study him by candlelight. When he is doing something, he is so focused and intense, unlike me. I hope the baby takes after him; he's so beautiful. He carries me into the bedroom, and I notice he has lit candles all around the room. He places me in the center of the bed.

"You are all mine, now and for always, my beautiful girl. I want to try something different with you. I'm not sure if you're ready for it, though. You have to tell me no if you can't, okay?"

My heart starts racing. "What do you want to do to me?"

He kisses me slowly, "I would like to blindfold you. I know from past experiences it might be too much to ask, so it has to be totally up to you."

I stammer. "I w-will try."

He strokes my back, calming me. "If it gets too much just tell me. I want you to experience pleasure without knowing what to expect; a total release."

He takes me to such new highs all the time. "I trust you, Jax."

He reaches over to the bedside table, and pulls out a blindfold made of silk. "Close your eyes." As he ties the blindfold around me, my heart beats wildly. I don't know if I can do this. I want to do this, to give him pleasure. More importantly, I need to do this for me. I will not let fear rule me; I rule fear. He kisses me long and slow, our tongues doing an erotic dance. "I want every part of you. I want to be your first and your last."

He's working his way down my neck, then back up to my ear, dragging his teeth as he goes. Just as I'm really getting into it, he stops. "Jax?"

"I'm still here, Raven, just getting some stuff."

Stuff, what stuff? I take a deep breath, releasing it very slowly. I trust this man.

"Are you still okay?"

I nod.

"I need to hear the words, Raven. Are you still okay?"

I let out a deep breath, "Yes. Yes, Jax, I'm okay."

He has the music on repeat; The Righteous Brothers singing "Unchained Melody." I feel his lips on mine and they taste like . . . Nutella! "Hmm, wow. So warm and silky." His tongue is full of Nutella, and he's working it around mine. This is so erotic, I don't want it to end. Now he's massaging my neck, his tongue follows wherever he's massaging. I realize he's massaging me with the warm, silky, chocolate hazelnut goodness. He works his way down my body until he's between my legs. I gasp.

"You okay, Raven?"

Every nerve ending is on fire. "Yes. Please don't stop, please. Oh my God, Jax."

His arms are locked around my thighs, and he is not letting up. The sensations are stronger because I can't see him. I'm pulling his hair and my hips are going wild. His grip on my thighs is strong like iron. "Are you really okay, baby, if not I'll stop."

I gasp, "Don't you *dare* stop! Jax, I . . . oh, fuck . . . Jax—I'm coming!" My core is shaking, and there is a buzzing in my brain. My body is so flushed; he's relentless. He works me down real slow as he kisses his way up my body.

"I'm not done, sweetheart, not by a long shot."

He enters me very slowly, so I can feel every rock hard inch of him.

"Oh yeah . . . do you feel that? Perfect, just fucking perfect, sweetheart. You're so beautiful. Enough of this blindfold, I need your eyes." He pulls the blindfold off and I'm hit with that beautiful smile. He has me totally cocooned with his body. In and out, then around to the right, and back around to the left. His arms reach underneath me, and he grips my shoulders, pulling me down as his hips push up—he's so fucking deep! Wow, this man has some killer moves.

"Look at me, Raven, now."

My eyes open wide and lock violets to blues. The depths I can see into this man's soul is . . ."Oh, fuck . . . oh, God . . . holy fuck, Jax!"

He slams into me, exploding with such force. He begins to slow down, giving me a chance to breathe. He rolls onto his side, taking me with him.

My brain fog begins to clear. "Jax, we should shower again, and clean up here."

He shakes his head, "Nope."

I look at him, "That's it, just *nope?*"

"Sweetheart, I could care less about the mess." He's in the *happy place* right now, and that's where I think he wants to stay. "Besides, I'm not done yet."

How could he possibly? "You're not done yet?"

As he laughs that beautiful raspy growl of a laugh, he tenderly kisses me, "With you, I know no end." He's moving slow and steady, in and out, but then he stops and pulls out of me. "I want to be in every part of you tonight." He crawls up to my chest and wedges his cock between my breasts, pulling my nipples, and pumping his cock.

"Oh, God, Jax, my nipples are on fire!"

He throws his head back, screaming and coming all over my breasts. "Raven, I. Love. You."

He leans down and kisses me real slowly. Working his way down my body, he enters me again.

"Jax, you can't possibly go again?"

He laughs, "No, now it's time for sleep."

I kiss him. "Shouldn't we shower?"

He shakes his head and gifts me with the most beautiful smile. "Nope, just like this—all night long." He pulls the comforter over us, and holds me in his arms, all while he's buried deep within me.

Raven

AS I SLOWLY OPEN my eyes, I realize Jax is still buried deep inside me. I laugh that this is the way this crazy, beautiful man loves to sleep. I have to wonder how he is going to manage that when I'm as large as a cow. We are stuck together and as I attempt to pull us apart, he tightens his grip.

"Where are you going?"

I never know when he's sleeping or just in, "Jax zone. " "I was going to head to the bathroom, and then the shower. I thought you were asleep?"

There's that smile. "I've been up for a while, waking up like this is shear heaven."

"I don't understand how you're able to sleep like this."

"Sweetheart, knowing that you're safe, and locked onto me all night long is a beautiful fucking thing."

"Why are you allowed to swear, and I'm not even allowed to think a swear word?"

He opens one eye, "Hush, the baby is sleeping."

I open my mouth to speak, but only a squeak comes out. Is he serious? "I hope you know how absurd you sound."

As I watch his face, I realize he's serious. "I think it makes perfect sense. When Bella was pregnant, I made her listen to soothing classical music so Junior could relax. There are studies, showing that babies can hear stuff in the womb. Why do you think those Einstein CD's are so popular?"

"Bella said you were nuts when she was pregnant, that you wanted health checks on everyone she came into contact with."

He gives me that smirk then leans down and kisses me. God, only knows what else he did to poor Bella. "What else did my *wonderful* sister tell you?"

I can tell Jax doesn't like to delve into the past, his body tenses quickly. "We didn't go into it any further because your mom looked upset."

He takes a deep breath. "It was a hard time for my mum when Bella found out she was pregnant. She wasn't married to Michael, yet. My mum is a very traditional woman. She eventually came to terms with it, and no one could love Junior more. When he was kidnapped, and Joseph showed up at my office, she really tore into him. What else happened at lunch?"

"I spoke to them about Max. I'm worried about him and Jackie." I watch his face, gaging his reaction.

He's mindlessly stroking my arm. "Sweetheart, I understand you want everyone to have their own happily ever after, but that's not always possible."

I of all people know life is not all rainbows and flowers. "I know, but they are both so lost without each other. There has to be something I can do to help."

As he begins stroking my back, he leans in and kisses my forehead. "Well, we are going to Switzerland tomorrow. I contacted Jackie's parents and they are very excited that you will be coming. We are also going to see your mum and, if all works out, she will be coming back to the States with us."

"Please tell me these are happy tears," he pleads softly as I lose the battle with my tears.

I laugh, "They are. Just when I didn't think I could love you more . . ."

He kisses me. "Enough talk, sweetheart, its time for the *happy place.*"

He tilts his hips, and kisses my lips. Just like that, everything else is forgotten.

Maxwell

AS I SIT ON the sofa, staring out over the New York skyline, I realize how much I miss her. I knew it would hurt, but it would hurt even more to keep her chained to me. Suddenly, there's a commotion out in the hallway. I hear her before I can see her; the hair on my neck is standing on end. I knew she would be coming—it was only a matter of time.

"Maxwell, you tell these guards to let me in, otherwise you will be even more sorry than you are right now!"

I wave her in because to fight her would be fruitless. "Do you want a drink, ma'am?"

She sits next to me on the couch and pulls my ear. "Should you be drinking, Maxwell?"

"Probably not. I knew you would be coming by, so I figured you could yell at me for everything in one shot."

Her face becomes red, and her jaw is tight. She's really mad, and I hate that it's me that made her this upset.

"Don't get smart with me, Maxwell."

We are silent for a bit. "I made my decision and I would like for you to respect that."

She glares at me. "Not when it's the wrong decision."

I have to laugh, "No matter, it's still my decision to make, right or wrong."

She jumps up, "Are you afraid that history will repeat itself, Maxwell?"

I freeze, staring at her in shock. How could she possibly know? I've told no one. "How long have you known?"

"I knew your grandmother, and she told me everything—even

why you went into Special Forces."

I can't believe she has known this whole time, never saying a word. "So you knew my grams before I even met Jax? Did you tell him? I mean, does he know the whole story? Is that why he tried to move heaven and earth to get me to work with him?"

Her eyes fill with tears, and she's losing the fight to hold them back. "No, of course not. It's your story to tell, not mine. Maxwell, it was a random act of violence, and there was nothing you could have done to stop it. Denying yourself love . . . is just so wrong."

"What if it happens again?" my voice cracks. "Look at what Jax is going through to keep Raven safe—all of you safe. I don't think I could live through it again. Jackie deserves a carefree happy life. She will never have that if she is with me, we both know that. The longer she is with me, the bigger the target on her back gets." I argue. She reaches down, taking my hand, and for the first time, I see such pain in her eyes. It breaks my heart, knowing that I'm the one causing it.

"Ma'am, some people are supposed to be alone."

She shakes her head, "Never, Maxwell, never."

"Either way, it's my decision and I need you to respect that."

"How about respecting Jackie. What you did to her was wrong. I understand your fear, but she didn't deserve that."

She squeezes my shoulder and heads out the door, leaving me to my thoughts.

BEFORE TOO LONG, Jax is back which is good. I need to be briefed on the trip. "Hey, sit down and run through your trip with me."

He's glaring at me. "Why are you drinking?"

I take a deep breath, "Calm down, Jax, it was just one scotch."

He growls, "I don't give a fuck! Are you trying to sabotage your recovery?"

"No, your mum was here earlier."

"Oh, do I need one of those, too?"

I nod, "Yeah, I need to talk, and you need to listen."

This is going to be so hard, but he needs to hear it all and it has to be from me. "Jax, there is a lot about me that you don't know."

"Max, whatever it is, it doesn't matter, mate. It's a little late in the game for this, don't you think?"

He's not going to make this easy. "Shut up and let me talk. This is very hard for me, and I never thought I would talk about it again, but then your mum came by and informed me that she already knew. Apparently, she was a friend of my grams long before we even met." I swirl my scotch around before bringing it up to my lips for a little courage. He sits down, his attention fully focused on me. "I told you my mum died when I was young, and I went to live with my grams in London. I went to the University on a full scholarship. I graduated early, and then went to work for Scotland Yard. I was young . . . about twenty. It was hard work, but I was good at it, always having an eye for the little details. Before I knew it, I was moving up the ranks rather quickly. During this time, I met a beautiful girl, Samantha; a Barrister. That was how we met. We worked so well together, I caught them and she put them away. We were married and she became pregnant shortly after. I felt that I had put everything with my mum to rest. And I was becoming a man that my grams could respect and be proud of. My son was born on a beautiful spring day in May. We named him Elliot, after my grandfather; he was a beautiful, blond haired, blue-eyed boy. Everything was going just as I planned. Well, you know what they say about that.

"One day in the early fall, Samantha took Elliot to the park; he always loved to be outside. When they were leaving the park, Samantha was taking Elliot out of his buggy, and two drugged-up punks' carjacked her. I was called to the scene, not realizing it was my wife and son. When I reached them, I found Samantha with Elliot in her arms . . . both of them were dead. I lost it. I was a crazy man, out for revenge. My whole world shattered that day. I quit my job, and took to the bottle."

Jax pours us another scotch. "My grams finally got me to a point where I could function and give up the drink. Then I joined the Special Forces. I didn't care about my life anymore. I didn't care where they sent me or what they asked me to do. I figured if I died, then I could be with my family. That's all I ever wanted—my family. The thing is,

I never died. Oh, I was hurt a lot . . . probably should have died . . . but never did. One day, I was asked to guard one of the Queen's grandchildren. He was wild and they thought I would be able to tame him, or if nothing else, keep him safe. Then, you came along. I took your offer because I had nothing to keep me in the UK. My grams was there, but she pushed for me to try and get a life. As much as your mum scares the crap out of me, she is the closest thing I have to a mum," I finally finish and wait a while for Jax to say something—anything. "Jax, say something please, mate."

"Why are you telling me this now?" he asks.

I take a sip of my scotch, trying to steady my nerves. "Your mum knows the story, and I never knew that she did. When she came to me today, she made me realize that you have a right to know everything. You're all the family I have, and I don't want you to hate me because of Jackie. I love Jackie, and I know that I broke her heart. I don't think I have anything left inside me to give. I'm a broken man, Jax. She deserves only the best. She needs to move on with her life. I don't want this to be a problem for you. I know she and Raven only have each other. Raven and the baby, they're your family now. I will back away and give you back the portion of the company that you gave me. I am also going to move back to Scotland as soon as I'm healed. Tony can take over for me."

He jumps up, "So that's it? You think you have this all figured out. Just like that and you're going to write me off? Well, guess again, mate. You're like a fucking brother to me, not some random employee. We're in this to the bitter end—so, enough!" He throws his glass across the room and storms out.

Jaxson

I KNOW THE WAY I just responded to Max was not the adult way to respond to things. Ha—fuck that! I'm not feeling like one right now!

I go across to my flat, only to find it pretty lifeless. I check on Raven. She must still be shopping for the trip. I told her not to bother;

we can get whatever we need when we are there. I think it is a way for her to settle her nerves, though. I'm glad she is not home right now; I need to be alone. I need to process all this shit and I know just where to start. I need to call my mum and find out exactly what she knows. I can't believe she has never said one word about this.

"Mum, I need to see you right now, where are you?"

"Why do you need to see me, Jaxson?"

I growl, "I just spent the last two hours with Max."

She lets out a deep sigh. "I'm on my way."

I always know I can count on her no matter what. I just wish Max could see that. How could everything have gotten so cocked-up for us? How did Max ever go on after his family was murdered? Three months without Raven nearly killed me. At least I had hope; hope that she was alive. Max had nothing.

The elevator opens, and my mum comes speeding in. "Okay, what happened?" She sits next to me. I see something in her eyes—fear maybe—I'm not sure.

"Max told me everything about Samantha and Elliot. He told me that you knew his grams. Why didn't you ever tell me?"

She fidgets with her bracelet, seemingly trying to find her words. "I made a promise to his grams, many years ago. Besides, it was not my story to tell, son, it was his heartache. He is like a son to me, and I want him to be happy. I tried to make him understand that what happened was a random act of violence. He can have love again, and a family, he just needs to open his heart to it. He's scared and lost. We need to support him."

She's going to be even more upset when I inform her of the latest development. "Well, you're not going to like this then . . . he has decided to go back to Scotland—permanently. He feels it would be better if he were out of all of our lives for good. What else did his grams tell you?"

Mum is visibly shaking. "She said it was Maxwell who was first on the scene; they were both shot in the head. He is in such a dark place right now, and I'm so scared. He said Jackie has a bigger target on her now. I can't imagine what he's feeling. He's hurting, we have to help him, son, *p-please*," Mum cries.

Oh fuck. "I know, mum. I will. Family doesn't give up on family."

I know what I need to do. "Raven and I are going to Switzerland; she needs to see her mum and Jackie. I will keep you posted, but please keep a close eye on Max. As a matter of fact, just stay here."

She nods, "I will, son, this is far from over."

I GOT MY MUM settled in before Raven and I had to head to the airport, accompanied by more security than normal. I'm not taking any chances. When we get to Teterboro, we meet the pilot at the plane. Max always likes to do a walk around with the pilot, so I figure I should too. He informs me of the flight time and weather conditions as we board. Raven has a tight grip on my hand and she's not letting go. "Sweetheart, I know you're nervous, but I will be there every step of the way. Max and I have already spoken to the doctors, so they are expecting us."

She's holding my hand so tight. "I know, Jax, I'm just scared. I don't want to traumatize her anymore than she already is. I'm also very worried about Jackie and Max. I know something happened because your mom is staying close to him, which means you're worried. Why won't you tell me what has you so upset? I thought we weren't going to have any secrets?"

I look into those eyes, and I try to find the calm that she always brings me. "Yes, I'm upset. Actually, very upset. Secrets were kept for the past eight years, not only by Max, but also by my mum. It's Max's story that he should have told me eight years ago. Raven, Max thinks he can just walk out of my life, but he can't. I'm not about to lose the closest thing to a brother I have. I told you, I can be a real bastard, Max, knows this, and I will throw everything I have at him if necessary."

"Does this have to do with why he pushed Jackie away?"

"Yes, it does, and also why he is so overprotective."

She squeezes my hand. "I won't push for answers, but I hope you know I'm not giving up on Max and Jackie. I told you, Jackie and I were roommates in collage. She is two years younger than me, so I always felt like her big sister. Did Max tell you about her family?"

I shake my head, "Not much, just that she has an older brother, but there is a large age difference. When you graduated, why didn't you continue to room with her?"

"I got the job teaching at the school about six months before she did. Marco followed me up to New York from D.C, and we moved in together. I wanted Jackie to live with us too, but she didn't like Marco. At times it was difficult, but she would make herself scarce when he was around, so I wouldn't have to choose. Jackie's parents are very nice; her mother is a traditional Japanese woman, always putting her husband first. If I didn't know her father on a personal level, I would be very afraid of him."

Well that's a surprise. "Really, why?"

She bites her bottom lip. "Maybe I should let you experience him for yourself?"

I lift her hand and kiss her wrist, "Oh no, sweetheart, you opened this door; no turning back now."

She takes a deep breath. "He is a quiet man, but he is very powerful. When he walks into a room, he doesn't need to say a word; his presence demands respect and he gets it."

"Max said Jackie has an older brother that owns a computer software firm. Are they close?"

"No, Dylan is much older than her, he lives in Japan."

"When was that last time you were at Jackie's parents' house?"

"I usually went home with Jackie during Christmas break. I wasn't able to go last year, but I was with them the year before. It gave me some sort of family for the holidays."

She unlatches her seatbelt and crawls into my lap. She begins kissing me with those soft lips, very gently.

"You know you should have your seatbelt on?"

"Yep, I should." She kisses me again.

"You know the flight attendant can see us?"

"Yep, I know." Another kiss.

"You know there are quite a few people on this flight that can see us?"

"Yep, I know that too."

She swipes her tongue over my lips, and I moan. "You know I

could make you get back into your seat and buckle up?"

"Yep, I know, but you won't." She deepens the kiss again, swirling her tongue around slowly.

"How do you know I won't?"

"Because I can feel how much you need me," she whispers into my ear and gives me a little wiggle and let's out a moan.

I smile and unlatch my seatbelt. "Did I tell you that there is an office on board and a master suite?"

"No, but I think it's time for a tour, don't you?" she laughs.

"We have at least another six hours of flight time, I'm sure we could find lots to pass the time, sweetheart." I lift her up and carry her into the master suite.

"Wow, Jax, this is beautiful."

I lean in and gently kiss her. "Sweetheart, you're beautiful, and all mine." I need to be buried deep within her, blocking out the rest of the world.

"Let me take care of you, Jax," she pants. She always knows when I need her like this.

I rest my forehead on hers, and I kiss her so softly. "Sweetheart, I'm all yours."

Maxwell

I SHOULDN'T BE SURPRISED, but I am. Jax had the balls to have his mum stay next door to watch me. He's such a bastard. It doesn't matter, my mind is made up. As soon as I can, I will be moving to Scotland. I don't know how she did it, but Jackie broke through all of my walls. I didn't realize it until the night Vincent tried to take her. Everything came flooding back that night, the fear of devastating loss; real pain. Thanks to me, Jackie's in more danger now than before. She needs to stay at her father's compound, where she will be safe. I was hoping to be gone by the time Jax returned. Now with his mum here, I doubt that will happen.

It's a nice day outside so I think I might go for a walk around the park; clear my head. I put on my gear and head out towards the elevator only to see Mrs. Phillips sitting in a chair with her book.

"What are you doing, sitting out here?"

She looks up at me, "Maxwell, what do you think I'm doing?"

I grit me teeth, "Spying on me for Jax."

"Where do you think you're going?"

I'm trying to be calm here. "I'm going for a walk in the park."

She gets up. "Did the doctor say you could?"

I'm so busted. "The therapist started me out in the gym. I'm bored; I know my limits."

She shakes her head, "You'll do no such thing, get back inside, right now."

I open my mouth to speak and she yanks on my ear. "Do I have to tell you again?"

I know better than to test her limits. "Ma'am, do you want to have tea with me? Or are you just going to sit out here and spy on me for Jax?" As much as I want to be left alone, I love having her here. I would never tell her that . . . but I do.

"Maxwell, I would love some tea."

She heads to the kitchen, and starts puttering around. "Ma'am, you know I'm quite capable of making tea."

"Yes, dear, I know that. But this is what I do, so behave and let me do it." I sit and watch her work her way around the kitchen with such ease. I will really miss her, but I have to do what's best for Jax; he deserves his shot at happiness. She sets everything up and sits next to me. She always gives me *Jammie Dodgers* with my tea, just like my grams did. "Jax, said you want to go back to Scotland, can I ask why?"

What do I say? I don't want to hurt her. "I was waiting to see how long it was going to take you."

She glares at me. "I was giving you some space."

I start to laugh, and I can't stop. Bless her, she is just sitting there with a straight face, waiting. "I'm sorry, ma'am, sometimes you're just too funny."

She rolls her eyes, "Well, I'm glad I can be your source of amusement, however, you still haven't answered my question."

I take a breath. "Jax has a shot at a happy life with a wonderful girl. He has a baby on the way. Raven's only friend is Jackie and vice versa. The situation with Jackie makes it hard for Jax, and he doesn't need or deserve that. He deserves to have his slice of heaven. Besides, if I'm in the picture, it puts a bigger target on Jackie."

She takes my hand and squeezes it. "What about you, Maxwell, what do you deserve?"

I stir my tea that's now cold. "That ship sailed a long time ago." We sit in silence for a while, sipping our tea. "Ma'am, can I ask you a question?"

She nods, "Of course, what is troubling you?"

I need to know this, but I don't want to upset her. "How did you know my grams?"

Her lip begins to tremble. "I knew it was just a matter of time before this story would have to come out."

A tear rolls down her cheek. *Oh bloody hell, what did I do?* "Please don't cry. I'm sorry. You don't have to say another word."

She shakes her head, "Unfortunately, it's not that easy. This story should have been told a long time ago, but I made a promise to your grams so I kept a lid on it. I knew who you were from a very young age. I was dating a young man, and I thought it was true love. I went against my parents' wishes and dated him. I fell in love; foolishness comes with youth. I found myself unmarried and pregnant. My father pushed for him to marry me right away, which he did. He said he was in sales and had to travel a lot. I was very young and very naïve, so I believed him. Things were good for a bit. He always made it home for the weekends to spend time with Jax. Then along came Isabella, and she was such a handful. After that, my husband came home less and less, until finally, he just never came back at all. I decided I would search for him, and what I found was his other family; you and your mum."

She stops talking, and watches me as if waiting for my reaction. Talk about dropping a bomb—Jax, Bella, and I are siblings!

"Your mum knew. He came home and told her everything, right before he left her, too. It wasn't too long after that, she overdosed. In the meantime, I decided to pack up my family and move to the States. When I found out about your mum's passing, I decided I wanted to take you with us. I wanted to raise the three of you together as a family. I went to speak to your grams; she was such a kind woman, Maxwell. Your grams was very gracious, but she wanted you with her. I couldn't blame her, you were all she had left. She promised me that she would keep me updated on everything in your life, and I kept her updated on Jaxson and Isabella's. When you married Samantha and had Elliot, she was so proud of you. Then when everything happened, she contacted me, thinking maybe I could bring you back to the States to live with us. She talked about maybe telling you the truth, but then you joined the Special Forces."

I take the rattling teacup from her hands. "Take as much time as you need, ma'am."

"Your grams wanted you to get to know Jaxson and Isabella. I think she wanted to know you had some sort of family before she died. You being in that bar on that night was not an accident, your grams and I arranged it. We couldn't think of any other way. And I knew how wild Jax would get after he closed a deal. We knew you would look after him."

I can't believe what I'm hearing; these two kind little old ladies totally pulled the wool over our eyes. "Does Jax know any of this?"

She shakes her head, "No. I would appreciate it if you let me tell him. He deserves the truth, and he deserves to hear it from me."

I stare into space, my mind racing, until I finally find my voice. "Of course, but why did you wait so long to tell me?"

"Shame." She looks down.

I don't know if I want to know this next answer, but I have to ask the question. "Of me?"

Her eyes grow wide. "Never, Maxwell! Oh, lad, never of you! Only of me."

"Why?"

I see her lip begin to quiver as she fights to hold back the tears. "No one likes to admit they were made a fool of. I fell in love with a man who was already married. I didn't know it, and I married him. My marriage was a sham, and my children would have to bare the shame of illegitimacy. It's my shame to bare—not theirs. I know in today's world it's not a big deal, but I'm from a different generation. Your grams never wanted him to know where you were, or anything about your life. I don't know where he is, or if he is even still alive. I really don't care. I made a promise to your grams that I would keep this secret as long as you needed me to. I tried so many times to convince her to tell you. Not just for you, but for Jax and Isabella. Your grams left a letter for you and told me that I would know when to give it to you. I have never read the letter. It's in a safety deposit box. When you're ready, I will give it to you."

We sit in silence, both of us not knowing what to say or do.

"Maybe tomorrow we can take a ride to the bank, ma'am, I would like to read that letter."

"Of course, and when Jax gets back, I will sit him and Isabella down and tell them the whole story."

I silently nod, not really knowing what else to say.

"Maxwell, I can only hope in time you will forgive me. I hope that by telling you this story, you will understand why you can't leave. Whether you like it or not, we are all family. "I'll leave you alone now."

I stay lost in my silence, soaking in all of this information, not realizing she's left until I hear a door shut.

Chapter Five

Jaxson

MY BEAUTIFUL GIRL IS fast asleep. It gives me a chance to do some research on Jackie's father. Wow, she wasn't kidding. This man is very influential. He holds a lot of power within the Japanese and Swiss governments. He's also very well insulated with security, which is a good thing. This is going to be a very emotional trip. I wish Max was here with me. I better check in with mum to see what's going on there.

"Hey, Mum, how's Max doing?"

"Well, he's not happy that I am sitting guard by the elevator, if that's what you mean."

I laugh at the thought. "Mum, of course I knew he would be mad, but how is he doing besides that?"

She sighs, "He's hurting, son, for many reasons. He needs us around him, now more than ever. You need to get through to Jackie and make her fight for him. I know she's hurt too, but she has no idea what this man has been through. It's his story to tell her, not yours, but she needs to be here."

"I get it, Mum, keep my mouth shut, but get her to come back with us. Just wish things would be easy for a change."

She laughs, "If it were easy, son, then it would not be worth fighting for. We will get to the other side of this, like everything else."

"Okay, I need to wake Raven up; we're getting ready to land. I will talk to you later, love you."

"I love you too, be careful."

I hang up and stare out at nothing, "When did life get so complicated?"

"Jax, your life got complicated the day you met me."

I jump up, "I didn't realize I said that out loud."

She strokes my face. "It's the truth, Jax. I understand your frustration and fear of the unknown. I feel it too, but all we can do is hang tough and lean on each other. Our love will get us through this, I honestly believe that.

I open my arms and she jumps into them, I'm holding her so tightly, that I'm afraid she won't be able to breath. "Raven, I need to speak to you about Max and Jackie."

She takes a deep breath, "Okay."

"I know why Max pushed Jackie away, but I can't tell you. It's Max's story. He needs Jackie, though, I know he does. But he needs to be the one to tell her why he pushed her away. I just don't know how to make it happen without revealing the things that should be told by him."

"Jax, I knew when you put your mom on as a watch dog that it was to make sure that Max didn't pull a *runner.* I also know that you are very worried and upset by all of this. I understand you can't tell me; I would never ask you to betray a confidence. Let me ask you this, with all your heart, do you believe Max and Jackie are better together or apart?"

I stroke my fingers up and down her back. The constant touch is comforting. "Together."

"Why?"

"I don't even have to think twice about it, Raven. Jackie got through walls in a matter of months, that I couldn't in eight years. She loves him for him, and not for what he could give her. She has brought my best friend back to life. His heart has been shut off since the very first day I met him, but with her, I have seen him come alive. I have seen him smile like he meant it, not because he had to. When I went to see him yesterday, it was the old Max, again—stone cold with dead eyes. It's not that I don't want that Max, I just want Max to be happy.

Does that make sense?"

She kisses me, trying to sooth me. "Yes, baby, it does. I don't need to know what was said between you and Max. I will work on, Jackie. There is no way I'm going to let her give up without the fight of a lifetime. It's just not in me to see her give up, and I know it's not in her."

I love this girl with all my soul. "Okay, this is just another reason why I love you. We need to get back to our seats, we should be landing soon. We are going to check into our hotel first, and then I will check on your mum to see if she is up to visitors today."

"Thank you, Jax." She gives me another soft kiss.

"Sweetheart, you never have to thank me for letting me love and take care of you. It's my life's mission."

Maxwell

I'M STUNNED BY THE story that An has told me. Not only that she knew my grams, but the fact that Jax and Bella are my siblings. I knew that I probably had other siblings out there, but never in my wildest dreams did I think it would be Jax and Bella. We are tied together for life. Not just by friendship, but by blood. How could I leave now? When the one thing I always wanted is right before me—family. After I had Elliot, I thought about looking for my father and possibly, any other siblings. But when he and Samantha were murdered, I died that day, too, so why bother. I can't believe my grams kept this a secret from me. An should be here any minute to go to the bank with me. I don't know how I can look at her and not feel betrayed; she knew all this time.

SHE MEETS ME BY the elevator and we silently head to the car. The ride to the bank is long and quite. Both of us, staring out the window. I finally have to ask her, "Why?"

"Why, what, Maxwell?"

I don't want to get mad, but I don't understand. "Why keep this secret for so long?"

She turns her gaze towards me. "Perhaps you will understand more after you read the letter."

I snap back at her, "Do you really think being cryptic with me now is the way to go?"

"What I think is neither here nor there, it is what your grams wanted. I don't know what's in the letter, all I know is, I made a promise to your grams. In the end, Maxwell, the only thing we have, of any value, is our word. If I didn't keep my promise, then I would be no better than your father. You need to try and understand, I had to respect your grams wishes. I had to do what she felt was best for you, not me. She never wanted you to be tainted by the actions of your father."

We go into the bank and An retrieves the letter. She hands it to me, and then starts to step outside the room, but I stop her. "I would rather we went back home before I read this." She nods and we leave.

The ride is silent for both of us, and that's okay. Right now, I don't think I could handle much more. We step out of the elevator and she takes my hand. "Maxwell, I will be next door if you decide you would like to talk."

All I can do is nod and head into my place. I sit by the fire for a long time with a glass of scotch and the letter, trying to get the nerve up to read it. After I finish my drink, I open envelope:

My Dearest Maxwell,

If you are reading this, then An must have told you everything. You are probably wondering why I never told you about your family. I wanted to, especially, right after Samantha and Elliot were murdered, but you were in such a bad way that I thought one more betrayal would put you over the edge.

Your mum was a dreamer. She was beautiful and naïve, believing in her husband. James Phillips was a very good-looking charmer. Right before An came to look for her husband, James confessed everything to your mum. He told her all about his other family. Your mum's heart was broken, and she felt like such a fool. An is a very strong women who was able to pick up the pieces;

your mum was not. She was young, so she brought you to me to take care of. She knew that I would love you with all of my heart. I blame myself for not realizing right then, why she brought you to me. She went home that day and killed herself. I tried to get in touch with your father, but I could not find him. It was at that point, I decided to change your name to Fleming, and erase all presence of Phillips from our lives. You need to understand, that man took away my only child, so I decided I would never let him near you, again. If he wanted to, he could have easily found us, but he never did. Right there, that should tell you the type of man he was. He never contacted An, either, which was probably for the best.

Don't blame An for your mum's death. I know she blames herself, but she came, in good faith, looking for a man that she knew as her husband. Unfortunately she was not his only wife. Your mum was not strong enough, and the betrayal is what killed her.

A few months passed, and An came to me offering to raise you with her children as one of her own. An is a tough woman, and even fiercer when it comes to her children. I knew that she would love you like her own; that was never a question. I really considered it, however, I needed you close to me. As selfish as that may sound, I just couldn't do it. The pain was too raw for me. I couldn't suffer another loss. You blossomed into such a wonderful man—a man I was so proud of. You met your beautiful Samantha, and then you gave me the greatest gift of all—my great grandson, Elliot. I thought life had come full circle. I wanted for nothing, until the world came crashing in around us. After that horrible day, I felt like I lost my child all over again. I realized that I needed to put my selfishness aside. I was ready to have An come, and we would tell you everything, but then, you joined the Special Forces. I really thought this would help you, until I realized you were taking ridiculous chances with your life!

Once again, I called An and we came up with a plan. She was worried about Jaxson, seems he was taking all kinds of risks when it came to business and women. An wanted him reeled in, so we set up a chance meeting that night. I knew you would never stand by and let someone be taken advantage of.

Please don't be mad at An, she was following my request to keep this secret. I told her she would know when to tell you the truth. Maybe I was wrong to keep this from you, but I didn't want you to blame Jax and Isabella for your mum's death. They're just as much the victim, in all of this, as you are. I hope that you will one day find love again. You have so much to offer someone, if you would just open your heart and get out of your own head. Life is too short, Maxwell, as you well know, so if you find that special someone, grab onto her and love her with all your might.

I love you so much, and I found peace in knowing that you will never be alone, again. I hope you can find that peace, too.

Love you,
Grams

I stare at this letter, trying so hard to wrap my mind around all of this. I understand what my grams was doing and why, but it doesn't make it hurt any less. The man I am today wouldn't blame anyone for my mum's death, but in my youth, I really couldn't say. I know I was bitter for a long time, that was until Samantha and Elliott came into my life. Having my own family helped me find some peace and stability in life. When they were murdered, I felt my heart turn to stone. I existed . . . one day leading into the next. Nothing ever really mattered, except keeping everyone safe. Then Jackie blew into my world, and everything has been turned upside down.

As I head next door, I see An sitting in a chair by the elevator and I have to laugh.

"Are you really sitting there, trying to hold me hostage?"

She nods, "Well, Maxwell, I'm trying to make sure you won't pull a 'runner' as Jaxson calls it. I'm also trying to make sure you are not doing anything stupid before you're one-hundred percent healed."

I smile at her. "You must be uncomfortable, sitting in that hard chair. Why not come in and we will have some afternoon tea."

"So you don't hate me, Maxwell?" her voice shakes.

I throw my arms around her, surprising us both. "I could never hate someone who would move heaven and earth to protect their loved ones. Come inside and make me some tea, I think we need to talk."

She reaches up and yanks my ear! "Ouch, what was that for?"

She laughs, "Manors young man—*please,*" she emphasizes.

As we walk inside, I look at her and realize she has always been there. She's been like a mum to me no matter what. I sit at the table and watch her putting together the tea and Jammie Dodgers. I realize I could never walk away from this, the thing I treasure most—family.

I have so many questions for her, but I need to take it slow. "I know you said you were going to tell Jax when he got back, but what about Bella? Have you decided when you are going to tell her?"

She takes a deep breath. "Well, Maxwell, you tell me what would make you feel the most comfortable? I can tell them together or separately, the choice is yours."

I smile trying to make her feel more at ease. "I have waited this long for a family, I can wait a little longer. Tell them together, so they have each other for support."

She hugs me, "It will be no big deal to them because they already consider you their brother. I think it was a bigger deal for you. I think that might be what your grams was worried about."

I know she thinks it's no big deal, but I'm still worried. "Ma'am, it will probably be no big deal to Jax, but I worry about Bella."

She laughs, "Don't worry about her, she will be happy to have someone that she thinks she can pit against Jax! Maxwell, why are you pushing Jackie away? I know you love her, and I know you're scared, but let me ask you this, do you think it is fair to her? She is paying the price for a lost love."

I feel my heart tighten in my chest. "I don't know what's right or wrong anymore. I don't know how she did it, but she broke through without even trying. She weaved herself into my soul. What if something was to happen to her because of me? Look at that night, when Vincent's people tried to get to her. That night, as I was racing to her flat, I saw Samantha and Elliot—dead—all over again. I love her enough to want her safe and happy. And if it means that I have to let her go, then I'm prepared to do that. This whole mess put a huge target on her back, and I don't think I can live with that. I need to let her go."

"What if she's not prepared to let you go, have you thought of that?"

I need to change the subject fast. "Ma'am, why did you never get married again, have you thought about that?"

She glares at me. "Maxwell, I'm a very strong person, and you will not push me away, so if that's what you're trying to do, you should just forget it. Now to answer your question, I made my children my life. I experienced love, or at least what I thought was love. I never wanted to put myself in a position to get hurt or fail again. You know the saying, 'hind sight is always twenty-twenty'? Well looking back, I could have found a man, and have gotten married, if I really wanted to. Life would have been easier for me, but I wanted more."

I stare at her, totally confused. "What did you want, ma'am, that you don't have now?"

"A man who would love and respect me for who I am now, and the choices that I have made. I want to experience true love. I've never closed myself off from that possibility, can you say the same thing?"

I stare into my tea, saying nothing.

"Maxwell, I'm going to go back next door, but before I leave, I would like to ask you something."

I'm thinking this is a first, both her and Jax just say whatever the hell they want, whenever they want.

"I know that you had a mum that loved you very much. I would never impose upon that, but I have loved you like I love Jaxson and Isabella for your whole life. I have watched you grow into the man that you are today. A man I respect, a man I'm so very proud of. Your grams and I exchanged letters and pictures throughout your lives. I only hope one day, you will feel comfortable enough to call me something other than, ma'am."

With that, she leans in, kisses my forehead, gets up, and leaves. I'm on overload today. I just don't know how much more I can take. I love Jackie but what do I do about it? Can I really have someone in my life that won't leave or be cruelly taken away from me? Her safety is priority number one for me, and right now, I'm not one-hundred percent. It's time I make some phone calls, starting with Tony.

Jaxson

WE LAND AND THEN get settled into our hotel. I know Raven is scared and I know, if it were me, I would be too, but there is nothing I can do to make this any easier.

"Raven, I spoke with the doctors. They said Gabriella is having a good day, so we will be going after lunch. It's okay to be scared and nervous, but I will be there with you every step of the way—no matter what. You need to prepare yourself that she might not even know who you are."

I see her eyes fill with tears. "Jax, what if she hates me? What if she sees me and is reminded of all the pain and loss in her life?"

I pull her close to me. "I don't think that will happen, but however she reacts, we will deal with it together. No matter what."

"Jax, did I tell you today that I love you?" She kisses me softly.

Those words make me smile, "Yes, but feel free to tell me as much as you want."

I lift her into my arms and nibble on her ear. I start to work my way down her neck when my watch alarm goes off. Oh fuck, she's going to pitch a fit now. As I stop, she looks at me.

"Jax, don't you dare, not now!"

I know she is going to flip out. "Sorry, sweetheart, you need to eat. Besides, the baby is up now."

"What makes you think the baby is not sleeping, Jax?"

"Well, if it's time to eat, the baby can't possibly be sleeping." I smirk.

She opens her mouth to speak, but nothing comes out. She closes it shakes her head. "Okay, Jax, what's for lunch?"

I lean my forehead against hers, "Do you see how much easier life is when you're agreeable?"

She rolls her eyes. "Lunch, Jax—now, because I'm not even going to dignify that with an answer."

"I'll order room service, what would you like?"

"The fruit and cheese platter with a cup of chai tea, please. I'm going to shower."

"I'll order, and then come in to wash your back."

"Ha, is that what we're calling it now?"

As I watch her arse sway, I know I'll be doing a lot more than washing her back.

I hurry up and order the food, then race to the shower, ripping my clothes off along the way. I open the door, and the sight before me brings me to my knees. *Oh sweet Jesus,* and all that is holy! She's standing in the shower with the water cascading down her back. She has one leg on the shower bench as she squats down. Her hands are clasped behind her back, pushing those beautiful breasts out. I'm frozen in place, staring at her.

"Um, sweetheart what are you doing?"

"Stretching after the long flight, Jax."

Stretching? She's not stretching—she's fucking trying to kill me!

Now she switches legs and I'm still frozen in place, mesmerized by her beauty.

"I thought you were going to wash my back for me?"

I snap out of my trance and race into the shower. I drop to my knees and worship that beautiful arse, kissing and nipping my way between her legs. Front to back and I'm not letting up. I'm working my fingers and my tongue; completely filling her. She's on the edge ready to fall, and watching her is a surreal experience.

"Jax, I'm there, please. I need you deep inside me now."

I get up and grab her hips from behind, slamming my cock deep inside of her. That's all it takes to tip her over the edge. She's shaking and screaming my name, over and over again. I pull out and turn her around, "My turn, sweetheart."

She knows what I want, and I can tell she wants it too. She kisses each one of my nipples before, dropping to her knees. She takes hold of my engorged cock and kisses the tip. She looks up at me before swirling her tongue around the head of my cock. I know she can taste herself on me and I can't begin to describe what that knowledge does to me. She works her way down very slowly, pumping me and taking me so deep.

"Deeper, please . . . *oh, God . . .* sweetheart."

My hips start to move, meeting her thrust for thrust. She squeezes the base of my cock to hold off my orgasm, while working my sac with just the right firmness. As she eases up on my cock, it swells, ready to explode.—She nips the head. I scream her name as I erupt fiercely. In one quick swoop, I reach down and pull her up.

"Turn around and put your foot up on the seat again now!" I bark then slam into her as soon as she does. I groan and nibble at her ear.

"Jax, how?"

"Fuck if I know, sweetheart, it's you, only you. I'm going to move now, are you ready, 'cause I need it hard."

"I'm there, Jax."

I grasp her hips for leverage and pound into her. I lose all control; I can't get enough. I want to be deeper, harder, further than ever before. "Fuck, Raven!"

We both explode. I pump into her a few more times, then collapse on her back for a moment before sliding out of her. I slowly turn to sit on the shower bench, bringing her with me to cradle her in my lap.

"Are you okay, sweetheart?"

"I can't move. Can we just sit here and nap for a bit?"

"Don't worry, I will wash us as soon as I find my legs."

I try to get up, but she's not helping at all. I look down and she's out cold. I need to get us up off the bench, and put her to bed. I get up without dropping her and rinse her off the best I can. I wrap her in towels, drying her off. I can't believe she's sleeping through all of this. I get us into the bed and tuck her into my side. When I get to watch her sleep, I realize how lucky I am. Now, I just have to figure out a way to convince her to marry me.

Chapter Six

Raven

WE HEAD INSIDE THE clinic in silence. My grip on Jax's hand is so tight. I'm scared to finally face my mother, especially since I read her journal. I know all that she went through, and the torment of losing the love of her life and a child. What she must have went through, being pregnant with the spawn of Satan. Knowing that I'm carrying a baby that was made from love, and feeling it growing inside me everyday, reminds me of that gift of love. My mother was reminded of horrific violence everyday that she carried Duke.

After signing all the necessary papers, the nurse leads us to a solarium where I see a beautiful woman with a sketchpad lost in her work. I realize that I'm shaking, and squeezing Jax's hand so hard I think I cut off the circulation. My God, she's beautiful. More beautiful than I remembered, with her: porcelain skin, crystal blue eyes, and golden blonde hair.

"It's okay, sweetheart, just be your beautiful kind self and take it slow."

Mom is busy sketching, and doesn't see Jax pull up two chairs. As we sit down, Jax introduces us, but she doesn't look up, she keeps sketching. I don't know what I was expecting, Max said she hasn't spoken since she was brought here. I guess I was hoping for some recognition; any sign of the mother I remember. I'm ready to bolt and

Jax knows it; he puts his arm around me, slowly rubbing circles on my shoulder. I lean in to see what she is sketching and I freeze—it's me!

I whisper, "Jax, look at the sketch."

He leans in, "Hello, Gabriella, my name is, Jax. Would you mind if I looked at your sketches?"

She smiles and hands him the pad. As he begins to flip through the pages, she closes her eyes. I look over as Jax turns the pages, and all of the pictures are of me when she last saw me. I realize this must be her way of remembering me.

Mom looks down at her lap, not saying anything. I have no clue what to do for her. I feel so inadequate, but Jax is a take action type of guy. He reaches in and runs his hand down the side of her face.

"Gabriella, you are safe. Can you look at me?" he asks.

Her eyes shoot up to his, searching them. "Ma'am, I'm going to show you someone, and I need you to look into her eyes. Can you do that for me?"

She nods yes, and Jax lifts her head towards me.

"Gabriella, look into her eyes, do you know who she is?"

My eyes lock onto hers, and I see the moment when she realizes who I am. Her eyes become wide and she starts to shake. *"Cara?" she whispers through her tears.*

I gasp, "Yes, Mom, it's me, your Cara." I can't hold back my tears any longer.

She reaches her hand up to my face; they are so small and delicate. She brushes her fingertips along my cheek, "You're so beautiful. You have my mother's eyes," she whispers.

I'm in shock. "Jax, get the doctor—she's speaking!"

She smiles, "Your father, he loved you so much. You have his hair, so dark and silky, like that of a raven."

The doctors come running, but stop when they reach us, probably to avoid scaring her.

"Cara, where have you been? I've waited so long for you."

I'm trying to keep it together. I don't want to overwhelm her. "Mom, I only just found out that you're alive."

Her eyes grow wide. "But where is Joseph? He knew I was here."

I'm at a loss, I don't know how much she could handle in her fragile state.

Jax takes her hand. "Gabriella, let's start out slow for today. I promise you, we will answer all of your questions, but right now, the doctors want to talk to you. Is that okay?"

She squeezes Jax's hand, "Who are you?"

He gifts her with his beautiful smile and twinkling eyes. "My name is Jax, and I am the man who is madly in love with your beautiful daughter."

She reaches her hand to his face, and runs it down his cheek. "You're such a beautiful man, and I can see so much love in your eyes."

The doctors step up, and begin to ask her questions, but she wants nothing to do with them. "I assure you, I'm fine. I would like to talk to my daughter."

"Mom, this is such a shock, can we take it slow?"

She sighs, "I have been here for twenty years, how much slower do you want me to go?"

I fight not to cry. "I just don't want to lose you again. I need my mother in my life."

"You never lost me, Cara. I've been waiting here for twenty years to see you again. Where is Joseph? He promised someday it would be safe to bring you back to me." She reaches up and wipes away my tears. "Shh, Cara, no more tears. I will go slowly for you. But please, tell me one thing—tell me you're happy . . . that it was all worth it?"

I don't want her to know how much hurt and pain I've been through. I don't want her to have a setback. "I'm happy, Mom, very happy."

She looks back and forth between Jax and me. "I have so many questions for you, but first, where is Joseph?"

Just then, the nurse comes with a tray of food. I look at Jax and by the look of disgust on his face, I know what's coming. I take a deep breath and wait. He gets up and excuses himself. Okay, not what I was expecting. I figured one look at what was on that tray and he would flip out.

"Mom, are they taking good care of you here?"

She nods, "It's comfortable, but it's not home. Where is Joseph? He hasn't come back in a very long time."

Interesting. "Did he visit you often?"

She shakes her head, "He would usually come once a month.

Those visits were becoming less and less."

I need information, but I also know not to push her. I need to keep it simple.

"What did he tell you, when he would visit?"

She has a faraway look on her face. "He would just sit here. Sometimes he would read, and other times, he would talk about a girl he called Raven."

I feel light-headed, and the faces around me are starting to spin. I hear yelling, and I realize it's my mom yelling for Jax, and calling out to me, right before everything goes black.

As I slowly open my eyes, I'm hit with those bluest of blues, I have come to love so much. I whisper, "Jax."

I see the fear in his eyes. "Hey, sweetheart, you're back. Don't scare me like that again, okay?"

I nod. "What happened?"

He growls, "You passed out."

I try to jump up, "The baby!"

He holds me tightly. "The baby is fine, but you need to rest. I guess now is a good time to tell your mum that we're having a baby."

My mom is kneeling next to me, "Is this why you came looking for me?"

Before I can answer, Jax takes her hand. "No, ma'am, we only just found out that you're alive. Once Cara knew, there was nothing that would stop her from getting to you. There is a lot that you don't know, but because of your health, we have chosen to take it one day at a time. I spoke with your doctors, and as soon as our business is finished here, we will be taking you back to the States with us. In the meantime, I need to feed our girl, and she needs some rest. If it's okay with you, I have ordered food to be brought here so we can all eat together. After, I will take Cara back to the hotel for some rest."

She smiles at Jax, "You're a take charge kind of man, aren't you?"

I can't help but giggle. "Oh, Mom, you don't even know the half of it!"

"SO, CARA, WHEN IS your baby due?"

I smile, my hands instantly go to my tummy. "Early August."

"Do you know what you're having?"

I shake my head, "No, I don't want to know, I just want a healthy baby."

She takes my hand and squeezes it tightly. "Did Joseph die?"

I don't know what to say, but I realize it's the truth that she needs right now more than anything else. "Yes, he died of pancreatic cancer."

She drops my hand and gets up. "I think I've had enough for today, and you need to rest. Will you come back tomorrow?"

I get up and hug her. "Yes mom, I will be here everyday until we move you."

"Thank you, Cara, and thank you, Jax, for all that you have done for my daughter."

Jax gets up and pulls Gabriella into his arms. "Ma'am, it's me that should be thanking you for giving me the most beautiful girl in the world."

She kisses us both. "Goodnight, I will see you tomorrow." And with that, she leaves.

As I watch her walk away, I think about the amount of information she *doesn't* know, and I'm not sure how much she can take.

"Jax, maybe I shouldn't have told her about Joseph?"

He strokes my arm, knowing that I need the constant connection. "Honestly, I think she needs the truth, right now. She is not as frail as you think. Everyone deals with grief differently. She mourned your dad, and maybe after the adoption, she grieved for you the same way. We need to take things slow with her. Giving her small amounts of information at a time. Remember, she has twenty years to catch up on, and we don't know what Joseph told her. Apparently, he spoke to her about you as Raven, but it seems that she didn't know that is your adoptive name."

I grab onto Jax. "I just want to scream, but what good will it do?"

He pulls me closer, "Getting upset is not good for you or our baby. Lets head back to the hotel, so you can get some rest."

I kiss him, so blessed to have him with me throughout all the madness. "Jax, right now, I'm so grateful that I don't have to think about anything. Have I told you today that I love you?"

He gives me that smile, "Yes, but you can never tell me too much."

J axson

WE GET BACK TO the hotel and Raven is so tired, I just want to carry her. She lets me. I put her on the bed and start to undress her.

"Sweetheart, I really need to get you something to sleep in other than my dress shirts." Her lip begins to quiver, and her tears are falling. "Hey, why the tears?"

"Jax, I love sleeping in your shirts. It's what saved me when I was kidnapped. I was able to smell you all around me. I didn't feel so lost and alone."

My heart aches for all she went through. "Well, that settles it, you can sleep in my shirts, and I will make sure I put everyone of them on before you do." I reach in and kiss her soft lips. "Do you want me to snuggle with you while you fall asleep?"

"Yes please, when I fall asleep within your arms, I feel safe."

"You don't have to explain, sweetheart. I love that you need me for the simple things." I open my arms for her and she crawls up into my lap. Before I know it, she is out cold. I could watch her sleep like this for the rest of my life. She is so beautiful. I wish I could shelter her from everything that would hurt her, but I know it's not realistic. Tomorrow is going to be another hard day for her. I haven't told her about Max, and what he is planning. I know if I do, she will push Jackie to come back and stop Max. I can't let Max leave. I know it's selfish but I never claimed to be a saint. Who am I kidding? I'm a self-proclaimed bastard when it comes to keeping my family together and safe.

MORNING COMES AND RAVEN is still snuggled up next to me, awake and kissing my chest lightly. "Good morning, my beautiful girl."

Hmm, "Good morning, my beautiful man. Jax, I need you."

My eyes open wide. "Well, you don't have to tell me twice. Are you ready for me?"

"Oh, I'm always ready for you. I only have to look into those beautiful eyes and my whole body tingles."

I try to flip her onto her back, but she stops me. "Oh no, mister, today, I'm driving the car."

Raven

HIS FACE LIGHTS UP as I kiss down his chest. I lick the V that I have come to love, and then right down the happy trail. His cock is so hard, yet silky smooth. I love that I can give him this. I slowly swirl my tongue around the head. He closes his eyes and tilts his head all the way back. When I look at him in this position, I can see him coming apart; it's breathtaking to watch. I want to freeze this picture in my head forever.

"Raven, baby, real deep and slow for me, *please,* sweetheart."

I give him what he wants. I take his cock really deep, and then slowly work my way up. When I reach the top, I stop and watch him— he's really trying to hold it together.

"Oh sweet Jesus and all that's holy, ride me, sweetheart, please. I need to be buried balls deep inside of you."

I love when he gets like this; it's just so erotic to see. I crawl up and slowly lower myself onto his beautiful cock, and when he is totally buried within me, I stop. "Look at me now, Jax. You are all mine and only mine, now and forever." I run my hands up my chest stopping at my nipples, playing with them just the way I know he likes to. When he reaches his hands up, I push them away. "Not yet, Jax, just watch." I slowly rock my hips back and forth, still playing with my nipples. I look down at him, relishing how beautiful he is. I go up and down again really slowly, using my core to clench his cock. He leans up and takes one of my nipples between his teeth and I'm coming and screaming. Jax is not far behind me.

He's breathing heavy. "Sweetheart, when you do that clench thing around my cock, I swear it feels like the poor fuckers head is going to explode."

I look at him, my eyes are wide and begin laughing.

"What are you laughing at?"

I'm really trying to control my laughing. "Oh, Jax, I can't wait to see how you will explain the birds and the bees to your son one day."

The look of utter fear on his face is not lost on me. "Now, it's my turn to have some fun, sweetheart."

He flips me over and begins kissing my neck really slow, when all of a sudden, his watch beeps. Before he can say anything I jump in first, "Oh no you don't, mister, you're not stopping now."

He stops kissing me, "Raven, you have to eat."

I reach over, pick up the watch, and fling it across the room! "That's what I think about that fucking alarm, and before you say anything about my mouth, the baby is sleeping now, so quit teasing me. I want you and I want you now!"

His eyes grow wide and his chin hangs down. "Wow, I kind of like this side of you, but did you have to throw my twenty-thousand dollar Rolex across the room?"

Tsk. "Well, who in their right mind would pay that much for a watch?"

"Oh, my beautiful girl, right now, I'm going to feed you my cock and then later, I'll feed you some food."

Chapter Seven

Maxwell

I NEED TO GET out of this house, before I go crazy. I think it's time for a trip to the office for a few hours. I know I'm not up to working a full day, but the silence is killing me. I open the door and An is sitting by the elevator again.

"Ma'am, are you going to sit there all day, everyday until Jax gets back?"

She looks up from her reading. "Maxwell, what do you think?"

I need to stand my ground here. "I'm going into work for a couple of hours." *She's not budging.*

"Maxwell, again what do you think?"

I turn to the guard and notice my regular guard is gone, and Mick is here. "Mick, I'm going into work for a couple of hours, you can stay here with Mrs. Phillips."

"Sorry, sir, no can do."

So help me, I swear I'm going to kick Jax's arse! "What do you mean, *no can do?* You work for me. I want to go, so either we go or I fire your arse!"

He's shaking his head, "Sorry, sir, Mr. Phillips said you would pull that card. He said I work for him now, not you."

"What else did Jax say?" I yell. I know he's just doing his job.

He shuffles his feet and clears his throat. "Well Mr. Jax said that Mrs. Phillips is supposed to stay stuck to you like glue, and if you give me any trouble, I'm supposed to shoot you in the arse. His words, sir, not mine."

"You wouldn't shoot me!"

An stops reading and looks at the two of us. "Maxwell, if I tell him to, he will, because he has the good sense to be afraid of my wrath, something you're clearly lacking right now. I suggest you get back inside. Breakfast will be here any minute, and then you have therapy. I have the schedule, and you will do as you're told."

I shake my head and go back inside. The scary part of all of this, is Mick would probably shoot me in the arse, and An would let him!

I head inside, take a few calming breathes and call Jax. I need to find out what the hell he was thinking.

"Hey, Max, how are you feeling?"

I take a deep breath, "Jax, you really are a crazy fucking arse! What the bloody hell, you told Mick to shoot me in the arse?! You have your mum glued to me. Do you know that she put a chair by the elevator and just sits there? No matter what fucking bloody time I go out there, she's still sitting in that fucking chair! She has a schedule, a fucking bloody schedule!" The phone is silent and I look to see if the call was dropped.

"Max, you need to calm down. This can't be good for your recovery. Does she really have a schedule?"

He's got the nerve to be laughing. *What the fuck?* "Jax, if you don't stop laughing, so help me . . ."

"Calm down, where do you want to go?"

I'm a fucking prisoner. I can't believe I'm asking for permission to leave my home! "I was going to head into the office for a couple of hours."

"Why? You know you're recuperating, so what business do you have there?"

"I just want to get out of here for a couple of hours and check on things. I need a change of scenery or I'm going to lose it, mate!"

"Tony, is doing just fine, and there is nothing that you need to check on." Jax says calmly like he's trying to talk a jumper off a roof.

I grit my teeth and begin pacing. *Fuck!* "You're not letting me out of here, are you?"

"No, but I do have to talk to you about some stuff, so get

comfortable. We went to see Gabriella yesterday."

I stop pacing and sit by the window. I need to keep it together for Jax; he's carrying my load right now.

"How is Raven?"

He takes a deep breath. "Well, I really wish you were here to see this. We found her mum sitting in the solarium, sketching. When we sat down with her, we realized she was sketching pictures of Raven, from when she last saw her," he starts to tell me about their visit. I listen for the next several minutes and get ready to interrupt him when he starts telling me the plans of bringing her back to New York.

"Wow, this has to be so overwhelming for Raven and Gabriella. I trust your opinion, Jax. I think we need to move her, but do a total name change and heavy guards on her at all times. Also, have the plane swept by your guards, not just the standard sweep. Do you think she is physically up for the move?"

"I do, and having Raven with her helps. She is opening up with Raven, speaking more and more. We had to tell her that Joseph died. She kept asking why he hadn't come back. Apparently, he would go visit her and talk about Raven, but never told her who she was."

"How did she take the news? Do you think it was too soon to tell her?"

"I don't think it was too soon, but it's hard to say. I'm clearly not a doctor, but I think, right now, its honesty that's needed the most. I don't think she's as fragile as we first thought, but I could be wrong."

I can hear it in his voice that something is off. "Okay, Jax, what else is going on over there?"

"Why?" he stammers.

I laugh, "I know you better than you know yourself, and I know you have something on your mind, so have at it. It's not like I have anything to do, that's for sure."

"Max, you know I really can't stand it when you're right. Okay, so here's the thing, I want to get married."

This is nothing new. "I know that already, Jax, what the bloody hell is your problem, mate?"

"I don't know how to go about this without being like a bulldozer. So help me, Max, if you don't stop laughing at me I will tell Mick to shoot you!"

"I'm sorry, Jax, it's just very funny that *big bad Jax,* who is always ten steps ahead of everyone else, is at a loss as to how to ask his girl to marry his sorry arse." *I can picture him pulling his hair out!*

"Come on, mate, how do I do this without being my usual bull-dozer self?"

I can't believe I have to give him step-by-step instructions. "Well, first, you need to get a ring."

"Done. Max, I'm telling you, I've wanted to marry her from the first day I met her."

"Jax, dare I ask when you got the ring?" *I know this man, and odds tell me he got the ring the first day he met her.*

"No, let's just skip that part. What should I do next? I don't want her to feel like I'm pushing or dictating how she should live her life."

For such a smart man, he can be so clueless. I need to try and make him understand. "Jax, you are in essence asking her to change her life. Granted—she is pregnant, so her life will never be her own again, but you need to make her realize that you want to marry her because of her and not because of an obligation to your child."

"I got that, Max, but how do I ask her?"

I have to laugh, "Sometimes you can be such an arsehole. Just tell her how you feel without demanding she see things your way. Tell her what you see in a future with the two of you, together as a team for life."

Okay, I got it. I'm scared I'm going to fuck this up, and if you tell another living soul, I will shoot you myself!" he threatens. I reply with a chuckle. As funny and neurotic as he's being, I can't help but feel excited for him. It's good to see my friend . . . my brother so happy. "Max, later today I'm meeting Gerhard. I know you ran a check on him, is there anything I should be aware of?" Jax pulls me back from my thoughts.

I get up, knowing I need to quickly end this call. "Nothing that you don't already know. Jax, I have to go, your mum is back with break-fast." I don't give him a chance to ask anything else; I don't want to hear her name.

I DECIDE TO CALL Tony for an update. "Tony, I need you to bring me up to speed." This is what I do best; taking care of others.

"Max, what do you want first?'

"Start with Vincent and work from there." I hear the clicking of the keyboard, and I know that Tony is in his element.

"His condition hasn't changed, no better no worse. Apparently, Vincent's sister, Annabelle, went to visit him and Duke, however, they wouldn't let her see either of them. I was able to compare the picture from the park with a current one on the surveillance camera at the jail, it was a match."

"Did you tell Jax that Annabelle was the woman in the park?"

"No. I never had a chance, I was waiting on confirmation. When it finally came through, Jax and Raven were already on their way to Switzerland. I just got the confirmation and I sent it to the guards."

Hmm, "Is that all Jax said?"

He pauses for a few moments. "Look, Max, I don't want to get in the middle of anything."

What the fuck is he hiding? "Just fucking tell me what he said, Tony!"

"I'm not to let you leave—no matter what. Max, don't make me have Mick shoot you, okay?"

I could just picture Jax, ordering him to have Mick shoot me. "No, Tony. I might be stubborn, but Jax is the one that's crazy here, not me. Besides, there is a lot Jax and I need to go over, so don't worry, you're off the hook." I hear him let out a deep breath and I can't help but laugh.

"Goodnight, Tony, I'll probably come by tomorrow, if An lets me leave the house."

Jaxson

RAVEN IS STILL SLEEPING. I'm worried if I can pull this off. Talking to Max helped; it always helps. I don't know why this man thinks he needs to get out of my life. My mum said he is lost and in a dark place. I just don't know how to help him. I do know that I need to be one-hundred percent honest with Raven and that means, I need to tell her everything.

"Hey, my beautiful girl, how are you feeling today?"

She looks into my eyes, "I'm good, Jax, but you seem troubled, what's the problem?"

She always knows. "I spoke to Max this morning."

She nods, "I won't press you for answers, just know I'm here for you, always."

I stare into her eyes and smile. "I told him about the visit with your mum. He agrees we should move her. I spoke with Tony, and there has been some noise from Annabelle, but he's not sure how much power she has, if any. He was trying to get an updated picture of her."

I see a look on her face that scares me. She instantly pales. "Jax, the day before we left, I was out running with Bo and my detail. There was a lady in the park, watching me and when she got up to come towards us, Bo freaked out. The guards got a picture of her and they were supposed to send it to Tony. Could that have been her in the park?" she asks. It's taking all of my control not to lose it.

"Why am I just hearing about this now?" I run my hands through my hair and pull at it. How could this have not been brought to my attention?

"Jax, I thought you were told. You know I wouldn't hold back something that important from you. Well, not intentionally." She sits up.

I get up, grab the phone, and put a call into Tony. "Hey, Jax, everything okay?"

I need to be calm—something I'm not good at. "No, why the fuck am I just finding out now about the woman in the park? Did you get a lead on her?" I seethe. I can feel the muscles in my arms and chest clenching, getting ready for a fight with an opponent that's not even in front of me. Raven's hands slide up my back and softly massage me, trying to calm me down.

"Jax, the picture was grainy and she had on large sunglasses. It could have been her, but we weren't sure. After she tried to get in to see Duke and Vincent, we got a better picture and compared them. I just informed Max, confirming that it was, indeed, Annabelle. I sent all this information to Raven's detail. They were supposed to give it to you. From what you're telling me, they didn't."

I take a deep breath. "Thanks." and I slam the phone down.

"Raven, please stay here and keep Bo with you. I need to talk to your detail."

I kiss her softly, I don't want to scare her, but I think it's too late for that. I step into the lounge and my eyes dart back and forth between Raven's guards. "Who took the information from Tony about the woman in the park?" They silently stare at each other until Daniel finally turns to me, "I did, sir, is there a problem?"

I mentally count to ten. "Did you feel that this was information that you should have withheld from me?"

I can't trust him. I know Max vetted him, but I can't trust him. I don't give him a chance to answer. "Collect your stuff, you're fired. There will be a ticket waiting for you at the airport. Now, get out of my sight."

I turn to my guards, "One of you take over for him. I will be fine with just one guard, and chances are Raven and I will be together on this trip, anyway."

I head back inside to assure Raven that I'm fine. I need to call Max, but before I can, he is ringing me. "What, did Tony call you?"

I know Max, and this can't be good for his recovery. "What the fuck, Jax? I vetted Daniel and Dominika myself. This is basic simple shit."

At this point, the only one I know I can trust is Max. "Max, I fired Daniel. What should I do about Dominika?"

"I think, for now, you should keep her so Raven has a female guard, but I would feel better if you never left her side. Try to finish up and get back here, quickly. I would rather have you here, where I have more control."

"We'll wrap it up as fast as we can and get home. If you find out anything else, please call me. I'll let you know when we are leaving."

As I hang up, I sit on the sofa and pull Raven onto my lap. She wraps her arms around me, holding me close. "Okay, Raven, let me tell you everything that I know to date about your family, so that you really get an idea of what we're up against. Your grandfather, Dion, was from Italy, and when he came to the United States, he brought his way of doing business with him. He had four children: Monti, Antonio, Vincent, and Annabelle. Monti was the eldest, he died in a bar room brawl. Your father never spoke of his family, and once he joined the FBI, he cut all ties with them."

She's tugging her ear, and I have to fight my urge to nibble it. "So, Jax, even though Vincent and Duke are in custody, there are other family members that could be a threat to us?"

I know it's a lot for her to deal with, but I realize she needs all the information. "Yes, but not just family members, these types of organizations are like roaches. You can never get rid of them. I think I would feel better if your mum was closer to us in the States. She has no family, her parent's died in a car accident while she was in college, and she was an only child. Having her close let's us keep an eye on her at all times."

She's searching my eyes as if she's looking for answers . . . answers I don't have. I can only hope I'm making the right decisions.

"Okay, I understand the risk, and I agree, I would feel better if she were close to us. But what else is bothering you? And don't say *nothing,* because I know better."

I take a deep, steadying breath. "Oh, my beautiful girl, I know sometimes you think you don't know me, but you really do know me so well. I'm going to tell you a story, and I need you to just listen. It's not my story to tell, but I think you need to know this before we go to see Jackie today." I proceed to tell her the entire story that Max shared with me.

"Do you see why it's really not my story to tell, and do you understand why he pushed her away? The murder of his wife and baby right before his eyes. I know I could never come back if, God forbid, something was to happen to you and our baby. It has to be Max's, decision to tell Jackie his story, not ours. She can't come back to him because of pity, she has to come back on her own."

I watch her, waiting for her reaction. She closes her eyes and pulls me close. "Look at me, please. Raven, tell me I'm doing the right thing here?" She opens her eyes and they seem distant. I'm watching her process everything I just told her. We say nothing for a long time. We just hold each other, lost in our thoughts. "Raven, I'm worried about him, he is in such a dark place. He wants to give me back his shares in Raiders, and move to Scotland. He thinks it would be best, so you can have Jackie in your life. I can't lose him, and I need to keep my family together and safe. I feel like I'm juggling so many things. I'm afraid of what will happen if I drop one."

"What has your mom said about all of this?"

My grip on her tightens, "That's just it, my mum is playing this pretty close to the vest. I know that there is something she's not telling me, but I can't force it out of her. My heart breaks for Max. I know he needs Jackie, even more now."

"Well, Jax, now that I know the whole story, it seems to me that Max is operating out of fear. Until he can realize that he can't let fear rule his life, then nothing will change for him. As far as your mother is concerned, I have to agree with you, there is definitely more that she is holding back. When I went to lunch with Bella and your mom, something was off. When I told her my concerns about Max, she could not get out of the restaurant fast enough. I knew she was going to head straight to Max. I think you need to have a sit down with your mom and get to the bottom of this. I know you felt Max should be the one to tell his story, but I think you did the right thing by telling me. I need to know, if I'm going to be able to convince Jackie to come home.

"Now as far as keeping Max hostage, will you ever learn your lesson? I know you want things done your way and on your timeline, but that's not how life works. You can't go around, threatening to shoot someone in the ass if they don't do what you want!" She smirks.

"How did you know that?"

"I heard you yelling this morning, but I figured you would tell me when you were ready."

As I stare at her, I try to keep a straight face (not easy here). "Raven, I wasn't really going to shoot him." *She is so not buying it.*

"No? Jax, somehow, I don't really believe that. What's even worse is you made your mother a watchdog, and we all know how much Max fears her. I'm surprised you haven't called in, Mrs. Osla."

As I watch her reprimanding me, I have to remind myself to stay focused on the problem, and not on that beautiful body!

"Well that was next on my list. Besides, I had to do something, and I knew he would never disrespect my mum. I told you I could be a real bastard when I need to be. I will fight to the bitter end to keep my family together and safe. Max, is the brother I never had."

"Max wanting to leave should show you how much you mean to him. He's willing to give it all up so you could be happy. Not many people would do something so selfless."

"Raven, knowing that only makes this hurt even more. How are you going to handle, Jackie? You can't tell her what I told you, that's for Max to tell." I pull at my hair again out of frustration.

She pulls my hands out of my hair. "I have no intention on breaking a confidence. I will have to convince her that running was a bad choice. Jackie and I have an unspoken trust between us. I have looked after her like a baby sister from the first day we met and I am not going to stop now!"

"Wow, this from the girl who spent the majority of our relationship running away from me. Well, I'm glad I made you see the error of your ways."

"Whatever, Jax, you just keep telling yourself that, if it makes you feel better. Now what is the plan for today?"

I hold up my shattered watch, "Well, first, I have to get a new watch, because someone flung mine across the room." I hit her with my usual smirk.

"Oh, don't smile at me, mister. I guess maybe you learned a lesson about trying to force me to do something I don't want to do."

She's got such fire in her eyes. "I'm just trying to keep you and the baby healthy, is that so wrong?" I grasp her hips and give her a hungry look that I know always gets her going.

"You really are a dirty bastard!"

"Oh, sweetheart, I love you!"

"Jax, while we look for a watch without an alarm on it, I would like to pick up some gifts to bring to Jackie's house. I know just the place to shop, it's called *Bon Génie,* have you ever been there?"

"Sweetheart, I hardly ever do my own shopping. If I really need something, I have my assistant pick it up. And as far as my clothes, I have my suits tailored from Savoy Tailors Guild in London. Everything else I have, a shopper at Barneys that takes care of me." I must have shocked her because her chin is practically on the ground.

"Wow, another first, Jax! There are seven floors of some of the most exquisite things in the world. Jackie and I would go every year, during winter break, and I would be honored to share the experience with you."

"Did you and Jackie travel a lot?" She smiles like she's remembering a happier time; at least she has those memories.

"We always came here for winter break and sometimes, her brother would come home if he knew we were going to be here."

I lean and kiss her, smiling at her beautiful face. "I'm looking forward to meeting Jackie's family, they sound interesting."

We get ready and head out.

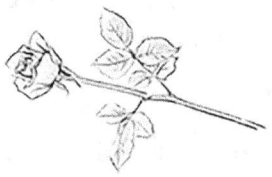

WE PULL UP TO *Bon Génie.* Raven wasn't kidding, the place is huge! We spend the next three hours, tooling around and picking up some cool stuff for Junior and the baby.

"Jax, I'm hungry. I don't even need your watch to tell me that, so let's get something to eat." she says with a sarcastic undertone that makes me laugh.

"Very funny, sweetheart. Thank you for my new watch but you really didn't have to buy it for me."

"I know, but I really did feel bad that I pitched your old one across the room."

"I need to feed you, sweetheart, what would you like to eat?"

"A grilled cheese sandwich and a chocolate fondue. What? Why the face?"

I lean in to kiss her, "Raven, please tell me you're not going to eat them together."

She rolls her eyes. "Come on, Jax, let's eat. And no, the fondue is dessert. If you're really good later, we just might have some fun with chocolate."

Raven

AS WE HEAD OUT to Jackie's, I feel nervous, though I shouldn't be. Jackie is my best friend, I tell her everything. Having to handle this without telling her anything of Max's tragedy, I'm sure, will prove to be difficult.

We pull up to the compound and glancing at Jax, I see a look of surprise on his face. "You okay, Jax?"

"Well, Raven, I can understand now why Max said she would be safe here. There's a gated guard entrance, electric fence, attack dogs, and a slew of armed guards. Is this the way she had to grow up?"

When I think of all the stories Jackie shared about her lonely childhood, it makes me sad.

"Yes. It makes for a very lonely childhood. Plus, there are no neighbors; this estate sits on 250 acres. Jax, do you think Max sent her away because of the threat and not because of his past?"

He looks around, shaking his head, "Sweetheart, I honestly don't know. Now that I see this place, it might make more sense that he might have sent her here for her safety."

We pull up to the house and even though I've been here so many times, I'm still in awe at the shear size of the place. As soon as the car stops, I'm out and rushing for the door. Jax is quick at my heels. Just as we enter the house, Jackie comes flying down the steps nearly tackling us. "Raven, oh my God, I'm so happy you made it. How is your mom? Did you see her? Did she recognize you?"

I laugh, "Okay, girl, slow down. First, let me say hello to everyone." I gesture just as her parents come into the room, giving me hugs and kisses; they really are my family, too. "Jax, I'd like to introduce you to Jeffery and Emi Gerhard."

Jeff takes Jax's hand, "Please, just Jeff and Emi; it's a pleasure to finally meet you, Jax. My daughter has told me so much about you. How has your stay been, so far?

Jax gives his charming smile that I love. "Wonderful, Raven took me to Bon Génie today."

Jeff laughs "Ah yes, that is her and Jackie's favorite place to go; they can tool around there for hours! Come in and let me give you a tour of the place while the girls do their thing."

We sit down and Emi pours some tea. "Raven, I am going to leave you girls to catch up. I'm glad you're here and safe."

I smile, "Emi, you don't have to leave," I say but she smiles and waves for us to carry on before she leaves.

"Okay, Raven, you need tell me everything." Jackie grabs my attention back.

I look at her and I want to scream, *Max needs you,* but I have to do this right.

"Where do you want me to start?"

Jackie takes my hands in hers. "What happened with your mom?"

My heart instantly constricts in my chest, "First, I have to tell you for her safety, no one can know whom she is."

"I understand, I haven't spoken to anyone about her."

"Oh, Jackie, it was surreal. I mean, she was sitting in a chair sketching pictures of me as a child. It was like she was trying to keep my face in her memories. Jax realized it, and he made her *really* look at me . . . at my eyes. At that point, we could both see recognition register on her face. A single tear slid down her cheek and she whispered my name, Cara."

Jackie's eyes fill with tears, and she's rubbing her arms. "Oh, Raven, I swear you're giving me fucking goose bumps!"

I need to lighten the mood here. "Okay, I have to tell you something, and promise you won't laugh." I know she's going to laugh.

"Okay . . . you're acting weird, Raven."

I take a deep breath. "You can't curse in front of me. Don't look at me like that, I know it's crazy, but Jax has this idea that the baby can hear us. He doesn't want the baby's first word to be . . . you know . . . a bad one. Jackie, are you okay?"

She's biting her lip and I know she is trying not to laugh.

"I'm trying with all my might not to get hysterical! Raven, you can't be serious. Oh my God—you are serious! You know how absurd that is, right?"

I nod, "Of course I do, but he's so cute, I can't burst his bubble. Apparently, he was a real whack job when Bella was pregnant. He wanted health reports on everyone she came in contact with!"

Jackie laughs, "Okay, I will humor him. So what are you going to do about your mom?"

"We are going to move her to the States."

Jackie's face lights up. "Well, I think that's a good thing. Then, you can keep a close eye on her. Maybe she will even get to the point where she can get back into mainstream life."

Jackie knows how much family means to me. "I wish, but I don't think the threat against my family is going to go away anytime soon. My father also had a sister, and apparently, she is making herself known." I take in a deep breath and decide it's time to shift the conversation towards the topic of one Maxwell Fleming. "So, are you going to ask me about *him?*" I watch as she closes her eyes tightly. I know she's fighting back her emotions. "Talk to me, Jackie, please."

She shakes her head. "What's there to say? I heard what he said to Jax, there is no denying it."

I need to get through to her, and this is probably my only chance. "Okay, Jackie, I need for you to listen to me. I mean *really* listen with an open mind and an open heart. *Nothing* is ever what it seems in life. I, of all people, should know that. I mean, look at Marco. A lot has happened since you left. Apparently, Max is in a very dark place, for reasons I'm not able to talk about. Jax has put guards on him with orders to—and I'm quoting here—'*shoot him in the arse if he tries to leave.*' He has moved his mom into our place and apparently, she sits by the elevator everyday—all day—making sure he doesn't leave. He's hurting and he pushed you away. Maybe in his mind, it was for the right reasons, even though it was wrong. I always tell you, never make a decision without having all the facts. You, pulling a *runner?* That was acting out on a knee-jerk reaction. You need to come home and get all the facts before you make your decision. Otherwise, you will regret it for the rest of your life. You will always wonder *what if.* I don't want you to end up like some old spinster with a hundred cats!" She doesn't say anything, but I know she is weighing her options. That was my one shot, let's hope she listens.

"Did Jax really have his mom stay there? Poor Max. For him, that's worse than getting shot!"

"Exactly, Jackie. That has to tell you how desperate and worried Jax really is."

"What about his health? Is he going to be okay?" It figures the first thing she wants to know is if he's going to be okay. She is such a tenderhearted person.

"The doctor said he should be okay. He started therapy, but he's lost. It's like a part of him died, Jackie. He seems so empty inside."

"I need a change of subject, please. What is going on with you and Jax?"

Where do I begin . . ."The man is nuts, but we already established that fact. Aside from the whole blue language thing, I found out from Bella that Jax had my building tented for non-existing termites."

She's looking at me like I'm nuts. "Why did he do that?"

"Why, Jackie, that's a great question. All I can figure is he did it so I can't go home."

As she smiles, I can see she's going to be on Jax's side here. "Oh, Raven, that's so romantic."

Tsk "Not only did he have the entire building tented for termites, he put all of the residents up in at the W Hotel—all expenses paid! He doesn't even know I found out about it."

Her eyes are like saucers. "Are you serious?"

"Yes!"

Jackie is laughing so hard that she is crying. Right at that minute, the guys decide to come in and see what's going on.

"Okay, ladies, what has you both in a fit of laughter?"

Jackie smiles at him, "Well, that would be you, Jax."

"Oh really, what did I do now?"

"Nothing, just you being you is always very entertaining. Did Daddy give you the grand tour?"

"Yes, I didn't know you ride. I was quite impressed with all of your awards."

"Thank you, Jax. Riding is a great way to pass the day. It gives me the freedom to think without interruptions."

Jax picks up one of the pictures of Jackie on skis. "Raven said you also love to ski. I didn't realize you started so young."

Jackie looks at the picture and smiles, "Yes, I probably skied before I walked. I like cross-country skiing the most; it helps build stamina. My brother, however, likes snowboarding better.

My body tenses at the mention of Dylan. He's made me aware that he is attracted to me from the first day I met him, to the point where I'm uncomfortable to be around him. "Jackie, how is Dylan doing?"

"Actually, you can ask him yourself. He went to town for something but should be home soon. He surprised me with a visit."

I just hope Dylan behaves. "Wow. I haven't seen him in a while. I'm glad you'll get to meet him, Jax."

The front door opens with a bang. "Oh, speak of the devil, here's my brother now." Dylan comes barreling into the room, bypassing everyone and attempts to pull me into his arms. Jax pulls me up against him, staking his claim.

"Dylan, let me introduce you to Jax."

Jax reaches out to shake Dylan's hand. Oh boy. He's pissed. He has a tight grip on me.

"Hello, Jax. So you're the man that has finally caught our girl's heart."

Jax is glaring at him. Okay, need to change the subject quick before the man blows a gasket.

"So, Dylan, when did you get here?"

"I got in this morning. Once Jackie told me you were coming, I couldn't stay away. How long will you be here for?"

Jax's tension is not letting up one bit; the more Dylan speaks, the tenser he gets. "Dylan, our trip here is very short, and then I'm taking *my* girl home with me—where she belongs."

Wow, major pissing contest, going on here.

"So, Jax, what do you do for a living? My sister really didn't fill in any of the blanks."

Jax is glaring at Dylan, and I think he might snap his neck. "I own a company called, Raiders Inc."

This is not going to end well. I look to Jackie for help, but she just rolls her eyes.

"Don't think I ever heard of it? What does your company do?"

"I assist companies that run into trouble."

"Ah, so you're a *corporate raider.* Is that how you assist them? Hence the name."

Oh no, he's growling; a growling Jax is never good.

"Well, Dylan, if you really are interested, my company invests in agriculture, technology and clean energy. I don't go out and just pick apart companies for the heck of it. I focus on companies that have a good idea, but either no business sense or lack of funding. If it's just the funding then I support them. If the company can't be saved, then I try to place the workers within my existing companies before I break it apart. I'm not the bad guy, Dylan."

Dylan is smirking, and Jax's whole body is tight. "I didn't mean to upset you, Jax. I just need to know that our girl is in good hands, that's all. When will you be heading back to the States?"

I'm holding onto Jax so tight; I fear he might explode. "As soon as our business here is done. Which reminds me, Raven, we have a meeting; we need to get going."

We head towards the door and make our goodbyes. I hug everyone, but Jax makes sure I'm glued to his hip when Dylan tries to hug me.

"JAX, ARE YOU GOING to sulk the whole drive to the clinic?" He's pouting like a little boy, and for some crazy reason it's a total turn-on.

"No, but you should have warned me that the fucker has the hot's for you! Don't look at me like I'm nuts, you know he does."

My crazy man makes this so easy. I have to try very hard not to laugh. "First, watch your mouth, the baby can hear. Second, yes I know that Dylan has had a thing for me from when I first met him. And lastly, Jax, look at me, please . . . you are my end all. Raise the privacy glass . . . *now.*"

"I'm all yours, sweetheart, have your way with me."

I am wound up so tight I think I might burst! This man drives me nuts, but I can't seem to get enough of him. "Jax, I will never admit this to you ever again, so listen carefully. When you get all Alpha male on me, it makes me so fucking crazy, I just want to jump your bones. Even though you make me crazy mad, you also make me crazy hot. Now get naked and fuck me hard!" Oh bless him, his eyes are wide and his chin practically hits the floor.

"Oh."

I'm the one growling now, "Yeah, *oh.*"

Jaxson

WELL, I'M NOT AN idiot. I don't need to be told twice. I only hope the driver has headphones on because I will make her scream. I slowly unbutton my shirt while she watches. I roll my shoulders back so my shirt slides down my back. She's watching my every move. I place my finger in her mouth and she sucks it like it's my cock. I pull it out and run it over my nipples. She's holding her breath. *Gotcha, sweetheart, oh yeah.* She is still fully dressed and I know exactly what I'm going to do next. I release my cock from his holding cell and start to pump him up and down while my other hand is stroking my nipples, first one and then the other. She's losing it; squeezing her thighs together for friction. I take the first drops of my arousal on my finger, and place it in her mouth. She moans. That's it sweetheart, get really worked up for me.

"Oh my God, Jax, I don't know how much more of this I can take!"

I'm not stopping, "Sweetheart, do you think you're ready for me?"

She nods her head.

"Show me baby."

She starts to undress, never taking her eyes off me as I pleasure myself. All her skin is flushed. "Jax, do you know how beautiful you are? Seeing you like this takes my breath away."

I reach over and rip her panties right off of her. "Kiss me, Raven, now!"

She gently presses her soft lips to mine. "I need you inside of me, Jax."

I'm on my knees between her legs. I slowly rub my cock up and down her; still making a show for her. I don't think either one of us will last much longer. I slowly work my way in and then out. I reach down and play with her nipples applying just enough pressure to make them peak for her pleasure. Her skin is on fire.

"You want me, baby, you've got me heart and soul." I pull back and slam into her, causing her to scream. "Jax . . . oh God, Jax . . . please."

I stop. "Look. At. Me."

Her eye's fly up to mine.

"Raven, I love you. All that I am, and all that I will ever be, in this world, is yours for life. I'm baring my soul to you now."

Raven

OUR EYES LOCK. WE are both screaming and shaking. My release is like a wave of never ending pleasure, rippling through my whole body. I search his face and I can see something is off. I fist my hands in his hair and pull him towards me, kissing him so softly. I whisper, "I love you, Jax."

He keeps kissing me softly, and then he nibbles on my ear. "Jax, talk to me, please. What's wrong?"

His beautiful blue eyes are filled with such angst. He rests his forehead on mine, "Raven, marry me, *please,*" he whispers.

I freeze. That was not what I was expecting. "Excuse me? Did you really just ask me to marry you while you're buried balls deep in me? In the back of a limo?"

He closes his eyes, "Well when you put it like that, it doesn't sound good."

"Jax, I think we need to get dressed." I try to move, but he holds me even tighter, pinning me beneath him.

"Raven, just stop for one minute and listen to me, please," he begs. "I know this is not the way I should be asking you this, trust me. I have been rehearsing what I wanted to say to you for a long time. I knew I wanted you for life the day I met you, but if I had told you then, you would have thought I was a nut." My eyes grow wide. "Don't look at me like that, I'm not a nut. Okay, so maybe a little, but still, let's put that aside for a minute. I love you with all of my heart and soul. You are my end all, and without you, I don't exist. I know this from when you were gone for three months. I was out of my mind, okay, maybe more of a crazy man. I sulked for three months, sat in your apartment, listening to your iPod over and over again. Some song called 'half a heart' every day for hours. I just sat on your bed, so lost without you. I can't go through life like that. I have so much love to give you and our child. I want to make a happy life for you and the baby. I want lots of babies. Okay, maybe we should get through the first one, but still, I see us growing old together. Geez, woman, I bought your whole fucking building and had it tented for non-existent termites, all so you wouldn't leave me! Okay, that didn't come out right, either. I really had no clue how to ask you this. I don't want you to think I just want to marry you because of the baby; I would marry you with or without a baby. When I asked Max what to do he said when the timing is right I should just bare my soul to you. Are you going to say anything?"

Jaxson

SHE LOOKS AT ME and begins to laugh, Not exactly the response I was expecting.

"I'm sorry, Jax, I shouldn't laugh at you, but really, you have to realize this will go in the history books as one of the funniest proposals ever. I don't think Max meant for you to be in this position, in the back of a limo, when you asked me."

"Well, Raven, are you going to answer me?"

She smiles and tenderly kisses me . . ."Jax, I already did, you are my end all. There could never be or will ever be anyone else but you."

Holy shit. I think she's saying yes! "You'll marry me? I need to hear the words, sweetheart, please."

She takes my face into her hands and stares into my eyes. "Yes, Jax, I will marry you."

I kiss him softly, "You crazy man. Make love to me now."

I instruct the driver to keep driving in circles until I tell him otherwise.

I lean in and kiss her tender lips; they are so soft. Our tongues begin a slow dance. I cocoon her whole body, and slowly begin to move. She needs me slow and tender right now. I'm giving her what she needs. In and out, holding her so close.

I search her face and I know she's there. I reach down and nip one of her nipples, and she starts screaming my name over and over again. That's all it takes, I explode with such force that I swear the head of my cock blew off. I rest my forehead on hers, both of us trying to catch our breaths. "Sweetheart, if it were possible to spend the rest of my life just like this, I would until my last breath on this earth."

Her eyes are filled with unshed tears. "Please, Raven, tell me those are happy tears."

She reaches up and kisses me, "Happy ones Jax."

I instruct the driver to head to the hotel, as we begin to make some sort of normal with our clothes.

"Jax, why are you staring down at your cock?"

Oh boy . . . I'm busted now. "I'm making sure he's still in one piece."

"Excuse me?"

"Okay, sometimes with you I explode so hard, I swear his head blows off," I admit. Her mouth gapes open. "Raven, are you going to say anything or just stare at me wide eyed?"

"I love you, Jax, and Mr. Cock is fine. You can put him away now."

She's amazing; she gets me like no one else ever could. "I love you more, sweetheart."

Chapter Eight

Raven

WE STOP AT THE hotel to get cleaned up, and Jax is pacing around the room. This is usually a sign that he is deep in thought, and that will mean trouble for me.

"Raven, if we didn't have to go to the clinic I would spend the entire day in bed ravishing your body."

We are all ready to leave when Jax takes my hand and drops to one knee. I look at him like he's a nut; I already said yes.

"Raven, I promise to fill every one of your days with all of my love. I will protect you and our baby. Everything I have, I give to you because without you I have nothing. I'm just a shell of a man. You're the half that makes me whole. When I look at us, I can see us growing old together. You complete me in a way that only you can. You get it; you understand me and all my crazy ways like no one else can. Will you please marry me and let me spend the rest of my life loving you?"

"You're my happy ever after, Jax . . . yes. Now and forever."

He slips the most beautiful ring on my finger. "I'm going to talk to your mum today about my intentions, I want her approval because I know you need it. But just know, no one will ever stand in our way."

We hurry up and get ready. I'm excited to see my mom today. I know I have to move slowly with her, but the sooner we are all safely back home, the better I will feel.

As we head to the clinic, I sit and think of how much my life has changed since that fateful morning at Starbucks. I can't believe I'm going to marry this intense, over the top, beautiful man. "Jax, when did you get the ring?"

"Do you really need to know this?" He strokes his chin.

"Yes, I do."

"The week I met you."

My eyes go wide and my mouth opens but nothing comes out.

"Raven, don't look at me like that. I just knew, that's all."

"You just knew what, that I would marry you? We had one date, how could you know?"

"I had purpose for the first time in my life. Everything I did or said mattered to me. That's how I knew."

Sweet Jesus, what this man does to me. "You'll always have purpose, Jax."

He kisses the inside of my wrist. "Raven, I never felt it until I met you."

There are no words left to say. I snuggle into him for the rest of the ride.

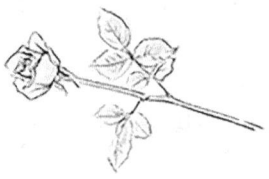

WHEN WE GET TO the clinic, I find my mom sketching again. This time they are of me now—not twenty years ago. "Mom, you're so talented; the likeness is unreal."

She smiles, "Cara, I never thought I would hear you call me mom ever again. Each time I hear it, it takes my breath away."

She seems at peace. I hope moving her is the right thing to do for her. "Mom, Jax and I have some things we need to talk to you about. Are you up for it?"

She grasps my hands, looking down at them. Upon noticing the ring, she looks at Jax and smiles. "Of course, what's on your mind?"

Jax and I take a seat next to her. Neither of us wants to make her nervous, but we really believe we are making the best move here for everyone. "Well, we would like to move you back to the States with us. What do you think about that?" Jax asks her.

Her eyes light up at the mention of it. "Jax, I want nothing more than to spend the rest of my days with my daughter and grandbaby, but is it safe for Cara?"

"Gabriella, for the rest of our lives, everyone will have to have constant guards. There is no way around it. Not just because of your situation, but also because of me."

I watch as my mother fights to hold back the tears.

"Jax, I don't understand, what do you mean *because of you?*"

It dawns on me how much fear Jax must have to live with every-day, not just because of my mom and me, but because of who he is and what he does.

"Gabriella, I am a very wealthy man. With wealth comes many crazy people, trying to take it away from me anyway they can. That wealth not only puts a target on my back, but everyone associated with me. I've come to accept that, and have made arrangements to always have protection." Jax pulls his chair closer and puts his arm around me.

"Jax, there are many wealthy people in the world. My parents were wealthy and we never had guards."

I need to give my mom all the information, so she can process it at her own pace.

"Mom, Jax's company, Raiders Inc., helps other companies that are struggling and sometimes the only way to help them is to dismantle them completely. You can make many enemies doing this, but unfortunately, it needs to be done."

My mom studies Jax. What she is looking for, I'm not sure.

"Jax, can I ask you some questions?"

He nods, "Yes, ma'am, just know that I don't sugar coat anything. If you want an honest answer, you will get it from me."

She smiles. "Wow, okay. Now what are your intentions?"

He hits her with the Jaxson smirk and his twinkling blues—God I love this man. Watching Jax is like watching a master artist at work. "Well, ma'am, hopefully with your blessing, I intend to marry your daughter, and love her endlessly for the rest of my days. I can provide nicely for her and our children. I want to support her in all of her dreams. I want to see the world through her beautiful eyes."

Okay, I'm officially crying. This man is so intense, he's so much more than anyone could ever imagine, and to think, that is what scared me away from him to begin with.

"Jax, you have my blessing. Now what's next?"

"Okay, the first thing you need is a total name change. I have all the security in place and they're ready to go as soon as the doctor gives us the green light. When we get back to New York, you will be at a clinic right near our flat. When the doctor says it's okay, you will be moved into your own flat. How does that sound for you?"

I hope my mom understands that Jax operates at one speed—his speed, and watch out if you get in the way.

"As long as I can be with Cara I'm okay. What name will I have?"

I know Jax is trying to slow it down a little, and bless him; it takes everything he has not to just dictate the way things will be.

"Gabriella, you can pick. Just keep it simple. You want something that will be easy for you to associate yourself with."

My mom looks to me. "Cara, what name have you been going by?"

I really don't want to upset her, but not being truthful would be worse for her. "Joseph named me Raven. He said my hair reminded him of a Raven."

She gets a faraway look in her eyes. "He would come to see me and talk about a girl named, Raven. I never knew it was you. I'm trying to remember all the stories he would tell me, but it's so overwhelming. Do you think he kept it a secret to protect you?"

I wonder what else he told her. "There is a lot that he hid from us, Mom. In time we will go through it all, but for now, let's concentrate on the here and now, okay?"

She smiles. I remember that smile. I'm trying so hard not to cry for all the years that have been lost. Years we will never get back again.

"Y-yes of course, and I must remember to start calling you, Raven. I decided upon my new name. I would like to be called Rose," she says and I can feel my eyes grow wide.

"Raven, you remember, don't you?"

I nod, but I'm speechless that she remembers something so simple.

"Jax, when Raven was a little girl, she would play a game called, 'Rose.' She and some of her friends, in the neighborhood, would dress up in their parents' clothes, pretending to be adults going to parties. They all called themselves 'The Rose Club.' They would drink juice out of champagne glasses and eat chocolates as Hors d'oeuvres."

Jax squeezes her hand. "Okay, it's settled. You are Rose Anderson. I will get the information to the lawyers."

"Jax, have you and Raven decided when you are going to get married?"

He shakes his head, "We haven't talked about that yet. She only said yes today."

My mom is laughing so hard she's crying. "Mom, are you okay?"

She smiles at Jax, "You're a very funny man. You may not have realized it yet, but I'm sure in the back of your mind, you have it all figured out. You don't seem like the type of guy who waits very easily."

I look to Jax, stroking his chin, and it hits me—she's right—he does!

"Jax, really, when were you going to tell me?"

His eyes grow large. He is so busted!

"Um . . . well, you see . . . oh crap. Am I in the doghouse now?"

I growl, "Yes you are! What did I tell you about dictating my life?" He gifts me with a huge smile, trying to charm me, I'm sure, but not this time.

"I know it's just—"

I grab his shoulders, "Just what, Jax? You're not getting out of this one—oh no, mister! Mom, stop laughing. You're not helping me at all here. You have no clue how nuts he is. Do you know that he went into my purse and took away all my credit cards, and then replaced them with one of his without even telling me?"

She's laughing even more now. "You two will be just fine."

Maxwell

I FINISH MY THERAPY and I'm starting to feel like myself again. Even my hair is almost back to normal. I would like to go for a walk in the park, but I know I won't be allowed to go by myself. I'm not going to fight it for now. I pick up my keys and head towards the elevator, and there she is, just like clockwork. "I am going for a walk in the park, would you like to come with me?"

She smiles. That's a first! Usually she's pulling my ear. "You know I am, but thank you for asking."

As we head down in the elevator, I figure I should tell her I spoke to Jax. "An, I spoke to Jax today, and everything is going well with Gabriella. He is making arrangements to bring her back to New York."

She seems happy about this. "Good. I think Raven will be happy having her mum with her."

The rest of the walk through the park is in silence. When we're done, I get pretzels and water from the vendor, and we head over to a bench.

"Thank you, Maxwell. I can never resist these warm pretzels. Have you thought anymore about your situation?"

I knew this was coming. I take a deep breath. "Actually, yes I have, I'm not going anywhere. I realize I really don't want to. This is where my family is. You were my family even before I found out that we *are* blood relations. I will have to find a way to make it work, now won't I." I take a breath, and close my eyes, knowing what she will ask next.

"Okay, Maxwell, but have you thought about Jackie, at all?"

I sit quietly for a bit. "I'm not ready to go there, yet. I hurt her very badly. She trusted me with her heart and I wasn't honest with her. I should have told her about my past. I shouldn't have gotten involved with her. The danger was too much, and now the target on her is even greater. Either way, I messed up. I'm not sure how to fix it, or if it can even be fixed."

She takes my hand. "Well, Maxwell, not that it's any of my business, but maybe you should start with a simple phone call."

I lean over and kiss her on the cheek, "Thank you."

She squeezes my hand, "What was that for?"

I fear this woman as much as I love her. "Just you, being you. I don't know where I would be without you. Now let's go back upstairs, I'm getting tired."

We get up to leave and I gather our trash, when I turn around I notice a woman watching us. I nod to one of our guards and he knows what to do. I lean in and whisper, "Come on, ma'am, we need to go right now."

I race her across the street and into the building. When we get into the elevator, I look over to An and see that she's as white as a sheet. "It's okay. I noticed a woman staring at us and it felt off. Our security is going to follow her and try to get some information, so don't worry." I try to reassure her. She takes a deep breath, and I feel bad that I scared her.

"Maxwell, I'm not good at all this cloak and dagger stuff. I wish Jaxson would get back sooner rather than later."

"I'll call Tony to get an update as to when we can expect them, okay?"

As we step off the elevator, she looks back at me, "Yes, and make sure you have a nap, then ring me for tea." She heads into Jax's flat, visibly shaken. Even if I was going to bolt, I would never leave An while Jax is out of the country and she knows it. I head into my flat, more pissed off than anything else. I'm worried about An. For the first time today, I saw real fear in her eyes. I grab my phone and call Tony.

"Tony, I just came back from the park with An. There was a woman following us, watching our every move. I sent one of our guards to follow her. Has he checked in yet?"

I feel bad that Tony is carrying my load, as well as his own.

"Not yet, but Jax checked in earlier. Gabriella consented to the move. Her new name is Rose Anderson. The doctors said she can be moved tomorrow, and I faxed you over some papers to sign for her release."

I walk over to the fax and flip through the papers. "Did Jax say anything else?"

He laughs, "He just reminded me that you're under house arrest until he gets home and you come to your senses, whatever that means."

"Funny, Tony, let me know when the guard checks in. I venture to say that it was Annabelle," I suggest. He only replies with a grunt of agreement before we hang up.

Next, I call Jax to find out the status of his return. "Jax, I just got off the line with Tony and he told me about Gabriella. I signed the paperwork and faxed it back to the clinic, so you are good to go."

"You sound better today, Max, does this mean that you have come to your senses?"

If he were here, I'd deck the cheeky fucker. "Jax, I'm not leaving you for many reasons. We'll save that conversation for another time. Right now, I need to fill you in on my day, so shut up and listen, mate." I tell him about the woman that was at the park, he's very quiet. "Jax, I have a feeling it's Annabelle. Your mum has been a rock through all of this, but today. I could tell she was scared and I don't like it. You need to have the plane under guard twenty-four seven and check it twice before you even get on it. Do you understand? I already put a call into the attorneys and they are going to issue a restraining order against Annabelle." Ugh, I just want to scream. Can't we just get through a day without any fucking drama?

"Got it, Max. This is why I need you with me always."

"How is Raven doing?"

"Well, she said yes!"

Knowing Jax I fear he might have bullied her. "Great, mate, congrats. How did you finally propose to her?"

"Let's just say it was unconventional at best, but she said yes."

I really wish they were back home and not so far away. "Have you figured out when you are going to do it? Knowing you, like I do, you probably have it already planned." He's really quiet now. "Jax, you can't do that to her." He takes a deep breath and I know what's coming, typical Jax "get it done yesterday."

"Max, I want to get married Friday. That would give her two days."

I almost choke, "Jax, are you afraid she will change her mind?" He's slow to answer and I know I hit the nail on the head.

"Max, I really can't stand you sometimes."

"Get it through your thick head—she loves you! She will only change her mind if you push her, so stop bullying her. Getting married is a big step, and every girl has a dream of what her wedding will be like. You are just the bloke that has to show up at the church! Try not to bully her, get home, and I will help you, okay?"

"Okay, I will keep my mouth shut about wedding plans."

$\mathcal{J}axson$

WE HANG UP AND I decide I want Raven, right now. God, I have no control when it comes to her. I come out of the office to look for her and I find a *fucking* note!

Jax,
Jackie is meeting me downstairs for coffee and chocolates. We are
going to have girl talk. I have Bo and my detail. No worries.
Xo Raven

Yeah, no worries my arse. I wonder if that wanker, Dylan, is going
to show up. Maybe I'll just sit in the corner and watch her. No, she
will know that I'm stalking her, and there will be hell to pay if it goes
anything like the credit card fiasco. I'll give her one-hour, and then I'm
looking for her. When did I become such a fucking whack job?

Raven

AS I WAIT FOR Jackie, I watch all the different people go by. It suddenly dawns on me, I'm getting married. I never thought it would happen to me. *And* I'm going to be someone's mom.

"Raven, you look lost in your thoughts, everything okay?"

I smile, "Jackie, he asked me to marry him!" I show her the ring.
She grabs my hand and gasps.

"Oh, Raven, I'm so happy for you. You deserve your happy ever
after. We need to celebrate and I know just the thing." She calls the
waiter over, and begins speaking rapid French. He smiles and leaves.

"Okay, what did you order? You were talking so fast, I only got
snippets of the conversation."

The waiter is back with two cups; he places them down in front of
us, and congratulates me.

"This is a liquid dark chocolate, hazelnut drink. There is no alco-
hol in it, but it's very addicting, so only one, my friend."

Words could never describe what I'm drinking, and I don't think I
will ever find this anywhere but here. I begin to laugh, causing Jackie
to look at me like I'm nuts.

"Raven, are you okay?"

I love her so much, and I know I can't leave here without her. "Oh
Jackie, only you and I could drink liquid chocolate and make faces like

we're having massive orgasms!" We're both laughing, and then Jackie takes my hand and squeezes it.

"That, my friend, is because you and I know the finer things in life."

"So, have you thought anymore about our talk the other day? Will you at least come back and talk to him?"

She clenches her jaw, and I can see the hurt in her eyes. I know if he would tell her everything, it would make a difference. In the end, it's up to Max to decide.

"Raven, you are becoming more like Jax everyday."

I smile, "Yeah, I know. It just works to get right to the point."

"I have and I've decided that I need to have some sort of closure with Max, before I can move on. I know you said there is a reason for his reaction, and I trust you. When are you flying back to the States?"

I bite my lip, trying to contain my excitement. "Well, if everything goes according to plan, we leave tomorrow. Will you be joining us?"

She nods, "Yes, if that's okay with you?"

I throw my arms around her. "Of course, you know I would do anything for you. Now, on another note, I would like for you to be my maid of honor." I hope she says yes, even if things don't work out with Max.

"I would love to. I'm sure Jax will have Maxwell as his best man. I want you to know, even if things don't work out, I would be happy to be a part of your special day."

I am so happy she's coming home with me. "Oh Jackie, I love you. You're the sister I never had." How did I ever get so lucky to have her in my life? "Okay, so next topic; what the hell was up with Dylan?" I know she didn't expect her brother to be such an ass. Heck, I know I didn't expect it.

"Yeah, I know. Raven, it hit him hard that you went and fell in love with the world's most eligible bachelor. I think he finally realizes that he will never have a chance with you."

I feel bad, but I never felt anything remotely like that for Dylan, and I hope I never gave him any ideas. "I'm sorry Jackie, but you know that I never had any romantic feelings for him."

"I know you never led him on. He will have to face it, and move on. Okay, so how did Jax pop the question?"

I start to laugh as I remember Jax's proposal. "Oh my God, Jackie, the man is crazy."

Jackie rolls her eyes. "Raven, we know that already, but how did he ask?"

I have to tell her everything; she's my best friend, but I know she is going to laugh her ass off. "We just left your place, having wild limo sex. While we were still deep in the throes of it, he asked me to marry him, followed by the most romantic declaration of love that I have ever heard."

Her eyes are huge, and she is trying not to laugh. "Do you think he was planning this?"

I take a deep breath. "Well, at first, no. But then, when we got back to the hotel, he did a traditional proposal with the ring."

"He already had the ring? Wow, he must have been planning this."

"Oh, Jackie, you don't know the half of it. Apparently he got the ring the first week we met!"

"Raven, you know he really is crazy and madly in love with you. I don't think that will ever change for him. It comes through in everything he does."

"I know, Jackie, I just need to find a balance we can both live with." I let out a long sigh and we glance at my ring again. When we look up, I see him. I knew he couldn't stay away long.

"Jax, congratulations on getting engaged, I'm so excited for you both."

"Thank you, Jackie, I'm sorry to barge in but I miss my girl."

Jackie gets up to leave. "It's okay, I'm leaving. I need to get packed."

Jax hugs her. I'm happy that he gets along so well with her, after all, she is my only friend.

"Oh, where are you going?"

She kisses us both as she leaves, "Raven will explain; love you both."

"Okay, Raven, what's going on?"

"Jackie is coming back to New York with us. She wants to talk to Max and get closure. She has also agreed to be my maid of honor, no matter what happens between them."

He kisses the inside of my wrist and I light up. "Wow, you have been a very busy girl. Well, I spoke to Max. He and Mum went to the park today and someone was watching them; a female. Max had one of the guards follow her to find out who she is. Tony and Max think its Annabelle. Max also contacted the attorneys, and they are issuing a restraining order against her. I told you I would not hide anything from you. We are leaving tomorrow, for sure. The doctor got the signed papers from Max, so we are good to go. Max has put the plane on a twenty-four-seven guard and it will be swept tomorrow before we leave."

Wow, this man thinks of everything. "Thank you for being honest with me. So, Max and your mom . . . in the park together . . . that's interesting."

He laughs, "Yeah, I don't even want to go there. What were you drinking?"

I know he is going to lose his mind when he finds out what this drink is. "Oh, you have to try this." I call the waiter over and proceed to order in French. "Jax, this is the most unbelievable drink I have ever had. You're going to love it."

He cocks his head and smiles, " You speak French beautifully."

I smile, trying to control the sparks. "Thank you. Now have a sip and tell me what you think."

He takes a sip and then calls the waiter over asking him to make it to go now. "You okay, Jax?"

He takes my hand and pulls me to my feet. "Yep, I'm good, sweetheart. We've been apart far too long, I want you now." He gently grabs me by the elbow. I throw my napkin down and rush off with him.

We get upstairs and he's trying to pull my clothes off, almost at a frantic pace. "Raven, please, just hurry okay—I need you now!"

Maybe I can take charge for a while. "Jax, you will do whatever I ask you to do, deal?"

He growls, "Right here and right now—*Yes!*"

"Well, then, Mr. Phillips, first, you have on entirely too many clothes and I need to rid myself of mine."

"I can help you with that, sweetheart."

I shake my head, "No, Jax, you get to watch." I make a show out of getting undressed. He's fighting his urge to touch me, fisting his hands and clenching his jaw. Now that we are both naked, I push him onto the bed. I open the drink and dip my finger in. I rub my finger over my lips and then slowly lick them. He tries to reach for me but I push his hand away. This is great; I finally have the upper hand!

"Woman, you're killing me. Please put me out of my misery."

Hmm, "Anticipation, Jax. You have to hold it."

He looks down at his cock, "You hear that, buddy? You need to just hold it."

"Oh my God, Jax, really? You know, having in-depth conversations with your cock could get you sectioned."

He's giving me the Jax smirk. "Well then, sweetheart, maybe you need to help him out here."

I dip my finger back into the chocolate. "Je tiens à lécher le chocolat hors de votre coq."

He takes a deep breath, trying so hard to let me have my way. "Oh fuck all that is holy, I have no idea what you just said, but I could blow just listening to you!"

I whisper, "I said, 'I want to lick the chocolate off of your cock,' now you need to breathe, Jax. If you pass out, it won't be fun."

"I'm trying sweetheart, but you are every fantasy come true, and then some."

I take the chocolate and trail it around his nipples and down the happy trail, making sure to not touch his cock. I look up at him and his eyes are wide.

"Sweetheart, please say something else in French."

As I slowly lick off the chocolate I tell him, "Je t'aime ma belle fou homme, which means: I love you, my beautiful, crazy man." I slowly cover his cock with the chocolate, and then swirl my tongue around the head. I don't know how much more of this he can take. He's really trying to keep it together as I work my tongue down to the base and back up to the head. When I reach the top, I nip it just the way I know he likes it. That's it—game over! He yells out my name, his hands squeeze tightly at my shoulders.

He pulls me up to him. "Come here, sweetheart."

He looks shattered. I love that I can do that for him. "You okay, Jax?"

He's nuzzling into my neck and giving me soft kisses. "Why wouldn't I be? You're my every fantasy, and then some. I need to make love to you, Raven, slow and easy. He takes his time entering me, and then stops.

"Open your eyes, Raven. Look at me."

Once I obey, he begins to move really slowly. Then he starts to grind into me the way that makes me crazy, I don't know how much longer I can last. "Jax, I can't hold it."

He softly kisses my lips, "Go, sweetheart, I need to watch you fall."

I look into his eyes and I can see the depth of the love he has for me and—I'm done. My body quivers and my heart begins to race. I'm riding the most unbelievable wave of pleasure.

"Oh, Raven, every time I watch you fall apart in my arms, I'm struck by how much love I have for you." he almost whispers before attacking my lips.

Slowly, we work our tongues into a sensual dance. He's buried in me, forehead to forehead, eyes locked. "You know what I want, don't you, sweetheart?" he asks.

I smile, "I know, Jax. Are you ready?"

He takes a deep breath. "Always, sweetheart."

I work my magic. "Oh my God, Raven . . . fuck!"

As he comes apart in my arms I whisper, "Jax, Je t'aime de tout mon coeur et de l'âme."

He pulls the covers over us, "I love you too," he whispers.

Chapter Nine

Jackie

I NEED TO TALK to my parents about my decision to go back to the States. I know they won't be happy, but in the end, I have to do what is best for me. I'm sure my brother will put his two cents in. Dylan's real problem isn't with me, it's with Raven. He's been in love with her from the first day I brought her home. I need to get this over with Raven and Jax will be here soon to pick me up. I head downstairs, suitcase in hand. My mother sees me, her eyes glance towards my suitcase and she begins to cry. I knew this would not be easy. However, I need answers and those answers are waiting for me in New York. I put my arm around my mom, "Let's go sit down, Mom."

My dad and brother are already in the drawing room, and I get the feeling that they know what's coming. My dad hands me an envelope.

"Jacqueline, before you make your decision to leave, that is a dossier on Maxwell Fleming. I'm not saying he is a bad man. All I'm saying is that he has a past, one that you should be aware of."

My brother is not as calm as my dad; he is fuming. "Jackie, he's thirty-eight and you're twenty-five. He is very experienced and you're not. Think before you jump in, blinded by lust. You're going to get your heart broken by this man, a man you know nothing about!"

I know I need to see this through and nothing anyone can say will stop me. "Dylan, life is about taking chances, and not always riding in the slow lane. Walking away from him broke my heart. There's not much more he could do to it now. I need to understand why. What ever is in the envelope means nothing to me. I need to hear it from Max."

"So, you're just going to up and leave? Do you even know anything about Jaxson or Maxwell? Do you know that Maxwell is twenty percent owner of Raiders Inc.? He might be Mr. Charming, but for fuck sake, Jackie, he's a glorified corporate raider—the lowest of the low!"

That's it, I've heard enough. I jump up, "Dylan, please stop. Your problem is not with me leaving. Your problem is with Raven. She fell in love with someone and it wasn't you. They are engaged, Dylan, and she is having his baby. It's time for you to move on."

I hated to throw that out there, but it's not fair for him to judge someone because he is hurt.

"Well, Jackie, are you going to follow in her footsteps and get knocked up, too?"

Before I can answer, my dad jumps up, "We have company."

I turn around and find Raven standing there with Jax. My father remains stoic not knowing how much Jax overheard. "I'm sorry, I wasn't aware that the housekeeper had let you in."

I think everyone is waiting for the explosion that is on the horizon. As Jax goes to step forward, Raven stops him. "Please Jax, let me handle this." She heads towards me and takes few steadying breaths. "Jeffery, Emi, you know that I love Jackie as if she were my own sister. I would never, knowingly put her in harms way. I promise you that I will look after her, and she will have round-the-clock security. Whether or not she decides to work things out with Maxwell is her decision and hers alone to make. Dylan, as far as your insinuations that she would get 'knocked up,' that is a very disrespectful thing to say about your sister. She has never done anything to warrant your behavior today. What I do with my life is my own business and none of yours. My fiancé, Jaxson, is a good man. He is kind-hearted, caring, and loving. Instead of disrespecting him, maybe you should strive to be more like him. Now, if you're ready, Jackie, we need to get going."

My dad pulls me into a hug. "I will let you go, however, you must take Samuel with you. The arrangements have already been made, since I knew what your decision would be."

"Oh, Papa, it will be fun, watching Samuel trying to adapt to living in New York City again!"

We say our goodbyes and head toward the door. Jax is very quiet, but his jaw is tight. I can tell he is fighting to control his anger. If Raven weren't here to diffuse the situation, Dylan would be in a heap, on the floor, right now.

As we head towards the door, Jax pulls my dad aside. "Jeffery, I don't know who Samuel is, and you're asking me to let him come on my plane with us. I hope you can understand why I'm apprehensive about this."

"Jax, I'm sure you understand how security conscious I am. I would never entrust Jacqueline's safety to just anyone. Samuel has been with our family for ten years, I trust him; he can't be bought."

"Jeffery, I need to make a call."

He nods, "Of course, Jax, we will wait for you in the drawing room."

"Raven, I need to call Max. I'll only be a few minutes," he informs her before we head back in.

*J*axson

"HEY, MAX, I NEED to run something past you." Before he can answer, I tell him what is going on with Jackie and this guy Samuel. I give him the guy's info, and I can hear him tapping away on the computer.

Finally he stops. "Jax, it seems that Samuel's info checks out. He has been with the Gerhard family for ten years. He was her guard when she went away to college. He has a very impressive history; he is former MI6. Have you met him yet?"

I stop pacing, "No, we are just getting ready to leave now."

Max, is quiet for so long that I have to look and make sure the call didn't drop. "Jax, I think it's okay but you have the final say. You need to trust your gut on this one, mate. In the meantime, I will pull a more in-depth report on Samuel and Gerhard. I'll also hit up all of my contacts at MI6 to find out what's not on paper. "

I just can't wait till there is some sort of normalcy in our lives.

"Okay, talk to you later." I end the call. I walk into the living room and meet Samuel. He is nothing like I was expecting, that's for sure. He looks like he just stepped off the pages of GQ Magazine. *And* he is sitting next to Raven—chatting her up! Jeffery looks over at me and I nod.

"Jax, let me introduce you to Samuel Kent."

I step in and shake his hand, my eyes locked on Raven. "Mr. Phillips, pleasure to meet you."

As I shake his hand, I hear Max, in my head, telling me to trust my gut. "You can call me, Jax. We have a stop to make. I will brief you on the way."

Everyone says his or her goodbyes and finally, we are on our way. The ride to the clinic is eerily quiet.

"Jax, do I even want to know what is going through your mind right now?" Raven asks from beside me.

"Oh trust me, sweetheart, you'll find out soon enough," I reply in a hushed tone.

"Okay, stretch, spill. What the hell happened back there?" Samuel asks Jackie.

"Dylan was acting up and Raven put him in his place."

Samuel laughs, "Sorry I missed it. He's always had a thing for you, Raven. Guess you showing up with Jax burst his bubble."

"Sammy, I've never showed any interest in Dylan. Whatever thoughts he's had were manufactured in his own mind."

"I know, Raven, but I'm still sorry I missed it. So what's the stop that we have to make?"

"Sammy, I came here on some personal business for a friend. I have to pick someone up and bring her to the states. She has top-level clearance. I would never let anyone near these girls if it wasn't safe."

"Jax, why wasn't I made aware of this earlier?"

"For the same reason I was not made aware of your presence earlier. My plane. My girl. My rules. You can trust me or I can let you out now—your choice."

"Jax, wherever Jackie goes I go."

The rest of the ride is in silence.

Raven

WE ACTUALLY MANAGE TO get my mom, and settle in for the long flight without any drama. My mom is showing Jackie her sketches. Sammy is reading a magazine. I snuggle up to Jax.

"Raven, what's on your mind?"

I love that we are really figuring each other out. "How can you tell I'm thinking about something?"

He laughs, "Sweetheart, I can always tell when your wheels are turning."

"Do you think I was wrong for telling Dylan off in front of his parents? They have always been supportive and respectful of me. I feel like maybe I disrespected them."

His thumb travels up and down my arm. "Look at me, Raven." His thumb stops and he pats my arm. My eyes fly up to his. "What you said was the truth, and you said it a hell of a lot nicer than I would have. When you were telling Dylan, off I was so proud. Not for what you were saying about me; I could give a royal fuck what anyone thinks. It was your passion to defend, not only Jackie, but also our baby and me. I never thought I could love you more, but in that instant, I fell in love with you all over again."

I snuggle into him. "I love you, Jax."

He laughs, "More, sweetheart, always more."

Jaxson

EVERYONE IS ASLEEP, EXCEPT for Samuel, so I figured I'd go into the office and get some work done. First order of business is to check in with my mum. I only hope that Max survived being locked up all these days with her!

"Hi, Mum, what's going on over there?"

She huffs, "Well, it's about time you called me. When will you be home?"

"We are in route right now. We probably have another six hours of flight time. Is everything okay over there?"

"Well, what did you think I was going to do to him? I mean, really, son."

I'm trying to get a lead on what's bothering her, but she's playing this pretty close to the vest. "I know, Mum, is he any better than when I left?"

"Actually, yes, he is. Is Jackie with you?" she asks, her tone lightening up.

Of course she wants to know that. "Yes, Mum, but they have to work it out on their own, so no interfering."

"Really, son, I never interfere in anyone's business."

I damn near choke on that one.

"How is Gabriella doing?"

I know my family will embrace Gabriella. "She is doing a lot better than the doctors expected. I think she might not need to be in a clinic. I'm thinking of putting her in a flat in my building. Raven, can be close to her all the time; she deserves that."

"I think that would be a great idea, but are there any available?"

Ha! "Mum, if not, I'll buy the whole building!"

She's mumbling something under her breath—which she does a lot, when it comes to me.

I take a deep breath, preparing myself to give her the news. "Mum, she said yes!" I say quickly.

"Well, did you doubt it? I told you, from the first day I met her, that she would be my daughter-in-law, you just need to listen to your mum more often."

I am never going to live that one down.

"So, when is the wedding? You know, the baby will be here before you know it."

That's mum's way of telling me she wants us married before the baby gets here. "I know, I haven't spoken to her about it yet. If it was up to me I would marry her the second this plane touches the ground. However, I'm not sure what Raven is thinking. Oh, and we had Gabriella's name changed. It's officially, Rose Anderson," I inform her.

This is also my way of changing the subject.

"Okay, now when you get home we are having a family meeting?" I can hear the apprehension in her voice; it's so unlike her and I'm worried.

I have to ask, but I know she won't tell me. "Mum, is something wrong?"

"Never mind, Jaxson, we will talk about it when you get in. Be safe and I love you."

"Me too, Mum."

Something is off and I'm not sure what. I decided to call Bella. "Hey, sis, I'm about six hours out, what is happening with Mum?"

"Ha, hello to you too, bro. What do you mean? Mum is guarding, Max and he's not happy about it."

I tell her what mum said about having a meeting. "She only calls them when one of us is in trouble, and I don't think it's me."

I hold while she yells at Vito. I swear that dog is a beast.

"Well, that's news to me. I know I didn't do anything wrong, either, for a change."

This is bugging me. "Alright, maybe Max fucked up. I'll call him next. She said yes, Bella." I add in quickly. I can't believe I almost forgot to tell her.

She laughs, "Of course she did, she loves you. Sometimes, you're such a moron. When is the big day?"

I guess I really need to get this nailed down with Raven. "I don't know, we haven't talked about it."

Bella is quiet for a minute. "Well, if you want, we can have it here. The garden is in full bloom, and you know I can get it together really quickly. How's her mum doing?"

That's not a bad idea. I wonder if I can sell Raven on it. "She is doing great. I will talk to Raven about what type of wedding she wants. Sorry to cut you short but I have to go. Love you, sis."

She laughs, "Me too, bro."

Next on my list is Max. He picks up on the first ring. "Max, I see Mum didn't kill you, yet. How are you feeling?"

"I'm doing better, and I'm getting used to having my watchdog."

He must be better, he's getting all cheeky again. "You better not let her hear you call her that; she'll be yanking your ears!" That shut him up real quick.

"Where are you, Jax?"

I'm pacing again, something I find myself doing a lot since all this started. Usually, it's Max who paces. "In the air. We should be home soon and before you ask, I still haven't talked to her about what type of wedding or when."

"Mate, what is your fucking problem?" he yells.

"Max, what if she doesn't want to get married for a year? I will go nuts. I really wish you would stop laughing at me." *I'm glad my life is so fucking funny!*

"Oh, Jax, I can't help it. You really are very funny. You can negotiate million dollar deals, yet talking to a beautiful girl—who is madly in love with you—renders you speechless. Please tell me you see the humor in this?"

"Fuck you, Max. What is going on with Mum?" I shift the conversation. "She said we are having a family meeting. I called Bella; she hasn't pissed Mum off. And I've been away, so that only leaves you." He gets really quiet, and now I know it's him. Fuck! What is going on?

"Actually, it has been quiet here. An, and I go to the park for walks. Then we have pretzels, sit on the bench, and people watch."

I know when something is being kept from me, but I can wait a few more hours. "Max, I have a job for you." Maybe this will get him excited.

"Well, *finally,* I get to do something."

Ugh. "Wise arse. I need a flat in our building for Raven's Mum. Before you even make the suggestion, the answer is no fucking way, you're not giving up your flat." I can just picture him pacing.

"I thought she was going into a clinic? I made all the arrangements, Jax."

I know Max will agree she needs to be around Raven, not in some clinic. "When you see her, you'll understand. She really doesn't need to be in a clinic. Between regular doctor visits and having Raven around all the time, we both feel that she will be fine."

"If there are no flats, then what would you like to do? I don't know why I ask, I already know the answer. Just buy the whole building, right?"

Finally, he gets it. "You see, Max, you know me better than anyone.

Oh and just so you know, you're my best man."

He's laughing, "Of course I am, mate, have a safe flight."

I GO CHECK ON everyone and find they're all asleep. I scoop Raven up and carry her into the bedroom. I'm such a lucky bastard. I know it. Now, if I can convince her that we should get married on Friday, all will be right in my world.

"Jax, where are we?"

I start by nibbling that ear. "We, my dear, are somewhere over the Atlantic, and I need you."

"Is everything okay?"

I laugh, "Oh it will be, just as soon as I get your clothes off." She slowly opens her eyes, "There she is, my beautiful girl." I nuzzle her neck.

"Hi." She kisses my lips so softly, I swear I could explode just from her tenderness. "Don't you ever sleep, Jax?"

I can't help but laugh, "Yes, but I sleep best when I'm buried inside of you." I love to kiss her tender lips and nibble on that ear. I don't know why it drives me crazy, but it does. "I need to make love to you very slowly, sweetheart. I don't know why, just know that I need it like my very existence depends on it." I enter her very slowly, and when I'm all the way in I stop and rest my forehead upon hers. "Raven, I have no control when it comes to you. I was so lost, and I didn't even realize it."

"Jax, I'm not going anywhere in this world without you—ever. I'm with you for life."

I take a deep breath, "I'm going to move now, and try not to explode, but I can't make any promises."

"Jax, flip me over. I want to be on top."

I'm a strong man, yet I don't mind giving Raven control in the bedroom. Sometimes she needs to take the power. It's a beautiful thing, watching her glide up and down my cock, taking me, as she needs me.

Let's face it; I'm not a one shot man!

Wow, "I love when you get all demanding, it's a real turn on."

"Jax, everything turns you on."

"Okay, yeah. When it comes to you, that's true. I have a confession, but I don't know if I can talk right now while you're gliding up and down on my cock."

She takes both my hands and stops. "Tell me!"

I take a deep breath, "Okay, don't stop. When you were giving Dylan the bitch slap, I was hard as stone; very exciting stuff, sweetheart."

She throws her head back laughing. "Oh my crazy man, I love you. Now hold on 'cause I need to let loose." She goes up really slow and then, slams down on my cock. She clenches and goes back up again, then repeats her actions. That's it—I'm done. "Fuck . . . oh, holy hell, woman." She is digging her nails into my shoulders and screaming her release. *Nails and clenching; she's trying to fucking kill me!*

She's gliding up and down really slowly, as I try to catch my breath. I slowly caress her growing belly, trying to figure out how to convince her that we should get married right away.

"Jax, you seem perplexed, what's bothering you?"

I tilt my hips up to meet hers. "I can't keep anything from you."

"No, and you know I don't want you to. We are on this journey together, so no secrets."

I don't know why I'm so nervous to talk to her about this. I know I shouldn't be.

"We need to talk about the wedding."

She's staring at me, trailing her fingers up and down my cheeks. "Is that what you're worried about?"

I nod, "Well, yeah . . . Bella said the garden is in bloom and we can have it there, but Max said that every girl dreams of her wedding day, and I need to give you free rein with the details. But you know me; I don't want to make you feel like I'm bullying you into the wedding. I want to make all your dreams come true."

She leans down and kisses me really slowly. "Jax, calm down and let's talk. First, did you tell everyone that we got engaged yesterday, and when did you tell them?"

"You know me, I have to bounce things off of my family, it's just who I am."

"Jax, when do you want to get married? Let's start with that."

I cringe a little at the idea of telling her.

"Please don't tell me you already have it planned?"

"No, well, not yet. If it were up to me I would want to be married yesterday." I say quickly, and then wait for my words to register with her. "Raven, are you going to say anything, or are you just going to look at me like I've lost all reason?"

"Are you serious?"

I take both of her hands, holding onto them so tightly: afraid she might disappear.

"Of course I'm serious. I want to be married before the baby gets here. My life didn't start until you came crashing into it. I want everyone to know that I'm one lucky bastard—the luckiest in the whole bloody world. I want to experience life everyday through your eyes."

"Just how do you plan on pulling this off so quickly?"

"Really, Raven, I don't like to throw my money around, but I'm one of the wealthiest men in the world. Surely, I can get a wedding pulled off in record time."

"Jax, how do you think I would feel?"

I chew on my bottom lip and squeeze her hands.

"Well, you see, sweetheart, there's my dilemma. I know how you would feel, I just don't know how to change that."

"Jax, I think a compromise is in order here, don't you agree?"

Suddenly, I feel a sense of relief wash over me. I think she may be onto something, here. "Okay, I can compromise . . . I think." Oh boy, not sure that was the right fucking answer. She looks like she's going to blow a gasket.

"You *think?* Jax, how the hell do you negotiate million dollar deals and not compromise? Please, I really need to understand this."

I give her my biggest smile, "I make them see the light."

"Okay, what do you mean by 'you make them see the light'?"

"Raven, I think you're making this a lot more difficult than it really is. I show the people what they can achieve when we all play nicely together, and then they see what life is like if we don't. It really is a no brainer, and I don't understand why more people don't do this for a living." *She's really quiet. I hope I didn't mess this up.*

"Jax, here is my list of *demands.* I would like a small wedding.

I would like Jackie as my maid of honor. I don't have anyone to give me away, so I think I would like Michael Jr. to walk me down the aisle since this all started with him. I want one long stem Abracadabra Rose. I would love to have it in Bella's garden. I want you in a violet bow tie. Wow, you're not saying a word? I would've thought you'd interrupt me by now."

I smile, "I'm processing. How long will it take you to find something to wear?"

"After all of that, your only question is about my gown?"

"I can pull all of that off within a reasonable time frame. I love all of this *negotiating,* it's making me hard."

"Oh, for the love of Jesus, Jax, everything makes you hard!"

"Yep, when it comes to you, sweetheart, everything does."

"Oh, and, Jax, I want a prenuptial agreement. I don't want anyone to think I'm marrying you for your money. Bad enough, people will talk when the baby gets here."

"STOP. I will not have you talk about our baby like that—EVER! I don't give a flying fuck what anyone says or thinks, it's what I know in my heart. That's the only thing that matters, the only thing that ever will. Our baby—our flesh and blood—was created out of love. No more talk like that and no prenup!"

"Jax, I thought we were negotiating?"

I growl at her, "That is non-negotiable."

"Wow, you scared me. Are you like this with the companies you deal with?"

"Sweetheart, I know what I want, and what I'm willing to give up to get it. I don't waiver on the important stuff, I do on the stuff I could care less about and that makes them feel like they had a victory."

"Okay, no prenup."

"Good, now that we have that settled, do you think you can decide on a dress by Friday? If not, I can have someone make you whatever you want."

Her mouth falls open. "This Friday?"

I'm still buried inside her; I tilt my hips. "I told you I don't want to wait. If we do it this Friday or six months from now, nothing will change. I will make it exactly how you want it." I start moving slowly again.

"Jax, I will try—oh who am I kidding? You know and I know that we are going to get married on Friday, come hell or high water!"

I attack her neck with laughter and kisses. "Sweetheart, I love negotiating with you, we should do this more often."

"That wasn't negotiating, Jax, that was you getting what you want. " Look at me, please." I stop my attack on her neck and look up at her. "I love you, but I need you to understand that you can't always push me around to get what you want. If you want something, talk it out with me, first, okay?" she pleads.

"Okay, but you need to understand that this was real progress for me. Normally, I would just take the ball and run with it. Try to be patient with me and all my craziness and I will promise to try and negotiate with you on the important stuff. I'm not going to run to you with every little thing, and I don't expect you to run to me with the small stuff, either. I trust you and your judgment. I need you to trust me. Are we all good now?"

"Yes, we're good."

"Okay, baby, you know what I would love right now?"

"I know exactly what you want." She smiles coyly at me. I grind my hips into her just the way she likes and I can see she's getting close; her breathing becomes erratic and she quickens her pace. "Jax, you ready, baby?"

I take a deep breath and I feel need in me, climbing. "Oh God, Raven, I'm ready . . . do it baby, *please.*" I beg. She clenches, squeezing my cock as she slams down. That's all it takes to send us both over the cliff.

I feel as if I'm about to pass out. "Jax, are you okay? Breath, baby, just breath."

I kiss her softly. "Raven, can we invite your Pilates teacher to the wedding?"

She laughs. "Go to sleep, Jax, I love you."

I whisper, "More, sweetheart, always more."

Maxwell

JAX WILL BE BACK soon, and then the calm, I've been experiencing, will be gone. There are no flats available in this building. I will see if anyone is willing to sell, otherwise, that crazy-arse fucker will buy the building, and then all hell will break loose. It's almost teatime with An; she keeps me on a tight schedule. I know she wants me to call her something other than ma'am, I just don't know what. Just like clockwork, here she comes.

"Maxwell, teatime."

I smile. She's so strong, yet she has let me see how vulnerable she really is. "Good afternoon, ma'am, how are you feeling?" She won't say it, but I know she's worried about telling Jax and Bella.

"I heard from Jaxson, they should be home soon. Raven said yes, so now we have a flurry of wedding events. Have you spoken to him?"

"Yes, ma'am, he called earlier. He was going to try and talk Raven into setting a date. You know what that means, he will move heaven and earth to get her down that aisle as fast as possible." I know she wants them married just as fast as Jax does.

"Well, I can tell you, I, for one, will be very happy on that day. I want them married and concentrating on my new grandbaby."

I'm more worried about Raven. "I know, but Raven has been through a great deal, and now she is taking on the responsibility of a mother, who, for all intents and purposes, died twenty years ago. I know she is thrilled that she has her mum in her life again, but it is an emotional time for everyone. And let's not forget that the threat is still out there."

Her face turns pale, and I feel bad that I even brought it up.

"Have you found out who that woman was? Did you think I didn't notice how worried you were?"

I laugh, "You're too smart for your own good, ma'am. I think it might be, Annabelle Gianconna, Vincent's sister. The attorneys are issuing a restraining order."

"Maxwell, we are going to have a family sit down later, and I would like you there. I plan on telling Jaxson and Isabella the truth about their father and you."

We are both quiet for a bit. "Are you sure you want me there? This is a very personal matter, maybe I should sit it out."

She's holding onto her teacup so tight I fear it will shatter.

"Maxwell, you really don't want to be on my bad side. You are family, whether you like it or not, you are stuck with us. I know that Jax and Bella will be overjoyed to know what they feel, in their hearts, is in fact reality. Do you have a problem with us?"

I shake my head and just begin to laugh, "Oh, ma'am, you really are a mini version of Jax. Yesterday, you said you wanted me to call you something other than ma'am. What would you like me to call you?"

She smiles, "You'll know when the time is right. We are having the meeting here, so you don't have to go anywhere. I already let Isabella know."

I need to change the subject. "Jax asked me to find a flat in the building for Gabriella."

"Maxwell, don't even think about it."

Ha. "Relax, An, Jax already yelled at me. However, there are none available."

"Well, I'm sure Jax will convince someone to move out!"

We sit in silence for a bit.

"Maxwell, did Jax mention Jackie?"

"She is with them." My heart constricts as I whisper.

"I know. Have you thought about what you're going to do?"

"I don't know what I'm going to do."

"Well, you can't sit here, wallowing in self-pity, can you?"

"I'm at a loss here. What would you suggest I do? I really hurt her. I pushed her away without a word. The worst part is, I made Jax do my dirty deed. What kind of man does that make me? She deserves so much better than me. My head keeps saying she would be safer, if she stayed away from me. Yet, my heart beats stronger at the mere thought of her."

She just sits there, stirring her tea. "Well, are you going to say something or just stir that cold cup of tea?"

She finally looks up, "Well, you're right. She didn't deserve to be treated like that. When you were shot, she put all her fears aside and sat by your bedside twenty-four seven. I had to force her to eat and sleep. She was willing to stay by your side, no matter what the outcome. That is not someone to dismiss from your life, like you're throwing out the morning trash."

Well that didn't help. "I feel even worse now. I thought you were supposed to be here making me feel better?"

"No, Maxwell, I'm not here to make you feel better. I'm here to make you feel. I think you should start with an apology. And from there, maybe explain to her why."

I don't know that I can do this. "The wedding is probably going to happen on Friday. You know I'm the best man?"

She laughs, "Of course, did you think he would ever ask anyone else?"

I only have a few hours till they land. I can feel my heart racing. "I'm so much older than her, and she has so much life to live."

"Maxwell, please stop the pity party and get on with life. I'm not saying that what happened wasn't a tragedy, but don't you think Samantha would want you to be happy? If, God forbid, the shoe was on the other foot, wouldn't you have wanted Samantha to be happy?"

I growl, "You're right, and if you tell another living soul I said that, I will deny it to the bitter end!"

She reaches up and pulls my ear, and all I can do is laugh.

$\mathcal{J}axson$

WHEN WE LAND, MAX has a limo and another group of guards waiting for us. I hope Gabriella is going to be able to deal with all of this craziness. Raven reaches up and pulls my hands out of my hair.

"Relax, Jax, we will be okay." She calms and grounds me. I don't know what I ever did before her.

Jackie seems very nervous . . . almost scared. "Jax, Sammy and I are going back to my apartment. I still have my tracking bracelet. Do you want me to have another guard?"

I know I can't stop Jackie from going home, but at least Sammy is with her.

"Okay, Sammy, take her back to her place, make sure the bracelet always remains on, and take another guard with you."

"Jax, he's gay. He's been in a committed relationship for the past seven years. His partner, Ian, has agreed to move and he will be joining

Sammy soon." Raven informs me of this news. Though, she could of saved my nerves from being on edge hours ago, I'm glad she finally did say *something.*

"I love that you understand me, Raven. The whole ride, all I could think was *Max is going to kill me if I let her go off with him.*"

She laughs at me but then glances at her mother and her smile fades. "Mom, are you okay?"

Gabriella closes her eyes and takes a deep breath. "I'll be fine, it's a lot to take in, all at once. I have been in that little clinic for twenty years. The world has changed so much, yet my life has stood still. Will I ever be able to catch up?"

Raven pulls her into her arms as the tears she was fighting to hold back begin to fall. "Mom, we will be here with you every step of the way. No one will hurt you, ever again. It's time you begin to live again. Daddy would have wanted you to be happy."

I watch my beautiful girl comforting her mum, and I realize this has to be so overwhelming for Raven too. She is so strong, and in this moment, I love her so much more . . . if that's even possible.

We pull up to The Tower and a confused look comes across Raven's face. "Jax, I thought we were going to bring my mom to a clinic?"

I take her hand, "I have been thinking that maybe it would be best if we got your mum a flat in our building. I would rather have her closer to us. I think it would be good for everyone. Until I can make the arrangements, I figure she can stay in our guest room."

"What if there are no flats available? Oh, why do I even bother asking such a stupid question? Don't worry, Mom, you will have a flat in this building if Jax has anything to say about it."

Chapter Ten

Jaxson

THE ELEVATOR DOORS OPEN, and my mum is waiting for us. One look and I know something is up. What else is going to be thrown at me? We make all the introductions, and Raven takes her mum to her room so she can get settled in.

"Mum, what's wrong?" I ask in a hushed tone.

"Jaxson, we are having the family meeting now at Maxwell's. Bella is already waiting for us. I would also like Raven to be there."

She really has me worried. "Are you ill?"

She shakes her head, "No, son, my health is fine."

Raven comes out takes one look at us, and she furrows her brows at me. "Jax, is everything okay?"

I take her hand, holding it tight. "We are having a family meeting at Max's and you have to come too." She strokes my back, trying to calm me. She is my rock, my light in the storm, and I thank God everyday that I went to that Starbucks a few minutes early.

We get over to Max's and Junior runs right into Raven's arms. He really is so attached to her. I glance over at Max, and I know something is up between him and Mum.

Raven is looking him over, "Max, you look wonderful, and all your hair is back!"

Bella laughs, "Raven, I was a cosmetologist before I met, Michael.

I told Max I could make some crazy hairstyles if he wants, but he won't let me near him with my shears!"

"Why did you give it up?" Raven asks.

She kisses Junior's head. "When I was pregnant with him I didn't want to be around the chemicals. After that, I fell in love with being a mum."

My mum stands up. "Okay, everyone, please have a seat. I have something I need to tell everyone." My mum seems really nervous.

"This is a very hard story for me to tell, but the situation being what it is, it must be told. I was a young girl of seventeen, living in Wales when I met James Phillips. We fell in love, and I thought the world started and stopped with him. Well, I was caught up in the rush of the romance and found myself pregnant."

Raven is squeezing my hand.

"My parents were very old fashioned and insisted that we marry right away. In the beginning, things were good. My husband was in sales and he traveled frequently, yet he always made it home on the weekends. When I found myself pregnant with Isabella, his time home became less and less, until finally, one day, he never came back. I decided to search for him. My search led me to Scotland . . . where I met his other wife and son. When I confronted her about her husband, I realized we were both duped. She said James came home and confessed everything to her, right before he walked out. I was stunned. I walked away that day a broken woman. So many lives were destroyed. The other wife's name was Cindy and their son was . . . Maxwell.

I leap up, "Are you telling me my father was nothing more than a bigamist? I never thought he was perfect, but a fucking bigamist?!"

"Jaxson, I'm sorry, son . . . so very sorry for all of this."

My mum begins to cry; she's trembling. I pull her into my arms, "Enough! Mum, I don't blame you at all."

"Please, son, sit down and let me finish. I left Scotland, went home to lick my wounds. I needed to figure out what I was going to do next. It was during that time that Cindy overdosed on pain pills. I reached out to Maxwell's grandmother, and we soon became friends. She never blamed me for Cindy's death, although, I will forever blame myself. She moved Maxwell to London and changed his last name to hers. I went to her, and pleaded with her to let me raise Maxwell as my own.

I wanted to have the three of you grow up together, but his grams felt that he was settled in already. And she wanted him with her. I made her a promise right then and there that I've kept all these years. I walked away that day so sad. Sad that one man caused so much heartache. Sad that Maxwell would never know he had siblings. Sad that Jaxson and Isabella would never know what a wonderful brother they had. But mostly sad at the part I felt I played in Cindy's death. That day, I made my decision. I would move my family to the United States. It broke my heart to leave Maxwell but I never had a choice."

No one is saying a word, my mum is trying to keep it together and be strong, but I can see she is going to lose it. I get up and take her in my arms. "Mum, I am so very proud of you. You took a bad situation and made it better for everyone involved, always putting the children first. I, for one, am very proud to call you my mum."

She begins to cry, and it slays me that she went through all of this alone. Max stands up, and takes her hands. His eyes, always on her. I don't know what happened when I was gone, but it seems like it was good for both of them.

"An, you should never have felt responsible for my mum's death. I'm so sorry that you carried this with you, all these years. You had no idea what you would find that day. You knocked on the door, looking for answers—answers you deserved. You were not there to hurt anyone. My mum just wasn't as strong. I've accepted that and you should too. Please stop blaming yourself. There is more to this story, and its time I told everyone."

Maxwell

I NEED TO GET this over with quickly. I know they need to know, but the pain in reliving it turns my heart to stone. "I did okay for myself. I met and fell in love with the most beautiful woman, Samantha. She was a barrister, and we worked well together. We married and soon after we had the most beautiful son, Elliot. I thought my life was complete, and I put the past behind me. Samantha would take Elliot to the park everyday. He loved to be outside. One day, while she was loading him into the car, some drugged up gang member's carjacked her. My wife and son were both shot. They died instantly. My life ended that day. I quit my job and drank myself into numbness. My grams was still in touch with An, and she told her what happened. An was getting ready to come and drag me to the States when I decided to join the Special Forces. I took every assignment there was, trying to get myself killed. I just wanted to be with my family. There is a saying: *'We make plans and God just laughs,'* well, God had his own ideas. I was then asked to guard the Queen's rebel grandson. I said okay, thinking the more danger, the better. Then one night I met Jax in a bar. I thought it was a chance meeting, only to find out, last week, that it was a set up by An and my grams. The rest, as they say, is history."

"Max, what do you mean, it was a set up?" Jax asks in shock.

I laugh, "Yeah, mate, your mum and my grams set the whole thing up. I was given a letter yesterday that your mum kept in a safety deposit box from my grams. She wanted your mum to give it to me when she felt I needed to know the whole story. If you want to read it, you can. Look, all of you, I've accepted that this is my life. I don't want your sympathy for what happened to Samantha and Elliot."

Bella jumps up and throws her arms around me, then smacks me in the chest. "You're such an arse."

We all freeze, watching Bella. "Of course we have sympathy, why wouldn't we? That's a terrible thing to have happen, and as a parent, I will never understand how you survived. When Junior was taken, I thought my life was over. I have loved you like a brother from the first day Jax brought you home and nothing that is said here will ever change that for me. What I always felt in my heart is real and I can use this to my advantage."

"Hey, Jax, why don't you come into my office and I'll give you that letter to read," I offer. He gets up and heads down the hall with me.

We get into my office and Jax is quiet. A quiet Jax is never a good sign. I'm worried about him I know this is a lot for him to deal with on top of everything else. "Jax, you're very quiet, mate, what's wrong?"

"Max, I have always thought of you as my brother. I'm blown away with the fact that you actually are. I couldn't be happier about that. I am in shock, however, to find out that Bella and I are illegiti- mate. I think I understand now why mum wants us married before the baby gets here, and why she was wild when Bella was pregnant before she was married. I know we live in a world where anything goes, but that's not how I fly, mate. You know I have morals and ethics that I live by, so how can I fix this for Mum's sake?"

"Jax, I honestly have no idea here, but I will do whatever makes it easier for everyone. Honestly, so much has happened since you've been gone. Your mum showed me a side of her I never knew existed. She acts all tough and brave, but she has been living with the fear that this will bring shame to her children. She's been carrying the guilt of my mum's death for all these years, a guilt she shouldn't have to bear. I think for everyone involved, we need to put this all away and move forward." I get the letter out.

Jax shakes his head. "That is personal, and I have no reason to doubt anything you tell me. Please put it away. What else happened while I was gone?"

As I put the letter away I take notice how tired he is. "Jax, we can go over this in the morning." He shakes his head no.

"No. Let's go over it now."

"Okay, if you insist. There are no flats available in the building. I put some feelers out to see if anyone wants to sell, but no responses. I got confirmation back from Tony, right before you landed, that the woman in the park was Annabelle. She has not made any more attempts to contact Raven. I am checking into new guards for Raven and Gabriella." I wait for a response from him. After a few moments, I lightly smack his upper arm. "Talk to me, Jax. I can't help you if you don't let me in." I open my drawer, pull out a bottle of scotch, and pour us each a glass.

"Will this cluster fuck ever end, Max? I want my family safe— safe and happy. Is that really too much to ask?"

"For everyone's sake, Jax, I hope so and soon."

Raven

THE GUYS ARE BACK and I see worry lines around Jax's eyes. My heart is breaking for this man. I need to get him to eat something and rest, and I know just what to do. "Jax, I'm hungry can we get something to eat?"

His eyes light up. "My girl is hungry, so I have to go feed her. I love you all, but this is a priority!" He is now pushing me out the door. Giving Jax purpose, and letting him know he is needed is what lights up his world. We go across the hall and everything is quiet. My mom is still sleeping, and I'm pretty sure she will be for a while.

"Raven, what would you like to eat?"

I reach up and kiss his soft lips. "Are you up for an adventure?"

He gives me that smirk I love so much. "As long as I'm with you, I will go anywhere."

Oh, how I love this man. "Jax, the only thing I need you to do is run a bath and I will meet you in there." He's about to argue, but I hold my hand up for him to stop.

" Remember, some things are non-negotiable. Right now, you need me to shut off your mind and let me take charge. Now, go."

His face lights up and his blues are twinkling. "Okay, you don't have to tell me twice."

I watch him stroll towards the bathroom, and I can't help staring at his beautiful ass. He stops just before the doorway and turns his head around, "Like the view, sweetheart?" I roll my eyes, so busted.

There is a little pizza place, not too far away, that makes a specialty pizza. I order it along with a ton of food, and give one of the guard's instructions where to pick it up. I head into the bathroom and there is my beautiful man, soaking in the tub. His head tilted back, eyes closed, and the room is filled with candles; vanilla and orange spice. I stand there and admire the view. I know he knows I'm watching, and I don't care. I get undressed and climb in with my back against his front.

"Jax, do you want to talk or would you rather shut your mind off, for the rest of the night?"

"I will take option B, thank you." He wraps his arms around me and pulls me tight. "Sweetheart, when we are locked away, just like this, I find a peace that I can't seem to get anywhere else. I'm worried about my mum, Raven, this shook her to the core."

Ah, so he does want to talk. "Give her time, Jax, she has held this secret for such a very long time. You know it had to be hard for her to admit everything. In her mind, she is afraid you and Bella will think less of her."

"I couldn't be more proud of her if I tried. To think, she put all of her pain and shame aside to give her children everything. Do you know what really got to me out of this whole situation?"

I turn in his arms so I can face him, "No, what?"

He pulls me tighter, "What really got to me is the fact that even though her husband was a bigamist, even though she was left with two very young children, she put all of that aside and offered to raise Max, along with us. That to me, shows what a strong and proud woman she is. I can only hope that I will set that type of example for our child."

I reach up and softly kiss his lips. "Maybe you need to let her know that, I'm sure it would help her." He doesn't say anything, but I know he gets it. I stand up, "We need to eat, and the water is getting cold." I offer him my hand, but he pulls himself to his knees, leans in, and kisses my growing bump.

"I love you, baby, and I love your mum, too." At this moment, I know I could never be without this man.

HE LEADS ME TOWARDS the kitchen. I stop. "I have a surprise for you, Jax, follow me upstairs." When we reach the rooftop deck, he looks at the spread and smiles. I know he's happy with the amount of food I ordered.

"Raven, this looks wonderful. I am starving, let's eat."

It's a beautiful evening, and this is the perfect place to enjoy the city, and each other. "Jax, do you think my mom is going to be okay, living in the city? I'm worried about her. This is such a change from where she has been living for the last twenty years."

"Raven, I know it will be an adjustment for her, but I think you being here, so close to her, will be a great help. I know you are fiercely independent, however, in this case, I think what would help her is to feel needed by you."

"I'm at a loss. How do I make her feel needed?"

"Sweetheart, your mum lost you when you were only seven years old. She missed out on all the milestones in your life. Yeah, she has you back, but you're a woman now, not a seven-year-old little girl. Helping you through the pregnancy, nurturing you, and helping with the baby will give her a sense of purpose. She will feel needed. Does that make sense?"

I nod, "It does. I can only hope that my pregnancy doesn't bring up any bad memories for her." Suddenly, Bo barks. I look over to see that my mom has wandered up to the roof deck. "Are you hungry, mom?"

"Yes, it looks wonderful."

Jax helps her to her seat. "Rose, I hope you feel comfortable staying here until I can secure a flat in this building. I know I can be a *bulldog,* so please tell me to rein it in, when I get overbearing." Jax is trying to make everything perfect for both of us.

"Jax, I'm excited to be close to Raven and the baby. Thank you so much for all that you are doing for all of us."

I know my tears will bring him to his knees, so I wipe them away quickly. Jax takes my hand and kisses the inside of my wrist, and I feel myself shudder. "Sweetheart, what's for dessert?"

I go about setting up the dessert, and I know he is going to lose his mind, but now that my mom is here I'm not sure how this is going to go over with him. I'm watching his face as I bring over a covered tray. "I hope you love it, Jax, it is one of my favorites."

I lift the lid, and the Jax's face is priceless. His eyes grow wide as he stares at the tray, speechless. I'm trying so hard not to laugh.

My mom smiles, but has a faraway look on her face. "Raven, do you know this is one of my favorite treats? Your father used to make this for me all the time."

I take a deep breath, to think that my mom and I both love Nutella. Something so simple, yet, so powerful. Jax still can't seem to muster a word. "My beautiful man, have I rendered you speechless?"

"I've never had a Nutella pizza. I am experiencing so many firsts with you."

I know Jax is trying so hard to control himself, but I can't help myself, he just makes it way too easy. I swipe my finger into the warm Nutella and pop it into my mouth. All the while never taking my eyes from Jax. I tilt my head back and let out a little low moan. He is frozen with a death grip on the sides of the table. Next, I swipe the whip cream and offer him my finger. He growls. I really don't know how long he is going to last, but I'm having way too much fun to stop now.

"Raven, I think I'm going to take my dessert and head back to my room. You both have fun." Mom giggles at us, shaking her head. I think she knows what I was doing to him just now.

My mom gets up and heads downstairs. The minute she is out of sight, Jax leaps up.

"I need you now."

I shake my head, "Nope, not yet, Jax. Tonight we are going to reverse roles here. I think it should be all about what *I* need." I inform him. His eyes grow wide, and he fists his hands like he's trying with all that he has for some sort of control.

"Sit, please." He does, but I can tell this is not going to be easy for him. I stand up and do a slow strip, just for him. I stand before him, wearing only my heels. He moans. I swipe my fingers through the pizza and smear the Nutella and whip cream on my nipples. "Oh my, Jax, this is wonderful. Warm Nutella and cool whip cream just making my nipples ache for you."

His eyes are gazing up and down my body, getting darker. I know he's not going to last much longer. I reach over and pick up his glass of Prosecco. I let it slowly drizzle down my breasts and between my legs. That's it—game over!

"*Fuck all that is holy, woman!*" he yells.

He leaps out of the chair, lifts me up, and runs with me to the cushioned chase lounge. He lays me down ever so gently, licking his way up my body, mumbling the whole way.

"You don't play fair, sweetheart."

He leans in to kiss me, but then leaps out of the chair. His eyes are wide with fear.

"Jax, are you okay?"

He stands there, silently, his bottom lip between his teeth. He runs both his hands through his hair, pulling it so hard I swear he will go bald. "The baby kicked me," he almost whispers in disbelief.

I have to try not to laugh but it's so hard not too.

"It's okay, Jax, the baby is moving a lot, lately." I take his hand.

"Talk to me. What's the problem?"

"The baby moved just when I was going to have sex with you. I don't know; it freaked me out."

Oh my, he's really rattled. "Jax, the baby doesn't know what you're doing."

"But I know," he barely whispers.

How can I convince this man that it's okay? "Look, the doctor said we could continue to be sexually active." I watch him; he seems to be battling between his fear and his need. "I have an idea. Maybe it will help you if I'm on top."

He rests his forehead on mine. "Okay."

I lead him back down on the lounge chair. I need to get him to relax. I slowly work my way up his legs, kissing from one to the other. On my knees, I stroke his beautiful cock up, twist, and then down. I lick the crown slowly, and he is finally relaxing. I climb over him and take my time lowering myself until he is sheath within me. "Give me your hands, Jax." I kiss one and then the other. I then place them on my breast. He's working each one of my nipples into a frenzied state. I pull myself up and slowly glide myself down, clenching all the way. His hips are coming up to meet mine. He puts my hands on his shoulders and he takes a hold of my hips. Leaning in, he takes one of my nipples between his teeth. I'm going to lose it real quick. Now he's onto the other nipple. "Jax, I'm not going to last, baby . . . Oh God, yes!" I can feel my whole body flush as I come, quivering and shaking. Jax's release soon follows.

I lie next to him and curl into his side. Both of us are quiet, and Jax is stroking my arm, lost in his thoughts.

"Raven, I don't know why I freaked out, it's just all of a sudden, the baby seemed so real."

I need to try and calm his fear, even though it's unfounded, it's real for him. " Do you think you're going to hurt the baby?"

"No, the doctor gave us the green light. It felt like I was walking in on my parents having sex."

I lean up, pulling his face towards mine. "Jax, the baby has no clue what we are doing. Making love with you is beautiful. Don't let the pregnancy take away from that."

He pulls the throw blanket over us, holding me closer. "I love you, and I love that you can take all my craziness, my beautiful girl."

"Jax, can I ask you for a favor?"

His smile is huge and his eyes are twinkling. "I would lay down the world at your feet, sweetheart, and just the fact that you need me for something is a total turn on!"

I can't help but laugh, "Oh, you're always turned on."

He's laughing and it's wonderful to be relaxed like this. "If we are getting married on Friday, do you think you can stay at Max's house, and Jackie can stay here with me and my mom?"

"We *are* getting married this Friday! You want me to stay away from you until Friday?" he asks. I kiss his soft lips and he smiles that beautiful crooked smirk. "Raven, I would lay down my life for you, surely I can do this for you. On one condition, you must keep your detail and Bo with you at all times—no matter what. That is non-negotiable."

Oh, how I love him and his wicked negotiating skills. "Deal."

He begins to move in and out really slow. "You had so much fun driving me nuts with the Nutella pizza, I think it's time I return the favor."

He helps me get onto my knees and puts gentle kisses up and down my spine. He reaches around and begins to roll my nipples with his fingers. They are so sensitive to his touch. He takes his cock and begins rubbing from front to back. He wants to consume every inch of my body, and I want him to.

"Push out for me, Raven, let me in."

As I push out, he slowly pushes through the barrier. He slowly begins to move. When he takes me this way, I can't think, maybe that's what he wants. The fullness is unreal, and my skin is becoming so hot. I know I can't last much longer. He leans down and slowly nibbles my ear. I'm trying so hard to hold it, not to fall too quickly. I want this to last forever. Then he takes his hand and goes right between my legs. Rubbing my clitoris and pushing his fingers deep inside me—every part of me is filled with Jax. I throw my head back, screaming. Jax is not far behind me. Time seems to stand still, both of us trying to breathe again. He pulls out and I'm tucked into his side, my head on his chest. When I finally open my eyes and I'm hit with the bluest of blues.

"There's my sweetheart, thought I lost you for a second. Are you okay?"

"Jax, are you even human?"

"Ha, of course I am, my beautiful girl. This is what you do to me. Let's shower, and then you need to get some rest."

He gets up with me in his arms. Pulling the throw around us, as he carries me downstairs. I'm so tired, but the thought of that wonderful shower makes me smile. I only hope I can stay awake long enough to enjoy it.

Chapter Eleven

Jaxson

I DECIDE TO GO next door and see Max. I left Raven a note in case she wakes up and I'm not there. I know Max will be up; it's been a long emotional day for all of us.

I find Max in the living room and I take a seat. "Hey, mate, I need to go over some wedding stuff with you. We are getting married this Friday, in Bella's garden. I need you to help me pull this off." He's sitting there, smirking at me. "Max, what is wrong with you?"

Ha, "I know you better than anyone, Jax. I knew you were going to go about this at lightning speed. I already started making the arrangements the day you left for Switzerland. Your mum has been helping me. You need to sign some papers for the license. The women need to get their gowns. Don't look at me like that, I needed something to do while you were holding me hostage in my own home."

He goes over to the bar and pours us both a scotch. "Jax, do you want to tell me what's really on your mind?"

"Max, I have more questions about our father, but on some level, I'm not sure I want the answers."

Max goes to his office and comes back with a file.

"Here." He passes it to me. "It's everything I know about the man. After he left, I vowed I never wanted to see or hear from him again. I carried on my life as if he were dead, because for me, he was. After I read the letter from my grams, I realized everything isn't always what it seems. I know that grams and your mum did what they thought was best for everyone involved, and I have only the utmost respect for both of them. I needed to know if he was still alive, and if there are other siblings out there."

I toss the file on the table and take another sip of my drink. "See, Max, I'm just not sure I want to go down that road. What made you feel you needed to know?"

He's pacing, which is comforting in a strange way, probably because it's Max's normal.

"Jax, we are as close as any family could ever be. What if there are more like us out there? I needed to know. I went from having no one to having a family, bound by blood, not just loyalty and friendship."

We sit in silence while I process this information. "Jax, now I need your help."

"Anything, Max. It's about time you ask me for something."

"Jax, can you help me with, Jackie? I know I really cocked the whole thing up. I hurt her badly, but in my defense, I was scared I wouldn't be me, again. My fear was that she would stay with me no matter what happened. She's so young, I just couldn't do that to her."

I sit for a moment, stroking my chin and thinking about all of this. "Max, do you love her, or is it just the sex?"

"I love her," his voice so low and vulnerable, I can barely hear him.

"Max, I know you love her, but are you *in love* with her? There is a big difference."

His jaw tightens and I swear he looks as if he's ready to punch me. "Yes damn it! I'm in love with her. There, I said it. Now, are you going to help me?" he asks almost angrily, fisting his hands.

I can tell he wants this badly, that's all I need to know. "Okay, mate, you work on the wedding and I will work on fixing this. In the meantime, what other information do you have for me? Don't look at me like that, Max, I know *you* just as well as you know me."

He pours us another drink. "Vincent woke up. They will not be able to operate; the bullet is in a spot that they can't access. I took my best shot, and the fucker still lived. The district attorney and the Feds wanted to meet with Raven tomorrow, but I put them off. I told you that we confirmed the woman in the park was Annabelle. She left an envelope for Raven. Before you ask, no I didn't open it, and neither will you. It's Raven's, and you need to let her decide what she wants to do."

I know he's right, and I can't bully her, but for fuck's sake, will there ever be an end to this?

"Max, we need to talk about Gabriella. I really don't think she needs to be in a clinic, however, I did notice that coming back to the city was hard for her." I change the subject, knowing I had no good argument on the other topic.

Max hands me another file. "Here is the file with the information on the flats in this building. I highlighted the residents that I reached out to, but so far, no responses. I think it's going to be hard for Gabriella, but she is stronger than you think. We just need to go slowly. Remember, it's not just Raven that has changed: the entire world around her has changed. Everything from technology to terrorism. She might still think the World Trade Center is standing."

I thank God I have Max to calm me down and juggle some of this. "I never thought about any of that, I'm just so focused on Raven and the baby." I sit silently staring out the window, sipping my scotch until I finally get the nerve up to ask him. "Max, do we have any siblings . . . is he still alive?"

He's silent, and after a while he hands me the folder. "When you're ready, read it. I think you will find it very interesting."

I pick up the folder and the letter, heading back to my place.

I LEAVE MAX'S FLAT and head next door. Everyone is still asleep; you could hear a pin drop. I sit in the living room, looking out over the park. I keep staring at the folder, wondering how it will affect my mum. She's been through so much already, how could I possibly open this can of worms? Do I really want to know? I know the answer, no need to contemplate it any further. I have lived my life by certain rules. My very first rule is to never make a decision without knowing all the facts. That's probably why Max had this folder ready for me—he knew. Just as I pick up the folder, Raven comes into the living room. She just woke up, her hair is tousled, and she is in one of my dress shirts. She is hauntingly beautiful.

She sees me and strolls over. I thank God everyday for how lucky I am. I open my arms and she crawls into my lap. "My beautiful girl." I nuzzle into her neck. She giggles, and it is the most magnificent sound.

"Jax, I woke up and you were gone."

I take a deep breath, and prepare myself to tell her about the letter. "I left you a note, sweetheart. I went next door for a bit. Max gave me this letter that was delivered for you from Annabelle. Vincent woke up; they can't operate. The district attorney and the Feds want to talk to you, but Max put them off. I also have some papers you need to sign for the marriage license."

She is staring blankly at the letter. "Raven, I promised I would not keep any secrets from you. You don't have to read the letter if you don't want to."

Finally she takes her eyes off the letter and looks at me. "When do I have to meet with everyone?"

I pull her tight so she can feel my body envelop hers. "Max didn't say, and I would prefer to deal with this after the wedding. I only want you to concentrate on a dress."

She picks up the letter and hands it to me. "I don't want this letter. Nothing she says will change the fact that my father is dead and my mother was taken away from me for twenty years. I could never believe anything she has to say, and I chose not to read it. If Max needs to read it for security purposes, then he can. Now what is in the folder?" She gestures towards it.

"I wish in some ways I was as strong as you are. That file is from Max. It's a detailed report on our father and if we have any other siblings. Part of me wants to know, and part of me doesn't. There is my dilemma."

"Tell me first why you want to know, and then why you don't. I need a pad and pen, so we can make a Pros and Cons List." She picks up the file and I carry her into the office. I watch as her mind flips to teacher mode and fuck me—it's sexy.

"So let's start with why you want to know."

"Well, what if I have more siblings? I mean, look at Max, he's the best brother and friend anyone could ever want. What if my father is still alive? What if I could possibly find out why he did what he did?" I start to ramble out the reasons.

"Jax, would it make a difference if you knew why?"

"No, I don't think so. Nothing he could say would justify what he did."

She's writing every word down. "As far as why I don't want to know, probably because of my mum. This could open up a whole new can of worms for her. I don't want to see her hurt anymore. She gave up so much for all of us. She has carried the guilt over Cindy for years. It wasn't her fault, but she will never believe that. I've never seen my mum so vulnerable as she was tonight."

She gets up, takes the file and puts it in the file cabinet. "Here is what I think you should do. If I were you, I would talk to your mom first. You know she must have some feelings about all of this. If she wants to know, then look at the file, but if you feel she wouldn't be able to take it, then just burn the damn thing."

I smile, "You know, Raven, when you get all teacher mode on me, it makes me hard."

"Well, there's a surprise!" Okay, she does have a point.

She's in my lap, running her nails through my hair. I reach up and bring her hands into her lap. If I don't, it will be game over—for sure.

"I need to talk to you about Jackie. I spoke with Max and he asked me to help him get her back. He feared he would never be back to normal, and he knew that Jackie would never walk away. We need to come up with a plan." She gets a faraway look in her eyes.

"Jax, you need to understand we are dealing with two very stubborn individuals. We need to get them in the same room and get them talking. That's not going to be easy. When Jackie makes up her mind about something, she's like a bull."

"Well, sweetheart, I have a plan just how to do that. Let's go have a nice soak in the tub, and I will tell you all about it."

Raven

I'M DREAMING OF FRESH baked pastry. As I open my eyes, I realize it's not a dream. The entire room is enveloped in the buttery sweet smell. Jax is not in bed, so I decide to follow the smell. I head out to the kitchen and find my mom and Jax having coffee and pastry together.

"Wow, something smells wonderful in here." I take in another whiff and sigh. My mom passes me a dish with some of the most magnificent looking pastries. "Mom, did you make these?"

"Yes. Do you like pastries?"

"I don't think I ever met anyone who didn't. How did you learn to make all of these?"

"When your father and I first got married, we took cooking classes together. Do you like to cook?"

Jax almost chokes on his coffee. "Oh, Rose, your daughter has such unique culinary abilities. Let's just say, with you here, there will be more to life than peanut butter and jelly sandwiches."

"Raven, I could teach you how to make some of these."

I don't have the heart to tell her that I hate to cook. "That would be great, Mom."

"Ladies, before I head out there are a couple of things I need to go over with you. First, no one but my family knows who Rose really is, and we need to keep it that way. Raven, for now, please always address your mum as Rose. Sammy doesn't know her true identity, and I would like to keep it like that. I know you have a bunch of things that you want to do today, however, never lose your detail, and keep Bo close. Rose, Max gave me a bracelet for you to wear. It has a tracking device built in. Remember to be back here to put our plan in motion for Jackie and Max," He barks out his orders quickly, not giving any chance to be interrupted. He leans down and gives me a kiss. "I wish I could stay here forever. I love you, sweetheart."

"I love you more, Jax."

He grabs another pastry before running out the door. My mom makes me a coffee, and we curl up on the sofa. "He's quite the whirlwind, Raven."

"Yes, I guess you can call him a whirlwind."

"Raven, will you tell me about your childhood? Were your adoptive parents good to you? I have so many questions, but I don't want to upset you."

I don't know what to do. She is looking for answers and they are not all sunshine and roses. I don't know how much I should tell her. "My adoptive parents were good until my mother died from cancer. I left home shortly after that. I teach second grade at a private school in Midtown. Jax's nephew, Michael, is one of my students. Jackie teaches at the same school; her specialty is math. We roomed together in college. Mom, maybe we should stay focused on the present; the wedding and the baby."

"Okay, Raven. I only hope that in time, you will share what your life was like growing up."

I feel bad, but I don't want her to know how much I've been through. I don't want her to blame herself. "Mom, the past can never be changed. All we can do is look to the future."

"We can take it slow, Raven. Last night, I made some sketches of gowns for you and Jackie. I thought if we went to the seamstress with some sort of idea, it would help." She pulls out her sketchpad and begins to show me what she came up with.

"Mom, these are absolutely beautiful." Jackie's gown is a charcoal gray with silver running through it. She placed the accent on her legs, with a slit running up each side. "You captured Jackie's style so perfectly." Then she shows me what she came up with for my gown—it takes my breath away. It's exactly what I had in my mind, simple, yet elegant. The back has a low v with lots of little buttons covered in lace. The way the front is gathered, it doesn't show my bump. "Mom, this is perfect. I can't wait to show Jackie."

"Do you think the seamstress can pull these off on such short notice?"

"I'm sure Jax is paying a ridiculous amount of money to have them make whatever I ask for. I'm going to need your help with Jackie, today. After lunch, I need to get her back here so Jax and I can get her together with Max. Will you please say that you're tired and ask me to drop you at home?"

"Well, of course, if that's what you need me to do. But can I ask why?"

I don't know what to tell her, or how much she could handle. "They are two stubborn people that need to be locked in the same room. They love each other, but they keep getting in their own way. Max asked Jax to help him with this."

"Okay, Raven, I won't ask any more questions, for now. You need to hurry up and get ready or we will never get everything done in time."

Jackie

THE TIME CHANGE HAS really thrown my body for a loop. I need to go for a run, but not too sure how Sammy is going to react to that one. I get dressed and head out to the living room, only to find him already dressed for one. "Wow, how did you know I would be running? Especially, this early."

He gets up and disarms the alarm. "Stretch, after all these years, I know you very well. Let's head out, and on the way back, we can grab a bite to eat."

We head out the door, and Sammy informs my other guard where we are headed. I haven't run with Sammy for a while, but we fall right into step. There is an ease about Sammy and I realize I miss this. When we finish, we head to the local coffee shop for some breakfast.

"So, Stretch, do you want to tell me why this guy, Max, has the family up in arms?"

Do I want to tell Sammy? How much should I share with him? "Well, he's different than anyone I've ever dated."

He stares at me over the rim of his coffee cup. "I can wait all day, if that's what it takes. Don't even think of trying to blow me off on this one. I've known you for a very long time. You don't give away your heart that easily. So, what is it about this man that has your panties in a bunch?"

Ha, "Yeah, they are in a bunch—that's for sure. He is older, thirty-eight to be exact, and he . . . I don't even know where to begin."

"Okay, let me ask you this. Do you love him?"

I nod, "Very much so."

"So, what happened that sent you running across the Atlantic in the middle of the night?"

I trust Sammy. I know he would never betray a confidence. "I will tell you everything, but it is between us, okay?"

I take a deep breath and tell Sammy how Max came into my life. All the months of craziness that ensued up to Max getting shot in the head. "I stayed by his bedside the entire time, and when he woke up, he barely said two words to me. Then I'm outside the door, and I hear him tell Jax to help him get rid of me. I can't begin to tell you how much that hurt me. I love him, but I'm not sure if I can survive another rejection like that. I gave him all of me, Sammy, so what do I do?"

A lone tear slides down my cheek. Sammy reaches over and wipes it away. "Well, Stretch, it's like this. Part of me wants to snap him in two, and the other part wants to shake his hand. He sent you away, even though it hurt you and probably him, because he didn't want you burdened with his recovery. You know, what if he wasn't one hundred percent? Knowing you, the way I do, you would have stayed by his side—no matter what the outcome. What kind of life would that be for you? The other part of me wants to throttle him for hurting you. I think there are two questions you need to ask yourself: can you forgive him, and do you even want a relationship with this man?"

I have ripped my napkin into a million pieces. "You know he's Jax's best man. The wedding is Friday, so I guess I need to figure this out real quick."

We leave the café and head towards home. I still don't have a clue as to what I'm going to do. Maybe I will when I see him. As we round the corner for my place, I see the limo sitting there, and I know it's for me. Raven and Bo get out of the car. Bo sees me first, and his tail is going crazy!

"Raven, why are you here so early?"

She grabs my hand, pulling me into the lobby. "You need to shower and make it really quick. The wedding is tomorrow afternoon at three o'clock, and we have a lot to do. I'll be waiting in the car with Rose, so hurry!"

Okay, I can tell the next few days we will be operating the way Jax does—One hundred mph!

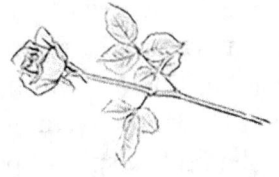

"OKAY, WHAT'S THE PLAN?" I ask, once Sammy and I climb into the limo, freshly showered and ready to take on the events of the day.

Raven opens up a box of my favorite chocolates and passes it to me. "Fuel for the adventure. Jax arranged a seamstress to make our gowns. She will be at The Tower later." She smiles over at her mom. Rose immediately pulls out a sketchpad. "Look what Rose did last night. They are unreal, Jackie."

My eyes grow wide as soon as I look. "Oh my God, Rose, they're unbelievable!" I'm glad I'm remembering to call her Rose instead of Gabriella. I'm sure it's hardest on Raven, trying not to slip up.

"I designed Raven's around her bump and yours, around your beautiful legs."

Sammy is laughing, "Now, you know why I've always called her 'Stretch'!" Everyone chuckles. I nudge him with my elbow, playfully.

"Jackie, I don't think the seamstress will have a problem having them done in time. I'm sure Jax is probably paying her a ridiculous amount of money for her to do it," Raven gets back to the topic at hand. "We have some errands to run before we meet with the seamstress. I need to go buy a gift for Jax." I'm not sure what I want to get him," she rambles. My friend is going to drive herself crazy if she doesn't calm down and take a breather.

Rose takes her hand. "What about a watch? You can get it engraved."

Raven starts laughing so hard, tears are rolling down her face. "Um, I had to buy Jax a new watch the other day because I took his twenty-thousand dollar watch and threw it across the room, shattering it. In my defense, he had the alarm set to feed me. It drove me crazy. *And* . . . who in their right mind would even spend that on a watch? Like really?!"

We are all laughing as we pull up to our first stop—Tiffany's. "I want to get a gift for An," Raven says before we get out, "and my mom," she whispers in my ear. She finds a beautiful diamond necklace with a little charm on it that says, 'Thank you for raising my happily ever after.' It's perfect for An. I help her to find a very delicate watch for her mom. She has them both engraved, 'Time to live again.' Now, it's off to Cartier, where she finds a special pocket watch for Michael Jr. She has them engrave the inside with, 'Future Time, Lord.' He'll definitely love that.

Maxwell

I DECIDE TO HEAD into Raiders for a bit. I have some things I want to look into. Tony should have the reports I ordered on Sammy and Gerhard. I'm not in the door five minutes and Mrs. Osla is all over me, asking a million questions about my health. I know I have to cut her some slack. She's worried, but I swear, she's like An on steroids! I don't have much time here before I need to be back to put Jax's plan in motion. I'm looking over the reports, when something pops out at me. *Fuck,* Sammy is still employed with MI6. Why would his file show that he's retired, yet, he is still employed? I need to get to the bottom of this. It helps that I still have many friends at MI6, even the Chief, himself, owes me. I call the Chief. After assuring him that I'm fine, he tells me what I need to know. I race out the door and head back to The Tower. I need to talk to Jax.

Raven

WE DECIDE TO TAKE a lunch break, which is good because I'm hungry. I take everyone to *S'Mac* for the best choices when it comes to Mac and Cheese. My mom is in shock when she sees there is a restaurant designed only around Mac and Cheese. I forgot that she has been isolated for twenty years; for her, time stood still.

"Raven, I've never been to a restaurant that only makes Mac and

Cheese." Mom leans in and whispers in my ear.

I want to cry at the loss she has gone through, but instead, I decide it's time for a mental pep talk. I am going to enjoy showing her the world, seeing it through her eyes for the first time. "Rose, there is so much to see. A lot has changed since your last visit to the states." I try to play our conversation off like she just hasn't been here in a while and not hidden away for so long."

We order four different types of Mac and Cheese, each of us passing them around to sample. I check my watch and realize time is getting away from us. It's time to set the plan in motion. "So, Jackie, have you decided when you're going to see Max?"

"Raven, you're more like Jax everyday. No, I'm not sure what I want to do yet."

I sneak a peek to mom, and she knows what we need to do next. "Raven, I'm feeling tired. Do you think you can drop me off at home, and finish up without me?"

Jackie takes mom's hand, "Rose, Raven and I can finish up. We will take you back to The Tower."

As we head out the door, I quickly pull Sammy aside. "You need to go along with the plan, and trust me, don't interfere."

He whispers in my ear, "Raven, I knew you were up to something. Not to worry, I won't interfere with your plan as long as I know she's safe."

We all pile in the limo and as we head towards The Tower I text Jax:

Plan in motion. On our way. Make sure you're ready. XO

WE GET TO THE Tower, and everyone is very quiet on the elevator ride up. "Jackie, Jax and Max are staying at Bella's, so we can stay together until the wedding. We set Rose up in Jax's guest room, for now. We have lots to go over and we will need both places. Jax texted and said he set the seamstress up at Max's place." I know Jackie; she can be very stubborn, so I have to give her a push. We get off the elevator and Mick is there, waiting for us.

"Hey, there are my favorite ladies. Did you get everything done?"

I am so happy for him, He finally feels like he has a purpose; little by little the night terrors are getting better. "Almost, Mick, just a couple of gifts left to get." I introduce him to Sammy, and they take to each other right away.

"Raven, some deliveries came for you, and the seamstress is waiting in Max's place. I believe you're up first, Jackie."

She is hesitating, and I think it's because the last time she was there, Max wanted her gone. I pull her into my arms, "Come on, I will go in with you. You'll be just fine. He's not there; it's just the seamstress." We go inside and head down the hall, towards the living room. Max and Jax are both standing there. Max stares at Jackie—neither one—saying a word. I keep my arm around her waist, so she won't bolt.

Jax steps up towards us, "Jackie, Max, the two of you need to work this out. Please hear me out and then if you still want to leave, I will let you."

Max cocks one eyebrow at him, probably because he knows that will never happen.

"You are both stubborn fools, too blinded by hurt and misunderstanding to dig your way out of this mess. You both need me."

Jax gives them both the biggest smile, and I'm trying not to laugh at my man. He is really trying. I hold my hand up to Jax, "I think what Jax is trying to say is, you both need to sit down and talk this out. You might decide it's too much and walk away, but you don't want to ever wonder—what if. Jackie, when Max woke up, he was speaking out of fear and love. You know you're a very strong person and would have stayed by his side, no matter what the outcome. Max, you need to tell Jackie why you built walls around your heart. Then, you both need to be honest about your feelings. After that, if you walk, well there is nothing anyone can do about it." So far no one is moving. "Jax and I are going next door. We are going to leave the two of you alone to talk this out."

Jax takes my hand, "Sweetheart, can I talk now?"

Oh he's smirking at me. God only knows what he's up to. "Go

ahead, Jax. The floor is all yours."

"Raven, is the nice negotiator, and she has been trying to help me with my *bulldog* style way of doing things, however, in this case, I have only one thing to say, you *will* sit down and talk this out. You *will* tell each other everything and, Max, I mean *everything*. If either one of you tries to leave here before that, I gave Mick instructions to shoot you in the *arse!* Okay, Raven, I'm done now."

Max is trying not to laugh and Jackie seems to be in shock.

"Jax, is Mick supposed to shoot me in the '*arse*' too, or just Max?"

He narrows his eyes at Jackie, "Seeing as your parents might get mad if I had you shot in the arse, I will have him tie you up until you listen to reason." Before anyone can say anything more, Jax pulls me into his arms and we are out the door.

Chapter Twelve

Maxwell

" JACKIE, WOULD YOU LIKE a drink?" I offer. Her eyes are glued to me and her silence is deafening. "Please, have a seat. I have a lot to tell you." I gesture to the seat next to me as I sit on the couch. She takes the chair. I push the coffee table in front of her and sit on that instead. Our knees are touching, and it takes all that I have not to pull her into my arms.

"I'm listening, Max, say what you need to," her tone, almost impatient.

I take a deep breath, preparing myself to relive this nightmare, yet again. "I have some things to tell you. Some of which, I only found out a couple of days ago. You need to know everything about me . . . why I'm so overprotective. Afterwards, if you hate me and decide to leave, I won't stop you." I wait a moment to see if she has any objection.

"My mum met a man from Scotland, got married young, and had me. He was in sales and traveled for business. His visits home became less and less, until one day, he just never came home at all. Shortly after, a young woman came to see us, claiming she was married to my dad. She had two children, Jax and Isabella." Just when I say that last bit, her face registers shock. "Yeah, I just found this out. It was not too long after that my mum committed suicide. An came right after that and offered to raise me as one of her own children. My grams kept me with her, but she kept in touch with An through the years. I made a life

156

for myself. After graduation, I joined the Police Force and my career took off. Not too long after that, I met a girl and fell in love. Her name was Samantha, and soon we were married."

She leaps up, "Max, you're married? That's what this is all about?"

"No, please hear me out. In the end if you want to walk, I promise, I won't stop you."

She quietly sits back down and I take a deep breath to continue. "Soon after we married, we had a son, Elliot. I thought my life was complete, it didn't matter that my dad walked out. I had the family I always wanted. Then one day, Samantha took Elliot to the park. Afterwards, she headed back to the car and while she was taking him out of his buggy, two drugged up gang member's carjacked Samantha. They pulled a gun and shot them both. My Elliot died in Samantha's arms, along with her. My heart died that day, too."

"Max, my heart breaks for you and all that you have lost, but it doesn't explain why you've pushed me away. I gave you my heart, my soul, myself, so completely. And you sent Jax to get rid of me. You broke my *h-heart.*"

I watch Jackie's face as the tears start to trail down. I want to take her in my arms, but she needs to hear it all, and then she can decide.

"Baby, you came into my life and you scared me. You blew my whole world apart."

She puts her hand on my knee and I jolt from the touch. "I scared you how?"

I take her hand and place in over my heart. "You made me feel hope, you made me feel love. You made me think of the future. That scared me half to death. The night that Vincent's men tried to grab you from your flat, I nearly died all over, again. I realized that night I was in deep. I can't take another loss. It's why I'm so over the top with security."

"That day I left you at the elevator to go after Vincent, I heard you when the doors closed. I heard the gut-wrenching wail, and I felt my heart crack in two. The whole time I was running through that mansion, searching for Vincent, I knew if I could just get this over with, I would be back in your arms. You're the light at the end of my tunnel, but then, my world went black." I squeeze her hands tightly for emphasis.

"I heard you at my bedside, crying. I heard Jax threaten me with bringing his mum to try and bring me around. I heard you and An, talking. Jackie, I heard you tell her that no matter what the outcome, you would sit by my bed and take care of me for the rest of your life. Do you know what that did to me?"

Her eyes grow wide and I can see she's shocked that I heard it all, that I could remember all of it. "It made me realize the best thing I could do for you, if I really loved you, was to force you to go, even if it meant that you would hate me. I didn't know if I would ever recover, and I couldn't, no—I wouldn't hold you back. You deserve to be happy and loved. When Raven was kidnapped for those three months, I would sit outside the school everyday and just watch you with the children. You love them, and they love you, how could I ever take that away from you? I just couldn't."

We sit there for a long time in silence. "Please, Jackie, you need to talk to me. At least tell me to sod off, if that's what you want, and I will."

She gets up and walks to the window, looking out over the park. "Would you have ever told me about your wife and son?"

I walk up behind her. "Jackie, please look at me," I plead. She turns and we're face to face. "Yes, I knew that I would have to when I felt the walls around my heart start to crumble. I knew I was in deep with you. You deserved to know my whole story."

She strokes my face, "How do you feel?"

I'm in shock. I pull her into my arms, "After all I told you, you want to know how I feel? I feel like I'm going to lose my mind if I let you walk out that door. I feel like my heart is beating again, now that you're in my arms. I feel like I've come back to life, like I've been given a second chance. I feel like I want to hold you, and love you all night long, never letting go. That's how I feel."

She leans up and lightly brushes my lips with a barely there kiss. "I meant your head, Max."

I lift her up, and carry her towards my bedroom; her long legs are wrapped around my waist. "Please stay, Jackie."

She kisses me again, "Not until you answer some of my questions."

I climb into bed with her still in my arms. She's sitting in my lap, her legs still wrapped around me. It feels so right, perfect. "Okay, you can ask me anything, and I promise to answer."

She searches my eyes, while stroking her fingers around my scar. "How is your head? What did the doctor say?"

She's worried about my health? God this woman is beautiful inside and out. "I get headaches, but the doctor said that is to be expected. They are becoming less and less. I don't have all my stamina back, but I hope to soon. I have been doing therapy, and the doctor released me to go back to work on a limited basis. I do a full workout in the gym. I don't think I am ready to be back in the trenches, but being in the office, behind the scenes—for now—is fine."

She leans in and kisses me. "First, thank you for your honesty, it is something that I need. Do you know what happened to your father?"

I wasn't expecting that one. "Yes I do, I just learned the other day that I am related to Jax and Bella, and I wanted to find out how many others there could be out there. Our father was a bigamist, and poor An has carried this knowledge, silently for all these years. I gave Jax a file that has all the information in it, but he's choosing not to look at it. Do you want me to tell you?"

She shakes her head, "No, I don't want to know. What is going on with Vincent and Duke?"

She's not holding back. "Vincent came out of the coma yesterday. I'm not sure if he remembers anything that happened that day. Either way, the Feds and the District Attorney need to talk to both Raven and I. There will be a trial. And it will be messy. Raven's aunt has surfaced, and we will be bumping up security on everyone, including you. I don't see this ending any time soon. Duke is in Sing Sing prison. From what I've been told, the Feds don't think he will be beneficial to them."

I need to know how she feels, but I don't want to push her. "Jackie, talk to me, baby. Please tell me what you're feeling. Just like you, I need total honesty."

She puts her arms under mine and pulls me close to her. She leans in and kisses my heart. I swear to Christ, I don't know how much more I can take.

"Max, I love you. I don't play games, I know what I want and what I want *is you.* That being said, I'm not going anywhere, but we need to set some ground rules."

I let out the breath I was holding. "Okay, baby. I can live with rules . . . rules are good. Just tell me what you need." God I have missed this girl so much; my heart ached without her.

"Real simple, Max—no secrets. I'm not running away and neither are you. If you have a problem with me, then tell me. If you're scared, then tell me. If you need a timeout, then tell me. If you ever pull this shit with me again, the only thing you will be looking at is my ass walking away from you. We are equal here, and it's best you remember that."

I kiss her and she deepens it. "Will you stay with me tonight?"

She rests her forehead on mine and closes her eyes. "Sorry, I can't. Neither can you. You're staying at Bella's house, tonight and I am staying at Jax's with Raven and Rose."

I whisper, "Okay, I've waited this long, I can wait another day."

"Do you think it will ever be safe for me to go back to teaching?"

I wish I had all the answers. "I honestly can't answer that. Has Raven or Jax spoken to you about Jax's idea of opening a private school at Raiders?"

She smiles and kisses my lips. "No, but it doesn't surprise me. Jax is crazy when it comes to Raven."

Maybe if I can convince Jackie, then she will convince Raven. I'm getting as nuts as that crazy arse fucker. "It's a good idea for many reasons." She cocks her head and smiles. "Okay, don't look at me like that, just hear me out. If the workers had daycare and a school, within the same building, then they could be more productive. If the parents don't need to worry about after care or before care, then they would be more productive in their jobs. We could have all sorts of after school programs for the kids. The parents would know their children are safe and getting access to more opportunities they normally wouldn't. For safety purposes I think it's great. Now, as far as learning, we wouldn't be relying upon the state or the federal government for funding, so we could offer a much better education. I went to school on scholarships and it really helped not having any debt when I was done. It would make the workers more productive, and it could be part of the incentive package for new hires. There are other companies with the same business model." I'm not sure she is buying this, and I know I'm starting to sound as desperate as I feel. "There is a company in North Carolina that does this. They also have other things available for workers, such as dry cleaners or car maintenance. By doing this, they are creating less stress for the workers. In the end everyone wins."

She leans in, and kisses my neck. "It's also good for you and Jax, this way you both know where we are at all times."

She kisses me, and I don't want to let her go. "Baby, I know you said I have to go to Bella's with Jax, but please, just let me hold you for awhile."

"Only for a little bit, then the seamstress needs to measure me. There really is a seamstress, right?"

I kiss her neck, working my way slowly down her beautiful body. "Oh, baby, there's a seamstress. I can help her with your measurements. I could tell her, in great detail, about every inch of these beautiful legs."

"Maxwell, you'll do no such thing!"

She's blushing. Oh God, if I don't stop now, there won't be a wedding. "Come on, baby, let's go find that seamstress."

Raven

ALL IS QUIET NEXT door. I wonder what is going on. I know Jackie loves him, and she will listen, but she can be very stubborn. The seamstress got everyone's measurements but Jackie's. Jax is in the office, working on something, and I'm enjoying the quiet time, relaxing and gazing out the window. My mom is meeting with her therapist for the first time, today. I hope she takes it slow. I need to figure out what to get Jax. He has no clue what tomorrow is, and I decide I'm not telling him until after the wedding. I need to let him know that I would like to write our own vows. I head to the office and am taken aback at the sight before me. Jax is talking to himself, crumpled paper is everywhere, and he's practically pulling all his hair out. "Jax?"

He leaps up, "Jesus, woman, you almost gave me a heart attack!"

I'm instantly worried, seeing how frantic he looks. "What's the matter, Jax? You look very upset."

He pulls me into his arms, and scoops me up so tightly I can't breathe. "I love you, Raven."

"Jax, you need to be a little more gentle, please. I love you, you know I do." I brush my lips gently over his. "Why are you so frantic?"

My heart races. "I want to write my vows, and I don't want to come across as over-the-top crazy, but I want them to have special meaning for us."

I can't help but laugh, "I was just coming in here to ask you if we could write our vows. I also need to see Michael and ask him about giving me away." I gaze into his beautiful blues.

"Raven, we're not a conventional couple. I knew that you would want something different, so I'm glad you're on board with writing our own vows. I know I'm obsessing about them but I want them perfect. I also wanted to figure out the most comfortable and secure way to introduce your mum to my family. I figured if we had an intimate dinner here, your mum could get to know everyone in a more relaxed setting. You could also talk to Junior about giving you away. I called in a caterer to make it easy."

Tears spill from my eyes at this. He leans down and kisses them away. "Please, tell me you're happy about this?"

"Everyday I love you more than I ever thought possible, Jax. What time will everyone be here?"

He looks at his new watch and smiles. "You have about five hours. And I love my watch, sweetheart."

"I have an errand to run. I'll have Bo and my detail with me. Try not to worry, Jax, I love you." I grab my purse before he can try and talk me out of it and head out to finish up my errands before everyone gets here.

I RACE OUT INTO the hustle and bustle of Midtown Manhattan. The energy in this city is exactly what I need today. I have to get gifts for Jackie and Jax. I also need to make a stop to invite someone very special to the wedding tomorrow. I finally decide on a gift for Jackie. It's a charm bracelet, and the first charm is a diamond infinity sign; my best friend forever. I figured I could add to it for every occasion. Next,

I need to get something for Jax. I have a great idea, so I head to a shop I love, in the East Village. I know they will make up what I want and have it delivered quickly. I decide to stop at Saks Fifth Avenue, and get some new clothes for my ever-growing bump before I head over to my final stop. I'm about to get into the limo to head home when Bo begins to freak out. My guards start pushing me into the car as a woman comes up to me. I know right away who she is, I've seen her before—Annabelle. She gets one look at Bo, baring his teeth and she turns away. We head back to The Tower. All the while, I try to calm my nerves; my adrenaline is pumping off the charts. Jax will freak out either way, but maybe if I were calm, it would help.

The elevator ride seems to take forever. When the doors finally open, Jax is standing there. *Oh hell, this is not going to be good.* Before I can say a word he pulls me into his arms, he is breathing so heavily. "Jax, calm down, please. I'm fine."

"Raven, I know I'm not supposed to freak out. I know that you have security with you, but it doesn't help me, at all. I want to lock you in this Tower and throw away the key. If something ever happened to you, I would die."

I want to cry when I see the fear in his eyes. "Jax, if you live your life in fear then fear wins. Let's go inside and sit for a while."

We head inside, and we snuggle up on the couch. He methodically strokes my arm up and down. "Jax, have you given the letter to Max?"

"No, I was focused on writing my vows and planning the dinner."

"It's fine. I'm sure it's just more ramblings. I will give it to him tonight."

"I love you, sweetheart," he whispers, pulling me close.

"Jax, have you heard anything from Max and Jackie?"

"Max had the seamstress go in and measure Jackie. I have not seen or heard from either one of them."

" Maybe I should check on them?"

"Nope. They will be fine. I think I need to have my way with you before everyone gets here."

"Really? Is that what you think?"

"Raven, what I think is if you want me to stay at Bella's house, then we need to go to the *happy place,* otherwise, I can't be held responsible for my actions."

I lean in and run my tongue up the side of his neck. I know what will put him over the edge of sanity—dirty talk in French. "Je veux sentir ta bite au fond de moi."

Jaxson

I'M A STRONG PERSON with an iron will, but—fuck me—when she hits me with the dirty talk in French! I want to blow. I lift her up and head towards the bedroom. I'm ripping off our clothes as she's biting my chest. I might not make it to the bedroom. I put her down, and she begins to unbutton my jeans. She pushes them down as she drops to her knees. She takes my cock in her hands and kisses the tip. I'm trying to control the urge to push all the way in. I thread my fingers through her hair, slowly pushing my cock into her warm mouth. When I'm all the way in, I stop, willing myself to last longer. I finally begin to move taking my time filling and emptying her mouth. With each push in, I go a little deeper. I pull out, and she nips the tip—that's my point of no return. I'm groaning, totally unhinged. I reach down and pull her up into my arms; her lips are puffy and her hair is wild. *Fuck.* I'm hard as stone, again! I manage to get us to the bed without breaking my neck, making quick work of my jeans as I go.

"I'm not done with you, Jax."

She's hovering over me, rubbing my cock over her clitoris. I reach up and gently flip her onto her back. "I need you now, Raven." I slam into her, and then stop. Her eyes are wide and she's biting her lip. "Are you okay?"

"I need you, Jax."

"How do you want me, sweetheart?"

"Tender and slow."

I slowly pull back and then sink into her, taking her gently, mindful of the baby. I kiss her neck and then nip her ear. Working my way down to her sensitive nipples. I know she needs me to be gentle. I swivel my hips just like she likes it. I can feel her quiver and know she's close. I'm trying to go easy, but then she clenches and that sends me spiraling out of control. I pull back and slam into her.

"Jax, I'm there . . . fuck."

Watching her body turn crimson, and knowing that I've sent her to heaven, sends me falling. I roll us onto our sides and pull the sheet over us, both of us trying to catch our breath.

"Jax, I don't know what's gotten into me, but lately all I want is non-stop, crazy sex. Maybe I should talk to the doctor about it. Bella said the pregnancy hormones made her bat shit crazy."

I grin mischievously while still keeping my eyes closed. "I would love to know what you're thinking right now," she says.

"I'm thinking if this is the work of pregnancy hormones, then I need to keep you knocked up all the time." I open one eye to look at her and see that her mouth is hanging open. "Sweetheart, if you keep that mouth open much longer I might have to put something in it."

"Don't make promises you can't keep, Jax," she sasses back.

"Is that a challenge, Raven?"

I tilt my hips up, showing her that I'm ready to go again. "Are you human?" she asks.

"I told you, sweetheart—it's you." I tilt my hips again. "This is what you do to me. From that first touch outside Starbucks, I can't seem to get enough of you."

I work my way in and out, real slowly. I crook my neck and take one of her nipples into my mouth, nipping and licking. "It doesn't always have to be hard, Raven." I hold her hands above her head, and cocoon her whole body. I kiss her, working our tongues in a slow erotic dance. I swivel my hips to match my tongue. Right, then left. In and out, really slow as she begins to quiver and shake. "Eyes. Now, sweetheart."

So soft and tenderly, she falls apart in my arms.

Chapter Thirteen

Raven

THE CATERERS HAVE EVERYTHING set up, people are filing in. However, there is still no sign of Jackie or Max. I'm really getting worried. What if it's too much for her to handle? "Jax, maybe I should go next door, since we haven't heard anything from them."

He smiles, "Don't worry, they will be here. You need to introduce your mum to everyone. My family knows to only refer to her as Rose. And . . . Raven? I don't think I told you how beautiful you look tonight."

He's trying to distract me and I think I will let him, for now. I introduce my mom to everyone. They are making her feel very welcome and at ease. Finally, I see Jackie and Max come out of his place, holding hands. I look over to Jax and he has the biggest smile on that beautiful face. He mouths to me, *"Faith."*

We all sit down, and Jax decides he wants to make a toast. "Thank you everyone for coming tonight and for sharing in our joy. Every single one of you has played a part in making this happen, and for that, I will always be grateful. Here is to good times and well-deserved happiness for everyone. God Bless."

The food is wonderful, but it's the company that makes this evening so special. I sit at the table, taking in each and every one of them.

Jax has even invited Mick to join us. He always treats everyone with such respect. We all make our way into the living room for coffee and dessert. Jax has all different pastries. I laugh as I notice there is no Nutella. I look over to Jackie and she's laughing, she seems very happy. I think they will be okay. Max has been through so much. I know to survive he had to shut down. Jackie has loved him back to life.

It's time for me to talk to Michael. I excuse myself and I ask him to join me in Jax's office. I notice all eyes are on us as we leave the room, and I'm sure Jax will explain it. "Miss Raven, am I in trouble?"

Oh, how I love this little boy. "Not at all, Michael, I have something I need to ask you in private."

I don't want to sit behind the desk; it's to imposing, so we sit on the sofa. "Michael, I need a very special favor, and since you're very special to me, I thought I would ask you."

He's watching me all wide-eyed, and I almost lose it when he starts to stroke his chin.

"With your uncle Jax and I getting married tomorrow, I'm going to need someone to walk me down the aisle and give me away. I would be very honored if you would do that for me." *Oh no, he looks like he's about to cry.* "Michael, are you okay?"

"Miss Raven, d-do I get to take you back after I give you away?" he stutters.

My eyes spring with tears before I can stop them. I love this boy with all my heart. "Michael, when we walk down the aisle and you hand me off to Uncle Jax, you are telling him that he gets to keep me in this family forever."

He gets it, his eyes become wide and his face lights up. "So, my mom said you will be my aunt, is that true?"

I hug him. "Forever, Michael. I have something to give you that I had made just for you. You have to wear it tomorrow at the wedding."

I give him the box, and he takes the pocket watch out. He opens it up, and when he reads the inscription he throws his arms around me. "I love you, Miss Raven, and I am your Future Time Lord! So, what do I have to do tomorrow?"

I stand up and take his hand. "We walk down the aisle together. When we reach the end, the priest will ask, 'Who gives this woman away?' You will say I do, and then you put my hand into Uncle Jax's."

He smiles, "No worries, Miss Raven. I got this."

We head back out to the living room, and Michael runs to show everyone his watch. Bella begins to tell him how his job is very important, but before she can finish he stops her. "No worries, Mum, I got this." He repeats to her what I just told him his duty was. "Then she becomes my aunt forever; piece of cake."

Everyone is laughing; he is such a sweet boy. "Uncle Jax, look what Miss Raven gave me."

Jax reads the inscription and he has the biggest smile on his face. It's the little things with this man that matter the most. I decide I will give everyone else their gifts right before the wedding.

I need to talk to Max about the letter, so I make my way over to him and Jackie. They look so happy together. I really hope they worked it out.

"Hey, Jackie, can I steal Max for a few minutes?"

She laughs, "Sure."

I take his arm and guide him into the office. I know Jax won't be far behind me. He has a seat while I get the letter. "Max, I need you to look at the letter from Annabelle. I don't want to read it. I don't want to be bothered with anyone in that family. I would just burn it, however, she tried to approach me today and—" Before I can finish, he is out of the chair.

"Why am I just finding this out now?"

Jax comes flying through the door. "Rein it in, mate; she's telling you now."

Max starts his usual pacing, "Jax, it's okay. Everyone needs to calm down." I hand Max the letter. "I know for safety reasons, you should read this. I don't want it back, nothing she can say will ever bring my father back."

"Okay. I am sorry that I flipped out," he apologizes.

"Apology accepted, Max, now go out there and have a good time." He grumbles under his breath, turns, and walks out of the room. "Jax, I have a question for you before we go back out there. Did you get Max a gift?" I can tell by the furrowing of his brows that he has no idea what I'm talking about. "Jax, you have to get him a gift for being your best man. I got something for your mom and mine. I got Jackie a beautiful charm bracelet and I got the watch for Michael."

"What should I get him?"

I kiss him, "Don't worry, you will figure it out." I think I have really thrown Jax for a loop. Just wait until tomorrow, when he finds out what day it is. I should probably tell him, but nope, I'm not going to. "Jax, what time do we need to be at Bella's house? Did you get the rings?"

He pulls me close to him, "Sweetheart, did you think I would forget the rings? They were delivered to Bella's house earlier today, and the limo will be here at 2 pm. Are you really going to make me sleep at my sister's house tonight?"

Oh I know what he's trying to do, but I'm not giving in on this one. "Just think how wonderful it will be when we go to the *happy place.*"

He's growling, and before he can say anything Michael turns to him, "Uncle Jax, are you going to Disney World too?"

Of course, I know exactly what he is thinking, and I turn a million shades of red, especially since Jax, has no clue.

"Junior, I'm not going to Disney World."

Michael looks up to Jax. "Mom said that we can go to Disney World on summer break; it's the happy place."

Jax's eyes grow wide, and I can't stop laughing. "Uncle Jax, what happy place are you going to?"

I bite my lip to squelch my laughter. "Junior, tomorrow I'm going to the happiest place in the world. I am marrying Raven, and my world will forever be the happy place."

I lean in to kiss him and whisper, "Nice save, Jax."

Raven

EVERYONE HEADS OUT, EXCEPT Jax and Max. They decide they can stay with Jackie and me, until one minute before midnight. Max pulls Jackie into his place, and I know she is thrilled. I'm tired, so Jax carries me to bed. "Sweetheart, you're so tired will you please let me take special care of you tonight?"

All I can do is hum. He takes off my shoes, sits on the bed, and starts to rub my swollen feet.

"Tomorrow night, at this time, we will be married. I know we can't go away right now, what between your mum and the pregnancy, but eventually, I would like to plan a proper honeymoon."

"Jax, you should have seen Michael's face when I first asked him to give me away. He was fighting to hold back the tears, he thought once he gave me away then I would be gone. After I explained it to him, and how important his role was, he was excited."

"That was a really cool gift you got him, what did you get my mum and yours?"

He's trying to get some ideas from me for Max! "Jax, you will know what to give Max, just think about your friendship and why it's special to you," I reassure him. He's stroking that chin and I know his wheels are turning. "Jax, did you finish writing your vows?" I figured after he was knee deep in crumpled paper, maybe I should ask.

"I assure you I will be at that alter and ready tomorrow. As much as I want to ravish you right now, I rather you and the baby get some sleep. Tomorrow is another busy day. Remember to keep Bo and the guards with you at all times. I will see you at Bella's, love you."

"I love you too."

Jaxson

RAVEN IS OUT COLD, so I cover her with a blanket and head over to Max's, but before I get there, Rose stops me. "Jax, can I talk to you for a minute?"

"Of course, come sit. What's on your mind?" I feel bad for her. This must be so overwhelming. I hope the therapy session went well.

"Are you going to be able to keep my daughter and grandbaby safe? These people are ruthless, Jax, and I'm scared—not for me, but for my family."

"I can assure you, I would lay down my life to protect them. What would really help is one hundred percent cooperation from everyone. One of the reasons why I pushed for the wedding to happen now was to build a barrier around everyone. If I could, I would lock Raven in this penthouse forever, but I know that's not realistic."

"No, Jax, that's not possible. So who is Annabelle? I heard her name mentioned tonight."

"Rose, I told you I would be honest with you. Were you aware that Antonio had a younger sister, Annabelle?"

She is quiet and I hope she can handle this. "Yes, Jax, I knew about her however, we never talked about his family. When he walked away from that family, he cut all ties with them. He hated the evil that surrounded them. Is she a problem?"

"Yes. She is coming around and trying to make contact with Raven. Vincent came out of the coma, but we are not sure if he remembers anything. The Feds and the district attorney need to sit down with Raven, but I want us to be married, first. There will be a trial, but we will cross that bridge when we get to it."

"Why was Vincent in a coma?"

I don't want to overload her, but I understand her need for the truth. "Max went after him and it didn't end well for either of them. They were both shot."

Thank you, Jax. After all this family has been through, what we need the most is honesty. I have so many more questions, but it's late, and we have a wedding tomorrow. Happy times are what we should be focusing on."

I hug her, "Get some rest and I will see you at the wedding."

Just as I head over to Max's, he comes out the door with Jackie. "Raven's fast asleep and I just sent Rose to bed." Jackie reaches up on her toes and kisses me on the cheek. "What's that for?"

She laughs, "Goodnight, see you at the wedding!"

"MAX, LET'S GO OUT for a drink." As we head out towards Bella's, we stop at a local Irish Pub.

"What's on your mind?"

"Did you read the letter? Part of me wants to know and part of me doesn't."

"Yeah, I read it. She is trying to sound like the wounded party, but I have no trust for this woman. I got the background check on her and she is very much like Vincent. I don't know how Antonio fit into this family."

"I spoke to Rose about Annabelle. She said she was aware that Antonio had a sister."

"What else is the problem, mate? After all these years, I can tell, so spill it."

"I found an island for sale, it's called *Jewel Cayle.* It's just off of the coast of Belize. It has two main houses, one on each side of the island."

"Jax, you can't hide her away on an island."

"Look, I know what you're saying makes all the sense in the world, but then there is the other part of me that wants to move us all there. You need to help me out here, mate, before I do something I probably shouldn't."

"Jax, take a timeout and think for a second. How would you feel if the shoe were on the other foot? You can't expect everyone to stop living his or her life, so you can feel safe. I, of all people, know that from experience. When my family was gunned down in the street like animals, I wanted revenge. Then after that, I didn't want to live any more. I closed myself off and shut down. I stopped living life even though life kept moving forward. I was stuck and determined never to let that happen to anyone, again. It almost cost me Jackie. Don't let your fear cost you Raven and the baby. We will work together, as a family, to keep everyone safe. I promise you, Jax . . . we will."

"So what am I supposed to do with this island?"

"Jax, you didn't, did you? Oh my God, you did."

I laugh, "Yeah, I did. Guess we have a new family vacation compound. Did you see Junior tonight? He was so excited." I then tell him about Raven asking him to give her away and what his response was. This reminds me to ask him, "Did dad ever watch 'Doctor Who' with you?"

Maxwell

WOW, THAT CAME OUT of nowhere, but I know Jax, and he's fighting both sides of the blade with this. "No, I was never really close with him. When he was around physically, he seemed distant. Did you read the file on him?"

"No, and I'm not sure I want to. I think we're doing okay. I don't need him, and if he came back into our lives now, I wouldn't trust him. How could I trust someone like him? I would always think he was in it for the money. You know what it's been like for me having money. Hell, you've had to step in on more than one occasion. You're a wealthy man, but we've kept your ownership in Raiders Inc. quiet. I've been the front man and that's okay, but I would never trust his reasons. I also have to think of mum, and how it would affect her. She gave up so much for us. I would never intentionally hurt her." We both sip our scotch in silence.

"Jax, while you were away, she asked me if I would ever feel comfortable calling her anything other than ma'am? I asked her what she would want me to call her, but she said I'll know when it's right. What does she mean?"

"Max, sometimes, for such a smart man, you can be such an idiot. I can say that because you're my brother, ha! Don't growl at me. She has loved you like a son. She is very protective of you. When you were in the hospital, she got on a plane and flew down to Florida, even though she hates to fly. She bullied her way past the guards, the police, and the hospital staff. She ordered the doctor around, and made sure you had everything you needed. She got the girls to eat, and held Jackie's hand the whole time. She never left that hospital. She slept in a chair, in the corner of the room, because she wouldn't leave you. When we flew you home, she suggested Jackie move in to stay close to you. She came by The Tower daily, for reports on you and Jackie. She hired the nurse, who by the way, annoyed the fuck out of us with her humming! Who do you think would do all of that, Max? Look, I know you had a mother, but she died while you were young. She felt responsible for that, and maybe her looking after you, all these years, was her way of honoring your mum by loving you as she would."

I don't know what to say, or even how to feel. It's too much, too fast; my head hurts.

"I get it, mate, but right now I'm so overwhelmed with everything. I need time to think and process it all. Give me that much." I close my eyes and rub my temples, hoping to ease the pounding in my head. "I need to talk to you about Sammy. I got a detailed report back, and it turns out he still works for MI6. I did some more digging, and found it's because of Gerhard. I spoke to the Chief this morning. He said, Gerhard was instrumental in peace talks. However, he's made some powerful enemies along the way. All of the guards that work for Gerhard are MI6."

He reaches over the bar and grabs the bottle of scotch. It's going to be a long night. "Is Vincent somehow tied into all of this?" he asks.

"Not that I can tell. Gerhard is clean, he's just a hard arse when it comes to getting his way."

"Max, no one outside of the family knows who Rose is, not even Sammy. I think we need to keep it that way."

"I agree. Let's get to Bella's house before it gets any later. We have a very busy day tomorrow. Did you get Raven a gift?" I ask. He's looking at me like I have grown another head. "Jax, you do know what tomorrow is, right?"

"It's my wedding day. Was I supposed to get her a gift? I could give her the island as a wedding gift."

Oh shit, he doesn't know. Fuck. "Sit back down, mate, we need to talk. Now normally, I would just mind my own business, but seeing how you are not only my best friend but my brother, I'm going to save your sorry arse." I look at my watch, "Today is Raven's Birthday." Oh I wish I could bottle that look: part shock and part horror.

"Why the *fuck* am I just finding out about this now?! Why didn't she tell me?"

I can only imagine her reasons. "Maybe because you're usually so over the top, and she doesn't want that. Maybe you could do something simple." He's really in shock and if he keeps pulling that hair, there will be nothing left.

"I'm at a loss here, Max. What the fuck am I supposed to do? *Fuck,* I'm getting married in less than twelve hours, and I need to come up with something special for her. It took me a whole day just to write my vows!"

"Come on, mate, we will figure this out." I get him outside and into the waiting limo. I tell the driver to head over to Bella's. "Jax, we are in the home stretch here. Don't give up now, trust me."

"I have an idea, but I'm going to need some help. We need to find an antique store."

I know I should probably tell him we can wait till morning but that won't work in Jax's world. I pull out my phone and find a dealer. Then, I do what I do best—track him down, in the middle of the night, and let Jax convince him to meet us at his shop now.

When we get to the shop, the man is none too happy to be here at four am. "Let me get this straight, you are going to pay me ten thousand dollars cash to open up my store, just so you can find your girlfriend a birthday gift?"

I tell the guy what I'm looking for, and it takes him all of ten minutes to find it. "Sir, here's an extra grand just for being such a good sport about all of this. And here is my business card, if you ever need anything, just call me."

The man seems in shock but I'm sure he's happy to have made a lot of cash for ten minutes of work. We head to Bella's, both of us lost in our own thoughts.

Raven

I WAKE UP AND have a wonderful stretch. When I open my eyes, there is a note by the bed with one Abracadabra Rose. I don't know when this man finds the time to do all that he does for me. I smell the sweet rose, and the baby starts kicking. I pick up the note. Behind it is a glass of orange juice and a warm croissant. Oh, even when he's not here, he drives me crazy!

My sweetest girl,
Today is a very special day. It is the
day our family becomes one. I hope
you love your breakfast. Please eat it
all! Don't worry, I didn't sneak in
and peek at you. I had your mum
help me out this morning with all of
this. I miss you and I love you.
Jax

Okay, I need to stop daydreaming about my beautiful, wonderful man, and start working on some personal notes for each gift. Everything was delivered yesterday, and Mick put it away for me. He really has become such a good friend. I head out to the living room to collect everything, and my heart skips a beat. I stand here, so overwhelmed by the sight before me. The man is nuts! I can't help my tears that are falling. There has to be, at least, thirty dozen Abracadabra Roses! They are everywhere. Every time I turn around, there are more. My mom comes in, hugs me, and wipes away my tears.

"He is extreme, but he does love you, Raven."

I'm speechless. I have no idea what to say.

"Raven, today is a special day. It's not only your wedding day, but it's your birthday too. I never thought I would get to spend another birthday with you, so this is so very special for me. When your father and I got married, my parents were already deceased. I had no one to give me any motherly advice, or pass any traditions down to me. I know that Jax loves you so completely. That man's love for you is in his eyes. I know he can be extreme and overpowering, just remember to stay true to who you are. Love him with all that you have. Life is full of compromises—some harder than others—that's just the way it is. If I can offer you only one piece of advice, it would be to never compromise on your love for each other. Hold onto that with all that you have and all that you will ever be. On my wedding night, your father gave me this Italian horn. He made me promise to wear it everyday, and I have. Even at the lowest point in my life. I think he would be happy to know that on this special day, I'm passing it on to you. I am so very proud of the beautiful woman you have grown into, and I know your father would be too. When I look at the woman you have become, I know that everything I have endured was worth it." She hands me the necklace and my heart swells from the significance of it.

"I'm going to give you some alone time while I start to get ready."

"Wait, Mom, Joseph left some stuff for me in a safety deposit box. There were some old pieces of jewelry in there, can you tell me about them?"

I hand her the box, but she hesitates. "Mom, if it's too much, we can wait."

"It's okay, dear, I just need a moment. I know what's inside the box. They were some of my mother's favorite pieces of jewelry. I asked Joseph to keep them safe for you. It seems like a lifetime ago. I'm sorry he's not here to see how happy you are."

She opens the box and pulls out the Cameo pin. "This belonged to your great-grandmother; she was French. The amethysts and diamond bracelet was your grandmother's. Your grandfather gave it to her on their wedding day, it was the color of her eyes."

I pick up the bracelet, and it glistens in the sunlight. "I will wear it today, in honor of her."

I hug my mom so tight. "It will be okay, Mom, we will get through this together."

"I know, Raven, let's focus on today, making a lifetime of memories for tomorrow. I'll leave you alone."

My mom gets up and goes inside, leaving me alone. I look around at the dozens of roses and I'm floored. I take one of the cards and open it.

I love you, sweetheart.

I go to the next one.

I will always have your back.

You rendered me speechless.

Looking at you takes my breath away.

I love negotiating with you.

Lock on, baby, Violet to Blues.

I hope I invaded your dreams like you invaded mine.

Sweet Jesus, and all that is holy—NUTELLA!

I'm laughing and crying at the same time.
Finally I find the last card.

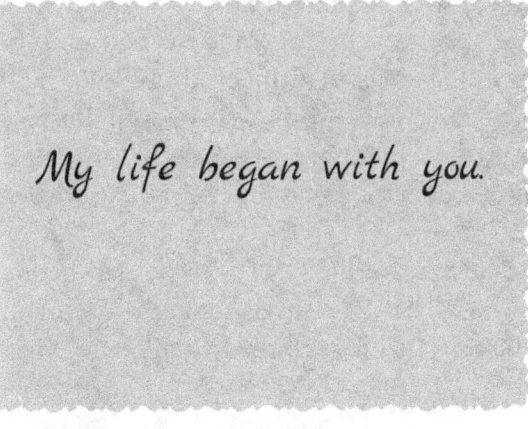

My life began with you.

I'm in shock; he captured all the craziness. I have to stop day-dreaming. I need to get the gifts together. I pull out his gift, certain that he will love it. I got him a beautiful, chestnut box, with a violet bowtie to match my eyes. I had the artist carve one of my favorite quotes by Chae Richardson, '*Courage is not living without fear. Courage is being scared to death and doing the right thing anyway.*' With everything that is going on right now, all we have is courage.

Jackie comes in from Max's place and grabs a cup of coffee. "Holy crap, Raven! It looks like he bought out the florist shop!"

"You know how crazy he can be. I'm surprised he hasn't done more."

"Raven, you didn't tell him, did you? You know when he finds out, he'll go nuts."

Oh, now I feel bad. "Jackie, I didn't want him to make a big deal. He's so over the top sometimes and I just want simple."

"Raven, simple left, the day you crashed into him at Starbucks. Where did Mick go? I heard him leave."

"He went to pick up, Ashlyn, my Pilates instructor. I invited her to the wedding."

"I'm so happy for Mick. His life is really coming together. Has he ever told you what his life was like before the war?"

"No, and he might never be able to talk about it. I wish there were more services for the men and women like Mick; those who end up falling through the cracks. So, totally changing the subject here, but . . . what happened with you and Max?"

"He explained why he pushed me away. I understand his fear, but it still hurt. I can get past it, as long as he is honest. I do love him."

"He loves you, Jackie, very much. I don't know if I would have ever been able to come back from what he went through."

Jackie nods, then jumps up. "We need to think happy thoughts today. Mick should be back any minute now, and we need to get going. Where is Rose?"

All of a sudden it's a flurry of activity. My mom gathers up all of my stuff just as Mick and Ashlyn come in. We are all off to Bella's house. I can't believe in a few hours, I'll be getting married.

Chapter Fourteen

Jaxson

I FINALLY DECIDED UPON a gift for Max, and I know the girls are going to stroke his ego over it. I don't know why I'm so worried about today, but I am. I decided to give her the island as a wedding gift. Yeah, she'll freak out, but it will be a good family vacation spot. Everything is set. I just need to find Max.

Bella's garden is beautiful, so many different colors. I find Max on the back patio, having tea with mum. I think having her guard him for a few days really did a lot of good for their relationship. They have a closeness and an ease that they didn't have before. I pull up a chair and mum pours me a cup of tea.

"How are you this morning, son?"

"I'm happy. I wish everyone could feel this way; it's different. Mum, before this day gets away from us, I just want to tell you how proud I am that you're my mum." Just as I say it, Max starts to get up to leave. "Max, stay please. Mum, you're the strongest person I know, and I love you."

"Thank you . . . both of you . . . for all of your support. Enough of this. Maxwell, what happened with Jackie?" She waves away the emotions threatening her eyes.

Max leans in and kisses her cheek while I'm laughing. "An, you're the best. We are working it out. She has accepted my apology, and informed me that she will not accept anything but total honesty. We have a lot to get through right now, and I want to take it one day at a time."

"I need to finish getting ready; I will leave you two boys alone." Just like that, Mum is gone.

"Max, I can't imagine this day without you standing by my side. You've helped make it all possible." Before he can say anything, I pass him a box. "This is a little something to remind you of today. Don't let it go to your head, mate."

"Jax, we got here together and we will face everything that comes our way together. You didn't have to get me anything, I will never forget today."

"Max, shut up and open the bloody box."

"Jax, this is fantastic."

"Yeah, well, the girls all think you're Bond, so now, you have Bond cufflinks that turn into USB drives. You better not let this go to your head." I laugh and swat his knee.

Bella comes running out to the patio in a flurry. "If you two are done with your little bromance, you need to finish getting ready; the girls are here."

$$\mathcal{R}aven$$

I NEED A MOMENT alone. I sit on the bed, and run through the events since I met Jax. It has been a whirlwind. So many lives changed. So many lost. I can't dwell on the negative. I need to stay positive, and focus on our baby.

"Raven? Oh. There you are, dear!" An comes in, seemingly happy. I think not having to keep her secret anymore will help her move forward.

"Hi, An." I greet her with a kiss on the cheek. I give her the gift I have for her. "I got you a little something to thank you for welcoming me into your family. I know there is so much stress and turmoil right now, and for that, I'm so sorry. I promise you, I will love him with all my heart—forever."

"Raven, it's me who should thank you. You have taught this old lady quite a bit these past few months. You've shown me that real strength comes from deep within. If it wasn't for all this craziness, I might have taken my secret to my grave."

"I'm glad you didn't. Max now has the family he always should have had. I know times were different, but no one should be alone."

There's a knock on the door. "It's almost time, Raven." Mom calls out.

An hugs me, "I'll give you some time with your mum."

"Mom, come sit for a minute, please." I hand her the present. "This is something for you to remember this day always."

She opens the box, and reads the inscription; *'Time to live again.'*

"Oh, Raven, it's beautiful. Today is so special for me. I never thought I would be here with you. I only wish your father were here to see what a beautiful, kind woman you've become."

I help her put it on. "Please don't cry, Mom. Today is a new beginning for all of us. I know my dad is watching over me. He is in my heart always."

"I will try not to cry, but I can't make promises." She smiles. "Now, you need to finish getting ready. I'll send Jackie in."

Jackie steps into the room, taking my breath away. "Jackie, you look beautiful." I slip the bracelet on her wrist. "This infinity charm represents my friendship and love for you, always. Don't even think of crying! Where is Michael?"

"Breathe, Raven, it will be fine. Michael is waiting right outside the door for you. Are you ready?"

I hear the music start and I know it's time. I whisper, "Yes."

Jaxson

I STAND IN THE garden—my nerves shot. I hope I can make it through this without passing out. Michael Sr. has the job of getting everyone seated. There is more security here than there are guests.

The music starts and it's the song I chose just for Raven. "How long will I love you?" by Ellie Goulding. Within a second, a fear that I will forget my lines comes over me. Max wraps his hand around my arm.

"Steady, mate, you'll be fine. Just remember to breathe."

Easy for him to say. Jackie comes into view; she's stunning. I look over at Max, and he's got a full fledge smile. Jackie reaches us, and then steps to the side. I finally get a full view of my beautiful girl. She takes my breath away, and my heart skips a beat. Junior is guiding her towards me. I'm so proud of the little guy. He whispers something to her, causing her to laugh. She is getting closer; my heart beats faster. I need to remember to breathe. I look up to the heavens and thank Antonio for this gift, a gift I will treasure with my life.

As they stand before me, the priest asks, "Who gives this woman away?"

Junior places her hand in mine and declares, "I do, Father."

She leans down and kisses Junior, turning him a million shades of red.

I'm holding her hand, staring at her in wonder.

The priest begins, "Raven, Jaxson, I understand you have written your own vows. Jaxson, please begin."

Hand in hand, she turns to face me. "Raven, the feeling hit me the moment I looked into your beautiful, violet eyes, the very first time. It was so immediate and powerful—far deeper and inexplicable beyond any calculation of time and place. You don't describe a feeling like that. You can't replicate it or force it. You just let it flow in and around you. You go where it takes you. I promise to love you with all that I am. I will support you and negotiate with you. I will challenge and protect you. I promise to grow old with you, every second of everyday. I will hold your hand through the good times and the bad. You are my lifeline in the storm. I'll love you beyond my last breath."

She brings my hand to her lips and kisses my palm. "Jaxson, my beautiful, intense man. Our love will transcend through all of time. I need you beside me, always, as my best friend, lover, and my soul mate. I will love you, honor you, and respect you. I will negotiate with you, and rein you in, when I have to. Through sickness and health, good times and bad, I will forever be your companion. You are my end all."

As we exchange the rings, there's not a dry eye in the house. The priest finally gets to the part I've been waiting for. "You may kiss the bride."

I lean in, "My beautiful wife, kiss me, please."

Raven

EVERYONE SEEMS TO BE having a good time. My mom is relaxed and laughing with Mrs. Osla. I almost forgot, I have to introduce Jax to my special guest . . . if I can drag her away from Mick.

"Jax, I would like to introduce you to someone very special. This is Ashlyn Adair, my Pilates instructor." I think he stopped breathing. I whisper, "Breathe."

"Ashlyn, let me tell you what a pleasure it is to finally meet you. Raven has shown me how wonderful Pilates can be. I ordered a Reformer for our personal gym."

Thank God Ashlyn is taking it all in stride. "Well, Jax, if you need any personal instruction, I'm sure Raven can show you. I also give private lessons and lessons for couples." Jax's chin is officially on the floor.

"I just might take you up on that. How long can Raven continue to do Pilates while she is pregnant?"

"As long as the doctor says it's okay, then up until delivery."

"Well, good to know, Ashlyn, I'm pretty sure we'll be taking you up on those private lessons." He smiles with a mischievous glint in his eye. I shake my head a little and bite back the giggle that wants to escape. "I can't tell you how happy we are that you could share our day with us. Please, make yourself at home. I need to dance with my wife, and then feed her. God, how I love the sound of that." He beams.

Jax pulls me into his arms, and the music suddenly changes. "Raven, I chose this song for you. The first time I heard it was on your iPod, 'Never Stop' by SafetySuit. The words say it all for me, wife. I love you."

The music starts, and my tears fall. It's such a beautiful song. As Jax glides me around, he begins to sing. His deep, smooth voice telling me how he'll never stop losing his breath when I look at him. You could hear a pin drop. My eyes lock onto his, and time stands still. It's a true declaration of everlasting love. I love this man, and all his crazy, intense ways. I wouldn't want him any other way. When the music finishes, he scoops me into his arms and carries me over to a table. I'm glad to finally eat and pick my feet up. Jax is slowly rubbing my neck, and I feel all the tension melt away. Max and Jackie come to join us.

"Hey, Max, you look wonderful. How are you feeling?"

"I'm doing better everyday, thank you, Raven. Did you see the gift that Jax got for me? They are Bond cufflinks that turn into mini USB drives."

"Wow, Max, I told you—Bond all the way!"

Jax rolls his eyes, "Please, sweetheart, don't fill his head."

"Max, Raven and I are leaving. I need you to take care of her mum while we are gone. We will be back for the deposition on Monday, but for now, we are heading out to Cape Cod for a long weekend."

"That's fine, just keep the detail with you both, at all times. Make sure you're back here for court at ten am, Monday. Jackie and I will keep Rose busy. You look very tired, Raven, go now, and we will handle the goodbyes."

"Thank you, Max." Jax scoops me up and practically runs out the door.

Maxwell

WHILE JAX AND RAVEN make a quick exit, I have other things to tend to, starting with Sammy. Jackie is talking to Rose and An. This is the perfect time to talk to Sammy. The guy's got the looks, but my understanding, from Jax, is that he bats for the other team, and is in a committed relationship. Lucky for him, otherwise, he wouldn't be staying at Jackie's.

I head over to him and slap his shoulder to get his attention. "Hello, Sammy, I think it's time we got to know each other. I understand from Jackie, that you have been her guard for a long time. How long do you plan on staying in New York?"

"I'm staying indefinitely, Max. Let's have a seat. I have questions, and I'm sure you have some for me."

"Okay, Sammy, what are your concerns? We are both in the same line of work, with similar backgrounds. I won't bullshit you, so ask away."

"Thank you. I'm sure you know I ran a check on you, so I know about your past. I never said anything to Jackie. I felt it was something that she needed to find out from you, not me. I understand why you pushed her away, but just so we're clear here, if you break her heart again, I will kill you."

Is he serious? Does he think he can intimidate me? "I assure you, my intention was to always keep her safe. Even now, I worry. Jackie will be staying with me. I have a guest room, and you're welcome to stay, also. We have to be in court on Monday for a deposition. I would appreciate you being there for Jackie, while I'm being deposed. I want eyes on her at all times."

"Let's get a few things straight, Max. I don't work for you. I'm here solely for Jackie's protection. That being said, I don't have a problem combining resources when it comes to her safety. Jackie has brought me up to speed on what she knows about Raven's situation. I also pulled everything I could find on Vincent. He's a real piece of work and I wouldn't be surprised if the Fed's offer him a deal."

I can play nice with others when I have to and now is one of those times. I will bite my tongue and let him feel like he has control. "I agree. At this point, I think his only option would be to turn state's evidence. That could possibly open a bigger can of worms. I heard today, from the district attorney, that Vincent's attorney is claiming it was self-defense for shooting me. He is also saying that Duke was responsible for kidnapping Raven. I'm not surprised that he would throw his kid under the bus." He's quiet, probably trying to absorb it all.

"What is going on with the case against Duke? Do you think he is going to fight the kidnapping charge or just go along with the father?"

"Sammy, this whole thing is so cocked up. Raven believes Duke is a *tortured soul,* but she sees the good in people. I think the kid did snap, however, he still needs to be held accountable for his actions. He killed two people at point-blank range. I think he deserves to be locked up forever. Either way, this is going to get a lot worse before it gets better."

"I notice there are many different guards here, but Mick seems to be a constant, and very protective of the girls. What's his story? I already ran a check on him, I want to know what's not on paper."

"Sammy, the one person I don't worry about is Mick. He loves those girls, and proved it when Raven was kidnapped. But I'm sure you already know that. He's a veteran, and a fine bloke. It looks like everyone is finally starting to leave, I'm going to collect Rose and Jackie."

As we head over to collect everyone, Mick pulls me aside. "Max, just want to let you know that Jax and Raven arrived safely. If you don't need me tonight I would like to take Ashlyn home."

I'm so happy that he is getting his life back. There is no one who deserves it more. "Mick, enjoy your weekend." I watch as he escorts Ashlyn out. I think she will be good for him.

I gather Rose and Jackie before we make our goodbyes. I want to get Jackie home, and spend time with her. God how I missed her. She calms me. I haven't felt this way in so long. I pull her close; she's my lighthouse in this raging storm. The entire ride is in silence. I focus on her slowly rubbing her thumb in circles over my knee.

When we get to The Tower, Jackie makes sure Rose is settled in next door. Sammy pulls me aside, "Max, I'm going to hang out in Jax's place with Rose. I have calls to make and some things I want to follow up on. If you decide to go anywhere, please let me know."

"Don't worry, I don't plan on leaving that flat, or Jackie, for the next few days. If Rose needs anything, let me know. I'm sure Jackie will want to check on her daily. Is there anything else you need from me?"

"No. I am, however, going to reach out to my contacts and see if I can get any further information. If I come up with anything, I'll let you know." And with that, he turns to walk away.

I take Jackie's hand, and we head next door. Finally, alone, at last.

Ashlyn

I SIT AND WATCH Mick drive. I realize there is a lot to this man that is unknown. He is always so quiet. I wonder if it's because it's his job or something else. "Mick, thank you for picking me up today."

"You're welcome. Would you like to go grab a cup of coffee?"

"I would love to. There is a local coffee shop, across from my house."

This man intrigues me. He's different. He's very quiet. Maybe he needs time to feel more comfortable with me. We pull up to the coffee house, and head inside. Mick orders our coffee while I find a table. It's not that busy and I'm able to get a quiet table near the back. He's back with the coffee, but he seems quiet again.

"Mick, how long have you worked for Jax?"

"Less than a year. I met him through Raven. How long have you been teaching Pilates?"

"I've been teaching for almost nine years. I also volunteer my studio and my services to veterans. I try to help them get some mobility back. I usually do that on a private basis. Makes them feel more comfortable."

He seems to tense at the mention of my work with veterans. "What about you, Mick, what did you do before this?"

"I was an Air Force pilot. I did six tours in Iraq before I was injured."

"Wow, six tours? That was a lot. What did you do prior to your service?"

"I only ever wanted to be a pilot. That ended the day of my accident. You don't have a New York accent, where are you from?"

"I was born in Los Angeles. My mom is a nurse at Children's Hospital in LA. My dad was a ship builder in Belfast. He met my mom when she was on vacation in Ireland, and followed her to the States. He died last year of a heart attack. Do you have any family?

"I am an only child, and my parents are both gone now. I was raised in Nebraska. When I got back from Iraq, I thought I would try big city living. I was living on the streets, when I met Raven. She helped me turn my life around. Showed me I still had purpose."

"Mick, everyone has purpose, you only need to believe you're worth it. If you're interested, come by my studio and I will teach you how to stretch out your muscles and work past the pain."

"I'd like that, Ashlyn, but for now, I better get you home."

He walks me across the street to my building. I don't know why I'm nervous. I hope he takes me up on my offer to train him. When we reach my door, he takes my hand in his and I feel all of his callouses, yet he's gentle.

"Thank you, Ashlyn, you're very easy to talk to. I'd like to get together again, if you would like to."

"Give me your phone, Mick." I hold out my hand. He reaches into his pocket and pulls it out for me. I call my cell from his phone, "Now you have my number. I would like to get together, again." I lean in and kiss his cheek. Finally . . . he smiles.

Chapter Fifteen

Jaxson

"**M**RS. PHILLIPS, WE ARE alone here, well, except for the guards and Bo, until Sunday evening. I expect you to take advantage of me in every way possible. Before anything, though, I want to wish you a very happy birthday." The look on her face right now is *priceless*. "Did you really think you could get something so important like a birthday past me?"

"I'm sorry, Jax. I didn't want you to make a big deal about it. You can be a tad over the top sometimes."

"Well, sweetheart, this time I think you will be surprised to know that my gift is not over the top." I won't tell her what I paid the guy just to keep things simple; she doesn't need to know that part.

"When I was in school, my teacher gave me an assignment. I had to write a small poem. It had to be something that I would want to give to someone someday. When she gave it back to me, she had me put it in an envelope and told me to keep it, until the day came when I would need it. I had no clue as to what she was talking about, but my mum did. My mum has held onto this for me all these years." I hand her the box, letting her unwrap it. Inside is a violet, antique, heart-shaped, glass bottle with a scroll inside. She pulls it out and begins to read:

Beauty
Thy gifted beauty is
vanquishing to my sight.
It pierces through my heart
with a sharp arrow of love.
Therefore, I would hate to part
with thy beauty.
I love thy more than everything
I've got and want.
More beyond than I can see.
Thy heart is more beautiful
than anyone can see.
I love thy in every way that I
know of.

"Jax, words escape me. This is precious and so special." Her eyes fill up.

"Sweetheart, those are good tears, right?"

"Yes, they are good tears. This came from your heart, so pure. It means more to me than anything, thank you. Right now, Jax, I need you. I mean . . . I *really* need you."

"Oh, you don't have to tell me twice." I scoop her into my arms and carry her to the bedroom. "I want to slowly peel you out of this dress and worship every inch of you all night long," I say as I place her back down on her feet.

She runs her fingers through my hair and brings my lips close to hers. "No one is stopping you, Jax."

I turn her around and start to unbutton each of the very frigging tiny buttons that are covered in lace. My crazy side wants to just rip it off, but my gentleman side is telling me to slow it down. "Sweetheart, how attached are you to this dress?" She tilts her head back and her lips are parted. Her silky hair, cascades down her back as her beautiful eyes lock onto mine. Fuck all that's holy—game over! I grab each corner of the dress and rip it right off her. *Fuck, I'll have the seamstress make her another one for keeps!* SShe spins around, standing before me—hands on her hips—in nothing but high heels, white—laced thigh highs, a sheer, white bra, and lace thong. She has fire in her eyes and my cock is screaming for freedom.

"Raven, I'm sorry . . . I um . . . I'll buy you another dress. I'll get this one fixed. Say something, sweetheart, please."

"You, Mr. Phillips, are extremely overdressed. You said I wouldn't have to ask you twice, yet, here I am, asking—again."

I grab her and kiss her wildly as I try to rip my own clothes off. She gets me, all my crazy ways and she loves me. *How the fuck did I get so lucky?*

I snap her thong and make fast work of the bra, but leave on the heels and thigh-highs.

"Breathe, Jax, close your eyes and breathe. I'm not going any-where without you."

She pulls me in for another kiss. Our tongues are doing their slow dance. My heart feels as if it will beat right out of my chest. I grab her face between my palms, deepening the kiss further as I back her up to the bed. I slowly guide her onto it before spreading her legs and sliding my cock inside of her. She throws her head back and closes her eyes like she's relishing in the feel of every hard inch of me. Balls deep, I freeze. She opens her eyes. "Jax, are you okay?"

"If I could spend the rest of my life in this moment, I would be a happy man. As strong as I am, is as weak as you make me. I love you so deeply, so truly, yet there is always more with you. You understand me like no other, even when I don't understand myself. My heart and soul is in your delicate hands."

Raven

HE DOESN'T HAVE TO move; he's throbbing deep inside me. He throws his head back and my name is his benediction as he floods me. I'm right behind him.

After a few minutes, he gets on his knees, takes off my shoes and stockings, all the while, buried deep within me. This is my over-the-top, intensely wild husband, whom I love with all my heart and soul.

"I need you, wife—again and again. Always more, never enough." He leans back down, careful not to place all of his weight on me. He nibbles on my ear, and I feel his magnificent cock pulsing inside of me.

He tweaks my nipples, both at the same time. "Oh, God, Jax, I need more."

He growls in my ear, "More what, sweetheart?"

He's swiveling his hips, "You don't play fair."

He takes both my hands and holds them above my head with one of his. He lifts my leg over his shoulder, so he can go deeper. "Jax, please."

"Tell me, wife, what do you want?" He's not letting up, he pulls out slowly and I'm trying to push him back in, but he's in total control.

"I want it hard."

"Want what hard, wife?" *Oh he's smirking.*

"Fuck me hard, Jax—*now!*"

"Yes! I love when you talk dirty, sweetheart."

He rolls onto his back and guides me patiently to climb on top of him. Once I am positioned above him, he grasps my hips and slams me hard onto his cock. He's holding onto one of my ass cheeks, pulling and digging his fingers into it, and then, he smacks my ass. This sets me off in a wild frenzy of riding him like my life depends on it. After several minutes, I feel him grasping harshly at my ass again. Smack! "Come now, Raven! Holy fuck, woman! he grunts. The explosion for both of us is endless. He's slowly bringing us back down, guiding my hips on him, his cock slipping in and out. I have nothing left; I'm totally and utterly spent. I can't even open my eyes.

"Sleep, my precious one. I will love you past the heavens and the stars. I will need you beyond this lifetime," he whispers to me as he lays me down and covers us up. I spoon back into him and fall asleep to the sound of our synchronized breathing.

Maxwell

ROSE AND SAMMY ARE settled in next door, and now I get my Jackie . . . finally! It has been a test to my strength and patience, waiting to take her completely. "Jackie, you look beautiful." I wrap my arms around her and nuzzle her neck. God, she smells wonderful, I want to bury myself in her forever.

"Thank you, Maxwell. We need to talk."

Talk? She wants to bloody talk now! "Okay, baby, what's wrong?"

"I know you're worried about Monday, but I can tell something else is bothering you. You seemed more on edge than usual at the wedding. Was it just the wedding or did something else happen?"

How does she do it? "Let's sit, and I will tell you everything. You know we are keeping Rose's identity a secret? Even from Sammy."

"Yes, Raven told me. I would never want to put her life in jeopardy."

"I got a call from my attorney. Vincent's lawyer is claiming he shot me in self-defense. He is also claiming that Duke kidnapped Raven."

I see her shock turn to rage like the flip of a switch. "Max, it's absurd that anyone would even believe him."

"I know, baby, but I think he is setting himself up for a plea deal. His best bet is to turn state's evidence. I'm worried how this is going to play out for all of us. On Monday, while I'm giving my deposition, I asked Sammy to stay with you."

"Maxwell, I will do whatever you need me to do. I don't want you worrying about me. I understand the danger, and I promise you, I will not take any chances."

We sit quietly for a while, gazing out over the park. "Max, if you squeeze me any tighter, I might snap in half."

"Oh my God, did I hurt you? I'm so sorry, baby."

"Relax, I'm fine, but you on the other hand, need some attention."

I smile and kiss the tip of her nose. "Do I now? What type of attention are you offering?"

"The kind that requires a lot less clothing."

"Well I wouldn't mind removing your dress."

She stands up in front of me, but my eyes are focused solely on her legs. "Max, if you don't take your eyes off of my legs, we are not going to get anywhere."

"Oh trust me, baby, I know exactly where we're going."

Jackie

HE GETS UP AND sweeps me into his arms. "The first thing I want to do is dance with you."

He puts on a beautiful song, 'Pieces' by Red and takes me in his embrace. He's a fantastic dancer; light on his feet. He nuzzles into my ear, and begins to sing. Max is singing. I might faint. Real slow style dancing with Maxwell Fleming, singing in my ear. I'm about ready to pinch myself when the music ends. "Max, you have a beautiful voice." Before I can say another word, my dress is a puddle around my ankles.

"I'm going to kiss you from head to toe, and I'm not stopping."

His kisses are soft, yet firm. He flutters them down my neck. His soft stubble, tickles in the wake of his kisses. "Oh God, Max, if you're going to do this to my whole body, I don't know that I'll be able to take it."

"Hmm, oh, you'll take it, baby, and then some."

My bra and panties have somehow managed to end up with my dress on the floor. He's kissing my arms, and I can't move. Every spot he kisses sends chills up my spine.

As he latches onto my nipple he brings me down to the floor. He nibbles and licks, followed by kisses. Just when I think I might burst, he goes to the other one. His fingers are fluttering down my ribs. He's kissing me everywhere. I'm so overwhelmed.

"Max, I don't think I can take it much longer." I know I sound whiney and desperate, but at this point I don't care!

"Baby, you are so responsive to me, and I love that I can give you such pleasure."

As he's kissing his way down my hips, his clothes are being tossed everywhere. He holds my legs open with an iron grip, leans down, and swipes his tongue over my clitoris. I'm screaming and riding a wave of unexplainable pleasure.

Maxwell

"I NEED TO BE inside you now, baby." I crawl up her body and take my time entering her, treasuring every movement, until there is nothing between us. I can feel myself all around her, and slowly begin to move. It's been so long since I've been deep inside of her. She's tight and warm. I trail my fingers up her legs; they are so long and lean. Her skin is soft and smells sweet. I need to slow it down. I can't let it end. I roll her nipples between my fingers then I stop. Her eyes open wide and she begs me for more. I give her what she wants, taking one of her nipples into my mouth, very gently sucking. She's yelling and I need to focus on her, what she wants. I pull her nipple between my teeth, biting down with just enough pressure while I roll the other nipple between my fingers, pinching and tugging. I can feel my blood racing through my body; every part of me is tightening up. She begins to shake and quiver, dragging her nails down my back. "Oh, bloody hell."

She throws her head back and digs her heels into my arse. She's screaming, and clawing her nails into me. I lose all control. I feel a dam inside me open. All of the stress and the loss, floods to the surface. I explode like I never have before. I hold her close, knowing that she is the one who has brought me from a world of darkness. She's the one who put together all the shattered pieces of my heart.

I carry her into bed, realizing that I could never be without her again. Cradling her in my arms, I fight to hold back all of the emotions that I've kept buried for so long. I pull the comforter over us. I'm never letting her go.

Jaxson

MORNING ARRIVES WITH RAVEN and I in a tangled heap. I smile and watch my wife sleep. Everything I need is right here in my arms. I don't want this peace and comfort to end, but come Monday morning, the craziness will start all over again. Mrs. Osla is overseeing the renovations on the island, which I've yet to tell Raven about. I love the mornings when I can hold her in my arms. The quiet and the feeling of knowing she is safe, overwhelms me.

"Jax, can you loosen your grip a bit, please. Are you okay?"

I pull her on top of me still buried balls deep, and I tilt my hips. "What do you think, sweetheart?"

"What's bothering you?" She narrows her eyes at me like she's trying to figure me out.

"I don't want this to end. I want to always have this feeling of total bliss."

"It will only end if you let it. We can't give up, and we won't give up—ever. Why do you fear it will end?"

I close my eyes and take a deep breath. "I'm worried about court, and everyone's safety."

Her fingers trace over the little lines at the corner of my eyes. "Have faith, think of *Die Hard* and how the good guy always wins."

I throw my head back and laugh. "Raven, I love you."

I tilt my hips again; she's so beautiful. Her hair is tousled, her eyes are bright and her lips are puffy. I'm a lucky bastard. "Ride me, sweetheart, take charge."

"Not just yet, my beautiful husband, first I want to kiss you everywhere." With that, she begins the slow process of kissing me over every inch of my skin. I know I won't last long. As she kisses each one of my nipples, I tilt my hips and grind into her the way that she loves. I don't think either one of us is going to last. She lifts her hips and slowly glides down. "Oh, it's so full this way," she whimpers before rising again and clenching as she slowly comes down. My eyes roll back, and I fist the sheets, trying to control the tidal wave. She does it again and I lose it, completely shattered. The sight of my undoing sends her over the cliff, I believe. She picks up the pace, the sounds escaping her keeping me hard for her finish. With one last guttural scream, she collapses into my arms. Neither of us move, we are barely able to catch our breath. Both of us silently lost in the intensity of our lovemaking.

She lifts her head after a few moments. " Are you okay?"

"Why wouldn't I be? My beautiful wife—who just gave me quite the morning shag—is sprawled naked across my body. I'm more than okay, sweetheart."

"Well, that same wife needs to crawl off your body like this. It's getting harder and trickier to do certain things with this growing belly. The same belly that is also rumbling for food." She climbs off. I jump up after her, lift her up, and head towards the kitchen. "Jax, you can put me down, I can walk."

"Nope, I'm spending the entire weekend just like this."

"You're out of your mind, we are not spending the entire weekend like this. Besides, I want to walk on the beach, what would the neighbors think?"

I frown. "I don't want to share you with anyone, is that so bad?"

"Jax, it's not bad. It's just not realistic. Let's look at it this way, when the baby is asleep we will be like this, and when the baby is awake we will let Mr. Cock take a snooze."

I stroke my chin. "Sweetheart, I'm really loving this negotiating stuff."

She rolls her eyes. "Jax, put me down, please. I want to give you something," She begs, but I don't give in. "Jax, the baby is up." And with that, I put her right down.

"I'm going to freshen up and you are going to get breakfast going."

"What would you like me to make you?"

"Surprise me." She kisses me and leaves me to it.

Raven

WHEN I GET BACK to the kitchen, after my shower, I see he has breakfast all set up on the patio. It's so beautiful here; the sound of the waves and the smell of the ocean. I sit down. I'm starving and before I realize it, I'm halfway through my omelet.

"Wow, sweetheart, you really were hungry. I can't let you get that hungry, anymore."

I have learned in life you need to pick and choose your battles wisely. I have come to know which ones I can win with Jax, and which ones are best left alone. As long as I don't let him dominate me all the time, I know we will find a balance.

"Jax, I really like the beach, and I was thinking maybe we can get a beach house for vacations. It would be nice with the baby to have a safe place to just be."

"Well, sweetheart, it's funny you should mention that."

He lifts his napkin and hands me an envelope. "My wedding gift to you."

I open it up and begin to read. I'm floored, but yet, I'm not. I look back up at him and see fear in his eyes, his jaw is tight, and I know . . . there is so much more to this than just a gift. I fold it up and say nothing, deciding to give myself time to calm down. I hand him a box. "My wedding gift to you, Jax."

He opens the box, his eyes becoming wide like a little boy. He looks at the bowtie, and smiles, but then he reads the quote by Chae Richardson. *"Courage is not living without fear. Courage is being scared to death and doing the right thing anyway."*

I brush my fingertips down the side of his beautiful face. "Now, Jax, do you want to tell me the whole story about the island?"

"Raven, I don't even know where to begin."

I get up and crawl into his lap. "Start at the beginning," I suggest. He says nothing. "Jax, when did you buy the island, how about that?"

He takes a deep breath and closes his eyes. "The same day I tented your building for non-existing termites." He opens one eye, probably to see if I'm going to flip.

"Why did you buy it? Go back to that day when you decided this was a great idea, and tell me why."

"You were always running away from me. Every time we were together, things would pull us apart. I just wanted to have someplace where we could be together and safe. I wanted to lock us away from the rest of the world. I know it's crazy, but in my defense, I wasn't thinking clearly."

"So, while we're locked away on this island, what about everyone else?"

"Full disclosure; my plan is to have houses built at all different points of the island. Everyone gets a house; we all live there. Mrs. Osla is overseeing all of the renovations."

"So, you're having houses built, and then you're going to lock the entire family away on this private island. Do you not see how crazy that is?"

"Honestly, up until the night before the wedding, it seemed perfectly normal to me."

I don't need to ask this, I already know the answer, but maybe if he hears it. "What changed? What, or should I say who, made you see how crazy this is?"

"Max made me see how unrealistic it was."

As I listen to his reasoning, I finally get it. This all goes back to the day his father walked out. Jax's fear of great loss came then. This is why he operates the way he does, so he never has to feel such pain, again. This is what drives the man.

"Jax, you have to stop operating out of fear. It's not good for you, and it's not good for everyone around you." I pull his face towards mine and kiss him. I hope that in time he will understand not all love comes with pain and loss. "Thank you, Jax. I guess we have a new vacation destination for the entire family."

"Let's go for that walk on the beach, maybe the baby will get tired and go back to sleep." He offers me the mischievous smile he's been sporting a lot lately.

Jackie

I TRY TO MOVE, but I can't. I open my eyes and Max is staring at me. He has an arm and a leg, locking me into place. "How long have you been staring at me?"

"I haven't been staring; I've been *watching* you sleep. Do you know when you're sleeping you look like an angel? I could watch you all day, but I've only been awake for ten minutes."

"Max, I need to check on Rose. What time is it?"

"It's eleven and I checked in with Sammy a couple of minutes ago. Rose is still asleep. What would you like to do today? I know you like to run, but honestly, I'm not up to a full blown run, yet."

"What I would really like to do is have a quiet, relaxing day alone with you. I still have more questions. And now that the flurry of the wedding is over, I just want a normal day. There is one thing we need to get cleared up right away. I'm not running away and I'm safe, so can you please loosen up your grip on me."

"Geez, I didn't realize I was holding you so tight. Did I hurt you?"

"I'm fine. Let's get something to eat."

WE HEAD TO THE kitchen where I sit and watch Max pull together a delicious breakfast. "This is amazing. I wouldn't even know where to begin."

"I take it, then, you don't cook?"

"No, I can make coffee and I can throw together a salad. Do you cook out of necessity, or do you enjoy cooking?"

"I never really thought about it, I guess a little of both. Let's take our coffee up to the rooftop deck, it's beautiful outside."

We head upstairs and I'm floored. "Max, this is so beautiful. I would be up here every morning."

"Sometimes I come up here just to think and forget, in a city this big, it's peaceful."

I pull him onto one of the lounge chairs. "Max, burying your head in the sand and trying to forget is never going to help you heal. Part of the healing process is talking about it. It's eating away at you like a cancer."

He's holding me and stroking my arm. "Elliot would have been ten. God, he was so beautiful."

Thank God he's talking. It's a start. I curl into him, wrapping my arms around him tighter. "It's okay, baby, take all the time you need."

"He was only eight months old. Seeing my wife and baby shot in the head is an image I will take with me to my grave."

"Don't focus on that, focus on the positive. Tell me about him, tell me what you remember."

"I remember his smell; sweet, so very sweet. His laugh would fill my heart. He loved music, and I would sing to him all the time. He didn't care what I was singing, just as long as I was singing. Samantha was good with him. She was fierce at work, but when she walked in the door, she was *mum;* she knew how to leave work at the door. I never could. I see danger everywhere and anywhere. After everything happened, I became worse."

"The healing process is different for everyone. You will probably be overprotective for the rest of your life. If you and Jax are honest with Raven and me, then we know the risk. We won't take stupid chances. Information is key. I never knew you sang, you have such a beautiful voice." I change the subject to something lighter.

"I haven't sung since my son died, at least, until last night. You're putting me back together, one shattered piece at a time. For the first time in years, I have hope."

"There is always hope, Max. First, you have to stop living to die and live to live. You need to realize that there are many people who love and respect you. You have been surrounded by so much love, but your heart has been closed to it all."

We sit in silence for a while. "Max, I would like to talk to Jax about setting up the school we spoke about. I realize I'm not going back to my job, and I need to do something."

"I have some questions for you; turnabout is fair play. What do you know about Sammy? I will admit, when Jax called me from your home, I pulled a file on him. I want to know what's not on paper, how you feel about him, and his partner."

"Sammy is very loyal to my family. I do know his partner, Ian, has agreed to move here. I'm very comfortable with him. He doesn't get along with my brother, Dylan, but in his defense, no one does."

"Are you close to your brother?"

"No. I tolerate him, at best. There is a large age difference, and he has been in love with Raven from the first day I brought her home. It's very awkward."

I lean in and kiss him softly. "What is it, Max, tell me what has you so twisted up inside?"

"I'm thinking of semi-retirement."

I see something in him, something beyond fear—I see hope. "Why would you want to do that, give up control? I thought you enjoyed what you're doing, making order out of chaos."

"I don't think I can go out in the field anymore. I'm not one hundred percent, and in my line of work, that could cost lives. The past six months, I've learned so much from you and Raven. All of this is just materialistic stuff, and if it went away tomorrow, it wouldn't really matter. I want to take a back seat and do more behind the scenes stuff. I'm ready to come back to the land of the living, and I want to start and end my days with you."

"Max, whatever your decision, I will support it."

He pulls me close to him and seems to be relishing in the peace he's newly found in life . . . with me.

Chapter Sixteen

Jaxson

THE LONG WALK ON the beach is wonderful, but my wife is tired. I scoop her up in my arms and carry her the rest of the way.

"Jax, I can walk."

I kiss her forehead and she nuzzles into my chest. By the time we reach the house, she is out cold. I put her to bed and decide to call Max. I want to check on Rose before Raven wakes up.

"Hey, Max, how's everything going?"

"Why are you calling me? Shouldn't you be spending quality time with your wife?"

"Relax, mate. She's sleeping, I wanted to check on Rose and I have questions that I want answers to before Monday."

"Well, Jackie just went next door to visit with Rose, so ask away."

"Okay, let's start with this one. Do you think Vincent knows that Rose is alive?"

"No, I don't. I think if he knew, he would do everything he could to get to her. His obsession with her was sick and twisted."

"Do you think he will turn state's evidence?"

"Yeah, I do. What worries me is Raven is the only living person who witnessed Vincent shoot Antonio. I've been trying to find the video that Raven told us about, but no luck. The statute of limitations for kidnapping in D.C. is six years, but there is no limitation on first-degree murder of a federal agent. Joseph left more questions than answers."

"What do you mean? What kind of questions?"

"Well, like why he didn't go after Vincent once he had Rose and Raven back. He was always preaching about following the rules and the laws, yet, he did none of it. The only thing I can figure is, Vincent's reach is far beyond what Joseph led us to believe."

"Max, do you think it would be better or worse if he turned state's evidence?"

"It would depend what kind of deal he gets. The best thing would be if he turned and received maximum jail time. Both D.C. and New York do not have the death penalty. If he does turn, it could incite a mob war. We will have our hands full, for quite some time."

"What about Duke?"

"He'll probably get life without parole, unless they can prove mental incompetence."

"Max, I'm worried about a trial. There will be a media circus, and rival families to think about. Who's been running his business while he's been in a coma?"

"From what I've heard, Vincent's consigliore has been running things. Vincent also relies heavily on Annabelle, which is unusual."

"Maybe it wasn't the best thing that I brought Rose back here."

"Jax, if someone were to dig hard enough, they would have found her. Joseph never even changed her name! Honestly, he was too emotionally invested to think everything through."

"How long do you think we can keep Rose's identity secret?"

"I honestly don't know, but as long as everyone co-operates, we have a fighting chance."

"How is everything going with you and Jackie?"

"Everything is good. Really good, actually. She's willing to try and so am I. Just need to take baby steps, something you know nothing about, mate. What happened with the gifts?"

"Fuck, Max, I'm not in the doghouse. I really thought she was going to flip out and tear me a new one, but she surprised me."

"Did you confess everything?"

"Yep, even when I purchased the island."

"Really, and when was that?"

I'm never going to live this one down. "When I tented the building. Stop laughing. I even told her about the houses that are going up on the island and how Mrs. Osla, is overseeing the project."

"Wow, you really did confess everything. How is she feeling?"

"She won't say it, but I know she is scared about Monday. I would feel better if Mick also stayed with Rose, on Monday. He's a good guy, and we all trust him. I think it would make Raven feel better, too."

"That's fine with me. I'm going next door. Let Raven know all is well here, and I will see you soon."

"Okay, thanks."

Maxwell

I'M THINKING THAT ISLAND is sounding better by the minute. Maybe Jax isn't *completely* off his rocker. Jackie and Rose are watching some mindless television show and Sammy is on the computer.

"Hey, Max, glad you're here. There's some stuff I want to go over with you."

"Why don't we go in Jax's office; it's quiet back there." I lead the way.

"Okay, Sammy, what's up?"

"Are you planning for Jackie to go to court with you on Monday?"

"As much as I want her stuck to me like glue, I know she can't be in the room with me when I'm giving my deposition. I was thinking Rose and Jackie could stay here. I will have Mick stay with them, along with an additional security team. I would like it if you stood here with them, too. This place is secure, and the lift has a private key and code."

"Good, I was thinking the same thing. There is no reason for them to leave here."

"Sammy, tell me everything you know about the situation with Raven, so I can bring you up to speed."

"Well, I know about Raven's father. I know who Rose really is. I know how sick Vincent is. I know that Duke probably snapped, and that Vincent is throwing him under the bus. I did find out that Vincent has some pretty heavy political friends, which will probably help him with a deal. I heard through the grapevine that the Feds are talking a deal. I also found out that Annabelle had one husband and two lovers that all died under mysterious circumstances."

"How do you know about Rose?"

"Max, the Chief called and he told me that he spoke to you. So, you know I still work for MI6. He told me about Rose, he wasn't going to let me go in here without full disclosure. You know I've been a guard with the Gerhard family for ten years. I can tell you that Gerhard is a hard, but fair man. He has a way of bringing people to the table. The government wants him and his family safe at all cost. I did some digging around and I heard the Feds were probably going to cut a deal with Vincent. Let's face it, they would be crazy not to. When Raven was seven, Vincent kidnapped her. This was the catalyst for everything."

"Sammy, what you don't know is Vincent videotaped everything that happened in that warehouse. Somewhere, there is a video of Vincent shooting his brother, a federal agent, to death. If we can find that video, it could prove murder. Right now, all we have is Vincent, saying he shot me in self-defense. The memory, from twenty years ago, when Raven was a traumatized seven-year-old, is not going to get Vincent convicted. Raven is the only living person who witnessed the murder. Rose watched the videotape, which is why we know it exists. Vincent is claiming that Duke kidnapped Raven, and that he had no idea she was being held against her will. With out that tape it's a he said, she said, and no evidence to back it up."

"Max, so what you're saying is, without that tape, he is practically a free man. How long do you think you can keep Rose under wraps?"

"I honestly don't know. I don't know why Joseph didn't change her name twenty years ago. Even if Rose came forward, she only saw a tape, a tape that we can't find."

"If we can find it, the best thing might be to leak it to the rival families that Vincent is turning; they will do the cleanup work for us."

"I thought of that, but then, what about Annabelle?"

"So we have until Monday morning to find that tape."

"Yeah, and trust me when I say, I've been trying."

"Well, I would bet that someone as sick as Vincent, would keep that tape pretty close to him, at all times. We need to get into his compound and find it before Monday."

"Keep in mind, if we obtain it illegally, then it can't be used in court."

"Max, you know there is always a way around everything. I'm going to make some calls, if I need to leave, I will give you a heads up."

"Sounds good. I'm going to collect Jackie, and go back next door."

When I get back into the living room, the ladies are laughing and chatting. It's good to see normal when we haven't had that in such a long time. "What are you ladies watching that has you laughing so much?"

"Rose never saw Friends, so I introduced her to Netflix and live streaming."

I keep forgetting all the simple things we take for granted that Rose doesn't know anything about.

Rose gets up and heads towards me, taking ahold of my arm. "Maxwell, please sit. I have some questions for you."

"I don't know that I'll have any answers, ma'am, but I will try."

"I would like to know what the plan is for Monday. You want me to stay here, don't you?"

"Yes, ma'am, I would like you and Jackie to stay here with Sammy and Mick. I need to know that you're both safe. I am trying to keep your existence under wraps for as long as possible."

"Will Vincent stand trial for any of his crimes?"

"Unless we can find the videotape that you wrote about, in the journal, then I doubt it."

She gasp, her face registering her fear. "How do you know about the journal?"

Oh no . . . I didn't realize she didn't know. "When Vincent kidnapped Raven, he gave her the journal to read. I'm sorry. I thought you knew all of this."

She begins to shake. "When d-did Vincent kidnap Raven? Oh my God, did he . . ."

I stop her before she continues. "Rose, he never touched her, I promise. I'm sorry. I thought you knew." I pull her into my arms. *Oh fuck* . . . she's shaking so bad. Oh my God, what have I done?

"Maxwell, so much is being kept from me. I'm a lot stronger than you think. I agreed to Raven's adoption to keep her safe. I would do anything for my daughter, even if it meant giving her up. Joseph looked for that tape for years. I'm not sure if he ever found it. Did you go through his private safe? If he did find it, he would have put it in there."

"I only met Joseph right after Raven was kidnapped. I don't know anything about his personal belongings, or where they would be."

"He had a cabin that belonged to his great-grandfather. Antonio and Joseph would go fishing there one weekend a month. I don't think they ever caught any fish. It was more to unwind. Before you even ask the question, yes, I know where it is. Raven owns the place. Joseph had no family, and when Antonio made him godfather, he put the cabin in Raven's name."

I'm shocked, "When I pulled a report on Raven, it didn't show that she owned anything."

"It's under Josephina Giaconna, not Cara Giaconna, or Raven Anderson. He probably never switched it. Maybe the answers you seek are there."

Sammy comes in the room, "Rose, where is the cabin?"

"It's in a small Virginia town called, Old Rag. It's about an hour and a half from DC."

I grab my phone and call Tony, "Hey, I need you to access all records for a Josephina Giaconna. I'm looking for real estate in Virginia. Send me the coordinates now, and get the jet ready. When we land, have a chopper ready to go. Tony, be on standby, I need to call Jax."

Sammy is about to grab my arm, but Jackie stops him. "He's in Max mode, let him be."

I hang up with Tony, and quickly call Jax. "Jax, I need to talk to Raven. We might have a lead on the tape, and only God knows what else."

"Slow down, mate. Tell me everything." I bring him up to speed on everything that we found out.

"Max, I will call the attorney and make sure it still legally belongs to Raven. I will have Tony coordinate anything that Raven needs to sign for the state, and have it sent it here. Physically, are you one-hundred percent able to do this?"

"Yes, and I will have Sammy with me."

"Double up security on Rose and Jackie. I will call Mick and have him head over there now. Max, am I on speaker?"

"No, what's wrong?"

"Head into my office and close the door."

Fuck, what else . . . "Okay, what do you want to tell me that you don't want anyone else to hear?"

He's quiet for a second. "When Raven and I went to Switzerland, I had the walk-in closet converted into a panic room. I didn't tell Raven yet, because she's been so emotional. Flip the light switch, next to the closet, and the door unlocks. Open the door and you'll see a number pad. The code is *violet.* You need to show this to Jackie and Rose. Everything they need to survive, for two weeks, is in there. Max, are you there?"

"I'm here. Just shocked and proud of you."

"Really, why?"

"Shocked that you pulled this off without anyone knowing, and proud that you did it. I'm taking Sammy with me. He knows who Rose is, Jax. It has to do with Gerhard, he's a powerful man, and his safety is priority one. I've got to run, I'll get the girls set up and call you when we land."

I head back into the living room and instantly see the fear in Jackie's eyes. I know what she's thinking, and I have to reassure her. She fights her tears back as I walk up to her. "Hush, baby, none of that. I'll be okay. It's nothing like the last time."

"Max, the last time I let you walk out that door, it nearly killed both of us."

"I'm not alone, baby. Sammy's got my back. I promise, I'll come back to you. I need you to be strong for my sake and for Rose's."

She walks up to Sammy, and grabs his shirt. "So help me, Sammy, you better bring him back to me in one piece, or there will be hell to pay!"

I pull her away from Sammy, and kiss her hard. With that, we're out the door.

Jaxson

I SIT ON THE deck watching the waves, wondering if this will ever end. That island is looking better and better. A text comes through from Tony, letting me know there are papers that Raven needs to sign, and that he's faxing them now. I turn around and she's standing in the doorway, watching me.

"What's going on, Jax?"

I open my arms and she crawls into my lap. "Apparently, you own a cabin in Virginia. Your mum said Joseph put it in your name when your parent's made him your godfather. The reason we didn't know about it is because it was in the name of Josephina Giaconna. Legally, you still own it, and I have some papers you need to sign. Max and Sammy are on their way down there to see what they can find before court on Monday."

"What are they trying to find?"

"The videotape that your mum spoke of. It could be the key to putting Vincent away for life. You're the only living witness to your father's murder. That puts you in a world of danger, sweetheart. " I hold her closer. I'm so worried for her safety and our baby's. A few minutes go by and I suddenly remember another tape that Tony had transferred for Raven and her mum. "Sweetheart, why haven't you watched the tape that Joseph left you?"

"I don't know if I'm emotionally ready."

"Have you told your mum yet that your dad left her a tape?"

"No, I was afraid to give her too much all at once. I was going to ask her therapist about it."

"I think, when we get back, you should at least tell her about it. It might be helpful for her.

I better tell her about the panic room before she finds out on her own. "I have a confession to make." Her eyes grow large, and she's tugging that ear.

"Go on, I'm ready."

"I had the closet in the office removed and a panic room installed. Jackie and your mum have been instructed on how to use it. I had it installed when we were in Switzerland. I needed some peace of mind," I admit. "Please don't be mad. I like order and organization. I never had to deal with so much crazy shit all at once. I felt better knowing it was there, in case we ever needed it."

Her hands tremble as they stroke my face. "Jax, I'm sorry that all this—"

"—Raven, never be sorry for something that was never your fault. I love you, and will move heaven and earth to keep you safe." I run my hands up and down her arms. "Hey, are you hungry?"

"Starving!" She widens her eyes. "Are you going to feed me?"

"Sweetheart, I'm going to feed you, and then I'm going to make love to you all night long."

"Well, while you're getting dinner ready, I'm going to have a re-laxing soak in that beautiful tub."

I kiss her and push her along, while I figure out what to do for din-ner. I'm so glad Bella taught me how to cook. She said it would come in handy someday, and she wasn't kidding, especially since my wife is totally clueless in the kitchen. I put the dinner in the oven and decide to go check on Raven. She is soaking in the tub. Her hair is pulled up, but some tendrils are cascading down. Her eyes are closed, and she's sing-ing a beautiful song by Nickleback, 'Never Gonna Be Alone.' I don't know why she thinks she can't sing—her voice is beautiful. I climb into the tub and face her. Her eye's fly open with a look that makes my cock jump to attention.

"I never heard you come in, is dinner ready?"

"You were very relaxed, and singing a beautiful song. You have a fantastic voice, so don't get all embarrassed. Dinner is in the oven, we have time. Relax and let me rub your feet."

She leans back and closes her eyes as I lift her foot. I work my thumbs up and down her arch, and then I graze my teeth along her big toe. She grips the side of the tub and just when she can't take anymore, I move onto the other foot.

"Oh, Jax."

"Feel good, sweetheart?" I give her a slight smile. My thoughts shouldn't be anywhere but with her, yet, I can't help myself from wor-rying about Max. What if, this time, my brother doesn't come back?

"Jax, he'll be okay." She pulls her foot away and moves to straddle me.

I let out a deep breath. "How could you know I was thinking about him?"

"Know that Max will be okay, or know that you're worried?"

"Both."

"I love you, Jax. When you hurt, I hurt. When you worry, I worry.

I feel what you feel. I know Max will be okay because I have faith. The same way I knew he would wake up. You need to do the same. Right now, I'm more worried about Jackie and my mom. Both of them are reliving a nightmare. Jax, can we head back home? I know that we were going to stay here another night, but I would feel better if I was there for both of them."

"I was going to suggest the same thing. Let's head back."

Jackie

ROSE IS MESSING AROUND in the kitchen, trying to keep busy. I am in dire need of chocolate. I know that Jax has a stash here somewhere. I find some and sit at the counter, watching Rose cook. "I didn't know you could cook."

"Actually, I love to cook. I find it very relaxing."

"Well, Raven didn't get that gene, that's for sure. Unless you consider a peanut butter and jelly sandwich cooking."

"Maybe that's something I can teach her now that we're together. Right now, I want to talk about you. You haven't been yourself since Max left earlier. What's going on?"

"The last time Max went after Vincent, it didn't end well." I cross my arms across my chest, rubbing at them to fight the chill I just got.

"We just have to pray that everything will work out, Jackie. Stay positive, dear." She offers me a warm smile.

Nothing else needs to be said; all we can do it wait. I decide to hang out with Mick in the living room for a little bit while Rose is busy cooking dinner. "Hey, Mick, how are you doing?"

"He'll be okay, Jackie."

"Am I really that much of an open book?"

He laughs, "Well, yeah, you are."

"What happened with Ashlyn? She's a very nice person, Mick. She does some great work with veterans."

"After the wedding, we went for coffee. I like her. We talked about getting together again, so we'll see where it goes."

"I'm going upstairs on the deck, for a bit. If you need anything, let me know. I'll let Rose know where I'm going, and my security, too."

I don't give him a chance to protest. I need to get out and get some air. I would love to go for a run, but not without Max. It's a beautiful night, and I can see stars, even with the lights of the city. I've decided to tell Jax I want to go forward with the school at Raiders. I need something to do. I never thought my life would turn out this way. I had it all planned out, but not like this. I want a life with Max, but I also need to be safe. Now that I know everything that happened to Max's family, I can understand the fear he lives with. I need to get him to a place where he can finally feel safe and loved. Suddenly, I hear a noise and nearly jump out of my skin. I turn, see Raven, and lose it. She is on me in a second, her arms around me, holding me tight.

"Jackie, stop with the ugly cry; he'll be back safely."

"If you believe that then why did you come back early?"

"I knew you needed me."

"Ugly cry, really?"

"Yeah, really ugly."

"Did you know your mom cooks?"

"Yes. The place smells wonderful."

"Raven, thank you for coming back."

"He will be back, Jackie, I have faith.
You ready to go back down?"

"Yeah, lets go."

Raven

WHEN WE GET DOWNSTAIRS, I see my mom setting up plates of food. Jax and Mick are deep in conversation. As we approach them, the elevator doors open and Max and Sammy step out. I let out a breath as Jackie runs to Max. The look on Jax's face is like a kid on Christmas morning. I walk up to him and whisper in his ear, "Faith, Jax."

Max lets go of Jackie, and kisses her forehead. "I told you I'd be back, no tears, baby." He then looks at Jax. "We got it. The videotape was in a safe, in the cabin. The authorities took possession of it, and I have a copy. It will be submitted Monday morning to the Feds. I'm not sure what is going to happen, but either way, we can use it to our advantage. If he turns state's evidence, we can leak it to the rival families, letting them know that he is a rat. Or they can use it to prosecute him for Antonio's murder. It is clear cut, and he can't talk himself out of it."

"Max, what else was in the cabin?"

"Nothing, Jax. It was just a basic fishing cabin, in the middle of nowhere."

"Let's all sit down and eat. Apparently, my mother-in-law is a wonderful cook."

Everyone sits down to eat Rose's wonderful food. Talk soon turns to all things baby. It's nice to see such normalcy for a change.

"Mom, what type of birth did you have with me?"

"I had a natural birth. My labor was very short, and you were early. Have you decided what type of birth you want to have?" She grabs her glass of wine and takes a sip.

All of a sudden, Max starts laughing. "Max, you already used up your one get out of jail free card, so if you know something, you better confess now," I order, having a hunch that his laughter was brought on by something Jax had done. That's usually the case.

"Raven, think of who you're married to. You should have seen him with Bella. I'm surprised we didn't have him sectioned."

Jax is very quiet, stroking his chin. I know he's done something. "What did you do, Jax?"

He's about to get up, but I grab his arm. "Don't even think about trying to worm your way out of this one."

"Thanks for throwing me under the bus, Max," he says with a bit of irritation "I rented a private suite at the hospital. I hired a team of nurses. I've been interviewing nannies and security guards. The baby never leaves our sight, and I hired a private Lamaze instructor to come to the house."

I'm reciting my mantra in my head over and over again. Pick and choose your battles wisely. I know it is fear that is driving him, but if I don't rein him in, it will only get worse.

I leap up and slam my hand on the table, and all heads turn towards me. "Jax, what about me? What about what I want, or don't want? I understand a lot of what you've done. I know the more private we operate, and then the safer we are. The one thing I will not go along with is a nanny. I'm not working. I will stay home and take care of our baby. Women have been having babies and taking care of them for years without the help of a nanny. I keep telling you the same thing over and over again. You have to talk to me before you go off and do all this crazy stuff. You just used up your last get out of jail free card, so like Max, you better think before you go off half-cocked."

You could hear a pin drop it's so quiet. I turn my focus to my mother. "Mom, how early was I?"

"You were only a week early, nothing to worry about. You do need to let the doctor know that I had a fast birth, as did your grandmother. It would seem to run in the family."

"How fast was it?"

"From start to finish, one and a half hours."

There's a loud clank as Jax drops his fork. He's frozen, my poor husband. If he survives this, it will be a miracle. "Mom, Monday afternoon I have a doctor appointment, will you come with me? It's the start of my last trimester. You can tell her the family history."

"Of course I will. Don't worry, Jax, I will be here to help with the baby."

Jaxson

I'm listening to everything going on around me, but all I hear is fast birth, over and over again, in my head. I never even thought it was possible, especially since my mum reminds me repeatedly how long she was in labor with me. I swear it gets longer every time she gets mad at me.

While everyone is cleaning up and getting dessert ready, Max, Sammy, and I head towards the office for a private chat. "Alright, bring me up to speed. What happened at the cabin? And thanks for throwing me under the bus, Max."

"Jax, you threw yourself under the bus. You need to dial it down, we will get through this together, mate."

He hands me a flash drive. "Put this in the safe. I had the tape transferred to a drive. There is no reason for Raven or Rose to ever see this. There were some papers in the safe, and among them was a letter to Raven from Joseph, explaining why he chose not to use the tape to go after Vincent. At first, I didn't understand it, until I watched the tape. I hope that neither of them will have to watch it again."

I take the drive and put it in the safe. "What's the plan for Monday?"

"I asked Sammy to help with security and transport. Jax, I know I'm not one-hundred percent for field work, plus I'm too closely involved to be clear-headed." He looks down. I can tell this is a hard adjustment for him.

Sammy steps up and begins to explain his plan. "Jax, I am going to stay here with Rose and Jackie. I have brought in some private security that I trust, and have used before for additional backup. They are all retired MI6. We will leave via the back entrance where a bulletproof car will be waiting for you. I emailed you both pictures of your driver and additional security that will flank you at all times. I also sent you additional pictures of Annabelle and her children. She has a son and a daughter; neither is in the business. The daughter is a director at a private school for the blind. The son is a research chemist for new drug development. Keep in mind; I never make changes to a plan. If anyone tries to tell you that I changed something—I didn't."

"Well, it sounds like you have everything covered. Where are you staying, Sammy?"

"I moved into Max's guest room, since Jackie is staying with him. After the dust settles, I will make arrangements for a permanent solution. Right now, I just want to get us all to the other side of this."

"Thank you. We better go back inside before I get into anymore trouble."

I look to Max, giving him a slight side nod of my head. No words ever need to be spoken, that's one of our many cues when we have something more to discuss in private.

"Sammy, Jax and I have some Raiders business to discuss, we'll be out in a bit."

I watch him leave, then go to my desk, bring out the scotch, and pour us each a hefty shot.

"Talk to me, Jax. What's going on in that crazy head of yours?"

"How did Sammy know who Rose is?"

"The Director of MI6 told him. I told you, Gerhard has quite a bit of influence." He takes a sip. "You never told me that Rose didn't know about Raven being kidnapped by Vincent. When Sammy and I were trying to figure out where the tape could be, Rose heard. I had to tell her. I assured her that Vincent never touched Raven. It's because of Rose that we found that tape."

"What was on the tape?"

" I would say, it is one of the most horrific things I have ever seen. The rage and pure evil from that man was sick. I would not have been surprised if he was really aiming for Raven, when he took the shot. Maybe Joseph told Raven the shot was meant for him to ease the burden of her father's death. We'll never know the answer; he took it to the grave with him. After watching it, I can understand what drove Raven into silence and Rose to recess into the darkest corners of her mind. Vincent made her watch this over and over again."

"What was in the letter from Joseph? Why didn't he put the bastard away?"

"Fear. He feared if it went to trial, Raven wouldn't survive, neither mentally nor physically. He feared Vincent would find out about Duke's existence, and that Rose was alive. He also knew that Vincent's reach was far and wide. That type of venom has connections in high ranking places."

"Max, are you okay with Sammy taking the lead on security for tomorrow?"

"I am. I know I'm too close to the situation, and I'm not one hundred percent. I'm still getting headaches, although they happen less, I never know when one will spring on me. The Chief said he would trust his children with him."

"Just one more thing, Max, before we go. I'm telling you this one time, and one time only. After what you put me through, getting shot in Miami, you're never going out in the field again. Your little stunt of going to that cabin when you knew I wasn't here to stop you—it really pissed me off. I have too much on my fucking plate! And yeah, right now, it's all about me. Pull that shit again and I'll shoot you in the arse myself!"

I slam my glass down and head out the door, leaving Max in silence.

Just as I head back to the living room, Mum gets off the elevator. *Could this day get any better?* "Hello, Mum."

"Don't you *hello, Mum* me, where is he?"

I'm so glad I'm not in trouble for a change. "He's in the office."

Before she can say anything, Max comes up behind us.

"I'm here, An, and I'm fine."

She reaches up and pulls his ear with no signs of letting go.

"Let me tell you something, Maxwell Fleming, if you ever do something like that again, so help me, Lord."

"Mum, I already warned him." I try to rescue him.

"Jaxson James, stop laughing, you're in just as much trouble as he is."

What the hell? "I wasn't even here, why am I in trouble?"

"You know the way he is. Next time, leave Mick here to guard him, and make sure he behaves." It doesn't matter how old I am, when she yells at me, I feel like I'm a kid all over again.

"An, I am an adult, and I can take care of myself. I was in no immediate danger, and I had, Sammy, with me."

Raven comes out, probably to see what all the yelling is about. She knows how to defuse a situation. *Must be all of that teacher training.*

"An, why don't you come inside and have some tea. My mom made some wonderful cookies."

"Honestly, Raven, sometimes they are like little boys in the school yard."

She is still talking away as Raven leads her inside. She looks back to me and I mouth, "*I love you, wife,*" while giving her a smirk. She rolls her eyes.

Chapter Seventeen

Raven

I T'S MONDAY MORNING, AND I open my eyes, only to find that the room is dark and I'm alone. I feel panic, but then I see him sitting in a chair in the corner of the bedroom. My poor, beautiful husband, he's so brave, yet so vulnerable. Everyone looks to him for strength and guidance, whom does he look to? I know he's watching me; I can feel it in my soul. I say the one thing that I know will make him come running.

"Jax, I need you." Without another minute passing, he's holding me, loving me, and consuming every part of me.

"I need you more, sweetheart, more than you'll ever know."

It's just a whisper, but I heard him. His fear about today is really off the charts. I know where he needs to be. The one place he can let go, the place that's reserved just for us. He's kissing my neck and nibbling my ear. I love when he is gentle, but I love when he is fierce. Right now, I know he needs fierce.

"Jax, I need you inside me now."

He stops and our eyes lock, "Hard and fierce, Jax—no holds barred."

He enters me slowly, his eyes still gazing into mine. When he's totally buried, just the way he likes to be, he stops. He lifts my legs up and places them on his shoulders. He slides his arms under my back grasping my shoulders. Our eyes never stray. He doesn't have to say a word; I see it in the depths of his beautiful blue eyes. He pulls back really slow and then slams into me, screaming my name. First fast, then slow. Time seems to stand still as I feel my heart pounding. He slows down, I think it's to give me a chance to catch up, but then he's swiveling his hips, first right and then left. He pulls back and then begins pounding again. I don't know how much time passes by; all I can concentrate on is his relentless pounding. He grabs my legs and pushes them towards me, lifting my pelvis to take more of him in. I grasp at the sheets, practically ripping them as he explodes, so fiercely, I fear he might pass out. He rests his forehead on mine, our eyes still locked.

"I love you, wife."

"I love you more, husband."

Jax loves to be needed, and taking care of me fulfills that for him. "I am jumping in that wonderful shower, and then I want oatmeal made with almond milk, with a poached egg on top, please."

"Raven, that's disgusting."

"Don't knock it till you try it."

Jaxson

I SLIP ON MY sweats and walk towards the kitchen, all the while muttering to my cock about how lucky he is. When I round the corner I see Max, pacing.

"Hey, mate, is there a problem, or are you just nervous about today?" I walk up to him.

"I'm having a problem leaving Jackie here." His hands are balled up; I know he's on the edge.

"Max, she will be totally safe here. The guards will be here, and Mick is staying here, too. Don't forget we also have the panic room. Would it help if I made them stay in there?"

"No, Jax, the only thing that would help is if I was here with her, and that's not going to happen. That fucking island is sounding better and better."

"Good, I'm glad you feel that way. I decided as soon as the baby is born, we are all going there for a couple of months," I inform him. Of course, right at that moment, Raven chooses to enter the room.

"Where exactly are we going, Jax?"

I jump, "I'm not keeping secrets, Raven, I swear I just came to the conclusion that it would be good to go away after the baby comes. The homes on the island will be done, and I think we could all use some relaxation." *God, I hope she's buying this bullshit.*

"I'm hungry, Jax."

She's not saying anything, so maybe I'm not *totally* screwed here. "I'm on it, sweetheart."

Raven

WHILE JAX ATTEMPTS TO make my breakfast, and get himself out of the doghouse, I walk up to Max. He is frozen in place, not knowing what to do with his raging fear, it seems. "Look at me, Max, please." His eyes shoot up to mine. "I understand your fear and I have an idea that might help you. You and Jax have every gadget under the sun. I know there is probably a camera in the panic room. You can watch her from your phone while Jackie and my mom sit in the room with the door open. I'm sure they can play poker with Mick and Sammy to pass the time. You will be able to keep your eyes on them without even being here, would that help?"

He throws his arms around me, and holds me tightly. "Raven, the best thing my brother ever did was marrying you. He really is a lucky bastard."

"Language, Max. Remember, the baby is up, right now."

Max laughs, then releases me so he can go next door to get Jackie.

I head over to the counter and sit down to eat. "Jax, this is wonderful," I say after my first few bites.

He makes a face of disgust at my oatmeal, and then shakes his head. "Are we going to talk about it, or are you going to let me squirm all day?"

"This is what you get when you don't talk to me. You can't just decide what we're doing without even giving me a vote. If you would have asked me, you would have known that it was my intention all along to go to the island, after the baby is born. I need a break, and so does everyone around us. My only concern is timing as it is hurricane season that time of year. Let's table this discussion for now. Right now, I just want to get to the courthouse; the sooner we get this over, the better."

I walk up to him and pull him into my arms. "I love you, Jax, and we will get to the other side of this together."

"Max is right, I really am a lucky bastard." He squeezes back.

WE GET TO THE courthouse without incident, and we're ushered through the back. Jax has an iron grip on me, and Max is glued to my other side. Security is tight and Bo is on high alert. We are led into a room where a well-dressed man is waiting for us, along with four federal agents and Jax's team of attorneys.

"Miss Anderson, please, have a seat."

Jax squeezes my hand tighter, "It's, Mrs. Phillips," I correct him. "Let's get this over with."

"I'm Leo Hage, Federal Prosecutor. I have watched the tape and I've spoken with your attorneys. Before anyone say's anything, I will not subject Mrs. Phillips to viewing it."

I let out the breath I didn't even realize I was holding, my voice barely a whisper. "Thank you, sir."

"I will tell you, up until we got that tape, there really wasn't a strong case against him. Now that his attorney has been given a copy, he is requesting a deal. No matter which way this goes, it will be ugly. He's claiming self-defense in the shooting of Mr. Fleming. He is also claiming that Duke was responsible for your kidnapping, and that he knew nothing about it. I, of course, don't believe any of it, however, it is a he said, she said situation. Duke is not saying a word, even after we made him aware that Vincent is blaming him for everything."

"Mr. Hage."

"Please, call me Leo."

"Leo, Duke shot Marco and Erica; I witnessed that. I also witnessed Vincent, pushing Duke, egging him on. I believe his exact words were, *'You gonna do her, son, or should I?'*

I think justice would be better served if Duke was institutionalized."

"I understand he is your half-brother?"

I hold my hand up, stopping him before he goes any further. "I only found that out right before he murdered two people. I assure you, I have no emotional connection to the man. Clearly, anyone could tell he snapped."

"Well, Mrs. Phillips, I have to look at everything and decide how I'm going to get the most out of this. If Vincent is willing to give up key figures in his drug cartel, then honestly, I might cut a deal."

Jax has my hand in a death grip. "What about my wife's safety, or is that not a concern of yours?"

"Mr. Phillips, we will do all that we can to protect, Mrs. Phillips. I'm not opposed to the Witness Protection Program."

That's the straw that snaps Jax. I see the exact second when the curtain comes crashing down. He jumps up and slams his fist on the table so hard, even Bo jumps.

Jax's attorneys are on him, trying to hold him back. The men in the back of the room come running towards us, and Max, instinctively, throws himself over me. I can't see him; I can only hear him.

"Do you even know what *the fuck* you're talking about? Do you realize she was in witness protection, and your bureau couldn't protect her? The Fucking Director of the FBI couldn't even protect her. We came here today in good faith. I won't tolerate your bullshit, Hage. I didn't get to where I am today by being some kind of fucking pansy arse follower. This is how this is going to play out, and trust me, you'll listen. You've got the fucking tape; use it to put that fucker away. If you don't use it, and you make some sort of deal, I will release it to the media. I will break apart Vincent's business, brick by brick, and anyone associated with him will feel my wrath. I have billions of dollars at my disposal and nothing but time. Time to protect my family. And if you think I won't do everything and anything to protect them, then you better go back and research me again. For all intents and purposes, this fucking meeting is over. My wife and Mr. Fleming will not be coming back here, again. Any other contact will be done through my team of attorneys, whom could keep you tied up for *years.*"

Before anyone can say another word, Jax is ushering us towards the door. Hage reaches out his hand to try and stop us and Bo nearly rips it off. Max whispers something to Bo and just like that, we're heading out the door, never looking back.

The ride back to The Tower is long and quiet. I look over to Max, watching his phone and smiling. "Max, why are you smiling?"

"I'm watching Jackie beat everyone at poker."

I laugh. "Max, she's a math teacher. She's probably counting cards. I'm surprised Sammy is even playing with her. He's never beat her at cards in all the years I've known them."

Max doesn't say a word, he only stares at his phone, smiling.

JAX IS QUIET—TOO quiet. A quiet Jax is not good; it can only mean trouble. I witnessed fierce Jax, for the first time, today. I've seen so many sides to this man, and every side of him brings a different element that I love. It's when he's quiet that I worry the most. .

When the elevator doors open, Jackie flies into Max's arms. His whole body visibly relaxes as he scoops her up and carries her towards his place.

We head into the kitchen, and my mom is making tea. "Raven, come sit down and tell me what happened in court today."

Jax pulls me towards him and kisses my forehead. "I have to go to the office for a little bit. I will be back to pick you up for our doctor appointment. Please stay here and wait for me."

It's not a demand or a request, it's a plea, and it breaks my heart. "I will not leave the house today."

He's holding me tightly and whispers, "I love you, wife of mine."

"More, Jax. I love you more. Now go."

I watch as he and Sammy leave, and then my walls come crashing down. My mom is on me in a New York minute. We sit on the couch and she rocks me in her arms. I can't stop crying; I'm overwhelmed. This emotional roller coaster can't be good for the baby.

"Raven, please tell me what happened."

"Oh, Mom, I don't see an end to all of this." I'm about to tell her everything and then it hits me like a ton of bricks. I don't really know how much she knows about everything. Thank, God, for once in my life, my brain-to-mouth filter was working.

"What are you not telling me? Don't even think of lying. You, my dear, are someone who should never play poker. I'm strong, and I can handle whatever it is you're hiding from me."

"Mom, how about you tell me what you know and then I can sort of fill in the blanks?"

She is stroking my arm and I don't know if it's to sooth her or me. "Well, you know I watched that tape everyday that Vincent held me captive. He raped me, sometimes two or three times a day. I didn't fight him, Raven; I thought he still had you." Her tears fall and my heart is breaking. We're both holding each other; a lifeline in this raging storm. "Finally, Joseph found me. He told me that you were safe. He wanted to go after Vincent, but he realized, right away, how physically and mentally abused I was. He knew I needed medical attention, so he stayed with me. Upon examination and tests, they informed me that I was pregnant. I knew it wasn't Antonio's baby, and I didn't know what to do. I knew that I could have had an abortion, however, that's a personal choice. I decided to have the baby, and give it up for adoption. You have a half-brother, Raven. I'm sorry, but I couldn't keep him. Looking at him only brought up such rage within me. Joseph found him a nice home, and I prayed for him every day in hopes that he would never turn out like Vincent.

"I was overwhelmed by everything, and tried to commit suicide. Joseph found me in time. He made me realize that I needed help, and you needed to be safe. Your safety was everything to me.

"Joseph, found your adoptive family through a friend of his at the bureau. It was all done privately. He had the records sealed and marked classified. He staged the accident in California. And just like that, we were gone. I know that Vincent kidnapped you, Max and Jax rescued you, and Vincent and Max shot each other. I don't know much of anything else, but I figured, when you're ready, you will tell me. And if you don't, it won't change anything for me. You're my daughter, and I would do anything to protect you. You need to tell me what you're holding inside you that's making you so upset. Think of your child, this can't be good for the baby."

"Oh, Mom, I wish it was that easy. Life has been crazy, and I don't see any light at the end of the tunnel."

"Nonsense, there is always hope. Your father always told me that I was the strongest person he'd ever met. *Quiet tenacity* is what he would always say, and I see so much of that in you."

"Do you really think knowing everything will help? For all intents and purposes, Mom, you're like a prisoner, just released from a twenty-year jail term. Life has gone on and left you behind. The world's moral compass has changed, and not always for the better." I take in a deep breath then bring up something I've been curious about. "You stopped talking for twenty years, why?"

"Raven, dear, the world will always have both good and bad. It's about finding a balance we can live with. If we make positive changes in our own little circle, then it becomes like a splinter in a glass. I kept up with the changes in the world. I read the papers daily, and I know a lot of bad things have happened. I stopped talking because my heart was broken. I lost the love of my life. I gave both my children away to save them, one I never knew. I know you have so many questions and so many years to make up for. I promise you I won't break. Please, tell me what has you walking on egg shells around me."

I take a deep breath and tell her everything. I leave nothing out from my first meeting with Jax, to all the craziness that got us here today. I tell her about my life with my adoptive parents, and all about Marco. I even tell her about Duke. She sits in silence as if she's absorbing every word I say, until I tell her about the tape that my father made. She gasps, and then she begins to cry. I pull her into my arms and rock her like a mom cradling a child.

"Raven, have you watched the tape?"

"No, I don't think I'm ready to do that yet."

"Why not?"

"Fear, I think. My whole life, I put my father on a pedestal, my knight in shining armor. I don't want anything to happen that would make him fall off that pedestal."

"Oh, Raven, nothing ever will. When you're ready, if you want, I will watch it with you."

"There is also one that he left for you."

She begins to shake, "Oh, I need to see it right now, please."

"Are you sure you're ready for this?"

"I've existed for twenty years without hearing my beautiful Antonio's voice, I don't want to wait a second longer. The only images I've had playing over and over again were Antonio getting shot, and you, terrified. This could erase all of that. Of course, I'm ready."

I take her into Jax's office and sit her down with the laptop. "Jax's, tech guy, Tony, put them on a drive for us. I'll leave you alone, just click play."

I close the door and head towards the kitchen. I realize I'm really hungry. *Damn I wish I knew how to cook.* I promised Jax I wouldn't leave, and I don't know if ordering a pizza is a safe thing to do. What if someone tries to poison us, or the delivery person works for Vincent. Oh God, now I'm getting paranoid. I'm not about to bother Jackie and Max, not after they finally have some alone time. I'm just about ready to scream when the elevator doors open, and in walks Mick with pizza.

"Mick, how did you know I was hungry?"

"I didn't, but Jax said you should be hungry right about now. I figured I would stop and get your favorite pizza."

"Mick, do you know how wonderful you are?"

"Raven, its just pizza."

"No, Mick, it's more than that. Come and join me."

"Where's your mom? Jax said she was here."

"Don't panic, she's in the office watching something on the computer." His whole body relaxes. Everyone is on high alert, and I feel so bad about it.

"I'm just going to check on her, I'll be right back."

When I open the office door my mom is crying and hugging the laptop. "Mom, what can I do to help you?"

"Oh, Raven, you don't even realize what you've done for me. For the last twenty years, the last image I have of my Antonio was of him getting shot, and Vincent laughing. You have replaced that for me with my beautiful loving husband. I could never thank you enough for that."

"Mick brought pizza, would you like to join us?"

"No, I need some time alone. Can you make my apologies, please."

"Of course."

I head back inside to eat and I think, maybe it was a good thing that I showed her the recording.

"Raven, please sit and eat something. Is Rose okay?"

"Yes, Mick, she's is going to have a nap before we have to leave for the doctor. It's been a very emotional day for all of us."

We sit, eating our pizza and enjoying the rare quiet moment.

Rose

RAVEN GIVING ME THIS video is a gift that I will treasure for the rest of my life. I want to watch it over and over again. Maybe I can erase Vincent from my head, once and for all. I stare at Antonio's face on the screen and press play again.

"Gabriella, I'm so sorry, baby. The evil that I tried to shield you and Cara from has finally caught up to us. None of this was your fault, baby. He was too far-gone for you to save. I'm sorry that Cara had to witness any of this. I will love you beyond this world. My life may be short, but I've found what some men never do. You're my happily ever after, Gabby. Take good care of our Cara. I know it will be hard for you, but Joseph will always be there for you both. I love you, heart and soul, my beautiful angel."

I pause it, I can't breathe. Oh Antonio, how could things have gotten so messed up? His voice after all these years is still too raw for my heart to handle. I take a few breaths and hit play again.

"Cara will need you close after all of this. Hold her tight, and love her with all you've got. I will watch over you both. Always remember what I told you that day on the beach, when I asked you to marry me. My heart, my soul, my life is yours.

I love you, Gabby."

I love you Antonio, and I will be strong for our Cara.

Jaxson

SAMMY AND I GET to the office. I'm in a foul mood. I'm not here five minutes and Mrs. Osla is on me for not properly introducing her to Sammy. I swear she is my mum on steroids. "I would be more than happy to introduce you, if you could give me a second, please." I realize I snapped at her and I quickly apologize, and move on to more important matters.

"First order of business, what is going on with the buildings on the island?"

"Well, it seems they will be ready ahead of schedule, especially when I told them I was going to personally come down to oversee the progress."

God, I love this woman. She could put fear in the Devil himself.

"Is what happened in court today making you this way, or is it something you did that you got into trouble for?"

I'm rubbing my temples and growling. "Both."

"Will you ever learn? Call your mum before you get into trouble with her, too."

"Samuel, it's very nice to meet you." And just like that, she's out the door.

"Wow, Jax, where did you find her?"

"Max found her after the whole Duke thing. I wanted someone different, and boy is she ever."

"She's different all right; kind of hard to understand."

"Yeah, you'll get used to it. Sammy, I don't pull punches and I don't sugarcoat anything. I know you're still MI6. I understand the government wants Gerhard protected, no matter what. What I don't tolerate is secrets. No matter what, I need complete honesty. Jackie is staying here with Max, forever. He's not going out in the field ever again. I can't handle him out there, and right now, it's all about me. Before you say anything about that," I put my hand up. "Max is the one who suggested that he take more of a behind the scenes roll. I need a replacement for him, but to come on board here, you would have to give up your day job. Around here, it's one-hundred percent or nothing. I'll give you a tour, and then you think about it. Once the baby comes, I'm taking everyone to the island. We're going in complete lock down, until this cluster fuck is over with."

"Are you done, Jax? Can I get a word in?"

"Sorry, I know I bulldoze, as Raven calls it, but that's me."

"I knew about the island, and I actually think it would be a great idea. It will give us some breathing space. I would like to see more of what goes on here behind the scenes."

"I'll put you with Tony; he is Max's right-hand man and knows everything. Let's go, I'll give you a quick tour and then introduce you before I have to call my mum. We are a very close family. If you decide to come on board, be aware my mum . . . She's a lion in sheep's clothing."

I drop Sammy off with Tony, and they seem to hit it off rather quickly. . I head back to my office to call mum and find my attorney, waiting. This can't be good. Mrs. Osla is in a tizzy.

"Mrs. Osla, it's okay."

I lead him into my office. "Mathew, what's going on?"

"Who was that, Jax?"

"My new secretary. Trust me, you don't want to ever get on her bad side." I shake my head.

"Well, I met privately with Hage, after you left there today. They don't take threats lightly. However, I did help them see the light."

"Look, Mathew, I'm not letting any of my family anywhere near these animals. We are all leaving right after the baby is born. I have an island off the coast of Belize where we'll be staying for a few months. After that, if this is not under control, then who knows? I might start looking at other countries. Nothing and no one will stand in the way of my families' safety."

"I get it, Jax, but you need to calm down. Let me be your voice, that's what you're paying me for. I will fight any deal they offer that we all don't agree upon. They were surprised to find out you have a copy of the tape. They were trying to order you to surrender it, however, I squashed that. Make sure it's locked up and not on the premises. Keep duplicate copies at different locations; but you never heard that from me."

"What about Rose? No one but us knows she's alive, can we keep it that way?"

"I buried her name change paperwork very deep. I'm surprised Joseph didn't do it when he moved her to the clinic. I understand she was dead to the world, but that could have been a disaster for everyone."

"All answers died with him. I need to get going, Raven has a doctor appointment. If you need anything else, I can have Mrs. Osla help you."

"No thanks, Jax, I'm no fool."

As we head out to the elevators, Mrs. Osla is quick to remind me again to call my mum. "Mathew, stop laughing or I will have her work for you!"

Jaxson

ON MY WAY HOME, I call mum to check in. "Hi, Mum, how are you?"

"Jaxson, what do you mean how am I? I'm worried. You went to court today and never called me. I had to find out second hand what happened."

Do I even want to know how she found out? "Mum, whom have you been talking to?"

"Never mind that; how is Raven?"

"She's trying to keep it together. I'm on my way now to pick her up for her doctor appointment."

"Okay, well, let me know what happens. Bella is making a family dinner tomorrow, make sure everyone shows."

"Mum, is everything okay? Am I in trouble?"

"Everything is fine, and you're not in trouble. We just need some normalcy. Bring Mick; I like him."

Well, at least someone else, other than Max and me, is on her radar. "Okay, Mum, will do. Love you."

She's quiet for a minute. "Love you more, son."

We pull up to The Tower, and I see the woman that has been trying to get to my wife—Annabelle. I step out of the car and my detail surrounds me.

"I want to talk to her."

"Sir, please do not engage her. Go inside. It's for your own safety."

My guard presses something on my bracelet and within seconds, all hell breaks loose. Guns are drawn and pointed towards her and the two men with her. Max comes flying out of the building with his gun drawn, yelling for the detail to get me inside.

"Max, I'm not leaving you here."

"Jax, for the love of God, do what you're told and get inside now!"

"Annabelle, I suggest you take your men and leave here now, and never come back. If you ever come back here, or anywhere near this family, it will not end peacefully. Leave now before your family has to decide on an open or closed casket!"

In seconds, she's gone and Max is back inside. Only then, I realize he's barefoot and half dressed. "Max, what the hell? I wanted to talk to her."

"There is no reason to talk to her. Mathew issued a restraining order today. If you engage her then it opens a can of worms we don't want opened."

"How the hell did you get down here so fast?"

"Your bracelet was activated."

"That explains your state of attire."

"Don't be a wise arse, I was having a wonderful time and you cut that short. I will get even with you, mate."

When we get upstairs, I realize no one is around. "Where is everyone?"

"They're in the panic room. I didn't know what was going on, so I didn't want them out here."

Max radios the guards to let them know we're coming in. *Will this nightmare ever end?*

Raven runs into my arms. "I'm okay, sweetheart."

"Jax, what the hell happened?"

"Annabelle tried to pay a visit, nothing to worry about. Mathew got a restraining order issued today. We need to get going to the doctor."

"Jax, I would like to go with you to the doctor, but only if you think it's safe," Rose walks up to us.

"Rose, I would like you too, but right now, I don't think it's a good idea. I hope you understand that I need to keep your presence unknown."

"I do. Remember to tell the doctor what I told you about quick deliveries."

Raven

WHEN WE GET CHECKED in, the nurse weighs me. Jax is excited to see I've gained weight. "So have you decided what type of birth you're having?"

Jax's grip gets tighter, and I know the pressure is getting to him, Hell—it's getting to all off us.

"We are going for a natural birth, in the hospital."

I whisper, "Relax, Jax, please. Everything will be okay."

Doctor Leanne comes in, and Jax seems to relax a little. "Raven, I hear congratulations are in order. The nurse will update your name change and marital status with the hospital for you. Have you scheduled Lamaze classes yet?"

"Jax, will be scheduling someone to come to the house for the classes. I do have some new information about my family history. It seems my mother and grandmother both had quick, early deliveries."

"How quick and how early?"

"Both a couple of weeks early. As far as quickly, apparently, my mom delivered me start to finish in an hour and a half."

"Okay, I think we are moving along schedule here, so I'm not concerned. You have put on weight, so I'm happy about that. Your blood pressure is a little high, but I know you've been under a lot of stress. I would like you to watch your caffeine and salt intake.

The best thing you can do for the last trimester is to enjoy the change. Relax, prepare for the baby, and concentrate on you because once the baby gets here then everything changes."

Doctor Leanne is watching Jax, and I think she's worried about him. "Jax, get those classes scheduled soon, so that you can both feel comfortable. The nurse will give you a list of everything you need to have done before your next appointment."

Just like that, she's done, and we're left alone. Jax is quiet, too quiet. "Jax, what's the matter?"

He pulls me into his arms so tightly. "I want to go home and be alone with you. I need you, Raven."

I pull away and look into his eyes. I can sense the pressure is getting to him and it breaks my heart. He helps me get dressed and we get everything we need from the nurse. I need to get him home and have some alone time with him.

Chapter Eighteen

Sammy

TONY SHOWED ME ALL around Raiders and it's quite impressive. Jax is so much more then he lets on. Tony hedged on giving me any details, though; typical tech guy. I checked in with Jackie's detail and she is in Max's flat. I decide to head up to Jackie's, flat where I will have some privacy.

First order of business, I need to call Gerhard and bring him up to speed on Vincent. I might as well get this over with. I know he's going to flip when I tell him, but better me than Jackie.

"Sammy, what's going on with my daughter?" His voice loud, forcing me to pull the phone away from my ear a bit.

"Sir, she is safe, and under tight guard right now. I think Maxwell is not going anywhere, anytime soon, sir."

"This is not the news I wanted to hear. Does she know about his past?"

"Yes, she knows everything. He's a good man, sir."

"So now you're a champion for Maxwell?"

"No, I'm a champion for Jackie."

"What is going on with Vincent?"

"Sir, there is a good chance he will get a deal. There is a video of him killing Antonio." I pause, giving him a chance to let the information sink in.

"That should at least get him locked away for life. What happened in court today?"

"Jax ripped the Feds apart. He made all kinds of threats, especially when they offered protection for Raven."

"I'm not leaving my daughter's protection in the hands of the feds. Maxwell has put a huge target on my daughters back. So, what's our next move?" His voice is getting louder and I'm not sure how he will react to the rest of the information.

"Sir, Jax purchased an island off the coast of Belize. He thinks after the baby comes he can move everyone down there, Jackie included. Might not be such a bad idea. It will give us some breathing room."

"Sammy, Vincent needs to be dealt with, and a message sent to all the families."

"I understand, sir, I do. Timing is everything right now."

"How is Raven holding up through all of this?"

"You know Raven, she's a survivor; tough and strong."

"Any chance I can get everyone to come back here? There is plenty of room at the compound."

"Sir, Jackie would never go for it."

"Yeah, I know. Why did my daughter have to be so much like me?"

"Sir, before you go, there's something else I need to discuss with you. Maxwell is thinking of semi-retirement, more of a behind the scenes role. Jax asked me to take over for Maxwell."

Gerhard is really quiet, almost too quiet. "Sir, you there?"

"Yes, Sammy, I heard you. He's awfully young to retire."

"Well, he owns a percentage of Raiders, and from what I saw today, money is not a problem. Jax doesn't want Max out in the field anymore. This could be good for Jackie. Jax is also starting a private school for the employees at Raiders. He wants Raven and Jackie to head it up."

"Sounds like Jax is trying to tighten his ring around everyone. If my daughter is going to stay in New York, then I want you there. If you need to work for him, so be it. Make sure he is aware that where Jackie goes, you go; that's non-negotiable. Let me know when the Vincent situation is handled."

I hang up and now I need to figure out what direction I should go with Vincent. He has political pull and street muscle behind him. It would have been so much easier if Max had killed the bastard. First things first, I need to check in with the guard I have on Annabelle. Then, put a few more key pieces in place.

Hage

I KEEP WATCHING THIS video over and over. I know that no matter which way I go with this, someone will be on the losing end of the stick. If I cut the bastard the deal he wants, I will get some top-level scum off the streets, but at what price? What a cluster fuck this is becoming. It would have been a lot easier if Maxwell had killed Vincent. Maybe leaking the tape and letting the world see the animal he really is would be the best way to handle this. As I hit play again, my intercom buzzes.

"Mr. Hage, Vincent's sister is here with their lawyer, Mr. Deveno, demanding to see her brother."

Can this day get any worse? "Send them in."

Annabelle Giaconna steps into my office with Mr. Deveno. I can't stop myself from staring at her; she is beautiful. I quickly remind myself she is a Giaconna, and as ruthless as her brother.

She places her hands on my desk and leans towards me. "I want to see my brother, and I'm not leaving until I do," she demands.

"Which brother do you want to see, Ms. Giaconna? Your brother Vincent, in prison, or your brother Antonio, being murdered?"

"Do you think you can scare me, Mr. Hage? I don't believe that tape is real. Family is everything to Vincent. He would have never killed Antonio."

"Mr. Deveno, how about telling your client the truth. The tape has been authenticated, Ms. Giaconna." I flip my screen around and hit play. "Enjoy the show, ma'am."

I watch as she stares at the screen in silence. It has to have some effect on her. Watching her niece being scared and brutalized by that animal, and seeing Vincent gun down Antonio, all the while laughing about it.

"Hage, that's enough. You made your point, but it won't change. We're here to see Vincent and Duke." Deveno snaps.

Everyone has rights, even that piece of shit Vincent. "Fine, now that he's awake. Vincent has been moved to isolation. You have thirty minutes, so make it good. He's being held at Attica. One of New York's toughest maximum security prisons, so I hope you enjoy your ride upstate."

They leave just as quickly as the information shoots out of my mouth. And now, I'm back to figuring out what to do with this giant cluster fuck that's been dropped in my lap.

Annabelle

ATTICA: WHAT A GOD forsaken place this is. "Deveno, where is Duke being held?"

"He is being held at Sing Sing. The Feds wanted them kept separately."

I haven't seen my brother since they transferred him here. I have not been allowed to meet my nephew. After watching that tape, I hope Vincent has a plan.

"Annabelle, we only have thirty minutes. We have to see him together. I have stuff to discuss with him about the case. You know how crazy he can be, so don't push him. I'm also trying to get permission for you to see Duke." Deveno's jabbering pulls me out of my fog.

This whole process has been a giant *hurry up and wait.* If I ran my business like this, I'd get nowhere. Finally, he walks in. *Jesus, what the fuck are they doing to him in here?*

"Vincent, if you've got to be in here, the least you can do is take care of yourself. You look like shit."

"Well, hello to you too, Deveno. I'm in a tiny room for twenty-three hours a day, maybe you should shut the fuck up and try it."

I can't believe how much he's aged in the past few months. "Vincent, I saw the tape."

"So?"

"You killed Antonio. You swore to me that you didn't. It's all there, in black and white. How could you lie to me, of all people? Do you have a plan? What about Duke . . . have you figured out what to do about him?"

"Anna, you need to get Duke to go along with everything I told the Feds. If he's a true Giaconna, he will do this for his father."

"I haven't been allowed to see him, so how am I supposed to do that? I tried a couple of times to talk to Cara, but Jax's men were all over me. Then today, I was served with a restraining order. That guy is over the top crazy, Vincent."

"Deveno, what the fuck am I paying you for if you can't even get her in to see Duke?"

"Vince, I'm working on it. Once the Feds got the tape, everything went into lockdown. I should be able to get her in today or tomorrow, at the latest. Have you thought about a deal?"

"I'm not sure what I want to do yet. Why did this tape surface now? Why was that prick, Joseph, hiding the tape? I mean he had it and could have put the screws to me twenty years ago. What was he trying to hide? Anna, did you get a look at Cara?"

"Only from a distance. I told you, Jax's men were all over me. She looks just like Antonio, except for her eyes."

"She acts like him, too. She kept trying to help Duke the whole time we were in Sicily; filling his head with nonsense. If Duke had grown up under my roof, he wouldn't be a fucking pansy-ass pussy. Just another thing to thank that bastard, Joseph, for."

"I won't be able to get anywhere near Cara again, Vince."

"Anna, what I really want is that fucker, Max's head, on a silver platter."

"I understand, but for now, let's concentrate on getting you out of here."

"Deveno, what kind of deal do you think they will offer?"

"After today, I'm not sure that they will offer any kind of deal. Apparently, Mr. Phillips has a lot of power in all the right places. He made some powerful threats today. It seems that the Feds are taking him pretty seriously."

"What kind of threats did he make?"

"My source said, Phillips, has a copy of the tape, and he will release it to all the families and the press. He will say you've made a deal to snitch, basically putting the final nail in your coffin.

Apparently, the only thing he will settle for, is you getting life with no chance of parole."

"That prick thinks because he has money, he can buy anything! Fuck that, I have more power than he could ever imagine. The difference is, I'm not afraid to use it."

"I wouldn't be too quick to count this guy out, Vince. He has a lot of power, and not just in this country."

"Couldn't have been too much power if I was able to get my hands on Cara."

"Do I need to remind you he was also able to find you, when no one else could? He infiltrated the entire United States and European banking system to do it. Does that sound like someone you should dismiss like a gnat?"

"Put some feelers out and see what they're willing to offer. Find out more about Phillips and that fucker, Max. Make sure you get back to me quickly. I'm paying you enough money, that's for sure. Now I want a few minutes alone with Anna."

Deveno gets up to leave, and I know to keep quiet until he is gone.

"Anna, we don't have much time left. Deveno is only as good as the money he's paid. He'd sell out to the highest bidder. Don't trust him."

"Then why are you using him?"

"I know what he's capable of. I want everything you can find out about Max. I need to know his weakness; everyone has one. The same goes for Phillips. Get your ass in to see Duke, and convince him to do the time for me. Find out what the fuck Joseph was hiding. Find out how many tapes this Phillips guy has and then get back here in a couple of days. I will get you a list of favors owed to me from other countries without US extradition. Now, go."

"How the hell do you expect me to do all of this, in only a couple of days? I know you want revenge, Vince. I get it. However, don't you think it would be time better spent to figure out how to get out of this mess and spend less time on revenge?"

"Anna, let me worry about that. Now, go!" Just like that, I'm dismissed. He wants all of this in a couple of days . . . is he fucking kidding me? As I get outside, I see Deveno on the phone, waving me over.

"Okay, got it. We're on our way."

"The permission for us to see Duke just came through. We are going to head over to Sing Sing now."

Could this day get any worse? "Now? I have some stuff to handle for Vincent. Can't we go later?"

"Look, we're up here and we're going, so deal with it. What else did Vince want?"

"Private family stuff that doesn't concern his case."

"If that's the way you and Vince want to play it, Annabelle, it's fine by me. I have work to do. If you need anything, tell the driver."

We get in the car and begin the long ride to Sing Sing in total silence.

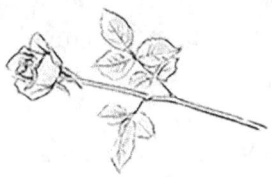

WE PULL UP TO Sing Sing, and it looks like another hellhole. I'm finally going to meet my nephew today. I have to convince him to take the fall for Vincent, and I don't even know him. Security is very tight as we are ushered into a tiny dismal room. Just like the Attica, the table and chairs are bolted to the floor. I have no clue what to expect, but then he walks in and I'm floored. His dark hair and chiseled good looks were not at all what I was expecting. *Jesus,* he's so young. He seems lost and dazed.

"Hello, Mr. Jensen, I'm your attorney, Mr. Deveno, and this is your Aunt Annabelle. How are you holding up in here?"

"Duke, just call me Duke. How do you think I'm doing?"

"Duke, I met with Vincent earlier and there is a lot we need to go over. Vincent said you killed Erica and Marco, right before you kidnapped your sister."

"I snapped and shot both of them, but I never kidnapped Raven. So, it's true, then? This is the way he's going to spin this bullshit?"

"Look, son, we need to get the story straight and get the best possible deal for everyone involved."

Duke

THIS GUY IS AN asshole if he thinks I'm buying his line of shit. "Look, Mr. Deveno, you work for my father and you're trying to get *him* the best possible deal. Looks like I need a new attorney."

"Duke, calm down, please, and let me talk. You have more options than Vincent does. This is your first offense, and there are extenuating circumstances. Deveno can work it to your advantage—plus—we have unlimited resources. If you get another attorney, you won't have that. Please give Deveno a chance to see what he can do before you dismiss him," Aunt Annabelle tries to convince me. Funny I've never even met this woman before today, and yet she thinks I'm going to do whatever the fuck she wants.

"Our time here is short, kid, so what's it going to be? Are you going to listen to your aunt or do I walk?"

At this point, I really have nothing to lose. "Fine, for now I will listen, but at any point, if I don't like the way things are going, then all bets are off."

"Great, I'll be in touch over the next couple of days. Keep your mouth shut and let me work your case. I'll give you some private time with Annabelle." Deveno gets up and leaves.

I size up Annabelle—she wants something, everyone usually does. "So, Aunt Annabelle, what is it that you want from me?"

"What makes you think I want something? Maybe I want to find out who you are."

"Look, since I found my family, I've had nothing but trouble. I've had a lot to absorb in the past six months. I'm not looking for a warm, fuzzy family that television shows are made of; I'm looking to survive this nightmare. So, I'll ask you one more time, what is it that you want from me?"

"What did Cara tell you when you were in Italy? Did she talk to you about Joseph?"

And there it is . . . she's here to fish for information. I don't know what she thinks I could possibly tell her. "She told me who I was and that I was the product of rape. She told me a little bit about our mother.

She gave me Gabriella's diary to read. Do you know what it was like to read about your father raping and beating your mother over and over again? Do you know how it feels to be considered the spawn of Satan? Raven never talked about Joseph or anyone, for that matter. Even if I get to the other side of this, I have no one—nothing."

"You have Vincent and me; you have a family now."

"Well, Aunt Annabelle, isn't that encouraging. Time's up, I've gotta go." I get up and give the corrections officer a nod of my head to let him know that I'm ready. He opens the door for me and I head out without hearing another word from my *loving* aunt.

Raven

AFTER THE RIDE HOME in silence, Jax and I are greeted by my mother as soon as we get off the elevator. "Mom, is everything okay?"

"Everything is fine, I was worried about you. What did the doctor say?" she asks after hugging me, her eyes on Jax.

"Everything is good. I told her about the family history and she was happy that I gained weight. Everything is going according to schedule."

"Jax, are you okay?" she asks him.

"I'm fine, Rose, just tired. I'm going to lay down for a bit, excuse me."

Before I can say anything my mom grasps my upper arms gently. "Go be with him, Raven. I think the pressure is getting to him."

I head into the bedroom, but he's not there. I hear the shower running. *That sounds really good right now.* I head into the bathroom and find him leaning against the shower wall, the water cascading down his body. I step in and notice his eyes closed and he's not moving.

" Jax, what's wrong?" I grab onto his shoulders.

"I'm very overwhelmed right now," he says softly, his eyes still closed.

"Damn it, Jax, talk to me! I know it's more than that."

He takes in a deep breath. "I'm beginning to doubt my decision to let Jackie come back here. Vincent is going to want to hurt Max in the worst possible way. Going after Jackie would do it. She is so stubborn; I know she'll never go for Max sending her back to her parent's compound."

"Jax, maybe we should go to the island now. We could all use an extended vacation . . . just until the Feds get everything sorted."

"Raven, have you forgotten something? You're pregnant?"

"Oh."

"Yeah, *oh.*"

"Jax, could I have a doctor on the island to deliver the baby?"

He's stroking his chin, which means he's either plotting or processing.

"I asked Sammy to join the company. I don't want Max in the field ever again."

"What did Max say about that?"

"It was his suggestion to bring Sammy on board. Max wants a more behind the scenes approach. He wants to spend more time with Jackie. Jackie is interested in heading up the school we talked about."

"Are you planning out everyone's life again? I warned you about that."

"I know, Raven. I'm not telling everyone what they should do. I'm practicing my new found negotiating skills with everyone."

I know how that goes. "What about me, what am I supposed to do?"

"I'm going to be real honest with you. I would like for you to be a stay at home mum. It was not something that my mum could do for Bella and me, and I would love to give that gift to our child. You could also use the time to get to know your mum better."

"You don't have to sell me on it, Jax. I want to be there for our child. Those years only come once, there is no second chance."

"Wife, have I told you lately that I'm madly in love with you?"

"No, my wonderful husband, you haven't."

"Well, sweetheart, I am, and I think I need to have my way with you.

In one fell swoop, he scoops me up and steps out of the shower. He pulls the towels off the warmers and wraps us in them as he heads towards the bedroom.

"Oh, my beautiful wife, I want to make slow passionate love to you for hours. Relax and let me take you to our *happy place.*" He places me in the center of the bed and slowly crawls between my legs. "I want to taste you and devour you."

He locks his arms around my legs, keeping me spread wide for him. He's nipping the inside of my thighs followed by a lick and a kiss. *Oh my God what he can do with that tongue; it should be illegal.* When he gets to the top he stops and switches to the other leg. When he finally gets to the center, he unleashes that tongue. Round and round, in and out. Swipe, nibble, lick, and kiss.

"Jax, I can't hold it . . . oh good God, Jax." My hands are fisting his hair and my hips are going crazy. I'm riding a wave of pleasure. Just as I begin to catch my breath, he enters me . . . every rock-hard, solid inch of him. My eyes fly open and lock onto his—violet to blues.

"Sweetheart, all that I am, and all that I'll ever be is because of you."

He pulls back and slowly enters me again. He's there but yet he's fighting it.

"Don't fight it Jax, let it go."

"No—I want more. I want it to last forever."

I do the one thing I know that will tip him over the edge—I clench. He throws his head back and begins to come, over and over again. "Oh, fuck all that is holy, Raven!"

Gently, he turns us so I'm on top. "Ride me down slowly, please."

Pacing myself, I glide up and down, watching a calm take over him. I lean down and kiss him softly.

"You don't play fair, sweetheart."

"Hmm . . . I never said I would."

"Well, my beautiful wife, neither did I."

As she's riding me down I'm pushing my hips up to meet hers, slamming into her clitoris. I lean up and take one of her nipples into my mouth, pulling and nipping. They are so sensitive to my touch. I gently roll her onto her back and I pull out of her. She whimpers at the loss of my cock, fuck it's so hot to watch. "I know what you want but not like this, baby."

I turn her and pull her up on her knees. "Hold onto the headboard." I command while taking my cock and spreading my wetness from front to back. I'm ready to take her again. "Push out, come on, baby, let me in."

I push through that barrier; she's so tight and so warm. I'm holding the base of my cock; prolonging my explosion. I take a few breaths and begin to move, slowly at first.

"God, Raven, you're so tight and warm."

"Faster, Jax, please . . . Oh, God . . . harder please, I won't break!"

I give her what she wants, what she needs. Taking her harder with each push. I reach around and glide my fingers in and out of her. "Raven, fuck I'm going, fall with me, *please.*"

I give her all I've got and she takes it, screaming my name with her release. I'm still throbbing deep inside of her. My legs and arms are quivering; it's never enough with her. I will always need more. I gently pull out of her and she rolls onto her side. Her eyes finally open and they are filled with tears. "Hey, beautiful, you okay?"

"Jax, that was so intense. I don't know what came over me, I was so demanding. Oh my God, I gave you a hickie! I'm so embarrassed." Her hands cover her face.

I look down at my chest, and sure enough, she gave my nipple a hickie. "Well, that's interesting. I love intense and it makes me even wilder when you get all demanding. Sweetheart, never be embarrassed for wanting more. You love me and you show it."

"I do love you, Jax." She smiles up at me.

"I love you more, baby. Let's go shower, and then I think I want to talk to Jackie."

"Have you figured out what you're going to say?"

"She's a very smart woman. I'm going to put all the facts out to her and see if she comes to the right conclusion."

"Don't you mean your conclusion?"

"Yep, the right conclusion."

Vulnerable Jax, is gone, and my take-charge husband is back . . . *poor Jackie.*

Jackie

IT'S BEEN ANOTHER CRAZY day. I'm glad Max is okay. There is a calm when I'm curled up into his side. He's finally asleep; today has taken a toll on him. He's getting better at letting me in, but I know it will take time. I very rarely get to watch him sleep, and I notice, even though he's sleeping, there is a worried look across his brow. As I stroke him there, he visibly relaxes. I tilt my head in and kiss one of his scars. He has so many both inside and out; my heart breaks for him. I trail my fingertips over his V. God he is so beautiful; imperfectly perfect. I lean in and kiss his chest very softly. I don't think I can ever get enough of this man.

"Hmm . . . I love to wake up from a nap like this, baby."

"I'm sorry. I didn't mean to disturb your sleep."

He pulls me on top of him. "Never be sorry for this. This is where I've finally found peace."

I lean down and kiss his soft lips. God, what this man does to me. "I'm worried about you, Max. You need to get more rest, and a lot less stress."

"What I need, is more of you, babe, just you."

"Then, more you shall have." I slowly work my way down his body. Kissing my way down his happy trail very slowly, I begin stroking his cock. I lean down and kiss the tip.

"Oh, baby, take me deep, please."

I take him in my mouth, swirling my tongue around as I go down. This is so new for me, but with Max, it's so comfortable. He lifts his head and watches me, chewing on his bottom lip as he fists his hands. He is *literally* coming undone, and it's all because of me. It's such a beautiful high, a high I've only known with him. He takes a hold of my shoulders and tries stopping me. I'm so lost in my ability to give him such pleasure. I don't want to stop.

"Jackie, if you don't stop now, I'm going to lose what little control I have left."

I'm not letting go. I want to know what it's like to take him all the way. I work my way down again as I'm pumping his cock. I take his sac and work it slowly and firmly. That does it for him. His head flies back and his hips are going wild. He's yelling my name as he explodes with such a powerful force. It's feels endless. I wasn't sure what to expect but then knowing that I can take him like this is such a heady feeling. He pulls me off of him and into his arms.

"Oh, Jackie, I'm never letting you go, baby."

"Max, we will get to the other side of this, I promise."

He strokes my back, carelessly. "Baby, what do you know about Belize?"

"I know about the island. Stop acting like Jax." I lift my head.

"I'm just thinking, after Raven has the baby, it would be good for all of us to go down for a break."

"Max, you have a *tell.* Everyone has one but yours is obvious, my love. Don't play poker."

"I'm really worried, Jackie. Why the fuck didn't that bastard die? There's an even bigger target on your back now. I was thinking maybe you should go to your parents' compound, just until the dust settles."

I can feel my body tighten as soon as he finishes his thought.

"Jackie?"

"I'm counting, Maxwell Fleming."

Maxwell

SHIT COUNTING *AND* FULL name. "How much trouble am I in?"

She climbs off of me and out of bed. She is standing before me, totally naked. That beautiful mane of golden hair and those legs—oh, dear God—those fucking legs are going to be the death of me. She's got one hand on her hip, and she has fire in her eyes. Fuck it all, I can explode right now from the sight of her.

"Let me tell you something, mister, I did not turn my life upside down for nothing. I will not be banished to the compound like I'm a child again. I knew the risk coming back here, and yet, here I stand. You will never ever order me to leave, and you will never decide for me what I should or should not be doing. I am an adult. I know what I want, and whom I want to be with. Do you understand?"

I've never seen this side of her, and fuck it all, she's really hot.

"Well, Max, if you have anything to say, you better say it now."

"Wow."

"That's it, wow?"

"Come here, baby." I lift her into my arms and place her in the middle of the bed. I begin kissing my way up those fucking legs, and I think I'm going to die. They seem endless as I work my lips gently up one side and down the other. There is a spot right behind her knee that I love to kiss, knowing every time I do, she moans. "I'm so fucking turned on right now, I'm going to take you every way I can . . . everywhere I can and when I'm done, I'm going to start all over. I want you screaming my name over and over again."

I reach over to the nightstand and grab a condom. Getting it on as quick as possible, knowing I need to be inside her now. I enter her very slowly and when I'm all the way in, I stop. I lean down and latch onto her nipple. Grating it with my teeth. "Oh God . . . more, Max . . . please."

I latch onto the other one as I slowly rock my hips up and down. Dragging myself across her clitoris with just enough pressure to make her quiver. I pull out and then slam into her again. I've got my arms locked around those fucking legs, and I'm not letting go. I feel it; dear God above, the wave that is coming over my body is going to fucking kill me. I'm looking down at her and she looks like an angel. I feel like I'm looking down upon the whole scene . . . everything, moving in slow motion. Her nails are digging into my arse, and she's screaming.

I rear back and slam into her, over and over again. "Oh holy hell, Jackie!" I explode with such a force and that's when it happened. Her eyes fly open and she knows it too. An explosion so forceful, the condom broke. The two of us are stunned. Neither of us knowing what to say or do.

"Jackie, it will be okay. Chances are, nothing happened. Look, we had so much sex the past few days, maybe they didn't really have time to re-group." I can't believe I just said that to her. She's too quiet. "Baby, talk to me, please."

"Max, I'm only twenty-five and no way am I ready for parenthood. We need to shower and then I need to get to the drugstore for the morning after pill."

I'm holding and kissing her, trying to calm my racing heart. "You go shower first, I'll be just a minute."

As I watch her walk away, I realize the broken pieces of my heart are coming back together. I want the whole deal with her, now I need to make her see the light.

Chapter Nineteen

Raven

WE HEAD NEXT DOOR to Max's place. Max let's us in and I see Jackie sitting in the living room, mindlessly flipping through the television channels. She waves at Jax, but she never looks up from the television. She seems really quiet. I know my friend and something is off. Before I can suggest that we have some girl time, Max takes Jax into his office for Raiders business. Jackie gets up and slips into the kitchen. I follow her, thinking maybe she wants to talk to me in private. She begins to put together a fruit and cheese plate.

"Jackie, how about you tell me what's going on with you."

"Oh, Raven, the condom broke!"

Okay, not what I was expecting to come out of her mouth.

"What did you do?"

"Really, what did I do? What do you think I did? I completely freaked out, that's what I did. I'm not ready for parenthood. Heck, I don't even know if that's on my radar. I made him take me to the store for the morning after pill. Condoms are supposed to have a low breakage rate, between 0.4 and 2.3 percent if used and stored properly."

"How many times have you read the box, Jackie?"

"A million times."

"Well let's stop worrying about how it went wrong, you can't change what happened. You took the morning after pill; maybe you will be fine. I do think that you should follow up with the doctor tomorrow, just to be on the safe side. Do you want me to call Dr. Leanne? I'm sure she will see you on short notice."

"Would you go with me? I don't want to go with Max."

"Of course I will go with you. Why don't you want to go with Max? You've been giving yourself to this man twenty-four seven. He is an equal partner in this and you need to realize that. You are both responsible adults, Jackie."

"This is all very new for me, Raven. I want to go on some sort of birth control. I'm not leaving anything to chance. And . . . you're right; Max should be a part of this."

"Good, it's your body, Jackie. You're in control, no one else. However, he is just as responsible as you are."

"Can you not tell Jax?"

"Jackie, I won't tell Jax but you know those two are joined at the hip, so there's no vouching that Max hasn't already told him."

"Let's get back inside, Jax needs to talk to you."

"That doesn't sound good."

"Keep an open mind."

Maxwell

JAX AND RAVEN CAME over and the timing couldn't have been more perfect. I need to bounce this off of Jax. I'm not that shocked that the condom broke. I'm shocked that I'm happy it did. I need to snap out of this, I know I said it was Raiders business but the reality is the condom breaking is the only thing on my mind. Jax and I head into my office, leaving the girls in the living room. I'm sure Jackie wants to tell Raven what happened. I pull the bottle of Scotch from the desk and pour us each a glass. He begins to take up my pacing and he keeps running his hands through his hair. "What's the problem, Jax?" I stare into my glass, dreading what's coming.

"I need to watch the video."

"Why? Jax, there's no reason to put yourself through that."

"I've put it off long enough. If that video needs to be released, then

I need to stay ahead of it."

"Are you sure you want to watch this?"

"It's the last piece of the puzzle, Max, I need to see it."

I open my laptop and set it all up. He pours another scotch and hovers over the play button. "Do you want me to stay, Jax?"

"Yeah, please."

Jaxson

I HIT PLAY AND the screen comes to life. I gasp when I instantly see a seven-year-old Raven. She's so beautiful, even as a scared little girl. She's crying, her little lip is trembling, and my heart is breaking. Max goes to stop it and I grab his hand. "No, I need to see this through."

The evil bastard grabs her by her ponytail and puts a knife to her throat. *"Shut the fuck up or I'll slit your throat."*

Joseph and Antonio storm in the room. *"Vin, let my daughter go, it's me you have a problem with."*

"I've got the brat and Gabriella. The price you're going to pay for walking away from your family. You think you're better than us? Well, guess again. The blood that runs through us is the same that runs through her." He's gliding the knife down her neck. The lump in my throat tightens with each swipe of the knife.

"Let her go, Vin, Gabby will perform the surgery, you don't need Cara."

"You're right, I don't, but maybe I'll keep her all for myself. Think of the fun I could have with her. I could teach her all about our family; make her one of us."

The next few seconds happen so fast. Antonio looks at Raven, nods, and then say's something I can't catch. She kicks Vincent in the shin, bites his hand, and begins to run. He drops the knife, yelling. Vincent pulls a gun out of his back. Joseph jumps in front of Raven, and Antonio dives in between them. Vincent fires, hitting Antonio. Joseph blankets Raven with his body. Antonio takes aim at Vincent, but he's hurt and he's down. His shot only grazes Vincent's shoulder.

Within seconds, agents are rushing in, shots are fired and Vincent is gone. The video is still running as Joseph gets up and Raven runs into her father's arms. There's blood everywhere, and Joseph is applying pressure to Antonio's wound. Then I hear her last words to her father:

"Daddy, Daddy, please don't die. I love you, Daddy."

"Cara, my beautiful, baby girl, don't cry. Daddy loves you, beyond this lifetime."

Then silence. She's rocking and crying in total silence.

Max stops the video and I can't hold back my tears any longer, I let them fall. She's so strong and brave. "Max, I never want her to see this ever, understand?"

"I understand, but it may not be up to us. We can try to shield Raven and Rose, as much as possible."

"Max, that bastard made Rose watch this everyday, it's no wonder she retreated into the darkest corners of her mind. I want him *dead*. The first time in my life I've ever felt like this. What does that make me?"

"Jax, after seeing that video, who wouldn't want him dead? It makes you human."

I take a moment to collect myself, staring into the glass of amber liquid in my hands. Finally, I take in a deep breath and look up at Max. "Rose watched the video from Antonio today. She thanked Raven for giving her Antonio, again. Raven still hasn't watched her video. I asked her why, and she said she might never be ready." I put my glass down, my hand still shaking from what I've just watched. "When all this is over, I am going to see if she wants to go to counseling. I think we could all benefit from it."

"Jax, maybe a counselor will be able to help Raven deal with the video. I think the pressure and the stress is getting to all of us. Hell, I think we could all benefit from counseling after this nightmare." He throws back the rest of his scotch. "Jax, what happened with Sammy today at Raiders?"

"I spoke to him about working for Raiders. I think he's interested. We need someone in the field who can be trusted, and I'm just not sure, when push comes to shove, where his loyalty would fall. I know he is very protective of Jackie, which makes me feel a little bit better."

"Jax, what's your take on Gerhard?"

"He's smart and direct, but plays it close to the vest. The brother,

Dylan, is a total arsehole. Apparently, he has a thing for Raven. When we went back to pick up Jackie, he was yelling, telling her she would probably end up knocked up like Raven."

"You didn't snap his fucking neck?!" He throws his hands out.

"Before I could, Raven gave him a total bitch slap in front of his entire family. I was very proud. Gerhard gave Jackie a complete file on you."

Max grabs onto the side of the table. "So she knew about Samantha and Elliot?"

"No, she refused to read it. She said, anything she wants to know she would ask you directly. She's tough, a lot tougher than she looks."

"Yeah, I know, but it's killing me that she's in danger because of me. God only knows how Raven feels."

"I met with Mathew earlier. He said the Feds were demanding we turn over our copy of the tape. How ridiculous is that? He said to keep a copy someplace safe, wouldn't be surprised if Vincent tried to destroy it."

"No worries, I've got multiple copies in many different locations, including one at the Yard. I called in a lot of IOU's."

"How connected is this fucker, Max?"

"He's got some judges in his pocket and he has some political connections. His lawyer, Deveno, handles a lot of his business, and surprisingly, so does Annabelle. You know money rules, Jax. He's got it and he's not afraid to use it."

"Yeah, well he just met his match."

"We need to be smart and operate without emotion, otherwise mistakes will be made."

"Trust me, Max, I understand lives are at stake here. No one fucks with my family or me. I'm going to break him into a million pieces. I'll rip apart his organization one brick at a time, until he's left with nothing."

"And what if he doesn't stop, have you thought of that?"

"He's made my family fair game, well, turnaround is fair play. He shot my brother, kidnapped my wife, kidnapped and raped Rose. By the time I'm done, he'll be begging for mercy."

I pour us each another Scotch. Something is bugging him, he takes care of all of us, it's about time he lets me take care of him. "So, Max, what's going on with you and, Jackie? Something seems off."

"I can't get anything past you. I brought up her going to her dad's for a while and before I could finish she tore into me like nothing I've ever seen before. It was actually quite hot, mate."

"What else?"

"The condom broke."

"Oh fuck, and?"

"We went and got the morning after pill, and I assured her I'm clean."

"What are you not telling me?"

He's quiet for a bit. "I never thought I would ever want another child again, but when that condom broke, I felt walls around me shatter with it. I want everything with her. I'm scared; there's a bigger target on her now than before, and I put it there. If I were a better man, I would have let her go. But God forgive me, I can't live without her."

I watch as Max picks up his glass and he's shaking. I realize I need to take charge here.

"Well, that settles it—we are going to the island. I will have a medical team brought in for the delivery. I need everyone safe. Raven knows this is what I want to do, and we came here tonight to discuss it with Jackie."

"Jax, you know she is going to fight you on this."

"I will negotiate with her. Stop laughing, mate, I've been practicing the art of negotiating. If that doesn't work, then, we go to plan B."

"What's plan B?"

"You don't want to know."

"How soon are the houses going to be done?"

"Well, now that Mrs. Osla told the crew she was going to go down to supervise, it seems they are ahead of schedule."

"I told you she's scary."

"Come on, I need to go negotiate with Jackie." I slap his back and we head out.

IN THE LIVING ROOM, the girls are deep in conversation. The look on Raven's face tells me all I need to know—she knows about the condom.

"Jackie, I need to talk to you about something important, and I need you to keep an open mind."

She jumps up, "Jax, before you start, I'm not going back to my parents."

"I understand from Max, that it's not an option. I have a plan and I would like for you to hear me out. Please, have a seat."

She sits next to Raven, and takes a hold of her hand.

"I know you're aware of the private island, I purchased, off the coast of Belize. I am having renovations done; adding cottages all over the island. I'm making it into a family retreat. I would like for us all to go down there for a while, until the dust settles. I'm having a medical team brought in for the baby."

"Jax, I understand that I'm at a greater risk now, but is running away really the answer? These people will know where we are. Do you really think you can stop them?"

"Baby, it's not running away." Max interjects. "We are trying to protect everyone and give ourselves some breathing room. It's not permanent, just until we can get a handle on the situation. The entire family will be there. Will you please do this for me . . . for my sanity?"

After listening to Max, she brings her focus back to me. "Jax, when would we have to leave?"

"Best case scenario . . . by the end of the week—at the latest."

Jackie grabs Raven's hand, and tilts her head as if she's unsure. "Raven, are you okay with all of this?"

"Yes, I think we all need a break. Security will be very tight."

"Jax, I have to let my father know what is going on before we leave."

"Of course. Max and I are working closely with Sammy on everything that is going on."

"Okay. Then, I will go."

I see a wave of relief wash over Max, and I'm happy my negotiating skills worked.

"Great, now that we've got that all settled, I'm taking my wife home.

I scoop her up and head towards the flat. "Before you tell me you can walk, I know, but humor me, wife. I need this."

Maxwell

STUDYING JACKIE, I CAN see how overwhelmed she is; rubbing her upper arms nonchalantly and staring blankly as if she's in a daze. "Talk to me, baby, tell me what's going on in that beautiful head of yours."

"I spoke to Raven about what happened with the condom. She's making a doctor's appointment for me in the morning. I would like you to come along."

"Were you afraid I wouldn't go?"

"I was unsure about asking you. It's my body and my responsibility, however, after talking with Raven, she made me realize that you're just as responsible as I am."

She's looking down and tearing up the napkin in her lap. "Look at me, Jackie. I would move heaven and earth for you. I am just as much responsible for taking care of this beautiful body as you are. We are in this together. Please, never feel that you have to hide anything from me." I open my arms, "Come here, baby."

She crawls into my lap, wrapping her legs around my waist. "I know that the next few days are going to be crazy, and very intense. I need you to understand that I'm not letting you out of my sight. I will get the doctor to come here. I know it's extreme, but I really need this from you right now. Please stay indoors, until we are on that plane. Jax has probably made all the arrangements, including the personal shopper to supply everyone with enough clothes for months."

"Maxwell, why was Jax so rattled when he came out of the office?"

I promised her complete honesty, I'm just not sure how much she can handle. "He watched the video of Raven's dad being murdered. You saw how rattled he was, do you understand why I need you to stay put?"

She's searching my eyes, not saying anything. She leans in and softly kisses my lips. "Okay."

I feel relief wash over me. "Thank you. Now, I need to make love to you all night long."

She leans forward and nibbles on my lip, "Max, I need it just as much as you do, probably more right now."

Raven

JAX IS STILL ASLEEP. I decide to make a cup of tea and watch the sunrise over Central Park. It has such a calming effect. The baby is so active now; it feels like I'm growing bigger by the minute. I think Jax is right, escaping down to the island might be just what we need right now. I'm more worried about Jackie and my mom. If Vincent finds out my mom is alive, he'll come after her. I have no doubt about his sick obsession with her. Max has aged through all of this, and now his fear for Jackie's safety has brought all his pain to the surface again. I'm trying not to blame myself for any of this, but sometimes it's hard not too.

Staring out at the sunrise, I realize I'm ready to watch the video, I've put it off long enough. Mom is right; my daddy will always be on that pedestal and *nothing* will ever change that. I get Jax's laptop and plug in the flash drive. I close my eyes, take a deep breath, and hit play. The screen fills with my daddy in his hospital bed.

"Cara, my beautiful angel. The day you were born, my life changed forever. I finally understood unconditional love. I'm so sorry you were touched by all of this evil. Nothing that happened was your fault. You defended yourself exactly as I taught you to. Vincent just got the better of us; never blame yourself. You're strong, my beautiful girl. I might not be there to watch you grow into the beautiful woman I know you will be, but my heart will always be joined with yours. You take hold of your mom and don't let go. Joseph will always be there to catch you, if you fall. Live your life to the fullest and love with all your heart. You're Daddy's ray of sunshine, Cara, the best thing I have ever done in my life was help to create you.

Daddy loves you, Cara, always."

The screen goes black, and I'm frozen. All of the memories that I have kept buried so deep from that awful day come racing to the surface. *I can feel him pulling my hair. I can feel the cold steel knife scraping up and down my neck every time Vincent laughs. He's yelling at Daddy, and Joseph. I'm trying to be a big girl, but I'm scared and I cry. He yells at me to shut up, and presses the knife harder against my throat. He's dragging me by my ponytail, waving that knife around. Everyone is yelling: Vincent, Joseph, and Daddy. Then Daddy gives me the sign, that it's time to protect myself just like he taught me. I run it through my head, the mantra he would tell me whenever I was afraid. "Kick, bite, run, Cara, always remember that." Kick, bite, and run. Kick, bite, and run. I can do this. I kick him in the shin, bite his hand with the knife, and try to run towards Daddy. I did it just like Daddy taught me, but then Joseph leaps and all I hear are gunshots. All I smell is gunpowder and the metallic smell of blood. I'm rocking in my daddy's arms, crying,* "Please don't die, Daddy, please don't die."

Jaxson

I OPEN MY EYES to find the other half of the bed empty. I know she can't sleep through the night without going to the bathroom—the joys of pregnancy I guess. As I head towards the kitchen to make coffee, I hear her crying. I race into the office, and find her, in a ball on the floor. Obviously, she became sick because she's covered in vomit. She's rocking back and forth, crying, "Please don't die Daddy, please don't die."

She finally watched the video that Antonio left her. It must have triggered the memories she's been fighting to keep suppressed. I scoop her into my arms, and carry her into our bedroom. She's shivering and I need to warm her up. I wrap us up in the comforter, holding and soothing her. "Raven, you're safe, sweetheart. I'm here with you forever, baby. No one can get to us." Finally the shaking stops. I pull her head up to mine. "Open your eyes, baby." She opens her eyes; there's my girl. "Hey, sweetheart, there you are. You're safe, I've got you, always."

"Jax, I watched the video my daddy left me. He loved me, and he didn't blame me for anything that happened."

"Of course he loved you, sweetheart, why would you think he would blame you for what happened?"

"He taught me to protect myself. He would say, 'kick, bite, and run' all the time. When he nodded to me I did it, only it didn't work; Daddy was shot. I thought I didn't do it right."

I have to tell her I saw the tape, and I know she was not to blame. "I watched the tape, Raven. You were a very brave little girl. You did everything right. You can't predict what will happen when you're dealing with a madman."

"You watched it? When?"

"Last night, when you were talking with Jackie. Max showed it to me. I needed to see it, to understand the depth of Vincent's depravity. It's another reason we are leaving for the island, sooner rather than later. Now that you've heard what your father said, maybe you can put your self-doubt behind you. We need to focus on the future with our growing family."

"I'm a mess, I need to get cleaned up."

"Let me help you, we'll have a nice hot shower and then some of that wonderful porridge that you seem to like."

"Okay, a shower would be wonderful and I do have some questions."

Great, anything to get her mind off of all of this. I carry her into the bathroom and put her on the counter, while I turn the shower on. I turn on the IPod and choose her favorite David Garrett song, "Bring Me Back to Life." The same one I played when we made our apple pie. It will relax and help sooth her. I lift her up and carry her into the shower, letting the hot water wash away all the angst. I slowly begin cleaning her up. She closes her eyes and let's me take care of her.

"What do you want to know, Raven?"

"I want to go over the arrangements you have made for us."

"Okay, but don't flip out on me. I need to be my usual self right now. I need you to understand it's for everyone's safety, and my own sanity. Everything for the baby is set up. Dr. Leanne has agreed to come down two weeks before your due date. I hired a nurse to stay with us for the next four months. I had a small hospital built and staffed. The staff has been triple checked. I arranged for my personal shopper to come and fit you, Jackie, and your mom for all the clothes you will ever need. Mick will be coming, as well as Sammy. I let Jackie's parents know everything that is going on, and when we will be leaving. Is there anything I missed?"

Oh dear God, she's crying. What the fuck did I do now? "Sweetheart, please, what's wrong?"

"I'm overwhelmed, Jax."

"Don't be, that's what I'm here for. Let me handle all the details, and you just be you. The kindest, most loving person I've ever known."

"I feel like I've disrupted everyone's life and put them in danger. Michael was looking so forward to going to Disney World this summer."

"Stop, just stop with the pity party. Junior will get his trip to Disney World, and I plan on surprising him with a very special trip in the fall to Cardiff Bay."

"What's in Cardiff Bay?"

Raven

HIS WHOLE FACE LIGHTS up like a kid on Christmas morning. "The Doctor Who Experience. Of course, we will take the baby with us."

Oh my God, he's serious. "Jax, the baby might be too young for that. Maybe it would be a good bonding trip for you and Michael."

"Turn around, Raven, let me wash your hair."

As he's massaging my scalp all I can think about is how much I'm going to miss this shower. He rinses out the shampoo and now he's working in the conditioner. I could get used to this really quickly.

He's rubbing my shoulders and leaving a trail of kisses down my spine.

"Jax, I'm really going to miss this shower."

"No worries, sweetheart. I had the shower duplicated on the island. I would never deny my beautiful wife anything."

Oh how I love my beautiful, crazy husband.

Chapter Twenty

Sammy

MAX'S GUEST ROOM IS nice, but I need a private place to work. I decide to go back to Jackie's flat where I will have some privacy. I step into the hall and, as expected, Mick is sitting by the elevator, having his coffee. He's always there, and always on time. "Hey, Mick, let Max and Jax know that I went to Jackie's place to get some more of my stuff, and that I'll be back. My understanding is no one is leaving this flat until we head to the island. If something changes, please call me."

"Sure, Sammy, I'll let them know."

I get to Jackie's, and the first thing I do is update Gerhard. "Sir, Jax, has everyone on lockdown. No one is leaving the flat until the end of the week. Then they will be heading down to the island. Jackie has agreed to go with them. I'm going to arrange the transport for everyone."

"Jax contacted me and advised me of his plans. Have the Fed's decided what they are going to do with Vincent and Duke?"

"My contact said they are going to deal. They feel Vincent can give up some top level people."

"What kind of deal are we talking here, Sammy?"

"They are going to go with diminished capacity for Duke, and give him a reduced sentence. As far as Vincent, they aren't saying. I think it would depend on who he gives up."

"Sam, that animal can't get a deal, do you understand me?"

Oh, I get *exactly* what he's telling me. "Understood, sir."

"Did you get a list of all his dealings outside the United States?"

"Yes, sir. The list of his drug dealings, outside the United States, is quite extensive, along with his political connections. The Feds have got to know, if given the chance, he would flee. However, I think they're looking at the big picture, how much of a dent they can put into the drug trade. There like roaches, they keep coming back, no matter how much the government cuts into their business."

"Sammy, do you have any idea how quickly all of this is going to go down?"

"Not an exact timeframe, however, what I'm hearing is the Feds want this wrapped up pretty quickly. They're afraid the more time that passes the more problems they will encounter. They know that Jax has a copy of the tape, and there is probably nothing they can do to get it back."

"If that tape gets out—they will know Jax released it—then what?"

"They'd have to prove it, and Max had about a dozen different copies made. He stored them at various locations all over the world, including one at Scotland Yard. Apparently, he has a lot of friends in all the right places."

"Let me know when my daughter is safely on that island, and give me a heads up on Vincent."

I get what he's not saying, the further away from this Jackie is, the more plausible deniability he has.

I hang up with Gerhard, and check in with Annabelle's guard. Seems she has finally gotten in to see Vincent and Duke. Everything is going to move pretty quickly, now that the Feds have decided to deal. I need to convince everyone that they need to get to the island tomorrow, the latest. I have a few more arrangements to make before my team is in place. I get an alert that someone is looking into the Gerhard family, mainly pulling information on Jackie. They are following the breadcrumb trail I set, which is perfect. This will buy us a little bit more time, but we have to move quickly. There is only so long I can string whomever is looking along before they figure out it's a dead end.

Time to call Max, and get the ball rolling. Fucking phone goes right to voice mail. "Max, I'm on my way back to the flat. Get Jax, I need to meet with everyone now. Be there in ten.

Jackie

ANOTHER MORNING I'M UP before Max, which now has me worried. He's always up before dawn. He has an iron grip on my leg and his other hand is fisted and shaking. He is in a pool of sweat. Maybe it's a nightmare. If it is, I don't want to startle him. I stroke his cheek and whisper, "Max, it's okay. Everyone is fine. Please wake up, Max."

His eyes fly open and he leaps up, nearly knocking me on my ass.

"Oh my God, baby, are you okay? I'm so sorry. Did I hurt you?"

"Calm down, Max. I'm fine, but clearly, you're not. What is going on? And don't tell me nothing."

"Jackie, it's just the headaches, that's all."

I watch him as he checks his messages and I see he's still shaking. He might think I'm buying his excuse, but I'm not. Clearly, I'm not going to get anywhere with him on this.

"Sammy called, we need to get next door. The doctor called, she will be here at noon. Please stop worrying, Jackie, I'm fine."

We get ready and head next door, but this is far from over.

WE ALL GATHER IN Jax's flat. Rose has set up coffee for everyone. I know that we are all on edge right now, but not even Jax and Raven notice that something has been off with Max. Why am I the only one who sees it? I know we are all stressed and tired, but something is not right . . . I'm worried. Sammy comes rushing in and he seems very intense. Knowing him, as I do, this can't be good.

"Hey, everyone, there have been a few developments overnight that I need to make everyone aware of. First of all, the Feds are going to offer Duke a deal. They're offering him diminished capacity with life in prison. They are also going to offer Vincent a deal. However, they are not saying anything more until they find out what he is going to give them. Someone started looking into Jackie, but the only thing they got, right now, was the false trail I set up. I think we need to move to the Island today. I have transport and security already set up."

Jackie

I NEED TO MAKE a stand here. If this is what I need to do so Max will see something is wrong, then so be it. I stand up and all eyes turn towards me. "I'm not going anywhere, and before everyone starts yelling, please hear me out." You could hear a pin drop. Well, at least I know everyone is listening. "So much has happened, in such a short amount of time. I'm a strong person and I can endure quite a lot. What I cannot—no—what I will not do is sit around while the man I love is in physical pain, and hiding it from everyone. Until Max gets his head examined—literally—I'm, not going anywhere." No one is saying a word, however, all heads turn towards Max.

"Jackie, I assure you, I'm fine. It's the headaches, but they are getting better."

I roll up my pant leg, "Max, is this better? You gripped my leg so hard in your sleep that I'm bruised. You sleep past dawn; you never do that. You wake up in a cold sweat. You fist your hands in your sleep, and grind your teeth. None of this is normal. You get a complete check-up or I don't leave."

Before anyone can say another word, Jax leaps up and heads towards his gym. "I need a time out, please."

Raven gets up to go after him, but Max stops her. "Raven, please, it's me he's mad at, right now. Let me handle him."

Maxwell

I HEAD INTO THE gym. I see him beating on a bag, and I know it's my face he's seeing.

"Talk to me, Jax."

"Talk to you? You're the one who should be talking to me. Aren't you the one who's keeping secrets? What were you going to do, drop dead and leave me to clean up the bloody mess?"

"It's not that bad, Jax."

"Not that bad, did you see her leg? Did you see the fear in her eyes? Do you know what courage it must have taken for her to stand up in front of everyone, and put you before her own safety? Get your head out of your fucking arse, Max, or do I need to do it for you?! How fucking bad is it?"

"I thought it was the added stress."

"Well, apparently, it's not. I'm calling the doctor and getting him here now. You will do exactly what he tells you to do. Do you have any problems with that?"

"Okay. I will, but calm the fuck down."

"If you tell me to calm down one more time, so help me, you know exactly what I'll do!"

That shut him up real quick.

Raven

MY NEED TO BOLT has never been as strong as it is right now. My husband is on the verge of losing it. I can hear him screaming at Max. I would not want to be on the receiving end of his wrath right now. My best friend's life is in danger. The man she loves has been shot twice because of me. I brought my mom back into all of this, and now I'm questioning that, too. I have a baby to protect, and I'm in a world of danger. My heart is racing and my head is pounding.

"Raven, are you feeling okay?"

"I have a headache, Mom."

"When was the last time you ate anything?"

"Mom, you're starting to sound like Jax." I feel bad I just snapped at her.

"Well, maybe you should listen to him more. I'm making you some chamomile tea."

I pull Jackie into my arms, "He will be okay, and I'm not going anywhere without you."

Suddenly, Jax and Max are back. Jax pulls Jackie out of my arms.

"Thank you, Jackie, you're a very brave lady. The doctor will be here within the hour to examine, Max. No one gets left behind!" he says and he encircles me in his arms and squeezes me tight. "Raven and I are going upstairs for some fresh air. Sammy, can you brief Max and Mick on the transport, please."

We head up to the rooftop deck. The warm morning sun feels wonderful. Jax pulls me onto the lounge chair, and nestles me between his legs. "Talk to me, Jax, please."

"I need the peace of mind, right now, that only you can give me." He kisses the top of my head and takes in a deep breath. "Dr. Leanne, will be here soon to examine Jackie. I would like her to take a look at you again before we leave."

"Max told you about the condom but not about his head?"

"Yeah, go figure. I honestly don't know what the hell he was thinking."

"Jax, what's really bothering you? Don't look at me like that, I know there's more."

He's twirling a lock of my hair around his finger, not saying a word.

"What kind of person does it make me that I didn't even notice my best friend is in pain?"

"You can't blame yourself; you're juggling so many different things."

"I can't afford to let anything fall between the cracks, there are too many lives at stake."

"We'll get there, Jax, to the other side of all this madness. I promise you, we will."

"I wish I had as much faith as you do. Come, the doctor is

probably here."

We get downstairs and I find my mom and Dr. Leanne, deep in conversation. My mom seems to be at ease with everyone she meets. I'm surprised how comfortable she is with other people since she was alone for twenty years. I think therapy is helping. Dr. Leanne pulls me away for a quick chat.

"Raven, I would like to give you another exam before you leave. I will be making periodic trips to the island to keep a check on you."

"I'm feeling good, except for a nagging headache."

"Your blood pressure was up the other day. I know you're under a lot of stress right now. When you get to the island, I would like the nurse to monitor your blood pressure daily. She can report back to me. Are you okay with that?"

"That's fine. Where is Jackie?"

"She went next door with Mr. Fleming; the doctor is here to see him."

"Dr. Leanne, I don't mean to be rude, but if we're done, I really need to get next door."

"Go, Raven, it's fine."

Jax is talking to Mick and Sammy, but his eyes are never far from me. I head next door to talk to Max's doctor. I don't have to turn around; I know Jax is right behind me.

Jaxson

"WHAT'S GOING ON, SWEETHEART?"

"Jax, I want to talk to Max's doctor myself. I'm not about to let Max sugar coat anything."

Right about now, I should probably feel sorry for Max. Raven has fire in her eyes, and for once, I'm not on the receiving end. Maybe he'll learn a bloody lesson.

"Hello, Dr. Steven, I'm Raven Phillips, we've met before. I want to know what is going on with, Max?"

"Well, that would be up to Max to share, not me."

"Well, Dr. Steven, if Max could be trusted not to hide when he's not feeling well, we wouldn't be having this conversation!"

"Raven, Dr. Steven, thinks it's scar tissue. However, he is going to run a few tests today just as a precaution. I promise you that's all there is to report."

"How soon will the results be in from the tests?"

"I will have them to Mr. Fleming later today."

"Okay, fine. We'll wait. Jackie and I will be upstairs. I'm sure you and Jax have plenty to go over."

I practically drag Jackie upstairs. I know something's not right with her; I can sense it. "What's wrong? I know when something is up with you, so spill—right now." She looks at me and begins to cry a full-blown, ugly-ass cry. "Oh my God, Jackie, what is it? Nothing is so bad that we can't fix it."

"Dr. Leanne said there is no guarantee that the morning after pill will work. She said many women still end up pregnant."

Okay, that's not what I was expecting to hear. "What did Max say?"

"That's just it, Raven, he said nothing—not one word! I can't start birth control until I know for sure. It's too soon to tell, yet. So, now, we wait. I'm not ready to be a mom. I might never be ready. What will my parents say . . . my brother, after he practically accused me of getting knocked up."

I pull her into my arms and let her have a good cry, rocking her and stroking her back. Jax comes upstairs. I lift my gaze to him and shake my head. Thank God, he gets it and backs away, giving us the space we need right now.

"Jackie, first, stop worrying about what everyone else will think, and worry about yourself. Secondly, maybe you need to talk to Max, find out what he's thinking. When is the earliest you can take a pregnancy test?"

"I can take the test the end of next week. I didn't get a chance to talk to Max because Doctor Steven was waiting for us."

"When Max gets back from taking the tests, I think the two of you need to sit down privately, discuss your feelings, and all of your options. Don't jump to conclusions."

"Okay. I think I'm going to lie down for a bit, my head is spinning from all of this."

As we head downstairs, I pray this works out for both of them.

I LEAVE JACKIE TO her nap and go next door to find Jax. I really want to be alone with my husband, but when I enter our flat I see it's filled with people. Everyone, that is, except for my husband. I find my mom. "Mom, where is Jax?"

"He went with Max to get some tests run. I made you lunch, come sit down, please."

"Well, whatever it is, it smells wonderful."

"I made salmon broiled with a mustard glaze and a salad. I know Jackie doesn't eat meat, and I wanted to make sure I had something to her liking."

I'm shocked how she can whip this stuff up. I'm lucky if I can make a sandwich. I'm starving, and before I realize it, I've cleaned my plate. Too bad Jax isn't here to see it. I decide to take a picture and text it to him:

'I cleaned my plate and thought this would make you smile. I miss you.'

XO ~ Always

My phone immediately beeps:

'Sweetheart, You were right! I miss you, too. How is Jackie?'

XO ~ More.

'She's trying to keep it together. How's Max?'

XO ~ More? I don't think so!

'He's not saying much. He told me what

Dr. Leanne said, that's all. Is anyone
there, yet?'

XO ~ Oh I know so.

'Yes, everyone is here and your mom is
worried. You better warn Max. How much
longer do you think you will be?'

XO ~ I need you.

'We're done here, I'm on my way,
sweetheart.'

XO ~ Happy Place here I come! :)

Jaxson

DRIVING BACK, MAX SEEMS lost in his own head. I've never seen
him this bad, not even when he sent Jackie away. "Max, if I'm going
to be able to help you, then you need to talk to me." I say, then set my
eyes on the rearview mirror to talk to Mick. "Mick, keep driving around
the park until I tell you, thanks." I raise the privacy glass. "Well, talk to
me, damn it! I know it's more than just the condom breaking. If she's
pregnant, would it really be such a bad thing?"

"It is if she decides she wants to terminate it."

I freeze, "Do you think she would? It doesn't seem like something
she would do."

His hands are fisted and his jaw is ticking. "Ultimately, it's her
body and her decision, but it would be the final nail in my coffin."

"Well, then we just have to make her see the light."

"I can't bully her, Jax."

"Did you talk to her about how you feel? I know it's her body, but
she needs to understand what you're feeling, too. This is a two-way
street, you both took a dip in that pool and you're both responsible."

"I never got a chance, we had to leave to take these bloody tests."

"Raven texted. She said everyone is already at the flat. When we get upstairs, you head into your flat. I'll get Jackie in there and divert everyone's attention away from you. It will be okay, Max, I'm sure it was a shock for her."

I let Mick know to head back as we sit there in silence, both of us trying to deal with everything being thrown at us.

WE ARRIVE BACK AT The Tower and the elevator ride up seems to take forever. The doors finally open, and any chance of getting Max out of there quickly is gone. My mum is all over him.

"Maxwell, when were you going to tell me about the headaches?"

"Please don't worry, Dr. Steven ran tests and said its scar tissue."

"You still should have told me. Will you ever learn, Maxwell?"

"Where is she?" Max says under his breath when he pulls me to the side.

"Rose said Raven took her into your flat. Go, I got this."

"Mum, Max needs to rest and I need to go over some stuff with you and Bella; come."

Maxwell

JAX STEERS HER AWAY as I make a quick exit. I race inside and find her asleep on the sofa. Raven is sitting in the chair next to her, making sure she is there for her when she wakes.

"Max, she just fell asleep. Give her some time to come to terms with everything, besides we really don't know anything yet. What did Dr. Steven's tests show?"

"It's scar tissue, and this is as bad as it should get. Hopefully, with reduced stress the headaches will diminish."

"Good, I'm glad that's all it is. I'll leave you alone, but if you need anything, come get me." She gets up and gives me a warm smile before heading out.

I sit on the chair across from my sleeping angel. I know I'm only going to get one shot at this. I have to be honest with her. I need her to realize that my heart is in her hands. From this point forward, all that I will ever be is up to her. She can make or break me. I need to do all of this without scaring or bullying her. Her eyes are starting to flutter open; its time for my A game.

"Max, what happened with the tests?"

"Scar tissue, nothing more."

"What time are we leaving for the island?"

"We are not going anywhere until you and I get some things settled."

"Max, I'm on overload right now. I really don't want to deal with any of this."

I have to calm myself down or I will flip out. "You don't want to *deal* with this!" Maybe yelling is not my A game.

"Yelling at me, Max, is not going to help the situation."

"I'm trying to be calm, I really am, but I'm finding it a little difficult to be calm right now when my whole world is hanging in the balance."

"Your world? How the hell do you think I feel? I'm not ready for any of this. I thought I was being responsible. When that damn thing broke, I raced to get the morning after pill, now I find out I can still be pregnant."

"Jackie, stop. We used a condom and emergency contraceptive, no one is to blame."

Her lip is quivering and her tears are falling. "B-but I'm not ready for this, Max, I'm only twenty-five."

"What are you telling me, that you would terminate it?"

She stops, searching my eyes. "Max, is that what you want me to do?"

This is it, it's my do or die moment. I drop to my knees in front of her and lift her chin. "I would rather die first, Jackie. I never thought I wanted another child again, not after Elliot died. You cleared the muddy waters and showed me that I can love again. I want you, God how I want you with me for the rest of my life. I want to hold your hand and walk on the beach. I want to watch the sun rise and set with you in my arms. I want to watch you have our children—lots of them. I've watched you with Junior, and with all of your students, you're a natural born mum. I would be honored to have you be the mother of my children. More than that, I would be honored to have you as my wife. Before you say anything, please hear me out. I'm not asking you to marry me because of the possibility that you might be pregnant, believe me that would be a bonus. I'm asking you . . . no I'm pleading with you, because I love you. You've made me whole. You've taught me to finally live my life and not wait around to die. You've mended my broken soul. You complete me like no one else can. When the condom broke, I felt the walls around my heart fall like broken glass. Will you please do me the honor and marry me?"

She sits in silence and I'm holding my breath.

"Maxwell, I love you, I really do, but I feel like everything is spinning out of control."

"Baby, our love is the one constant thing through all of this. I won't rush you, but I'm not going anywhere without you. I can't."

"Can we have a long engagement?"

"My beautiful angel, if that's what I have to do to get you to say yes, then, hell yeah."

"And if I'm not pregnant?"

"Nothing changes for me, baby, absolutely nothing. We are all books, waiting to be opened, the pages filled with all of life's unknowns just begging to be shared. Please share the rest of your life with me."

"Yes."

I lean in and kiss her swollen lips. "Oh, my beautiful angel, you've saved me. God how I love you." I lift her up, and she wraps her beautiful legs around my waist while kissing me gently. She leans her forehead against mine, "I need you to hold me, Max, please."

"Forever, baby, always and forever."

Jaxson

RAVEN COMES OUT OF Max's flat, visibly shaken.

"Raven, how's, Jackie, doing?" I wrap her in a hug.

"About the same as Max is."

"They will be okay, sweetheart, I promise you they will be."

"How could you know that?"

"I know that because my wife's faith is rubbing off on me."

"Oh."

"Yeah, *oh.*"

"Jax, is Mick going to come with us to the island?"

"Yes. I gave him the option to stay here, but he was adamant about going."

"I feel bad that everyone's life is being turned upside down. Mick was just getting to know Ashlyn. Maybe I should talk to him about staying here. He needs routine and structure in his life, not all this drama."

"Would it make you feel better if you talk to him? I already did and he was adamant about protecting you and Jackie. If you want, you can ask Ashlyn to come, too."

"Jax, she has a business to run and then there's her volunteer work. I'm sure she would come for a vacation, but not an extended stay."

"Why don't we just take one day at a time? Let's get down there and settled in first."

"I think I'm still going to talk to him. Have you heard anything more from the Feds?"

"No. Only what Sammy told us this morning. Once we get to the island, I'm prepared to release the video, if necessary. We will be leaving later for the airport."

"Well you go check on Max and Jackie while I go talk to Mick."

I tighten my grip. "Jax, what's the problem?"

"No problem, but I need you to come with me for a few minutes, please."

"Go where?" She raises a brow at me.

"Um, office. Yep, that'll work." As we head towards his office, Bella try's to stop us. I make a quick U-turn and practically run into the bedroom.

"Jax, what the hell are you doing?"

I scoop her up and walk faster, trying not to judder her too much.

Raven

HE'S RACING TOWARDS OUR bedroom and in an instant he has me in our walk in closet. "Jax, why are we in our closet?"

"Look, sweetheart, when you get all demanding with me, it's so fucking hot, I can't think about anything but the *happy place.* It's been a crazy arse day and I need you, dear God, I need you now!"

I've never seen such urgency in this man before. It must be the stress, it has to be. He pushes the clothes on the pole aside.

"Hang onto the clothes bar for support, Raven."

I reach up and hold onto the bar. He quickly rids me of my pants as he drops to his knees. That beautiful strong powerful tongue hits me like a lightning bolt. He pushes my legs wider as his tongue is working front to back. His fingers are working their way inside of me very slowly but his tongue is moving with such urgency. Fast and slow at the same time. I can't take much more and he knows it, but he's not letting up. "Jax . . . oh, Jax . . . please."

"Please what, sweetheart? Tell me and I'll give you what you want."

"You know what I want, Jax."

He's slowing down! "*No!* Please don't slow down."

"Then, tell me what you want."

"I don't know how much longer I can hold on, Jax, please."

He grips my ass with both his hands and begins to lightly nibble on my clitoris. His fingers are moving in and out matching the tempo of his tongue

"Jax, baise-moi maintenant et me baiser dur."

I know what talking dirty French does to him and I swear he growls, his grip tightening. "Sweetheart, are you saying what I think you're saying?"

"Jax, fuck me now and fuck me hard!"

"Yes! Sweet Jesus, woman!"

He's off of his knees. "For the love of God, Raven, don't let go of the bar.

Oh *happy place,* here we come."

He lifts me up so my legs wrap around his waist, which is not easy with my belly getting in the way. He takes his cock and strokes my clitoris with it, right before he enters me. I want him hard but he's determined to go slow. All the frustration and the fear from the past few weeks come flooding to the surface. He picks up the pace and finally gives me what I want. "Oh fuck, Raven, I'm going. You there, baby?"

He doesn't need to wait for me to answer; I'm screaming his name over and over again. Fast, furious, and so fucking hot. He's holding me up, and we're both shaking.

He finally finds his voice, "Oh, baby, you can let go of the pole now."

"Jax, I can't, my hands are cramped and stuck to it."

He pry's my fingers loose and we sit on the floor. I'm curled in his lap, both of us trying to catch our breath.

"My beautiful wife, I think you're trying to kill me."

"Jax, do you want to tell me what that was about?"

His eyes are closed, and he's got the Jaxson smile going full blast.

"I needed you, sweetheart. We were away from each other for way too long. When you get all teacher mode on me, it makes me crazy."

I'm snuggled into his chest and he's stroking my back. "Hmm . . . Jax, I could stay like this all night, but the baby is kicking like crazy. I need a shower and I'm hungry, yet again."

"Let's shower and then I'll get you something to eat. What would you like?"

"A toasted bagel with cream cheese, a cup of tea, and those wonderful cookies that your mom sneaks into Max's flat when she thinks no one is watching."

I sit up, "Wait, my mum is sneaking cookies to Max? What cookies is he getting that I'm not?"

"Some type of shortbread cookie with jelly in the middle."

"Oh my God! Max is getting Jammie Dodgers and I'm not! This is war, Raven, trust me."

"Sometimes, Jax, you're such a little boy. Let's go before anyone misses us."

Chapter Twenty-One

Annabelle

I GOT PERMISSION TO see Vincent, again, and he's not going to be happy with the news I have. My brother sits in front of me, on the other side of the glass. Every time I come here he looks worse. We both pick up our phones.

"Anna, what have you found out for me?"

"Apparently, Maxwell has gotten back together with Jacquelyn Gerhard."

"I thought he threw her out like yesterday's trash. When did this happen?"

"From what I can gather, Jax and Cara brought her back from Switzerland."

"What were Jax and Cara doing in Switzerland? I'm sure they didn't fly over there just to bring the little bitch home for Max."

"I'm trying to find out more, but right now, Jax has a wall up around everyone and everything. I did find out that he purchased a private island off the coast of Belize. There is some major construction going on there. Word is, that he is taking everyone there for a while."

"Anna, if he's planning on going to that island, then that means he's going to release the tape. Any luck on getting it back?"

"Apparently, Max has many friends in high places. That tape has been duplicated, and word is, Scotland Yard also has a copy."

"Anna, I thought Cara was dead. I only found out when Duke got in touch with me that she was alive, and that I had a son. Makes me wonder what else has been hidden from me."

"I don't know. All I do know is we need to figure a way out of this mess. I spoke with Duke and he is at least willing to listen. He will be keeping Deveno as his attorney, for now. I will tell you, Vince, Duke is a broken man with nothing left to lose."

"I know, and that's the most dangerous type of man. I'm meeting tomorrow with Deveno and the Feds to see what they are going to offer me. In the meantime, you need to stop Jax from getting everyone to that island. If they make it to there, then he'll release the tape. If that happens, then were all *fucked!*"

Duke

MY PARENTS HAVE TRIED to get in touch with me, but I declined to have any contact with them. I've fucked up their lives enough; they don't need to be part of this giant cluster-fuck. The Feds are on their way to talk to me, along with that weasel, Deveno. My father is willing to throw me to the wolves. At this point, who the fuck cares? I have my ace. I wonder about Raven and how she is doing. I hope her and the baby are okay; she deserves some sort of happiness.

I make my way toward the holding room, hoping my plan will put an end to all of this, permanently. I enter the room, and the guard locks the chains that are around my ankles and wrists to a ring on the floor. They act like I'm some sort of deranged serial killer. Maybe in their minds, I am. In walks the weasel and the Fed; let the games begin.

"Hello, Mr. Jensen, I'm Leo Hage, Federal Prosecutor for the United States government. I'm here to discuss your options. I understand you have retained Mr. Deveno as counsel?"

"Call me Duke and yes, Deveno is representing me at this time."

"Duke, as I informed Mr. Deveno, at this point, we are prepared to offer you diminished capacity with a prison term of twenty-five to life. Originally, it was life without parole, however, upon speaking with Mrs. Philips, I believe that you were under an extreme amount of pressure. Part of the agreement is you must sever all ties with the Giaconna family. You must also, undergo counseling. Do you agree to these terms?"

I'll play along with him, letting him think he's got a win. "So, Raven went to bat for me. When did she get married?"

"I'm not here to discuss Mrs. Phillips."

"Where will I be held?"

Deveno grabs my arm; the thought of him touching me makes my skin crawl. "Duke, does it matter to you where they hold you?"

"Well, seeing how my father is probably going to sing like a fucking canary, I don't think my life will be worth much. So, yeah, it matters, Deveno, it matters a lot."

Hage, shakes his head and mutters something under his breath. Clearly he despises Deveno, about as much as I do. "I've already made one concession on your sentence. Do you have something to offer me that would make me want to put you someplace easier?"

"Yeah, Mr. Hage, I do." Deveno's face turns red and he's about ready to stroke. Hage smiles, and I venture to say, he will be smiling even more.

Deveno jumps up, "Until I have time to talk to my client alone, this meeting is over."

"Mr. Hage, can you guarantee my safety? Not that it means much, look how well the Feds protected Raven."

"That would depend what you have to offer us, Duke."

"I have to object. Duke, stop talking, you're digging yourself into a hole. Let's talk about our options privately."

"Deveno, you're fired. I told Annabelle I would keep you, as long as you were useful. That usefulness just ran out."

"Hage, I'm filing an objection with the judge. Apparently, if you're willing to give him diminished capacity, you're aware he is unstable."

Hage's eyes light up, "Duly noted, Mr. Deveno. However, your client still fired you. Goodbye."

Thank God, that weasel is gone. I'm not going to rot here and be someone's bitch for the next twenty-five years.

"Okay, Duke, you do understand that you have the right to another attorney, and that you're waving your right to new counsel?"

"Yes, Hage, I understand. I will tell you what I have, but I won't show you everything, until I have a signed deal."

"What do you have that you think is so valuable?"

"I have the original FBI file on the entire Giaconna, family. I have Gabriella's hand written journal, detailing everything that Vincent did and said to her. He raped and tortured her. Made her watch her husband's murder over and over again. He made her believe he still had Cara, and he threatened to rape Cara if Gabriella didn't comply. I have journals and files that I lifted from the villa in Italy, when my father was fleeing the country. There are details of wire transfers, and lastly, there is a thumb drive. On that drive is a list of all of my father's business contacts; dealings and holdings that I conveniently copied. Hage, I've got the Holy Grail. You can lift your chin off the ground now and let's discuss what I want."

"How do I know you actually have all of this?"

"I have a sample saved in a drop box online. I will give you the passwords and you can confirm the information. I want total immunity, name change, and relocation. I don't trust your witness protection program. I've seen how well that worked for Raven. I want $20,000,000.00 in an off shore bank account and a clean passport. I also want safe passage out of the country to anywhere I choose. I want to stay in solitary until everything is done; it's my only chance to survive."

Hage

"GIVE ME THE INFORMATION and let me verify it. If it checks out, then we have a deal."

Duke gives me the information and heads back to his cell. This day just keeps getting better and better. I hope, for his sake, he can deliver the goods. I'm sure Deveno is on his way now to deliver Vincent the bad news. I would rather have Vincent locked away for life than give him any sort of deal.

Deveno

VINCENT'S GOING TO GO fucking ballistic when he finds out what went down with Duke. I don't have a clue what the fuck this kid has that makes him think he can get a deal. Time to face the music; Vincent enters the room.

"Deveno, what the fuck is going on? Hage, was supposed to be here today to discuss a deal and the last minute, he canceled."

"We met with Duke this morning. Apparently, he has something on you. He fired me and struck a deal with Hage. Before you even ask, I have no idea what the kid has. I have asked every one of my contacts at the bureau, but it's on tight lockdown. Whatever it is, it's big. Do you have any idea what it could be?"

"How the fuck would I know? I picked the kid up with Cara at that dump in Woodstock. We were at the villa the whole time, until I had to flee. I told the kid we would go our separate ways, and I would hook up with him in the states. Everything happened so fast; Jax and Max's men were all over the place."

"Was there anything at the villa he could have gotten his hands on?"

"There were some banking ledgers that I had to leave when we fled. I keep everything that's important on a thumb drive but I grabbed it when I left."

"Could he have gotten a copy of it?"

"I honestly don't think so. But if he did, then I'm fucked—which means—you're fucked too, Deveno. Everything you have ever done for me is also on that drive. All of my business dealings and contacts are on that drive. Judges, politicians, leaders in other countries, bank accounts—everything. You better fucking find out what the kid has, and then how to get your hands on it—now!"

"Why the fuck would you put everything on there?"

"Well, would you rather I kept written copies? It was easy and I could carry it everywhere."

"Where is the drive now?"

"I put it someplace safe before that fucker, Max, came after me and shot me."

"You're not going to tell me, are you?"

"No, there is no reason for you to know where it is. Find out what is going on and get back to me." Vincent gets up and walks away, leaving me sitting here, holding my dick.

Maxwell

I NEED TO TALK to Jax, something doesn't feel right.

"Jax, am I on speaker?"

"No, what's up?"

"Come next door, and bring Raven." I don't give him a chance to answer.

Within a few minutes, Jax comes flying through the door. "What's the problem?"

I begin my usual pacing which I find a comfort. "Jax, it's my tingle sense, it's firing up again."

"Oh *fuck,* no!"

Raven and Jackie have a deer in the headlight look. "Raven, Max's tingle sense was the key to finding you in Sicily."

"And I'm just finding out about this now!"

Max holds up my hand, "In Jax's defense, a lot has been going on, Raven."

Jax sits on the arm of the club chair and pulls Raven into his arms. "Go on, Max."

"I don't think it's safe to go to the island. I think we need to go with plan B. Let everyone think we're going to the island. And yes, Jax, I have a plan B." I hand Jax a scotch and the ladies water. "When Jax was holding me hostage, I was determined to leave here. With the help of a friend, I made a purchase abroad."

Jax looks like he's about to explode. "Who's the friend, Max?"

"Mrs. Osla."

The shocked look on everyone's face tells me that my plan worked. "I knew that above everyone else, I could trust her. With the help of Mrs. Osla, I purchased a 2700-acre equestrian farm in Angus, Scotland.

When I realized I was never leaving my family, I figured, eventually, I would do something with it. Then when everything got crazy at the deposition, I knew I needed to do something. So I had the place updated. It has been equipped with everything we will ever need, including a clinic for the baby. It has its own airfield, and it has been completely staffed. I made the purchase in Mrs. Osla's maiden name. Vincent and Duke are getting a deal. The island is too isolated; we would be like sitting ducks." I look at Jax, and he's pulling his hair every which way. "Jax, if you keep pulling that hair, you will be bald, mate. Talk to me."

"Max, you're sure about the tingle sense?"

"One-hundred percent, Jax, I can't let the family go to the island, I just can't."

"Max, does my dad or Sammy know?" Jackie asks.

"No one but Mrs. Osla and us."

Jackie closes her eyes, "Will I be able to tell my father where I'm going?"

"Not until we are all safely tucked away."

"Max, how are you going to get us there, it's not like it's just the four of us." Jax brings my attention back to him.

"Well, we aren't getting on that plane tonight, that's for sure. I think if we do, it's game over. I called in a favor from a certain Turkish Prince. His private jet is waiting for us. I will let Mick in on what is going on. He can get the rest of the family to the hanger. We will be leaving by helicopter from the roof."

"What about Sammy? He's not going to be easily fooled." Jax throws his hand out.

"You're right, Jax, he won't be. Do you remember the night we first met? I was on assignment, protecting the Queen's grandson. Well I helped him out so many times that now, he has agreed to help me."

Jax gets up still keeping his arm around Raven. "Wait, Max, how will Mick know where to bring the family?"

"By now Mrs. Osla has everyone at Bella's house. Mick is on his way to pick them up and bring them to the airport. Mrs. Osla has his new instructions and a burner phone, so he can call me to verify."

Everyone is quiet, seemingly processing everything. "I'm sorry I had to keep everyone in the dark for so long. I needed to make sure I could get everything done as quickly and as safely as possible."

Raven lets go of Jax, comes over and pulls me into her arms. "Max, I could never repay you for all that you've done for my family and me. I know how hard this must have been for you. The added stress probably didn't help with your healing. Thank you."

"Raven, you're my family, I would lay down my life for everyone of you." I hit the remote and the TV comes on, showing the entrance hall.

The only thing we see is Sammy, and some of his guards waiting for us.

Raven gasps, "Max, when were these cameras installed? Are they all over the flat?"

"Raven, your privacy is intact. I had these installed after the night you pulled a runner on Jax. I'm sorry, but I had no choice; you were driving me nuts."

"Max, part of me wants to hug you and part of me wants to wring your neck."

"Well, Raven, I would much rather have the hug."

Jax and Raven are staring at the screen. We all see it at the same time, the elevator doors open and out steps the director of MI6 and a half a dozen guards. They block the door to my flat and that's our cue.

"Jax, grab Raven and Bo, we're heading up the back stairwell to the roof. NOW!"

Jaxson

SOMETIMES IN LIFE IT seems as if time is standing still. This is one of those times. Max scoops up a shocked Jackie as Raven gives Bo a hand signal to run. I realize Raven doesn't know where the stairwell is. Instinct kicks in as I reach down grab her hand to lead her. We run into the kitchen, behind the pantry door. We hit the stairs, taking them two at a time. When we get to the roof, there is a chopper waiting, along with a slew of men, guns drawn. I freeze, but Max grabs my arm. "They're ours, Jax, get in the chopper *now.*"

It seems like forever to get us in the chopper and airborne, but in reality, it's seconds. These men are trained for this sort of thing, we, on the other hand, are not. Max is co-piloting, which makes me feel better. All we can do is pray his plan works.

Sammy

I'VE TOLD THEM NO one is to divert from the plan, so what do they do? Divert from the fucking plan. Just as I get most of the family loaded into the van, Mrs. Osla tells me they are going back to Bella's house for some shit they forgot. That woman is a pain in the ass and she doesn't back down. I instruct their driver to take them to get whatever it is they forgot and head straight to Teterboro Airport and we will meet them there. The elevator doors open and I'm in shock. The Chief of MI6 steps off with an elevator full of guards. They form a barrier in front of Max's door. "Sir, what are you doing here?"

"Special request from the Queen. You need to stand down."

"Sir, what about, Miss Gerhard?"

"She's already been removed and is being transported to safety."

"Does Mr. Gerhard know, did he order this?"

"For everyone's safety, we are going dark. Let's go."

I've been at this long enough to know when to shut up, and now is the time.

Hage

WELL, THE LAST THING I ever expected was to walk out of Sing Sing with the gift that Duke just handed me. If this checks out, it's going to catapult my career. I open the drop box and there it is, a file and a video. The video is a short clip showing the FBI file and the Journal. I open the file and Bingo; it's a nice portion showing Vincent's holdings. Some of his contacts in other countries. Holy shit this is big. I need the rest of this list and I need to keep this all a secret, not just for Duke's safety but for my own, as well. This kid just bought himself a deal. If this is going to work, it needs to go down fast.

Duke

I'M BEING PULLED FROM solitary. Apparently, Hage is back already. For once, the tables of luck are on my side. They bolt me to the table, yet again, before they let Hage come in. "So, you're back? Guess you're happy with the information."

"You delivered, Duke, now how do I get the rest?"

"As soon as you get everything else I requested, then it's yours. Do you have the immunity agreement?"

"Yes, and the offshore account has been funded. You never said what name you wanted so I picked something simple. Patrick Brown, easy enough to remember. Due to the extent of high-level people in the information that you provided, only three people know of this deal: myself, the President of the United States, and the Prime Minister of Great Britain."

"How's Raven?"

"Mrs. Phillips is fine. You understand you can never have contact with her or any of the Giaconna, family?"

"Hage, I get it. Duke Jensen dies when I sign those papers. She was innocent through this whole mess. Even at the worst point, when she thought she and her baby would be a prisoner for life, she tried to help me. I just want to know that she's safe and happy."

"I assure you, with a husband like Jaxson Phillips, her safety is not an issue. How do I get the rest of the files?"

"I have a letter I want you to personally deliver to Raven."

"That was not part of the deal, Duke."

I slide the letter in front of him. "Yeah, well without this, there is no deal."

I grab the letter, "Fine, now give me the rest of the files."

"I'll give you the rest on the plane, let's go."

I sign the paperwork, giving birth to Patrick Brown, and leaving a world of hurt behind.

$\mathcal{J}$ axson

WE LAND AT A private hanger at Logan Airport in Boston. A car is waiting to take us to our jet. When we get on board, everyone breathes a sigh of relief. Max gives customs our passports, while Raven runs to check on her mum. Jackie's very quiet, and I'm worried about her. A lot has been thrown at this girl, today.

Max comes back and he seems relieved. "Jax, we're clear for take-off. Let's get everyone seated."

It's only now that I take a look around and realize this is not a plane, it's a frigging resort.

Once we're airborne, everyone seems to relax. "Raven, I'm going to meet with Max for a bit. Try and get some rest."

"Come on, Max, we need to talk."

"There's an office in the back."

We get into the office, and I'm floored—this place is beyond words.

"Max, are we safe here?"

"Jax, this is the Turkish version of Air Force One. What do you want to know?"

"Why did you keep this from me?"

"Honestly, Jax, you had so much on your plate, and I wanted everyone to believe they were going to the island. I had to in order to pull this off."

"What about, Jackie? This girl has had so much shit thrown at her today.

"Don't you think I know that? Once we get to Scotland, she can contact her parents. I had no choice, mate. I had to keep everyone in the dark."

"What are we going to do about Vincent? Are we going to release the tape?"

Before Max can answer, his Blackberry buzzes.

"Apparently, Jax, we won't have to."

"What's going on now?"

"Text from Mathew."

"Stay away from New York right now. Shit hit the fan. Duke threw Vincent and the entire organization under the bus. Feds are NOT going

to make a deal with Vincent. Don't tell me where you are. I will let you know when it's safe. Make sure Raven and Rose don't turn on the news; the tape has been leaked."

"Holy shit, Max, could this be the light at the end of the tunnel?"

Max turns on the TV and it's everywhere.

"Breaking news: Mafia Drug Lord kills his Federal Agent brother as agent's seven-year-old daughter watches."

"Jax, it's not just the tape. What the hell did Duke have on Vincent?"

"Oh my God, Max, it's that slimy lawyer, Deveno, being taken away in handcuffs."

"Jesus Christ, Jax, we got out just in time. Hage is slated to give an interview."

"I'll be right back I want to check on Raven."

"ARE THE GIRLS OKAY?" he asks as I walk back in. He hands me a scotch.

"Yeah, everyone is asleep."

Hage walks up to the podium:

"Hello, I'm Senior Federal Prosecutor Hage. Today will go down in history as the day The United States Government shut down a major Mafia crime family. It is also the day many people will be answering for their crimes. Arrests have been made, and many more to follow. If you've done any business with the Giaconna family, there will be no place you can hide. The United States Government is in possession of the Mafia's equivalent to 'The Holy Grail.' It's a list of anyone and everyone who has had any dealings with this family. Every payoff, every country, every government official is listed. Vincent Giaconna murdered his brother, a decorated Federal Agent, in front of the agent's seven-year-old daughter. He kidnapped, tortured, beat and raped his brother's wife everyday. You've seen the tape. At this time, Vincent Giaconna has been charged with murder, major drug trafficking, and treason. All of these are punishable by death. No more questions at this

time. Thank you."

Max and I sit here, stunned. How the hell did Duke pull it off?

"Max could this possibly be over for us?"

"We need to stay clear for a while, let the dust settle."

"We have to tell everyone. I don't want them to see that tape!"

"Jax, we might not have a choice. I'm glad we will be hidden away for a while; totally off the grid."

I'm swirling the amber liquid around my glass, trying so hard to keep it all together. "Max, do you think everyone will like this place?"

"Yeah, mate, it's beautiful. There is so much to do. I think Junior is going to love it there. Once everything gets settled, if anyone wants to leave, they can."

"Do you have everything set up for the baby?"

"Of course, that's the first thing I took care of. Hold on; let me pull up the pictures. The main house looks like an old castle and has enough room for all of us. There are a dozen cottages that are for the staff. There are stables, a lake, and an airstrip."

"What were you planning on doing there?"

"Do you really want to know this?"

"Of course, I want to know."

"I was going to make Scotch whisky. It's something I always wanted to try."

Jax is stroking his chin and sipping his scotch. I think the simple life I was dreaming of just got a whole lot more complicated.

"Jax, I have something else to tell you. I asked Jackie to marry me."

"And?"

"She said yes, as long as we can have a long engagement."

"Congratulations, mate, and to think, you owe it all to me and my negotiating skills. Did you get her a ring?"

"Jax, it wasn't planned from the first day I met her."

"Nonsense, that night on the dance floor, you were done. It just takes you longer to see the light."

"I have one question for you, why Mrs. Osla? For fuck's sake, Max, you're petrified of the woman."

"Have a seat, Jax. I've got something to tell you."

What the fuck else could possibly be thrown my way today?

"You've got my full attention now."

"You've never once asked me how I found Mrs. Osla."

"That's because I trust you blindly, so why would I? Where are you going with all of this?"

"You know that she's a widow? Her husband was killed by a drunk driver, and she never had any children. What you don't know is Mrs. Osla is, Samantha's, aunt. When my family was murdered, it not only destroyed me, but Mrs. Osla, too. She was like a mum to Samantha, and she doted on Elliot. She came to see me when I was at the lowest point in life. It was with her help and support that I pulled myself together and joined the Special Forces. I never forgot her and when you were in need of a new assistant, I reached out to her. I knew I could trust her, and I respect her. In a way, it was like having a part of Samantha with me. She knew my past and never told anyone, not even your mum."

"Why are you telling me this now?"

"Raven and Jackie have taught me a lot, mainly that there can't be any secrets amongst us, our family. True love is about honesty, trust, and respect. I need you to understand Mrs. Osla is a very special lady, and without her help, none of this would have happened today."

"Have you told Jackie?"

"Not yet, but I will when Mrs. Osla feels comfortable with everyone knowing."

"One more question, are you really afraid of her?"

"Hell yeah!"

" After we land, we should let the family know what's going on."

WE ARE GOING TO be landing soon. Max and I watched the news all through the flight. So many people, arrested for having any dealings with the Giaconna family. The last one we watched was Annabelle. If I have learned anything in my life, it's that there is no easy way. Work hard and stay true to who you are, everything else will follow. Gaining power any other way but honestly only puts you at the top of the house of cards, waiting for it to tumble. Watching that tape, and seeing what Vincent did to Raven, made me want to kill him. If I personally went after him, it would have made me no better than him. I need to be better than that. I hope that I've set an example for Junior. I know I will for my own children.

I find Raven in one of the many suites in this flying palace. She's still asleep, in my dress shirt, of course. I undress and crawl in bed next to her, pulling her in my arms. Even in sleep, she wraps herself around my body. I know the next couple of months are going to be very emotional for everyone. I can finally say I have faith, the same faith that she has. We *will* get to the other side of this. I gently kiss her lips and her eyes flutter open.

"Hey."

"Hey, yourself, sweetheart. We're going to be landing soon."

"Jax, you look different, are you okay?"

"Yeah, I'm great, actually."

She reaches up and kisses me, pulling my lower lip between her teeth. "I know you're great, but what happened?"

"It's over, Raven. The tape was released. Apparently, Duke had some sort of evidence that the Feds are calling, 'the holy grail.' They charged Vincent with numerous crimes, and they are seeking the death penalty. We don't know everything yet, but so many people were arrested, including Annabelle. We will stay in Scotland until the dust settles, unless you love it there and decide you want to stay." I look down and I see the stunned look on her beautiful face. "I know it's a lot sweetheart, but it's all good. We'll be okay, I have faith now." I smile and plant a kiss on her nose. "I have some other news. Max asked Jackie to marry him and she said yes. She wants a long engagement."

"I know she told me. So much has been thrown at her today."

"I know I was worried, too. I know that Max had Mathew check on her family, and they are fine." I rest my hand on her growing belly and I can feel my baby kick.

"Max showed me pictures of the place and it looks surreal. The main house looks like a castle. Junior is going to have a blast."

"Jax, is there anything else?"

God, she knows me even when I don't. "I decided I'm going to read the file."

"Did you talk to your mom about it?"

"No, it has to be my decision, not hers. I'm the one that needs to see this through. She's made peace with her decision when she moved to the States. I need to find that same peace."

I've made love to her in so many places, and in so many ways, but right now, I need her. Our room is beginning to fill with a golden hue as the sun starts to rise. I shift so she can climb on top of me and slowly lower herself onto my cock. She stops, takes my hands, and kisses each palm.

"God, Raven, how is it you always know what I need?"

"Because I need you too, Jax, just as much as you need me."

She kisses me, our tongues doing their dance. Maybe now, with all of this behind us, we can finally relax. I watch her as we unravel together. I'm buried deep within her, knowing that she can be safe, sends me over that cliff of extreme pleasure, taking her with me as I fall.

Were both quiet for a while, enjoying the calm, and watching the dawn of a new day on the horizon.

"Raven, how do you feel about making scotch?"

"Excuse me."

"Let me tell you a story."

*J*axson

ALMOST THREE MONTHS HAVE passed since we got to Scotland. Junior is in love with the castle. Everyday, I take him to explore the different secret rooms. Bella and Michael went to Italy to tend to Michael's winery, but I asked them to leave Junior with me. I love our private time together. Construction to add more homes on the estate has started. With Mrs. Osla in charge, I don't doubt they will be ahead of schedule. Between this place being so big and Raven, nearing the end of the pregnancy, I now have everyone carrying two-way radios. While Raven is resting, I decide to find Max and give him my decision. I radio him to meet me in the study.

He comes racing in. "Hey, Raven okay?"

"Yeah, nothing yet. Everyone in her family went early except for her. I want to talk to you about Raiders. I want to sell it. Before you say anything, hear me out."

"Go ahead, Jax, I'm listening."

"I'm tired of that lifestyle. We're young and I think we are due for a new adventure. I know that everyone loves it here. I spoke to Jackie and she wants to teach children with special needs how to ride and take care of the horses. I really want to get this Scotch idea of yours off the ground. It would also be easier for Michael to run the winery. Mum, Rose, and Mrs. Osla agreed to it, as well. Jackie would be closer to her parents, too. All the way around, I think it's a great idea. If you don't want to sell, you can buy my shares at whatever you think is fair. Are you just going to sit there or are you going to say something?"

"Well, it sounds like you have everything already planned out for everyone. How does Raven feel about this? Did you run any of this by her?"

"Yes, as a matter of fact, I did. I'm really trying hard not to bully anyone, Max. She wants to stay here. She loves the country. She wants to be a full-time mum."

"I'm okay with it, Jax. I would be very happy, living out the rest of my days here. We can keep the flats in New York for vacations, along with the island. What else is bothering you? I can tell, so don't even try to hide it."

"I also decided that after the baby comes, I want to read the file. I need answers."

"Jax, what if the answers you're seeking aren't in the file?"

"Then, we will find them out together, but either way, I need to know."

"What about, An, have you spoken to her about it?"

"She made her peace, now I need to make mine. Does that make sense?"

"Okay, get the ball rolling on everything."

"Have you and Jackie thought about setting a date? I know she was relieved that the pregnancy test was negative, but that doesn't mean she wants to wait forever. Bella can't have any more children, and I want lots of babies in this house. That leaves me and you, mate."

"Actually, Jax, we're thinking late spring. Does Raven know you want lots of babies?" he chuckles.

"Stop laughing at me. Yes, she knows. She probably figures after this one I might not want lots more. I think I've calmed down a lot since we've been here. All the arrests have helped to calm me down."

"Jax, you can't possibly be serious. You're a crazy arse fucker and you always will be!"

"Thank you very much, Max. On that note, I'm going to bring my lovely wife some freshly squeezed juice."

As I get up to leave my radio goes off, "Jax, help me!"

Max starts barking orders behind me as we're flying up those steps three at a time. As I burst through the door, I see Raven, kneeling on the floor. "What the fuck are you doing on the floor?!"

"I'm having a damn party, Jax! What the hell do you think I'm doing? I don't think I can make it to the clinic."

"What the fuck do you mean, you can't make it? You have to make it to the clinic, that's the plan! The plan is in place for a reason!"

"Max, please call my mother and the doctor."

"I already did, Raven, they are on their way. Jax, snap the fuck out of it and get her on the bed. Where is your labor bag, Raven?"

"It's behind the door."

Max grabs the bag and pulls everything out, finally finding a night-shirt and tosses it to me. "Jax, help get this on her now."

As I lift her up, there's a gush of water. Raven is screaming and panting. My heart is ready to leap out of my chest. I'm never going to survive this. Fuck all that is holy, stop this ride, I want to get off!

"Jax, what are you waiting for? Help her get undressed."

"Turn around, Max. Don't roll your eyes at me, I'm serious, mate, turn around."

He turns around and I quickly help her change. I get her comfort-able in the bed with the sheet pulled up.

"Can I turn around now, Jax?"

"Don't be a wise arse, yes, you can turn around. What's the status on the doctor?"

"He's still a few minutes out."

"What do you mean, a few minutes out? He was supposed to be here on standby."

"One of the staff's children fell and broke her arm. He was

tending to her. Look, forget about that right now, and start timing her contractions."

Raven is following her Lamaze lessons, doing all the breathing we learned. She has a death grip on my hand and the other on Max's.

When the contraction finally passes, Raven leans back into my chest. "Oh no, Jax, I feel like I have to push."

"What the fuck do you mean? The doctor isn't here yet! *The. Baby. Has. To. Wait. For. The. Doctor!*"

Max grabs my arm, "This baby is not going to wait for anyone, Jax, and that includes you. Get your head out of your arse—*now!* Raven, I need to see if the baby is crowning. I know this is not the ideal situation, but we are out of options."

"Max, do whatever you have to but please make sure our baby is safe."

"I promise, Raven, I will. I'm going to pull the sheet up and take a look at what is going on okay?"

Max rolls the sheet down and gently pushes her legs apart. His eyes become wide as he announces the baby is crowning.

"Looks like I'm delivering my niece or nephew. I've done this before, don't panic. Raven, I'm going to need you to pant and then push. Jax, you need to help her with this. Massage her back like you learned in class. Talk her through it. I'll tell you when."

"Max, can't we wait for the doctor, he should only be a couple of minutes."

Raven grabs my hair and pulls my face to hers. "So help me God, Jax, you do what he tells you to do. If you don't, I will pull every last hair out of that glorious head of yours!"

"If you two are done arguing, it's time to deliver. Raven, do you feel the urge to push again?"

"Yes."

"Start now. Jax, count it out for her."

"Raven, you're doing great. Now pant like you're blowing out a candle."

"Jax, you need to breathe. If you pass out, you'll miss this. You need to help her with the breathing."

"Jax, so help me, if you pass out, you and Mr. Cock are never going to *cock heaven* again!"

"Don't worry, I'm good." *Damn she goes right for the jugular.* I lean up against Raven's back and help her push. I look down to see what's going on and see a shock of black hair. I'm in awe of the sight before me.

"Jax, start counting for her again. One more push, Raven, come on you, can do this."

"I'm tired, Max, I don't think I can."

"You need to push the shoulders out. Come on, girl, you can do it!"

My beautiful wife gives it all she's got. The doctor and Rose come running in just as we hear the baby cry.

"Jax, Raven, meet your beautiful daughter." Max places her in Raven's arms and wrapping my arms around her, we cradle this angel together.

The doctor steps up and offers me the chance to cut the umbilical cord. I'm nervous but I give it a go, wiping my tears away, first, so I can see. The happiness I'm feeling is overwhelming. We fought hard for this and won. Life has come full circle . . . for all of us.

"So, does my niece have a name?"

Neither one of us is saying anything. We are too busy huddling together, watching her with wonder and love. Finally, I get up and hand the baby to the doctor and Rose to examine.

I turn to my brother. "Max, if it's okay with you, Raven and I would like to call her Antonia Samantha Phillips. You are my best friend and a great brother. You've been shot twice, protecting my wife and daughter. Now you've helped bring my beautiful baby safely into this world. I would be honored to give her Samantha as her middle name."

Maxwell

I'M STUNNED. "THANK YOU . . . both of you. I'm honored that you would do that."

I look over at Rose, coddling my niece, and I know that Samantha would be proud to have her name carried on. Proud of how far I have come. I back out of the room, giving them some privacy. I need to find Jackie, and let her know what's happened. As I head downstairs,

Jackie, An, and Mrs. Osla come rushing in. "It's okay everyone, they have a beautiful, healthy, baby girl."

"Is Raven okay, and did my son survive this?"

"An, Raven is fine and yes, even Jax survived this, although, he might be rethinking his need for lots of babies right now."

An and Mrs. Osla head upstairs, but I pull Jackie back towards me. "I need you, baby."

"Are you okay, Max?"

"They named the baby Antonia Samantha Phillips. It was just a little overwhelming for me. Sometimes I feel like I've come so far, and then, I feel like I've hit a wall."

She pulls me into her arms and holds me tightly. "Max, there will always be a time when something or someone will stir up memories of Samantha and Elliot. Cherish the fact that you have some happy memories. Remembering them will always keep their spirits alive. It's okay to feel, Max, it's when you stop feeling that the walls go up."

I lift her head up to mine and look into those beautiful golden eyes. "Let's head upstairs, and you can meet my new niece. After that, I want to be alone with you for the rest of the day. Did I tell you I delivered the baby? You should have seen Jax. It's a wonder Raven didn't kill him."

"Why did you deliver the baby? What happened to the doctor?"

"Come, I'm sure Raven wants to tell you all about it."

We walk into the room and An is on the phone with Bella. The whole family is gathered around, and I realize, I've come back to life. It's taken ten years, but I've come full circle. I wish my grams were here to see this, to see I'm happy and loved.

I'm sure she's looking down on me now.

"Max, what are you thinking right this second?"

"I'm loved, baby; truly blessed."

AS I WATCH MY beautiful Antonia sleep, I look out over the sun rising in the meadow. So much has happened to me—hell—to all of us in this past year. Things I never thought or dreamed of, have become my reality. My mom is alive and getting stronger everyday. Jackie has found the love she always dreamed of, a true soul mate. Max is healing, one day at a time. He's feeling again, learning to live life. My Jax, oh how my skin tingles just thinking about him. I've finally figured out his over the top ways, but more importantly, why he does what he does. He's so wonderful with Antonia. I don't think any boy will ever have a chance with her. To think, I was worried that he would want lots of staff around to take care of her. He won't let anyone within ten feet of her. I'm glad he still wants lots of babies, this place is huge and I wouldn't want Antonia to be an only child.

He's been a little off, lately and I know it's that damn file. I wish he would just burn it, but that's not Jax. I know he has to see this through to the end, but at what price? I scoop up Antonia as she begins to wake. She has quite the appetite, which I'm sure, makes Jax happy.

"Hello, my beautiful Antonia." I watch her as she latches on. She makes a fist near her jet-black hair and I have to laugh, she really is her father's daughter. "There's a whole world at your doorstep, my sweet daughter, just waiting for you. I can't wait to explore it with you, one day at a time."

Jaxson

A COUPLE OF DAYS have passed and Antonia is already getting into a routine. Raven is a natural with her. I have a beautiful daughter, and rest assured, no man will ever be good enough for her. I pity the poor bastard that even tries. My wife and daughter are asleep. I know it's time; I can't put this off any longer. I head to my office and pull out the file. I've been waiting for the right time to do this and now seems as good as any.

"Are you ready for this, Jax?"

"Jesus Max, you scared the living daylights out of me."

"I figured you'd want to get started on this. Are you sure you really want to look?"

"Yes, I have to."

"Well, then, let's get started."

I open the file and there are pictures, lots of them. "Who are all these people?"

"The first picture is our father as he looks today."

"Who are these other people Max?"

"Read the file."

I begin to read and I'm floored. Our father is a career bigamist. He's lived off of all these women. When he is done with them, he moves on to the next one. Never caring about the devastation he's left behind. There are other children like us out there. "Jesus Christ, Max, we've done business with some of these people and never knew! Now what? Do we contact them?"

"Well, I don't think it is a decision we have to make right this minute. I think we need to talk to Bella and An about this. They need to be aware of everything. Jax, he's alive and well, living in Capri."

"Well, Bella will be home tomorrow. We will let her and mum know everything, and then I guess we're off to Capri."

Raven

I WAKE FROM A nap and look for Jax, but I know he's not here. I get up to find him, although I know I won't have a long search, he's never far from me. I stop outside Antonia's room and I hear him talking to her.

"My beautiful daughter, I am yours for life." He stares down at our daughter and I don't know what is going on in his head right now but he seems a little upset.

"My beautiful Antonia, you're so sweet like your mum. How could I go without seeing these little pouty lips everyday, or those beautiful crystal blue eyes? How can I leave Raven?"

What's this? "Jax, are you okay?"

He brings his focus to me. "No, sweetheart, I'm not. I read the file and, apparently, my father is a serial bigamist, living in Capri. I need to confront him and right now I'm struggling with leaving you and, Antonia."

"Are you worried about our safety, or something else?"

I watch his struggle as he tries to find the words, words I already know. My heart tightens in my chest. "Would it help if we went with you?"

"I thought of that, believe me, I have. I need to get a handle on these feelings. Feelings I've never had before."

"What feelings, Jax?"

He's quietly stroking Antonia's, cheek. "*Fear,*" he barely whispers.

My heart breaks for him, and I know that only I can help him through this. "What are you afraid of Jax?" Antonia, falls back to sleep and he puts her in her crib.

"I'm afraid this might all go away."

There it is, that little boy whose family was rejected for another. I take his hand and pull him towards me. "Look at me, Jax." His eyes shoot up to mine, "You are not your father. You're a kind and loving man. We made promises to each other, promises that I plan on holding you to, until my dying day. I will never leave you." I stroke my fingers across his worry lines, I see his angst. "I know your craziness stems from your father abandoning your family for another. That's an awful hurt for anyone, especially a little boy who idolized his dad. You're not your dad and you never will be, you don't have it in you. You're a good man, Jax, one I plan on growing very old with. We have a long, full future ahead of us. A future we need to be working on."

"Raven, the doctor has not given us the green light yet, and I struggle with this every minute of every day."

I lean into his chest and kiss his heart. "My beautiful man, come back to bed, please . . ."

He lifts me into his arms and nuzzles into my neck. "Sweetheart, you don't play fair."

"I never said I would."

Maxwell

IT'S ANOTHER BEAUTIFUL DAY, and fall will be upon us soon. I know Jackie has already gone to the barn. She is so happy; her riding academy is a huge success. She's adding two new horses today. The kids love her, but what's not to love? I hate that I have to leave her, but Jax and I are supposed to be heading out to Capri today. I'm not sure either one of us can do it. Jax has put three guards on Antonia, one that Raven and Jackie call T-Bear. Mick is always within view, so I'm not worried about their safety. I just don't want to leave. I watch in the distance as Jackie mounts up. God she's so beautiful. Her golden hair, cascading down her back—and those legs! I watch, in a trance, as my mind wanders.

"Maxwell, are you sure you and Jax will be leaving today?"

"Jesus, An, you scared me half to death."

"Maybe your apprehension to leave is really a sign. What is it going accomplish anyway? The past is just that—the past. Nothing will change what was, only you can change what will be."

"For once, I agree with you, but Jax needs to do this and I won't let him go alone. Is there some other reason you don't want us to go?"

"No, I just don't see any good coming from it. Jax fears he is like James, but he's nothing like him."

"What about the other siblings out there, shouldn't they know the truth, An?"

"Maxwell, maybe they already do, have you thought of that? Maybe they know and they just don't care."

"I've thought about that, but I know Jax needs answers. Answers he can only get from our father."

"Do what you must." She walks away, leaving me to my thoughts. As I walk towards the barn, my phone beeps. It's Bella.

"Meeting. Now. Kitchen!"

She sounds upset. I better get over there now.

Isabella

JAX AND MAX TOLD me everything about my father. I have siblings I never knew about. They are getting ready to go to Capri. They think they can head out and leave me here.

Jax comes running into the kitchen, half out of his mind, as usual.

"Bella, what's wrong?"

"Calm down, bro, I'm fine."

"Then, why the meeting?"

Max steps into the room, "What's the urgency, Bella?"

"I'm going with you to Capri."

"Oh no you're not," Jax jumps in.

"Look, you can't stop me from going. I will be perfectly safe with the two of you. I need to do this just as much as you do."

"Your mum is upset that Jax and I are going, you going, as well, will be too much for her."

"Max, don't bring my mum into this. She doesn't need answers, I d-do." I stammer, trying to fight off my emotions.

"What kind of answers are you looking for?"

"Max, it was after I was born that he walked out, why?"

Jax pulls me into his arms. "I've heard enough, you are not responsible for his leaving. It was his choice to make. I tried to give you all the love and support I could, Bella, and I'm sorry if I failed you."

"Jax, you didn't fail me, but I still need to know."

"Well, then, I guess the three of us are going to Capri just as soon as I can pull myself away from my wife and daughter." He pulls back from me. My brothers and I all stare at each other in silence; this is going to be hard on all of us.

The End . . . *for now.*

Book 3: Untitled

James Phillips

The day has finally come, the day I've feared the most. The day my oldest son comes to find me. I knew it would be soon. It was only a matter of time before my past would collide with my future. His family murdered because of me. My grandson and daughter in-law gunned down like animals. How can I face him, knowing what I've done? I've stayed away for their own safety, but what did that get me? They are still dead because of me. I have managed to keep the rest of them safe, but for how long.

There's a knock on the door that startles me out of my daydream. "Come in, Reynolds." Reynolds has been my Valet and confidant for twenty years, the keeper of all my secrets.

"Sir, I just received word that their plane has landed. It's only a matter of time now. What would you like to do?"

"Well, Reynolds, what we won't do is run anymore. The time has come to face my demons. I must own up to what I've done. They are not children anymore, and they deserve the truth, no matter how ugly it is."

"Sir, what about their safety?"

"Well, the better question should be, what about ours? When Maxwell finds out my role in all of it, I venture to say, I'm a dead man."

"Sir, you did everything you could, clearly, he will understand."

I squeeze my eyes shut, trying to get that image out of my head I whisper, "Everything but save them."

Acknowledgements

Rick, thank you, for always having my back. You're unwavering love and support is priceless. No matter what the course may be, I know you're always by my side. My end all. I love you.

My mom, Jean, my sister, Fran, and all my family and friends, you have all been so supportive through all of this, making sure I never give up. Your constant love and support has taught me to be a better person. I can only hope I've passed this on to others in my lifetime.

Erin, Charles found you so I could have you. You listen to me even when I don't want to hear myself. I know no matter what happens in life, you will be behind me; kicking me in the arse when I need it, and holding me up when I fall. Always and forever.

Thank you, Kelsey Dobbins, for naming Raven's Pilate's instructor Ashlyn Adair.

The girls at Chocolate Smiles of Cary, North Carolina. Throughout all the craziness, it has been your constant supply of the best, dark chocolate, covered graham crackers that has kept me somewhat sane.

My street team, Theresa's Sinfully Sexy Angels—you girls rock!

Clementine Catapano, thank you for continuingly showing me all the new uses for Nutella.

Thank you to the little boy who agreed to let me use his published poem as long as I kept him anonymous. Your secret is safe with me.

Finally, my son, Leif. I learn from you everyday. I have the pleasure of watching the world through your eyes. Your loyalty and courage are beyond reason. You're more than I ever dreamed possible, and I thank God every day for the gift of you.

About the Author

I was born in Brooklyn New York. I am old enough to know there is no luggage rack on the hearse. I am married to a Professional Chef. I have a son who is a Research Chemist and a wine maker. Yep I'm covered from the food to the drinks. I have 2 dogs Vito and Godiva. I live in the United States. I've had so many different jobs, even I can't keep count.

I believe if you give a girl espresso and Nutella she can change the world!

www.ingramcontent.com/pod-product-compliance
Lightning Source LLC
Chambersburg PA
CBHW071106250626
47159CB00002B/620